Hive

By

Ischade Bradean

Mal Cortado

ISBN: 0-7596-7774-3

This book is printed on acid free paper.

1stBooks - rev. 12/03/01

CHAPTER 1

Heliotrope sat still. To been seen or heard was death. She reminded herself that once her princess was Queen she would have to destroy this useful little spy hole. It would be sloppy to leave the listening post for use by potential enemies. 'Humph,' Heliotrope thought, 'there is no such thing as potential'. There were always enemies.

The tiny peephole in the wall allowed only a limited view of the Queen's chambers. But Heliotrope could see enough. Some of the Queen's attendants were buzzing about the chamber trying to find a way to be helpful. Others sensed the futility and simply stood looking on at the horrific scene. The Queen was wounded, perhaps mortally so. She lay gasping in her bed in a growing pool of her own blood.

The Royal Physician's back was to Heliotrope. She could not see the expression on the Physician's face, but the set of the Physician's shoulders said much. The fact that the Physician was not actively working to save the Queen told the rest of the story.

There was a commotion at the door to the Queen's chambers. The Royal Guards dragged in a worker.

'We've brought the attacker!' The Captain of the Guard announced. With a dramatic flair the guards cast the worker to the floor.

Heliotrope gasped audibly, a sound thankfully not heard by the inhabitants of the Queen's chambers. She knew this attacker. It was Oxalis, nursemaid to one of the other princesses.

The Queen struggled to rise. 'How dare you sting your own Queen?'

Oxalis began to shake violently. Stinging the Queen was a death sentence not only to the Queen, if the sting was a mortal blow, as this appeared to be, but also to Oxalis. Workers such as Oxalis could only sting once. As the worker plunged her stinger into her victim the stinger detached from the worker's body,

1

disemboweling her. Only the Queen had the ability to sting repeatedly. Workers tended to sting only as a last resort. Usually the sacrifice was made in defense of the Hive. Assassination attempts like this were almost unheard of.

Heliotrope's mind raced. This was a planned assassination attempt, but why? No mere worker would benefit from the death of the Queen. However, there were five individuals who would benefit from the Queen's assassination, the princesses! The plan was clear. Someone was making a grab for the Throne.

Heliotrope jumped from her hiding place and ran to the chambers of Princess Aynia, the princess that Heliotrope served.

The Captain of the Guard heard a strange thump apart from the noise of the Queen dying before him. Captain Thorn's eyes narrowed as he starred at the seemingly innocent wall across from the Queen's bed. His lips thinned, showing his displeasure. The Queen's imminent death was apparently no longer a secret.

Princess Aynia's other attendants jumped as Heliotrope slammed open the door to the chamber and rushed into the room. Heliotrope took in the scene, which attendant was available, whom she trusted. 'You, Verbena, and Freesia, go right now, no questions, get the Royal Jelly. Prepare for violence. The vaults may be guarded.'

Verbena jumped up, grabbed Freesia's hand, and ran from the room to do as instructed. Heliotrope had trained them well. They did not hesitate or question her.

'The rest of you, start preparing the princess's inner chamber for the transformation.'

Princess Aynia heard the commotion in the outer room of her chamber. She was studying, the main occupation of her life, with the eldest of her attendants, Sister Passiflora. Aynia was a tall strawberry blonde with a heart shaped face and a chin that came to a point. Those who served her loved her wit, but shyness stopped her from displaying her quick mind in public. This cost her followers among the Seelie Court, the nobility.

Princess Aynia and Passiflora exchanged a glance. Something was up. They stood at the same time and went to the main room of the chamber.

Sister Passiflora had long passed the time of her life when subtlety and intrigue interested her. She valued directness. 'The Queen is dead?' Sister Passiflora asked Heliotrope.

Heliotrope wavered. These attendants were loyal to Princess Aynia. They pledged their entire lives not to the Hive, not to the Queen, but to the princess that they served. But no matter how loyal they were they knew the law. To feed a princess Royal Jelly before the death of the Queen was treason. It would mean the death of them all, including their beloved princess, if they were found out.

Heliotrope wanted to lie but she was sister to these attendants. They deserved to know the truth. 'No,' Heliotrope shook her head, 'the Queen is not dead, yet. She lies mortally wounded, a sting to her abdomen. The Royal Physician is no longer working to save the Queen's life. She is only making the Queen's last moments more comfortable.'

'A sting to the abdomen?' The attendant Sister Sweet Pea asked with suspicion in her eyes. Sweet Pea looked to the other attendants. There was agreement here. Everyone understood that it was an assassination.

'Who did it?' they demanded.

'Oxalis.' Heliotrope told them.

There was a sharp intake of breath.

'Princess Carman! Her cell is behind this!'

'What an infamous way to seize the Throne.' Princess Aynia murmured. Her mother was dead. The words did not seem to want to have meaning for her. Princess Aynia lost her beloved father years before, a loss she still felt keenly. And while the Queen was not close to any of her princesses, Aynia was most often commanded to be at her mother's side.

'You see why I sent for the Royal Jelly? If they planned the assassination they probably have already begun feeding Royal Jelly to Princes Carman. We can waste no time. If Princess

Carman emerges from her sarcophagus as a new Queen too far ahead of Princess Aynia she will kill our princess. If we delay until the official announcement of the Queen's death it will be too late,' Heliotrope pleaded her case to her sisters.

Freesia and Verbena returned with the Royal Jelly. 'We had no problems, but the vault was already breached and the guards were dead.'

Sister Passiflora stepped forward and held up her ancient hand. 'This is wrong. I'm sorry Heliotrope, I love our princess, but this is wrong, and no justification will make it right. Princess Aynia must think about this decision. She must reflect upon her actions. Her Royal Mother is not yet dead.'

Princess Aynia opened her mouth to say something, but what she was planning to say was never heard. Heliotrope took a handful of the Royal Jelly and shoved it into Princess Aynia's open mouth. Princess Aynia had no choice but to swallow if she wanted to breathe. As she swallowed and opened her mouth to gasp in air Heliotrope shoved more Royal Jelly into her mouth.

The other attendants jumped into action. As soon as she digested the Royal Jelly Princess Aynia would begin the transformation from a juvenile female into a Queen. They needed to build a snug chamber to protect the princess while the change took place. Using the thick wax the attendants secreted from their abdomens they created a sarcophagus, a standing coffin.

Princess Aynia doubled over. The sweet, thick, potent Royal Jelly did not so much enter her digestive track as it was absorbed by the cells in her mouth, stomach, and intestines. Like water to a sponge the Royal Jelly seeped into her cellular structure. Immediately her body began to respond. For over one hundred seventy years she had be in a stasis state, a prepubescent child. Now in the short span of a month she would become a fully developed female. The speed of the process was painful.

Heliotrope gently picked up Princess Aynia, undressed her, and placed her in a standing position in the chamber of wax. Then the attendants began sealing her in. For a month she would not talk, would not eat, and would have no contact with the outside world. Then on the thirtieth day she would tear apart the chamber and emerge as a Queen.

As the other attendants sealed Princess Aynia inside the chamber Heliotrope poured a cup of nectar for Sister Passiflora and handed it to the outraged nurse. Heliotrope sat down on one of the comfortable chairs on front of the stone fireplace and faced her critic. With a smug smile Heliotrope placed her hands across her rounded abdomen. 'Now that Princess Aynia is taken care of we have time to leisurely discuss the morality of the situation.'

There was urgent pounding on the outer door of the chamber. At Heliotrope's direction the attendants pulled curtains to hide Princess Aynia's sarcophagus. Freesia took a calming breath and opened the door.

A Royal Messenger stepped into the chamber and bowed. He glanced around the homey room with gray stone walls and a well-worn wooden floor. Deep leather chairs were pulled in front of a stone fireplace. It was an intimate scene.

The Royal Messenger took a deep breath. 'I bear sad news. Our Royal Sister, the Queen, is dead. The vaults have been opened. Go take Royal Jelly and prepare your princess for the transformation to Queen.'

In a performance worthy of the greats of the Royal Theater, Freesia swooned.

Heliotrope dropped her cup of nectar.

Verbena took the hand of another attendant. 'Come; let us get the Royal Jelly. Time is of the essence.' The two scurried off to the vaults for more Royal Jelly.

Sister Passiflora began to cry genuine tears.

The Royal Messenger stepped out of Princess Aynia's chamber. He had several more chambers to visit. He had been given explicit instructions as to the order in which he should notify the five Royal Princesses about the death of the Queen. Princess Aynia was on the top of the list, Princess Lily was

5

second, and so it went until the least favorite of the princesses were given the news. It was perhaps unfair but this method gave the favored princess time to emerge from their transformation into a Queen just ahead of the less favored females. That made dispatching of potential rivals easier. If the other princesses were still entombed in their sarcophagi the new Queen would not have to look upon the faces of her sisters as she stung them to death.

The Royal Messenger was aware that the vault of Royal Jelly was breached before the official pronouncement came of the Queen's death. He was under strict orders to observe all of the chambers as he delivered his message. One chamber would show preparations already underway to transform the princess, exposing the culprits. But he did not suspect the attendants of Princess Aynia. Their shock at the news of the Queen's death had been too genuine.

Princess Lily's chambers were decorated in a fussy manner. Overstuffed chairs and tiny tables draped with layers of material and little trinkets were crammed into the room making it seem small and cramped. Worse, masses of lilies were everywhere. The flowers were so strongly scented that one alone could perfume a whole room. The effect of dozens of the princesses' namesake flower was overwhelming. The scent gave the messenger an instant headache, the overabundance of flowers seeming funereal, not cheerful.

The visit to Princess Lily's chambers resulted in much the same reaction of shock and dismay as the Royal Messenger witnessed in Princess Aynia's chamber, but the messenger remembered something as he looked at the tear-stained face of the Princess Lily. He hadn't actually seen Princess Aynia. He shook his head. It was too late to turn back. Aynia's attendants would already have her well along in the transformation process by now even if they had just heard the news. No worthy attendant would wait long to act after hearing of the Queen's

6

demise. There was nothing for the Royal Messenger to do but to continue on to the next princesses' chambers.

Princess Carman's rooms showed a taste for the regal. Delicately carved furniture with the barest hint of gilt filled the outer room. The floor was wood, but a rich red carpet covered most of the area. Little backless chairs were grouped together in sets of threes and fives around the room. The messenger recognized the decor immediately. The room was an exact replica of the old Throne Room, except that a conference table sat in the place of the Queen's Throne. On top of the table was a yellow wax sarcophagus.

There was no question in the messenger's mind as to who was responsible for the death of the guards at the vault of Royal Jelly when he saw Princess Carman's sarcophagus on the table. Carman was already suspected of complicity in the assassination of the Queen, as it was her nurse who committed the act.

The Royal Messenger nodded to the blue uniformed nurses who let him enter the chamber. 'I see that the good news already reached you,' he said sarcastically.

The nurses gathered in a ring around him. Too late, the messenger realized the great danger that he was in. He knew their secret. He had the proof that would send them and their princess to instant death for treason. And they knew that he understood what he saw.

Sister Snakegrass came up behind the messenger and clasped a rag soaked in ether to his mouth and nose. He sank to his knees. 'Bring the last of the Royal Jelly,' she commanded.

The well-trained attendants fell into formation behind their leader. The first two held the Royal Messenger. Those in the row behind held a cup with Royal Jelly. The next two attendants held swords. The remaining two took positions on either side of the wax sarcophagus.

'Guard our princess with your lives,' Sister Snakegrass commanded.

7

The two remaining attendants struck their left upper chests with their fists and then straightened their arms to finish their salute. They did not speak.

Sister Snakegrass turned on her heel. 'It is time to pay a little visit to Princess Gladiola.' The seven attendants headed out of the chamber, dragging the unconscious messenger with them.

Sister Snakegrass did not bother to knock on Princess Gladiola's chamber doors. She knew that no one would answer if she did. It always amazed her how trusting the attendants in the other chambers could be. She would never be so careless as to allow a basket of sweets into Carman's chambers that were delivered anonymously.

When the last of Carman's attendants entered Gladiola's chambers they closed the doors. They did not want anyone walking past the chambers to see Princess Gladiola and her attendants lying on the chamber floor.

The smell of ether was subsiding, but Princes Carman's attendants wore handkerchiefs over their mouths as a precaution.

Sister Snakegrass looked down at the crumpled figures and laughed. 'The fools, they should have known better. Never, never take a gift from the hand of your enemy.'

The Royal Messenger began to come around. He could not make sense of things at first. This was a not Princess Carman's chamber. 'Are they dead?' he asked in a groggy voice as he gestured towards the prone figures on the ground.

'Not yet,' Snakegrass said.

'You two,' Snakegrass turned to the attendants with the chalice of Royal Jelly, 'force-feed the little princess some Royal Jelly. Then start building her sarcophagus, but don't waste too much time on it. It's not as if she'll be allowed to live once Captain Thorn finds the messenger's body in here.' Sister Snakegrass laughed unpleasantly.

The messenger tried to struggle. The two guards holding him did not let him go.

'Who is the head nurse here?' Sister Snakegrass asked.

'That one,' one of Princess Carman's attendants pointed out a female on the floor near to Princess Gladiola.

Princess Gladiola was beginning to come around and was fighting off the attempt to force-feed her Royal Jelly, but with her nose pinned closed she eventually had to open her mouth. The two attendants forced her jaw open and poured the thick sweet substance down her throat.

'Bring the messenger,' Sister Snakegrass commanded.

The messenger dug in his heels, trying not to be taken across the floor. This time he knew that it was death. But he could not stop them.

Sister Snakegrass rolled Princess Gladiola's head nurse over and exposed the female's stinger. The messenger fought back violently. He kicked and screamed.

The attendants on either side of the messenger held him with strong grasps. He could not loosen their fingers from his arms.

The messenger was slowly lowered, his abdomen getting closer and closer to the exposed stinger.

The messenger bent over at his waist so that his vulnerable stomach was not exposed. The attendants pulled him forward by the arms.

Sister Snakegrass was enjoying the scene immensely but their time was running out. She walked behind the messenger and pushed his bottom forward with her booted foot.

The messenger lunged helplessly forward. The stinger punctured just below his ribs. He thrashed around as the two females who held him let go. The messenger stood up and staggered back. The stinger was still in his stomach. As he moved away from the nurse whose stinger had been used to kill him the stinger detached from her body and pulled her intestines out across the floor.

The nurse's body convulsed as she was disemboweled.

The messenger was trying to scream but no words came from his mouth. Foam formed at his lips. His eyes rolled back, and then he pitched forward onto the ground, the tip of the stinger plunging out through his back with a slick, wet sound.

The failure of the Royal Messenger to return to his post was noted within half of an hour. Cabinet members who were aware of the breach of the vault of Royal Jelly were by now fully comprehending that the assassination was not the act of a single lunatic. The assassin was obviously part of a conspiracy to replace the Queen.

In the long history of the Hive from time to time rumors floated about the Royal Court of a princess growing impatient to take the Throne. This actual coup attempt was, however, unprecedented. It was also kept quiet. Few in the Royal Court or the military knew of the assassination. Efforts to stop rumors were well underway, but just because the plot was being swept away from public view did not mean that one of the princesses and her attendants would be allowed to get away with treason.

An armed search party was sent out to find the Royal Messenger. They began at the chamber of the youngest princess, Peony. The Royal Guard was shocked to find that news of the Queen's death had not yet reached this chamber.

Princess Peony's attendants panicked. All of the other princesses already knew of the Queen's death and had at least an hour jump on Peony in the transformation process. Princess Peony's attendants rushed to the vault for Royal Jelly. Deep in their hearts they knew that it was already too late but they had to try.

The next stop the search party made was to Princess Lily's chambers. The attendants there told the military what they knew of the messenger's visit. Then the guards moved on.

There was great panic in Princess Gladiola's chambers. Half of the attendants were still unconscious. The Head Nurse's disemboweled body still lay on the floor. Not far from her body lie the Royal Messenger and her stinger.

Princess Gladiola's attendants who were awake were working feverishly on the sarcophagus. Made hastily and without care by Princess Carman's attendants, the thin shell of wax forming the sarcophagus was not enough protection for Princess Gladiola during her transformation to Queen. But fixing an existing sarcophagus was much harder than constructing one correctly from the start.

The Head of Security, Captain Thorn, notified the Cabinet via a messenger of the situation.

'Well, this seems fairly obvious,' Lieutenant Sage commented to his superior.

Thorn frowned. 'What is obvious to you is not what I find obvious, but please, tell me what you think that you see.' The frown did not mar the face of the Captain of the Guard. His high cheekbones and strong jaw line accentuated his sunken cheeks. In sleep the Captain would appear to be a young male. And, in a way, he was. Having avoided marriage he was not a drone, a mating male, and thus was locked forever from the final stages of physical maturity. But like human eunuchs Captain Thorn's face did carry the weary burden of time and responsibility.

'The Royal Messenger came here to deliver the news of the death of our Queen. When Princess Gladiola's attendants opened the door the messenger discovered that they were already in the process of building the sarcophagus. In order to stop him from reporting their treasonous acts the nurse here stung him to death. This put the attendants further behind on their work. In order to preserve the princesses' life they left the bodies here hoping to dispose of them later.'

Thorn shook his head. 'You only see what you were meant to see.' He walked around the room, twice stopping to sniff the air. 'Do you smell that?'

'I smell an odor.' Lieutenant Sage admitted.

'And did you happen to notice the bodies on the floor?'

Lieutenant Sage stooped down and checked the pulse of first one, then another attendant. 'They are alive.'

'I suspect that they were overdosed on ether. The person or persons who drugged them forgot about the lingering odor. Those who remain passed out seem to be fairly close to this table. Look! Crumbs! Some sort of cake or other sweet I think. They were drugged by a sweet left on this table for them.'

'Someone framed them?' Lieutenant Sage began to understand his superior.

'I think so. Where is the cake? There are crumbs, but I see no cake. Whoever did this took that piece of evidence with them.'

'The nurses here could have eaten it all.'

'We will ask Princess Gladiola's attendants,' Captain Thorn said, but as he turned to see the females working with grim determination he stopped Lieutenant Sage. 'No wait, don't interrupt them. But observe them at work. Their actions are a clue too. The princesses' attendants act like dam builders desperately reinforcing a damaged levy before a rising river.'

'I see, but how is this any different from the frantic work going on right now in any of the other princesses' chambers?'

Thorn was a male of infinite patience. He did not loose it now with Sage. 'Let us suppose for a second that you put together a very clever plan to place your own princess on the Throne. You send out an assassin to kill the Queen. But before hearing of the plan's success you break into a vault containing Royal Jelly and feed it to your princess, starting the transformation process at least half an hour before the other princesses learn of the Queen's death, giving your princess a distinct advantage. The first hatched is usually the one who survives.'

'A dangerous plan. What if the attempt failed?' Lieutenant Sage asked. He was beginning to wonder why he thought being assigned to the Royal Palace would be dull.

'The mind that created this plan was willing to take big risks for a big reward, the Throne.'

'But how do you come to the conclusion that these are not the conspirators? They do have a rather damming dead body on their floor.'

'There is that,' Thorn admitted, 'but if you went to all the trouble to create such a complex plan, wouldn't you think to create the sarcophagus before hand so that it was ready when you needed it? And wouldn't you construct it with great care? After all, the plan is to end up with your princess on the Throne. A shoddy construction job on the sarcophagus would only jeopardize her life.'

'I suppose,' Lieutenant Sage admitted reluctantly.

'These workers knew that they were framed for treason. They had time to dispose of the bodies. But they did not. Instead they put one hundred percent of their energies into saving Princess Gladiola's life. Whoever did this to them tried to make sure that Princess Gladiola would not survive the transformation process even if this chamber escaped a charge of treason.'

The armed guards turned and watched the frantic efforts of Princess Gladiola's attendants to repair the sarcophagus. Captain Thorn's logic helped the guards under his command understand that the females working in front of them were not traitors to the Hive. And the guards understood that a desperate race against the clock was taking place before them. But the males did not have the physical ability to make the wax that was needed. Nor did they know how to help reinforce the sarcophagus. Despite their real desire to do so the males could not help Gladiola's attendants.

The remaining attendants woke from their stupor. Within seconds they staggered over and began to assist their Sisters.

'No!' An anguished cry arose from one of the nurses. She put her hands in front of her eyes.

Other attendants rushed to the spot where she stood. Their hands flew to the sarcophagus. They tried to stop the growing tear but could not. The faulty wax of the original sarcophagus was too wet for the patches to adhere to. Cracks formed everywhere and the entire structure began to give way. The frantic efforts of the attendants to shore up the sarcophagus failed.

Once a princess ingested Royal Jelly she began her final metamorphosis from larva to adult. The change was at a cellular level. If a sarcophagus breached in the middle of the thirty-day transformation the princess would not be revealed in a half-grown state between child and adult. Instead the sarcophagus would contain primordial soup, cells rearranging themselves over the thirty days into the adult form. It was this primordial soup, the cells of the unfortunate Princess Gladiola, which was leaking from the sarcophagus.

The whole structure gave way. In a sickening wave half-liquefied body parts and smelly green-yellow ooze spilled over the floor. Several of the guards threw up. The attendants started to keen in high-pitched wails of grief.

'We should have built a whole new sarcophagus around the old one instead of trying to shore up the old one. We failed our princess,' one of the nurses cried out. She was facing Thorn but was talking to her Sisters.

The attendants moved as one to form a ring around the failed sarcophagus. They fell to their knees and began to pray to the Goddesses.

Thorn realized what was happening too late to act. Each attendant unveiled her stinger and fell on it. The suicides convulsed gruesomely as they died.

Captain Thorn surveyed the horrific scene before him. Bodies seemed to be everywhere. Thorn was a soldier but this was beyond the scope of his ability to remain distanced. To all outward appearances he remained calm and in control, but his jaw was clenched tightly and his eyes were shinning with unshed tears.

Lieutenant Sage was not as experienced as Captain Thorn was at hiding his thoughts. A tear rolled down Sage's cheek. 'What is it Captain, twenty four?'

'Twenty four?'

'The body count Captain. We lost twenty-two workers and two Royals today. It is a black day for the Hive.'

Thorn began counting off the devastation. 'The Queen, her assassin, the Royal Messenger. The two guards at the Royal Jelly vault. Then there was the Princess Gladiola and her attendants. That's twenty-four today. But this deed is darker by far than you realize. The blood bath has just now begun.'

Lieutenant Sage blanched. 'Where will it end Captain?'

'In thirty days the killing will begin again. We have three possible Queens.'

'Four Captain,' Sage interrupted.

'No, only three. The traitors saw to it that Princess Peony had no chance to emerge before the other Queens. She will be slaughtered, as will her attendants.'

'So whichever Queen is victorious will kill all of the other princesses' nurses? That's not fair.'

'Fair? This is a military operation. Civilians are not protected. Each attendant is loyal to her princess, loyal to the death. Would you leave alive such potential enemies?'

'I suppose not.'

'Trust me; the ones who thought out this plot are not the type to draw the line at a few more deaths.'

'So the total body count is going to be more like one hundred dead?' The number shocked Lieutenant Sage.

'Or two.'

'Can't we stop it?'

Thorn grew weary of this conversation. It was making him maudlin, and he had no time to feel today. He needed to take charge of this situation before it completely spun out of his control. He straightened his spine so that his entire frame exuded military authority.

'You,' Thorn pointed to a young male near the door, 'call for morgue workers,' and be sure to warn them about the clean up,' Thorn's voice nearly broke in anguish, 'of Princess Gladiola's remains.'

The male nodded. The smell of death settled around the room and the scent was not pleasant. He was glad to escape.

'The rest of you pick two bodies to examine. Look them over carefully. We need positive identity on each attendant. I need to find a roster of all attendants to Princess Gladiola so that we know if all of them are here. Once the Royal Messenger's body is at the morgue have another messenger come and identify him. We don't want to overlook a possible body switch.' Thorn swung into action. Action was good. Action left him no time to think.

Thorn was in the nineteenth hour of his shift. He needed rest. His mind was losing the sharp focus that was so critical to him now. Every little nuance, every glance, every word could be an important clue. He knew that he had to sleep, but when he went home to his comfortable little cell near the Queen's chambers he could not fall asleep. He sat in front of the fire and sipped his single malt whiskey, a gift from the late Queen. He already knew who the traitors were. The fact that they were fairly sloppy about their plan worried him. Could it be that they thought that they could get away with treason anyway?

Thorn reflected on this and saw that perhaps the traitors could expect to escape punishment. With two of the five princesses unable to transform into Queen, at least in time to have any effect on the outcome of the succession, the traitor had only two remaining rivals. And she had a seemingly insurmountable head start on those two. If Carman managed to emerge from her sarcophagus a full hour ahead of Aynia or Lily then Carman would be able to kill both and seize the Throne with minimal struggle.

Another factor was that for the next thirty days the Hive would be without strong leadership. With news of the assassination and the treason withheld from the workers it would be difficult for the Cabinet to publicly justify action against one of the remaining princesses. Besides, who in the Cabinet had enough guts to commit to decisive action? There was no one. The late Queen tightly controlled Parliament. No one in the Cabinet would have a clue as to how to take charge. Without a

Queen the Hive was adrift and without direction. The traitors knew this.

In addition, members of the Cabinet could argue that the princess who acted with the most determination and foresight to take the Throne would logically make the strongest leader for the Hive. Cabinet Members would certainly argue against executing Carman for treason if persuaded by gold, sword, or stinger.

Thorn leaned forward. Three princesses left, three strong females, each capable mentally and physically to rule. And what if Lily or Aynia managed to emerge as Queen before Carman got to her chambers? The timing of the transformation was inexact. Even if all three took Royal Jelly within seconds of each other they could all emerge hours apart. Having two such strong rivals left a large element of risk to Carman's plan. But what if the traitor decided to increase her odds by sabotaging the other two princesses? Would her plotting go that far? Thorn couldn't take a chance. Somehow he would have to help shore up the defenses of the other potential Queens.

Thorn was a soldier. He despised court intrigue. He liked simplicity. He hated things that were not as they appeared to be. Be that as it may, perhaps his well-known desire to keep out of politics would help him to get away with the plot that was now forming in his mind. But before he took another step in his plan he decided to force himself to get some sleep. In the following month he would need all of his wits about him.

CHAPTER 2

The next morning Thorn woke up and reviewed his plan. He wanted to make sure that his reasoning was not clouded by fatigue. With a few minor adjustments he saw his plan as workable. After a small breakfast he put on his best dress uniform and set out to make a few social calls.

The dress uniform tunic was cut a trifle short and the hose were incredibly snug but Thorn knew from experience that the nurses who attended the Princesses were partial to a male in uniform. He rarely visited a Princesses' chambers without being patted, squeezed, or cupped by roving hands. Even the late Queen made it quite clear that Thorn was to wear his tunics as short, and his hose a little tighter, than propriety allowed.

The quarters of the Royal Guard were attached to the Royal Chambers where the new Queen would live. Beyond that hallway and up a flight of stairs was the hallway that housed the individual cells where the princesses lived. If there were Princes they would live in a common room on the floor above their sisters. But the late Queen had no sons.

Thorn walked out of his personal chamber, through the common chamber for the Royal Guard, and out into the main hallway of the Royal Palace.

The halls had white limestone floors and walls. To minimize the echoes bouncing off the stone great carpets stretched the length of the halls and tapestries were hung at regular intervals on the walls.

Once, years before, Thorn had stopped to examine the tapestries that hung in the hallway outside of the Queen's chambers. Most portrayed all manner of court life from several centuries past. Some, however, were decorated with scenes more fitting to the harem than a public hallway. The details were vivid, the sexual positions varied, and the entire tapestry an enlightening education for a curious male. It was years before Thorn was able to pass through the hallway without blushing.

Across from the tapestries the hallway revealed the French roots of the architect. Three-story high French doors opened out onto a small terrace that ended in several flights of shallow steps leading down into the Hive center.

From the opening at the peak of the roof of the Hive sunlight streamed in and lit the Hive center, bounced off the granite walls, and finally passed weakly through the great glass French doors of the Royal Palace. It was the only natural light ever to reach into the Royal residence.

At one end of the hallway was the Throne Room where the Queen held Royal Court. The hallway terminated at the other end at the massive doors that protected the Queen's Royal Chambers, a spacious suite of rooms nearly equal in size to the public rooms of the Palace. Beyond the Royal Chambers another hallway branched off which led to the largest section of the Royal Palace, the princesses' chambers. There were eight chambers provided for princesses. Each one consisted of a large front room equal in size to the Throne Room. Behind it was a small personal room for the princess in residence. All of her attendants, usually about twenty females, slept in the front room of the chamber. Also included in this wing of the Palace were schoolrooms and the vault for the Royal Jelly.

Thorn walked to the hallway leading to the princesses' chambers. Here the hallway was just as wide as the front hallway of the Palace, but it was enclosed. Unlike the front hallway of the Palace there were no carpets and no tapestries here. The sound of Thorn's footsteps echoed loudly off of the vaulted ceiling. There was no sneaking up on the princesses' chambers. In this hallway every sound carried to curious ears. More than one chamber door was cracked open as Thorn passed by.

His first visit was to Princess Peony's cell. He was curious to see if the attendants there had thought of a unique strategy to save their princess. It was possible to hold a princess in reserve and not feed her Royal Jelly at the death of a Queen. That way if something went wrong during the fight for succession and no viable Queen emerged to take the Throne the reserve princess could then take the Royal Jelly and ascend the Throne with her way already cleared. It was a very risky strategy, but a logical one for a princess terribly far behind on the transformation process.

Thorn saw with that Princess Peony was sealed in her sarcophagus. It was too late to offer the alternative and even mentioning it now seemed cruel. Although Peony's attendants well knew that she had no chance to emerge in time to fight off any other Queen they had never the less done their finest work. It spoke well of these females.

Thorn took a deep breath and told a lie. He informed the head nurse that Princess Gladiola had been found guilty of treason and that she and her attendants had been summarily executed. His conscience did not at all bother him as he told this lie. Nothing would bring Princess Gladiola back to life. This way her death was not entirely in vain. As for the cloud of suspicion over her head, well, the future would possibly rectify that injustice. Until then it was a necessary precaution.

'Unfortunately not all of Princess Gladiola's attendants were caught. We are, of course, searching for them. I doubt that they will remain on the loose for long. The Cabinet did not inform the general population about this incident, as we did not want the workers to panic during this sad time.'

'Then why tell me?' The Head Nurse asked sourly.

She was direct. Thorn liked that. 'Because the traitors have made it clear that if Princess Gladiola is not to be Queen then they plan to make sure that no one becomes Queen. They are planning the annihilation of the entire Hive.'

The Head Nurse gasped. 'My princess!'

'Exactly. Don't be obvious about it, and tell no one, but increase your guards by double if you can. The Cabinet does not want me to interfere with the 'natural selection' of our next Queen,' Thorn made a face showing his disagreement with their policy. 'So this is not an official visit. It's just a friendly warning. Remember; don't let anyone know that you've

increased your guards. Then if they do attack they won't be ready for the extra fight.'

Thorn rose and exited Princess Peony's chambers. He was confident that within twelve hours the number of guards in Princess Peony's chambers would be tripled, not merely doubled as he had suggested.

Thorn's arrival at Princess Carman's chambers caused an interesting commotion. They did not expect this visit. From the consternation on the faces of the attendants Thorn was convinced of one thing: the brains behind all of the plotting were currently in a liquefied state in the yellow wax sarcophagus displayed prominently in this room. None of the attendants was a General. Sister Snakegrass came close, but even she was just the Second in Command. These attendants were well drilled but they lacked the ability to act on their own. This made Thorn's job much easier. Those who were not used to thinking for themselves could be easily manipulated.

Thorn smiled at Sister Snakegrass as she sat across from him in a highly agitated state. Traditional Hive manners demanded that a visitor be provided with food and drink upon arrival. It was a good measure of the panic in Carman's chambers that Thorn was seated a full ten minutes before anyone in the chamber thought to offer the basics of hospitality. Not that Thorn really wanted a cup of nectar. This was his second cup of the sweet liquid in half an hour. Before long he would be floating in the stuff. So he took only a little in his mouth, but kept the cup at his lips long enough to make a show of taking a big sip.

Thorn gladly set the cup down. 'I have disturbing news Sister Snakegrass.'

'Oh?' She tried to seem unconcerned.

'This is strictly confidential. I am not coming to you in my official capacity.' The fact that Thorn was wearing his most formal uniform belied his statement. The deep blue tunic of the Royal Guard was decorated with minimal silver braid. As

21

Captain of the Guard Thorn was allowed to wear fringed epaulets on his shoulders and an array of medals across his chest but he shunned those as being unnecessary. Besides, how well could he perform his job if his clothes jangled every time that he moved?

'Go on.' Sister Snakegrass said.

'You may not be aware, but the Queen was assassinated by Nurse Oxalis, a member of your princesses' staff. We have reason to believe that Princess Gladiola's staff somehow corrupted Oxalis. At first, I must admit, we were suspicious of your Princess Carman. Subsequent events have changed our view of the situation.'

The smile on Sister Snakegrasses' lips made Thorn's blood run cold. She was proud of her part in the day's events. And she really believed that she had gotten away with her evil deeds. 'Thank you for not condemning us based on the actions of a rogue member of our staff,' Snakegrass said.

'All of this information is of course a State Secret. No one is supposed to know.'

'You have my word that I will hold all information coming from you as confidential,' Snake Grass said in an unctuous tone. 'However, I will inform our princess of your faith in her upon her emergence after transformation. I'm sure that she will be, how shall I say, grateful?'

'Grateful?' Thorn echoed. He was a little puzzled at this turn in the conversation.

'Captain, you are an attractive male. You are very physically fit.' Sister Snakegrass let her gaze cover every inch of Thorn's body. 'Your military background is evident in you carriage and demeanor. Our princess likes a soldier. She wants someone whose physical strength will match her own.'

Thorn began to feel very unclean. 'I am no drone.'

'Exactly!' Sister Snakegrass said as if they understood each other. 'She will not want some over-bred, fat, lazy male to sire her princesses. She will want a strong male, like you, someone

with superior genes, and someone who will help her to breed a better, stronger Hive.'

'You know perfectly well that I am not a breeder. I'm not a drone; I can not sire a child.'

Sister Snakegrass leaned forward and gave Thorn a sleazy but tight-lipped smile. 'Do you know what the difference is between an ordinary male and a drone?'

Thorn was very uncomfortable. He did not want to have this conversation with this crazy worker. He shifted in his seat. 'They are able to sire offspring. And the drones of the Seelie Court have wings.'

'But why?' Sister Snakegrass hissed. 'Because they are allowed to drink the Queen's milk. It makes them virile. When Princess Carman becomes Queen, if she chooses you, and if she feels that you deserve the reward, she can let you suckle on Queen's milk. As a chosen consort you could join her in the mating flight.' Sister Snakegrasses' eyes shone with fanaticism. 'Think about it. When Princess Carman becomes Queen she can reward her friends.'

Thorn stood. His face seemed to betray an awful temptation before him. It was all a show for the sake of Princess Carman's attendants. In reality he had no desire to become a drone. 'I didn't come here for this. I only came to warn you.'

'About what?' Sister Snakegrass was instantly alert.

'Princess Gladiola was executed for treason, but we have reason to suspect that Princess Peony might have been involved as well.' Thorn stammered.

'Princess Peony? What threat could she be?'

'I don't know, but she was already in her sarcophagus when we went to her chambers. It means that she might have had advanced warning about the plot to kill the Queen.'

'How could she possible have heard news of the Queen's death? She was supposed to be the last to be notified. But the Royal Messenger never made it there.' Snakegrass protested.

Thorn wondered if Sister Snakegrass would ever realize how she had just betrayed her involvement in the death of the Royal

Messenger. Only someone who killed the messenger would know that the messenger never made his way to Peony's chamber.

'How did Peony learn of the Queen's death before the others?' Sister Snakegrass wondered out loud.

'A question that we asked ourselves. But we will never be able to prove that she was involved in the assassination plot, at least not with enough evidence for the Cabinet to act against her. So just take this as a friendly warning, just between the two of us, and the Princess Carman. Beware of Princes Peony. She could be the first to emerge, and she just might be an enemy of the Hive.'

Sister Snakegrass patted Thorn's behind and led him to the door. 'See how easy it is to be a true friend to my princess? If you hear anymore news like this be sure to let me know. I will tell Princess Carman as soon as she emerges. I will tell her what a good and true friend you are to her.' With the last words she gently squeezed his buttocks.

Thorn bowed to Sister Snakegrass, moving away from her hands. 'I thank you for making me a friend of her Highness.' Thorn saluted the attendants before he closed the door to the chamber.

Another of Princess Carman's attendants joined Sister Snakegrass at the door. 'What do you think?'

'I think that we have found a very important ally. And I think that I have dangled the ultimate temptation in front of him. No male can pass up the idea of being First Consort, especially a male who couldn't even dream of such an honor ten minutes ago.'

'What about Princess Peony?'

Snake Grass frowned. 'That is a matter of some concern. I didn't think that any of her attendants had enough imagination or guts to try taking Royal Jelly before they got the official sanction. But it could be that they had a spy in the Queen's chambers, perhaps it was a member of the Queen's personal guard, or even the Royal Physician. Maybe they saw us breaking into the vault and simply stumbled onto news of the Queen's death. Bad luck like that can happen. I heard that more Royal Jelly was discovered missing from the vaults than the amount we took. At the time I didn't think much about that report. Now I see that it fits with the facts we know about Peony from Thorn. The fact that Princess Peony could emerge second after Princess Carman is a problem. I wish that we had a better idea of when she started her transformation to Queen. We can't risk her growing strong before Princes Carman gets to her. Peony will have to be moved up to the top of the list. Carman will have to kill her first.'

'It sounds as if the entire order we had is wrong. We thought that Princess Carman would take out Aynia first, then Lily, then Peony.'

'We'll just move Peony to the top of the list. It's not a major change of plans. Just a change in the order,' Snakegrass argued.

'I still think that we should have Aynia at the top of the list. She's our biggest threat.'

'I would agree, except that she was not at the top of the list to be notified. Who would have thought it? The Queen's favorite daughter moved down on the list. That must have been quite an embarrassment to Heliotrope,' Snakegrass laughed.

'You'll have to remind her of it.'

'I will just before our princess stings her to death. Or maybe I'll cut Heliotrope's throat myself.'

Thorn resolved to spend as little time in Princess Lily's chambers as was possible. Every item in the room was over-decorated. Tables were swathed in cloths with ornate floral prints, on top of which sat another cloth in a complementary solid color, and above that was a small round of Battenberg lace. Additionally every item on top of the table sat on a crocheted doily. Every square inch of space was stuffed with paintings, figurines, or vases of flowers. The chair that Thorn sat in was so soft that it was impossible to sit up straight.

For the third time in less than an hour Thorn was holding a cup of nectar in his hand. At least this cup was small. It was very small, too small for a male's hands. And the china was very thin. He could see his fingers through the side of the cup. He had never felt so ungraceful in his life. He felt that by merely blowing on the cup it would break in a million pieces in his hand.

Thorn was feeling awkward, big, and clumsy. He was sure with every movement that he made some of the bric-a-brac clutter would get knocked over. Never in his life had he been made to feel this way. It was the fault of the decorators of Princess Lily's chambers. The place was designed to make a male feel like a klutz.

Despite the tiny size of the cup of nectar given to Thorn he ended up drinking much more nectar in Princess Lily's chambers than in the other two cells combined. Here the fussy attendants checked to see if he actually drank the nectar and constantly insisted on refilling the cup.

The overly warm room with its claustrophobic decorating was getting on Thorn's nerves. So were the attendants. The abundant and heavily scented floral arrangements made Thorn long for a fresh breath of air.

It was time to get down to business. Thorn cleared his throat. 'I have come to warn you about a plot against Princess Lily.'

'Would you like more nectar?'

'No.'

The attendant looked hurt. 'Are you sure?'

'Yes. I mean no, I do not want anymore.'

'Didn't you like it?'

'Yes, but I'm fine. I don't need any more.'

'If you don't like it I can get another batch. Has it gone bad? Daisy, taste this nectar. Has it gone bad?'

Daisy gently tasted the nectar. 'I don't think so. It seems fine to me. Doesn't it taste fine to you Captain Thorn?'

'Yes, it tasted fine.' Thorn sighed.

'Then would you like some more?'

'I have had quite enough, thank you ladies. Now please,' Thorn tried to get back on track.

'Let me just go get another batch then. Wait a second,' Daisy sang out as she went to get another pitcher of nectar.

'No, really, this is fine. I'm just not thirsty.'

Daisy came back with a fresh pitcher. 'Here you are. Let me pour you a fresh cup.'

'No. I don't want it.'

'But I went all the way over there to get you a fresh pitcher,' Daisy said, tears welling up in her eyes.

Thorn sighed. If his soldiers were this tenacious he would never lose a battle. He handed over his cup. 'Just a little please.'

Daisy happily filled his cup to the brim. All of the attendants watched with abated breath while he sipped a little from the cup.

'Thank you, that's very nice. Now, can I get to the reason why I came?'

'Cookie? Cake?'

Thorn closed his eyes for a second and willed himself to barrel through his speech regardless of the nurse's feelings. 'Your princess is in grave danger.'

'Lily?'

'What danger is Lily in?'

Thorn gave a silent prayer of thanks that there was something besides nectar parties that interested these females. Their tenacious devotion to their princess was about to shine through. 'I will not mince words. Princess Lily is in great danger. Princess Carman and Princess Peony both ingested Royal Jelly before official word came of the Queen's death. Both princesses will emerge from their sarcophaguses before Princess Lily has a chance to. They may attack each other first. If they do Princess Lily will only have to face one of them. If they don't attack each other first you will have to be able to fight off both Carman and Peony until Princess Lily has a chance to emerge. After she emerges she has to fight for herself, but I want her to at least have a chance to emerge before they get to her. If you increase your guards you can help to hold the other Queens off until Lily has a chance to hatch. If they find out that you have increased your guards then they will increase the number of attendants that they bring along on the assault. So you must add to your guards quietly and let no one else know.' Thorn delivered his entire speech on one breath. Now he paused to refill his lungs.

'But this is supposed to be just a fight between the Queens. Since when are attendants involved?'

'Since now. This is going to go down in Hive history as the dirtiest fight ever for the Throne. Princess Gladiola and her entire chamber were already killed.'

Of all the words that Thorn said to Princess Lily's attendants, these were the ones that sunk home. The females exchanged worried glances. 'Princess Carman's attendants killed Princess Gladiola's?'

'It's being hushed up. I could be put to death for telling you this State Secret.'

'When did it happen?'

'They tore apart Princess Gladiola's sarcophagus. She never had a chance. Her remains were spilled all over her chamber floor.'

The females gasped. Some looked back at Princess Lily's sarcophagus. 'Our Lily is defenseless.'

'You must protect her. I am not allowed to get involved. Technically I am not even here. I can not be seen talking to you again.'

'We will increase the guards.'

Thorn stood and bowed to the attendants. He had to escape this chamber. 'Good luck to you and your princess.'

'Thank you Captain. We will not forget your help. Princess Lily will be most grateful. When she is Queen she will want to show you her gratitude.' Daisy's twinkling eyes gave Thorn a once over. Then she winked at him, slowly.

Thorn escaped Lily's chambers before the conversation became uncomfortable again.

Thorn sank thankfully into the brown leather wing chair in front of the fireplace in Princess Aynia's chambers. Despite the fire the air in the room had a cool crispness to it, like an autumn evening. But it wasn't cold. The room was just right. Thorn smiled a little to himself. Although this chamber was much larger than the one he lived in there was a similarity to his own home. A good chair, a nice fire, some books, all that he needed was a nice drink.

It was as if Heliotrope read Thorn's mind. As she settled herself into the chair next to him she handed Thorn a glass of whiskey. 'You look like you've had a rough day Captain. If you would like something to eat we have a small cold luncheon. We don't have any sweets I'm afraid. Princess Aynia was not especially fond of cakes or cookies, and the last batch that we were sent had a suspicious odor.'

Heliotrope's hand patted Thorn's shoulder lightly, like an old friend comforting him. This was the one chamber where even a male would be taken seriously.

Thorn nodded. 'Thank you Nurse Heliotrope. This will be fine.' He sipped from the glass. It was much better quality than the whiskey the late Queen had given him. This was amber fire. 'Quite fine,' he said and took another sip.

'To what do I owe the honor of this visit?'

'I wanted to tell you a brief history of the day's events, and to give you a warning.'

'Indeed?' Heliotrope never showed a sign of panic, but she did wonder for a fleeting moment if he suspected them of taking Royal Jelly early.

'As you know, our Queen was assassinated yesterday morning. The culprit was a nurse from Princess Carman's chambers. Approximately the same time,' Thorn interrupted himself, 'I'm sorry to say that the attack on the Queen caught us so off guard that the Royal Guards were not functioning at peak

29

performance,' then he continued 'two guards at the vault holding Royal Jelly were killed and the vault was breached. We suspect Princess Carman's Head Nurse Sister Snakegrass heavily in this raid on the vault. And we suspect that Princess Carman ingested the Royal Jelly at least half an hour before the other princesses were notified of the Queen's death. Unfortunately, in another badly calculated move, we sent out a Royal Messenger by himself to deliver news of the Queen's death. We decided at the time,' Thorn's use of the word "we" left no doubt in Heliotrope's mind that the idea had not been Thorn's, but being a good soldier he did not break ranks. 'We decided at the time that to spy on each princess's chambers without arousing suspicion we would use a single messenger to deliver news of the Queen's death, as if we suspected nothing. This mistake cost the Royal Messenger his life.'

Heliotrope murmured regrets on the death of the messenger. Being a messenger was supposed to be a fairly easy position. Most of the young males who performed the job were either Princes or sons of nobility who were waiting to be married off by their families.

'The Royal Messenger made his first stop as ordered by the Queen.'

'Where?' Heliotrope interrupted.

'Here.'

'Ah,' Heliotrope smiled. 'It is good to know that the late Queen treasured our Princess Aynia above her sisters.'

'The choice of Aynia over her elder sister Lily was a matter of concern in the Cabinet. Be aware of that in the future.' Thorn said seriously.

'In the future there will be only one living Queen. Who will care about past alliances?'

'I'm surprised to hear you make such a naive comment Sister Heliotrope. You know as well as I do that where there is statecraft there are undercurrents.' Thorn watched Heliotrope with a measuring look, and then decided that her statement had been misdirection. Of course Heliotrope knew that even when only one Queen was left to rule the Hive there would always be court intrigue.

'Who did the Royal Messenger notify next?' Heliotrope asked.

'Princess Lily. Then he went to the chambers of Princess Carman.'

'A true nest of vipers.' Heliotrope commented.

'Of course, since Carman's nurse Oxalis was the assassin we suspected Carman of treason right away. Apparently the Royal Messenger stumbled onto some damming evidence in Carman's chambers.'

'Like what?' Heliotrope asked innocently.

'He probably saw Princess Carman already in her sarcophagus. Since no one was supposed to be aware of the Queen's death until officially notified the presence of her sarcophagus would have been sufficient evidence to bring a verdict of guilty of treason at trial.'

'Yes, I think that would be enough evidence.'

'We would have sent troops to her chambers and breached her sarcophagus. Then we would have executed her attendants. It would have made the following thirty days all that much easier on me. Unfortunately the Royal Messenger did not have an armed accompaniment. As a result I believe that the following chain of events took place:'

'You mentioned that you received a basket of sweets in this cell that smelled suspicious. Well, so did Princess Gladiola. Unfortunately for her, her attendants allowed the basket to be brought inside her cell. The basket was heavily laced with ether. Princess Gladiola and her attendants fell unconscious, and I'll bet that Sister Snakegrass was well aware that they would be incapacitated.' Thorn told Heliotrope.

He continued as curious nurses moved closer to hear his tale, 'I think that Sister Snakegrass and most of Princess Carman's attendants entered the chambers of Princess Gladiola. There they used the stinger of Gladiola's Head Nurse to kill the messenger, planting evidence at the scene, so to speak. The next step was to force feed Princess Gladiola Royal Jelly. Then Princess Carman's attendants built Princess Gladiola's sarcophagus.' Thorn noticed that Heliotrope's hands clutched the arms of her chair.

Heliotrope's eyes went wide. 'They didn't, tell me that they didn't construct the sarcophagus of thin wax.'

The other attendants in the room began to weep quietly.

Thorn nodded. 'When Princess Gladiola's attendants came to they saw through the plot right away. They knew that they had just been framed for treason. But they immediately started trying to secure Princess Gladiola's sarcophagus. That's where I came onto the scene.'

Heliotrope heard the catch in Thorn's voice. Soldier or not, what he saw in Princess Gladiola's chambers upset him to his core. Heliotrope put a reassuring hand on Thorn's arm. 'The sarcophagus failed.' She said quietly.

'Yes,' Thorn nodded his head. He fought back to wave of emotions he felt welling up. Successful as always, he mastered his voice and feelings. 'Once the sarcophagus failed the attendants stung themselves to death.'

'How horrible for you and your guards.'

'Of course, once the Royal Messenger was dead he could not go on to notify the next princess.'

'Princess Peony!' Heliotrope said. 'This was indeed a villainous plan. Carman killed off two of her rivals before the transformation even began. But I have to wonder why didn't she attack the stronger princesses? Why did she eliminate her weaker sisters first?'

'I think that the basket of ether laced sweets delivered to your chamber answers that question. Princess Carman was testing to see whom she could get to. The chambers with the strongest defenses turned the baskets away. She made her strikes where she could with the least amount of trouble. After all, every Queen is deadly.'

'Did Peony ever get word of the Queen's death?'

'I informed Princes Peony's chambers myself, but they began too late to be a real threat.'

'But Princes Carman has a half-hour jump start on us. That gives her enough time to break into our chambers and kill Princess Aynia before Aynia even has a chance to hatch. The same goes for Princess Lily.'

'It would appear that the fight is won even before it has begun.'

'Indeed,' Heliotrope agreed glumly.

'That's what the attendants in Princess Carman's chambers are thinking. I'm sure that they feel pretty smug about now.' Thorn leaned closer to Heliotrope and lowered his voice. 'I'll let you in on a little secret though. I think that things might not be as dark as they now appear. You see, my sister once told me about a small hidden alcove with a spy hole that looks into the Queen's chambers. I think that perhaps a very clever nurse might have been sitting there spying yesterday and she happened to hear about the Queen's death first hand. I think that she might have taken the initiative to start her princess on the transformation before the official notification of death came from the Queen's chambers. What I need to know is,' Thorn lashed out with amazing speed and grabbed Heliotrope's arm in an iron grip so that she could not get away, 'did this very clever nurse have the guards at the vault killed, or were they dead when she got there?' Thorn's bared stinger hovered inches away from Heliotrope's heart.

Heliotrope's face showed no fear. But her heart pounded in her chest. How did he bring out his stinger so quickly? She wondered. Heliotrope never saw the movement that bared it. It simply appeared.

'Verbena, Freesia, come answer this male's question. Tell him the truth.'

Verbena and Freesia walked closer to the chairs so that Heliotrope and Thorn could see them. 'The guards were dead when we arrived. The vault was already breached when we got there.' Freesia said.

'Is this true? You would swear on Heliotrope's life?' Thorn asked.

'I vow on my princesses' life that what we say is true,' Verbena said.

Thorn let go of Heliotrope's wrist. 'If Verbena swears it then it must be true.' He withdrew his stinger. 'We will never mention this again.'

'Agreed.'

Thorn allowed himself to smile. 'Actually, I was hoping that Princess Aynia got a head start on the transformation. Despite overwhelming evidence of treason against Princess Carman the Cabinet forbids me to execute her. They believe, as so many of our workers do, that survival of the fittest is the best way to determine our next Queen. If they knew of Carman's plots they would say 'don't condemn her, she's showing the skills we need from a Queen to protect the Hive'. The only hope is that your princess began her transformation within minutes of Carman. That will at least give her a fighting chance.'

'Princes Carman knows that Princess Aynia was first on the list to receive notification about the Queen's death. The second that Princess Carman emerges she will swarm this chamber,' Heliotrope was thinking out loud.

Thorn shook his head. 'I don't think so.'

'Why not?'

'A little misdirection on my part. I told Sister Snakegrass that somehow Peony got word early and was well on the way through the transformation before I arrived to tell them of the Queen's death.'

'Will Sister Snakegrass believe that Princess Peony is a real threat?'

'I think so. She's not the one calling the shots in that chamber. Carman is. And those who think up plots like this easily believe that others plot just as much. They won't be able to risk not attacking Peony first.'

'So that buys us what? About ten minutes?'

34

'Longer. I think that when they do go to Princess Peony's chambers they will find about sixty attendants defending her instead of the usual twenty.'

'Oh you are a clever boy,' Heliotrope smiled indulgently at Thorn.

'Not to mention,' Thorn continued, 'that attacking Princess Peony's chambers first puts Carman all the way on the other side of the Royal Chambers from Princess Aynia. It will make sense to hit Lily's chambers next because it is on the route to this chamber. Besides, I told Sister Snakegrass that Lily was the first to be notified. That was believable since Lily is the eldest princess. So logically Lily would be the biggest threat to Carman after Peony. Again, Lily will have an increased guard. Hopefully this will help cut down drastically on Carman's forces before she gets to this chamber.'

'Okay, that could buy us as little as twenty minutes, and much as an hour. It's not much but it will have to do.' Heliotrope sighed. 'And we have, of course, already increased our guards.'

'I knew that I could count on you.'

Heliotrope cocked her head to one side, looking at Thorn critically. 'Why do you help us?'

'I am not helping you. I am forbidden to interfere with the selection of the Queen.'

'Humph. And yet you do meddle. You sent Carman's attendants scurrying in the wrong direction and you alerted other chambers to increase their guards. All of this seems to be just for the benefit of our Princess Aynia. Why?'

Thorn looked down at his hands. Why had he put himself out to interfere with the selection of the Queen? Seemingly it was against everything that he believed in. It was against the Parliament that he was sworn to serve. It was in its own subversive way against the very Hive itself. After all, wasn't the strongest Queen the best Queen? But deep down Thorn believed that a strong Queen would not have committed treason against the Hive in order to take the Throne. A strong Queen did not

35

have to kill off half of her rivals in devious ways before the transformation even began. No, if Carman were going to fight against nature then he would fight against her until his dying breath. That was the true way to protect the Hive. That was upholding everything that he believed in.

'Why?' Heliotrope asked again.

All of his noble thoughts about the Hive were true, but could Thorn ever admit the truth? Wasn't Princess Lily or Princess Peony entitled to as much protection from Carman as Princess Aynia was? Probably. But Thorn was in love with Princess Aynia, not the others.

CHAPTER 3

Heather, a stern blonde with a square jaw and a brusque demeanor, took the steps to the Temple two at a time. It was winter in Russia, no time to be outside. As the massive door of the Temple swung open a heavy cloud of incense billowed out into the sub-arctic air. Black robed Priestesses ran for the door to close it behind Heather. She took no notice of them as she swept past with the gait of one fully accustomed to her surroundings.

The interior of the Temple was huge. Marble, gold, silver, no surface was unadorned. Filigreed, outlandishly baroque, Moorish, a jumble of styles and fashions came together in an overwhelming mass of bad taste and excessive wealth. And all of it for what? The few worshipers who scattered themselves among the pews? Heather allowed herself a snort of contempt. The folk were falling from the ways of religion. She had served in many Hives and in all it was the same story. The Temples were empty, the faithful few, and the strength of the folk was ebbing away.

Heather knocked on the door of the confessional. Why had the High Priestess summoned her to meet here? This was not the usual day of confession. Besides, Heather usually gave confession in the privacy of the High Priestesses' personal chambers. After all, neither one would want the confession of the Queen's confidant exposed to prying ears.

A figure sprang out at Heather from the confessional.

Heather whirled away, using her black, fur-lined robe to create a whirling shield. In the dim lighting of the Temple she could not see the knife, but she knew it was there.

The assassin stabbed wildly at the robe, not sure where Heather's body was in the mass of moving fabric.

Heather stumbled back against the pews. Arms grabbed at her throat from behind. The worshippers in the Temple were part of the attack! Heather freed herself from the second assassin and worked her way down an aisle. She quickly tried to count. How many worshippers had she seen? And how many false Priestesses had she seen at the door of the Temple? How many? Seven, maybe ten.

In frustration Heather threw her cloak to the ground and took to wing. If she was lucky the assassins were of low birth and did not have wings. If she was not lucky, well, who knew how many other killers were hidden among the cherubs and gargoyles that adorned the sixty-foot high ceilings of the Temple?

A projectile hit Heather in the wing from behind with enough force to knock her towards the ground with dizzying speed. Her wing was not broken, but she could not support herself enough to fly.

Heather landed on the back of a pew. Using her strong legs she hurled herself in a backward somersault to the back of the Temple. She was getting closer to the door and most of the assailants were behind her. One of the drawbacks of not having wings was the difficulty in remembering that your prey did have them. Heather did not mind this lack of foresight on the part of her enemies. It left her with only three assailants between herself and the doors.

The three at the door formed into a triangular defense, the middle female slightly in front of the other two. The idea would be to draw Heather to the middle female while the other two flanked her, thus putting her in a position of having to fight on three sides. Heather was having none of it. She lunged towards the female on the left flank.

The assailant's eyes were narrowed in hatred. 'Ferengi,' the female hissed.

Heather recognized the word. 'Foreigner' was the polite translation, a very polite translation. In fact that translation almost obscured the meaning of the word. The assailant obviously meant it in its more literal terminology.

'What have I done?' Heather demanded.

'Let our Queen breed,' a different female hissed. 'You have corrupted our Queen.'

Heather had little time to discuss the nature of the female's complaint. The other assailants were closing in fast. The door of the Temple was near. Heather pushed the closest female down on her own blade and rushed for the door. She flung it open only to throw herself into the breast of the Captain of the Queen's guard.

The Captain saw the body on the floor oozing blood. He looked up to see the other assailants running away. The message was clear. He signaled his troops. They surrounded the Queen and marched her away from the Temple.

Wearily Heather followed the Queen's entourage to the gates of the Palace only to find it locked down tight as the Royal Guard assessed the situation. It could be hours before they allowed her inside. Disgusted, Heather headed to the nearest tavern for some icy vodka. Some days it was the only thing she liked about Russia.

'You over-react darling,' the Queen laughed at Heather much later in the evening.

Heather was not the type who enjoyed being laughed at. She frowned.

The Queen stretched her hands out to Heather and wriggled her fingers. 'Come, come. Don't frown so.'

Heather took the Queen's hands and sat as she was commanded to on a small footstool by the Queen's feet.

The Queen stroked Heather's hair. 'You are so darling to be worried about the life of this Queen, but I am fine, as you can see. And I am having the Priestesses tortured right now to see who let those assassins into the Temple. I will get to the bottom of this.'

'Majesty, one of them called me a Ferengi. I think that they were attacking me,' Heather said gently.

The Queen laughed again. 'Ferengi? This is not even a Russian word. Besides, why would they attack someone as unimportant as you? The attack was meant for me. They probably just wanted to stop you from warning me.' The Queen dismissed Heather's concerns with an imperious wave of her hand.

After the Queen was asleep Heather quietly exited from the Queen's bedchamber and went into her own room. She could not sleep. Something about the attack greatly troubled her. Despite the Queen's egotistical belief that the attack was not meant for Heather, Heather knew that it was. Obviously someone sent a false note summoning her to the Temple. As for the use of the word Ferengi, no, it was not a Russian word, but this Hive was close enough to the border that there was strong influence from other cultures. Besides, the word conveyed in no uncertain terms how the assailants viewed her. The Russian folk were not exactly welcoming to strangers.

Heather poured herself a brandy and went to the chair in front of her fireplace. She frowned at the glass. This drinking of alcohol was getting to be habitual. Heather was beginning to drink more often and in greater quantities at each sitting. When she first came to Russia from Bohemia Heather rarely drank at all. It was those damned unending Russian winters. What else was there to do but drink?

Setting the brandy aside with a determined expression on her face, Heather saw the letter she received three days ago from her sister Deidre. The letter was still unopened. Heather sighed and took the letter in her hand. Time for one of those awful catch up letters where all of the year's deeds were listed in triumphant detail along with dull news passed on from the other two sisters, Rose and Camellia.

'Good old Deidre, at least this letter will put me to sleep,' Heather commented to the air. She opened the letter and began to read the predictable news. As she turned the missive over to read the second page, however, Heather sat up and took notice. There was news about the Hive at Balnacra, in Scotland. Heather held the letter close to her breast. Home. It was a chance to go home, or at least the next closest Hive to home. And there was something else. Three of the five princesses were red heads. If Deidre knew one thing about her sisters, it was how to get their full attention.

Deidre could not believe her luck. She was still very young, but here she was, the new Chief of Staff for the future Queen of the Hive at Balnacra. It was a real honor. Of course she could not discount the assistance that her sisters gave her. Few Chiefs of Staff could assemble the team that she could just by appealing to her family connections.

The idea of leaving Chambord was a bit difficult to face. The Hive de Chambord epitomized the age of chivalry, an age long past but in ways so much alive. In response to the growing pressures of the outside world most Hives in Western Europe were becoming insulated. Few Hives enjoyed the richness of the earth around them anymore. This was not true at Chambord. Many days of summer were spent at the hunt, and many nights were passed in the rituals of courtly love. Weeks went by when the entire Hive de Chambord lived al fresco.

Deidre, for her part, would not miss the frivolous rituals of courtly love. She found it amusing to watch but was not truly interested in taking part. She was too busy to think of love and too ambitious to take on a mate. This caused the Queen of Chambord to make jokes at Deidre's expense, but the jests were not meant as ridicule. Unfortunately there were those at court who failed to understand the difference between gentle teasing done in real affection and outright vicious barbs. Deidre would not miss the Ambassador from the English Hive at Norfolk who fell into the latter category.

'Scotland? How can one give up life in this cultured place for life among the barbarians of Scotland? But I forgot. You're used to that. You're one of them.' The Ambassador from Norfolk said with a curled upper lip at the state dinner when Deidre's new appointment was announced.

Deidre knew better than to rise to such bait. Instead she took a small sip of her raspberry cordial then settled back into her chair. The only sign of her agitation was a finger that twisted a lock of her dark blonde hair endlessly through the evening.

The Queen was watching Deidre closely. Although she did not seem to watch Deidre knew that the Queen's eyes were on her every move. Weeks ago the Spanish Ambassador made quite a scene over some small matter, much to the French Queen's displeasure. That Ambassador was now unhappily serving in a junior position in a German Hive, a political fate worse than death.

It would not do to show a slip of temper here. Even though Deidre was leaving she still desired this Queen's good opinion.

'That Scottish Queen died under such peculiar circumstances. There was no word of an illness, just sudden news of her death, which was never followed by details. Good heavens, what are they doing up there on the moors?' The Norfolk Ambassador, Cowslip, added with a mocking laugh that was not echoed around the table.

The Queen of the Hive de Chambord frowned. She too was curious as to the cause of death of the Queen at Balnacra. There were rumors though, the type of rumors no Queen wanted to hear. Her gaze flicked over to the faces of her own three princesses for a moment. Nor did any Queen want her Hive to dwell on such rumors. She didn't want the workers getting ideas. 'You may find out for yourself Ambassador Cowslip. You're being sent to Balnacra in two months. I received a note from your Queen Norfolk this morning.' The Queen waited with a benign smile on her face as those around the table snickered at the horrified expression of Ambassador Cowslip.

The Queen gave an exaggerated yawn. 'This talk bores me. Tell me Deidre, what is that wicked sister of yours, Camellia, up to? Her exploits always amuse me.'

Deidre knew better than the let family pride stand in the way of the Queen's amusement. Leaning forward she recounted the latest news of Camellia's scandalous behavior, a tale that never needed embellishment to keep a royal audience riveted.

Camellia, the second youngest of Deidre's sisters, looked most like Heather, the eldest. But she shared her taste in males with her sister Rose. Curly hair, the darker the better, and a Mediterranean complexion, set both sisters pulse's racing. There were two important exceptions. Rose was only interested in the drones that met her specific taste. And, being a traditional sort, married the males she wanted and kept them as her drones.

Camellia, however, was willing to forego her favorite features for any male who was willing and available. She also viewed males as being strictly for recreational purposes. Camellia vowed never to marry. And she would have nothing to do with a male already made drone.

Males in most Hives had the freedom to move about the Hive until they were married and made drone. At that point the male entered a harem and was never seen in public again. Social norms demanded that a male in full sexual maturity was for the private use of his wife alone. A drone exposed to public viewing was deemed shamed and therefore for the use and abuse of any female in the Hive demanding his services. Free drones, as they were called, were not generally tolerated and were eventually evicted from the Hive.

In some Hives even young males were not allowed out of the harem. Camellia knew this and could have kicked herself for not checking before she arrived at Tunis if that was the case there. While she was only visiting, and could have left at any time, Camellia was currently without direction and thus was in no hurry to go elsewhere.

This did not mean that she was enjoying her stay in Tunis. Certainly the Hive was beautiful and the folk there friendly and generously warm, but Camellia was itching for male companionship. She had not set eyes on so much as an adolescent male since arriving in Northern Africa.

Camellia sipped her strong coffee slowly in the café. She observed folk as they passed by, an occupation that ate up hours of her morning.

'Miss, rug?' A vendor hustled up to Camellia's table and began to show her samples of prayer rugs.

Camellia pretended not to be able to understand the language.

The vendor was a persistent type who did not seem to notice how Camellia ignored her. Finally the proprietress of the café and inn where Camellia was staying came out and shooed the vendor away.

'Why didn't you tell her to go away?' The proprietress asked.

'What makes you think that I didn't?' Camellia responded fluently in the local language with little trace of her native Scottish accent.

'Lady Camellia, why do you sit here every morning for hours and let those vendors buzz around you?'

'They make me laugh,' Camellia responded in a flat, humorless tone.

'I will never understand your jokes.'

'What makes you think that I was joking?'

The proprietress shrugged. 'A letter came for you.' She handed the letter over to Camellia and went back inside the inn. The proprietress already read the letter. It was from Camellia's sister Deidre, asking her to return to Scotland. The proprietress hoped Camellia would respond to the call of family. Having Camellia in one's house, the proprietress mused, was like keeping a cheetah in the pen with your goats. In this case the cheetah was paying very handsomely for the lodgings, but it didn't make the innkeeper any more at ease about the situation.

By the progress of the sun across the floor of the Hive Camellia guessed that she sat there for an hour before she picked up Deidre's letter. Camellia didn't really want to read it. Deidre's career was going extremely well, Rose was solid as ever, and Heather, well, Heather was heading into possible trouble with that Russian Queen, but Camellia was easily the black sheep of the family. Usually she enjoyed this distinction. Lately it was an annoyance.

'Well, what do you have to say?' Camellia asked the envelope. She turned over the letter. A frown settled on her lips. The seal was broken and clumsily repaired. Well, if a stranger wanted to be bored to tears they were welcome to read private family news. Camellia read Deidre's letter.

'Miss, rare frankincense, myrrh? I have here the finest and rarest fragrances.'

The strong resin smell of the amber and brown chunks filled Camellia's nose. Camellia pushed the vendor's hand away and rebuked her forcefully and fluently.

The surprised seller's mouth dropped open. But not one to miss a sell, she persisted. 'But Miss, I sell only the finest.'

Taking the pages of the letter with her, Camellia stormed inside the inn, leaving behind a trail of blazing profanities.

'Is everything fine Lady Camellia?' The proprietress asked. 'No bad news, I hope?'

'I'm sure that you know as well as I do. Have you packed my bags yet?'

'I took the liberty…'

'Well, once you've taken one, what's another?'

'Hmmm?'

'Never mind, I will leave tonight. I don't need to tell you why, but we will observe the rituals of hostess and guest. I will pretend that you don't know what I am going to say, and you will pretend to be very sorry to see me go.' This comment went right past the proprietress but Camellia continued. 'My sister offers me a position as Mistress of the Harem for a new Queen in Scotland. It is very near to my home Hive, which is either a blessing or a curse, which one I have not yet decided. And I have a chance, for the first time, to serve with a Queen's primary staff entirely consisting of my family. Again, this could be either good news or bad news.'

The eyes of the proprietress had gone wide. 'You are a Mistress of the Harem?' she asked, incredulous. The letter was not specific about the position Camellia was being offered.

'It is my profession,' Camellia said stiffly.

'If you watch the drones, who watches you?'

Camellia was beyond insulted. 'Madame, I have never, ever, touched a drone that did not belong to me. How dare you insinuate such a thing?'

The proprietress had Camellia's money already so she was not afraid to speak her mind. 'I know your type. You have an eye for the males. This you can not deny. It must be hell, no? All of those willing males within your grasp.'

'In all honesty I have never once been remotely tempted,' Camellia spoke with sincerity.

The proprietress shook her head. 'Maybe you've never be caught, but you must have been tempted.'

'No. Not even once.'

Camellia decided to take one last walk around the Hive before she started her trip north. She had to admit that she would miss the warmth of Tunis. Scotland was going to be much colder, and damper. Camellia sighed about that, but then she sighed again as she thought of the deep greens of the forests of Scotland.

She paused to laugh at herself. 'Homesick? Me?' And the normal good humor of her disposition, which had been missing since she arrived in Tunis, returned.

She looked up at the towering Hive structure over her head. The air was dry and hot, the sky uninterrupted turquoise. The walls were all washed in a soft honeyed hue. Colorful doors of cerulean blue, scarlet, and yellow marked the entrances to family cells. Arched windows inset with patterned grills allowed light into the harems without allowing females passing by a glimpse in.

Camellia took two more steps. A rose landed at her feet. She spun around and looked up. Three stories above her head she could see a young male face at the edge of a balcony. His large brown eyes met hers. Slowly, he winked. Camellia could not stop herself from smiling.

'Come away from that balcony at once!' A female voice shouted from inside the chambers.

Camellia made a hasty decision. Looking up and down the alleyway to see if she was observed, she looked up and made a sign for midnight, then for two hours past that. The male nodded.

'What are you doing by that balcony?' The female voice demanded to know.

Camellia rushed down the alleyway and turned the corner so that when the female looked suspiciously out of the chambers she saw no one in the street.

At two in the morning Camellia leisurely made her way to her rendezvous. In the moonlight the shadows of the Hive were cool blue. Most of the Hive was sleeping. For once the streets and shops were silent. Ten minutes late, she saw a sliver of light through the curtains of a balcony and alit on the edge of the balcony.

The male was worried and growing impatient. Camellia silently watched him for a moment. He was a beauty with skin the color of caramel and black ringlets of hair cropped at his shoulders and pulled back into a ponytail. His overly large eyes gave his face the virginal look that Camellia found irresistible.

As the male seemed ready to give up and leave Camellia threw his rose on the table in front of him.

'You came!' he whispered.

'How could I refuse such an invitation?' Camellia purred. She moved across the room to him. He stood up and backed away, unsure of what to do with his guest.

'We must be quiet,' he stammered.

'Of course. And we should go to a room that is more private, yes?'

The male nodded.

'Take me there.'

He stepped cautiously into the hallway and led Camellia to a small room in a turret overlooking the water. Camellia locked the door then went to the window. She looked out across the bay. 'The moonlight is beautiful on the water,' she told him in a quiet whisper.

He joined her at the window and looked out too. Finally he turned to her. 'I've never done this before.'

'Of course not,' Camellia said in a reassuring tone. 'I know. You're just tired of waiting to become a drone. I can tell,' she whispered into his ear, lightly brushing the lobe with her lips.

He shivered. Then he began to untie the laces at the throat of his tunic.

'No, allow me to undress you.' Camellia kissed him on the lobe of his ear, then on his neck at the nape. With exaggerated slow movements she untied the lacing at his throat, and then pulled the tunic off of him. Her fingernails lightly grazed over the surface of his skin, touching his nipple, sliding down well-defined ribs, then down the center of his stomach. She stopped her hand just at the top of his tights though.

Camellia went behind the male and ran her fingers lightly down his back. 'Who did this?' she asked. The male had been punished recently with a heavy hand.

'My sister.'

'Why?'

'I did not come away from the balcony quickly enough today. She suspects me.'

'She did a poor job,' Camellia commented with a frown. 'This is not the proper way to discipline a male.' Camellia pressed her lips to each lash mark on his back.

The male did not know if the kisses were more painful than pleasurable, but when Camellia gave his buttock a playful bite he realized that she had managed to remove his hose without him noticing.

Camellia lifted each of his feet to fully remove the tights. Then she pulled him over to the center of the room were she could see him better in the light of the single candle.

His hands went automatically to cover the small thong that hid his genitals.

Camellia shook her head. 'No, never hide yourself. When you are drone your body belongs to your wife. You must never hide yourself from her. You must allow her to view what rightfully belongs to her. This is part of your first lesson.' She moved his hands to his sides.

'What is the other part?' he asked and trembled.

'You exist only for her pleasure. Don't ever forget the female. She is first, she is last, and she is everything in between.'

Camellia walked across the room with an exaggerated sway to her hips. Then she sat down on a chair and crossed her long legs so that her thigh was uncovered much higher up than was proper. 'Come to me.'

The male started to walk across the room.

'No. Move slowly. This is not a race. The female will assume that you want her. Give her a moment of uneasiness.'

'Why?'

'Do you want to be just another drone or do you want to be the one she remembers on cold nights?' Camellia snapped. 'Now, if I were to let you touch me, where would you first place your hands?'

The male's hands rose in an immediate gesture as if to grab at her breasts.

Camellia snorted and rolled her eyes. 'Could you be more of an idiot? No, I guess not. Males,' she said with contempt.

'What do I do then? Show me,' he pleaded.

Camellia's smile resembled a contented cat's. 'Touch is so important. But it can not be rushed. You must be so into the whole of her and every part of her that you are willing to invest the time to seduce her properly.'

Camellia stood up and turned her back to him. 'Walk up to me slowly and place one hand on my upper arm.'

'What if she does not have her back to me? What if she is sitting down?'

'We will cover all of these situations in time my pet. But for now be a good boy and do exactly as I command.'

'Like this?'

'You can add a little more pressure but never let your fingers press hard enough to make marks. Now sweep my hair away from my neck just enough to give you a place to kiss me at the base of my neck. Feel the warmth of my body with your lips and smell the scent of my hair.' As he kissed her she murmured, 'very nice.'

For Camellia there was a very specific scene she liked to create. It bordered on fetish for her. In order to get every part of it right she left nothing up to the male. She controlled every aspect of the fantasy.

'Should I press my body against you?' He asked.

'Yes, but don't you dare grind your pelvis into me. That is never, never alluring.'

'And next?'

'Let your other hand slid around my waist to my stomach. While you are doing this remember how I kissed your neck and ear? Do the same to me.'

It took a second for the male to figure out the coordination. Then he began to dare to move his kisses to her shoulders.

'You do this well. I like a male with full lips. They have the softest kisses.'

'But how long do I do this?'

'If she takes a deep breath or sighs give her two more lingering kisses. Then if she does not lean against you take your hand off of her waist slowly, take your hand off of her upper arm, and move across the room to a chair or some other place. She is not ready for you yet, but you will have left her wanting more. This is always good.'

'If she leans only the top half of her body against you it means that she is interested but not persuaded,' Camellia continued the lesson.

'What do I do?'

'Move the hand on her arm down beside the hand on her stomach, hug her closely and bury your face into her hair for a moment. Then whisper in your deepest voice some fittingly non-sexual comment such as 'Can I fill your wineglass?' Or

'Shall I have the servants take away the dinner plates?' Gently release the hug and again move away from her. Let her come to you.'

'The best of all scenarios is when she leans her body fully against you.'

'What does that mean?' The lesson was going very fast for the young male. His mind was swimming with the heady scent of Camellia's perfume and the forbidden touch of a female's skin.

'Then you have her.' Camellia turned to face him. 'Once you are face to face with her slip one hand about three inches below her shoulder blades. The other should be at the small of her back, not,' she told him with a sharp slap to his hand, 'on her buttocks, not yet.'

'That hurt.'

'You have no idea boyo. That was a gentle reminder. When I punish males they shed tears.'

He gulped.

'And sometimes blood.'

Camellia knew that his hand would now stay where it belonged.

'Now for the kiss. These things must be done with such a delicate touch. First give me a kiss on my lips for about five seconds with gentle pressure. Then stop and look into my eyes. If you are then allowed to move on to a real kiss my expression should let you know. If not, well, you'll know.'

The male kissed her and then pulled back to look in her eyes. 'Is this yes or no?' He asked.

'If I don't turn away and I don't talk, the answer is still yes.'

He smiled and went for another kiss.

Camellia slid her hand around the back of his head and pressed him in close for a longer kiss. Her tongue pushed his lips apart. He was surprised for only a moment.

'Mmm, nice. You kiss well. If you're in bed with her remember to use your lips on the back of her knees, down her back, down her stomach, almost anywhere. Touch her gently.

Run your hands along her body, caressing everywhere. Take your time with her.'

'Then what will happen?'

'She will be crazy for your touch and you will have earned a chance at a greater reward.' Camellia took the male's hand and guided it between her legs. 'Do you want a taste of this?'

He nodded.

Camellia looked about the room. There were not a lot of furniture choices. She could sit on the chair or she could lie down on the table. Under no circumstances would she get down on the floor. She led him to the table.

'Put your hands on my hips and lift me up onto the table.'

They kissed for a time as he stood between her legs. He grew increasingly bold as he trailed his kisses down to the swell of her breasts above her corset. His hand went to caress her breasts through the black leather. His desire to take her milk nearly vibrated through his body but he feared Camellia enough that he did not attempt to unhook the cups of the corset and expose her nipples.

Camellia slipped his thong off. As they kissed her hands slid down to cup his testicles. Although his penis could not grow hard enough for penetration until he was a drone, the male was not entirely flaccid. Camellia opened her corset at the crotch and rubbed her pelvis against him.

'Why is that bad when a male does it but okay for you?'

Camellia slapped his buttock with her open hand. 'Because it is. Now listen very carefully. I want you to bring that chair over here to the table and to sit down right in front of me. You are going to use your lips and your tongue to their best advantage. If I do not like what you do I will put my hand onto your head and pull your hair until you stop. If I do like it I will not hurt you. Is that a fair trade?'

He nodded and brought the chair to sit in front of Camellia. She placed one booted foot on one arm of the chair and then the other foot on the other side. Then she gently but firmly brought his face to her. Her eyes closed. His talented lips nibbled at her.

Camellia was already fairly wet. The danger of seducing a young male in his own home had an intoxicating rush to it. And she loved the way that males not yet introduced to the life in the harem were so in awe of sex. But most of all she loved the power that she had over them without having to use her usual punishments. These young males were so desperate for her physical touch that her mere voice was whip enough.

'Mmm, yes, like that,' Camellia instructed him, but he needed little instruction. Males who grew up in a harem heard often enough from the drones around them how to please a female. She rarely had to go over basics.

His tongue darted inside of her.

Camellia felt the rush coming. She pushed her pelvis up into his face, riding his tongue. He slipped his fingers inside of her and worked her as she came with muscle cramping intensity. Her back arched up, pushing his head away. She was, for the moment, lost in her own pleasure.

Suddenly she realized that he took advantage of her lapse in attention to unhook the cup of her corset. He was almost latched to her breast. 'No,' Camellia yelled out as she pushed him away.

The shout echoed in the room, down the flight of stairs, and into the ears of the eldest sister, who was a light sleeper.

'You little fool,' Camellia hissed. 'You just had to try didn't you? I told you and told you, you must take time with a female. And in the end you blew it by rushing things.'

Suddenly the hallway outside the door was filled with angry voices. Someone tried to open the door then swore loudly when she found it was locked.

Camellia turned to the nude young male beside her and asked the obvious question. 'Is that your sister on the other side of the door?'

The male nodded. Both of them leaned against the door and braced against the floor with their feet. It was a losing battle. There were at least five females on the other side of the door who were determined to get into the room. One was throwing herself against the door with gusto.

'Boyo, if you think that you got punished for not obeying her earlier today, just wait until your sister breaks down this door. That cute little ass of yours is going to be so pink that you won't be able to sit for days.' Camellia paused to consider the image in her mind. 'Pity I won't be here to see it.'

Suddenly the pounding stopped.

'Either they know another way into this room, or they've gone to get a battering ram. I'm sorry to leave you with so much explaining to do boyo, but I must fly. Family obligations and all. You understand.' Camellia grabbed the young male and kissed him hard. Then with a bound she was at the window of the turret room. Unlike the male, Camellia was fully dressed. She learned long ago not to strip off her black leather corset, skirt, or thigh high boots when seducing young males. Running for her life from enraged mothers and sisters was an easy way to lose expensive clothing.

'Take me with you,' the male pleaded. 'I'll be your drone.'

Camellia laughed. 'Why on earth would I want a drone? I so prefer you fresh, young types. Besides my sweet, you can not follow where I go.' Stepping onto the ledge she blew a kiss to the male.

The door behind him splintered into a thousand pieces. A battering ram was dropped onto the stone floor as the male's sister ran into the room, sword drawn. 'You! Come back here! You've spoiled my brother and you must pay!'

'Spoiled? My dear, he is still marriageable. And with the tricks I taught him he should fetch an even better price.' Camellia purred.

The sister's face went red. Her murderous intentions were clear as she ran towards the window.

Camellia merely laughed at her and plunged out of the window.

'No! My darling!' the male cried. He ran to the window, looking down at the dark waters of the harbor below the window.

The sister knew better than to look down. She found her target, silhouetted against the moon. 'Look, there she is!' The sister pointed out Camellia to the other females. Frustrated, she pounded her fist into the sill of the window. 'Fucking nobility! Those damn wings make them think that they can get away with anything.'

Of the four sisters Rose had the shortest distance to travel to Balnacra. She served in a Welsh Hive. Somehow contemplating moving the distance to Scotland wearied her much more than it did her sisters. Her sisters didn't have to carry the burden that Rose did though. Rose had mates, a harem of her own, as well as several children. The logistics involved with moving her five lovely Turkish drones across the length of the Island of Britain while keeping them from prying female eyes was almost more than Rose cared to think about.

The Queen of the Ellylion, the Welsh Hive, was quite surprised that Rose intended to take the position at Balnacra. Rose explained that her sister needed her. Although this was the only reason Rose gave it was not the true reason why Rose felt that she needed to leave. Deidre's request simply came at a very convenient time.

In a bid to stop incursions the humans of the nearest village from encroaching on the land of the Ellylion the Queen began taking the village children hostage. Rose was strongly against this policy. The Queen ignored her protests. To make matters worse the Queen treated the hostage children as pampered pets. Then when they grew too big or old for the Hive to house the Queen simply abandoned the children in the surrounding woods. Having been taught no survival skills the children usually died within a week. Even those who managed to return to the village were destined to be outcasts. Rose could not abide such cruelty to any living thing.

Rose felt that she could not serve a Queen that she did not respect. But she would never tell the Queen that this was her true reason for leaving. So she pleaded family problems and began the awesome task of moving her harem to Balnacra.

The Council meeting was not harmonious. This was not unusual. However, the late Queen kept a tight reign over the meetings and would not have allowed one to disintegrate into the chaos that plagued this one. Thorn sat far down the table from the others. His opinion was not asked for so he did not give it.

'How could the council hire a bunch of outsiders to be attendants to the next Queen?' Thane Adders-Tongue yelled.

The High Priestess looked to Thorn like a cat with a saucer of cream before it. 'They are highly qualified.'

'They are not from this Hive.'

'A point you have mentioned at least six times in your past six breaths,' the Minister of Food Production noted tensely. 'Thane Adders-Tongue, you are not a member of the Council. You have no place here at this meeting, and you have no say in our decisions.'

'Your bad decisions.'

'Thane Adders-Tongue, I warn you…'

The High Priestess pretended to yawn. 'I can't think what your objection is Thane. These sisters are well regarded.'

'By whom? One is a noted seducer of young males, another is, well, a little too intimate with her Queen, and the other is a very young and untried female.'

'Our French allies are quiet impressed with her.'

'If they like her so much why don't they keep her at their court?' Adders-Tongue grumbled.

'What would make these females acceptable to you?' another council member asked. The evening was growing late and they were tired of the argument.

'What if we were to place an insider from the Hive into the Queen's chambers, just to keep an eye on the others?' Adders-Tongue suggested as if the thought just occurred to her. In fact, this was the only reason she was present at the meeting.

'I suppose that you have a candidate in mind,' the High Priestess asked.

'Family connections aside, she is the best qualified member of the Nobility here at Balnacra to serve a Queen, and to look after our interests as well.'

'You mean your niece Cobra-Lily? She's an idiot.'

'I do mean Cobra-Lily. And she is not an idiot,' Adders-Tongue said defensively.

The High Priestess snorted and rolled her eyes.

'If it will make you happy...' The Minister of Food Production said. She wanted desperately to get home to her warm bed and the newest drone in her harem.

'And get this meeting ended,' the High Priestess added.

'That too. We are willing to hire your niece on. All in favor?'

Hands went up around the table. Except for Thorn's, but as a male he had no voice in the vote.

'Very well. Meeting adjourned.'

CHAPTER 4

Princess Carman woke to find that she was floating in a warm liquid. She panicked for a second then collected her thoughts. She was now a Queen! But she had to be the only Queen. She had a sudden urge to go kill.

Princess Carman, no, Queen Carman, slammed her fist through the wax wall of her sarcophagus. The wax crumbled. The bright lighting in the room blinded her.

'Lights,' Queen Carman managed to mumble as she stepped forward from her sarcophagus and fell to the floor.

Her attendants rushed to her side.

'Put out some of the candles,' Sister Snakegrass hissed. She held Queen Carman's head up protectively. 'My Queen! Take this and drink it. The nectar will give you strength.'

Queen Carman choked on the nectar going into her mouth. She raised a weak arm and pushed the cup away. 'Fool! Get me up. I need to walk. I need to go kill my sisters.'

Sister Snakegrass nodded. 'We will get you accustomed to your new body in a moment. My lady, there has been news that may change your plans.'

'What news?' Queen Carman demanded as several attendants helped her to her feet and steadied her as she took tentative steps.

'Princess Peony somehow heard about the Queen's death ahead of the others. According to sources she began her transformation before the other Princesses.'

'How can this be?' Carman demanded. 'How did she know? What sources?'

'Captain Thorn of the Royal Guard let word slip. He thinks that Peony was in on the assassination with Gladiola.'

Carman thought on this for a moment. 'Thorn is no fool. Was Gladiola charged with treason?'

Sister Snakegrass shrugged. 'No one is talking. The Cabinet hushed it all up. However, everyone from Gladiola's chambers is dead and her sarcophagus was destroyed. Not that it wasn't bound to fail anyway,' Snakegrass smiled smugly to another attendant who grinned evilly.

'One down, three to go,' Queen Carman murmured. 'Let go of my arm,' she snapped at an attendant. 'I can walk perfectly well on my own already. Who are you anyway?' Carman peered at the attendant, realizing that she did not know the worker at her side.

'We took the precaution of hiring forty extra guards for you my Queen. This is one of the new attendants.' Sister Snakegrass explained.

Carman gave a curt nod. 'I approve. You finally had a thought of your own. I was beginning to despair for you.'

'What of Peony, my Queen?'

'I haven't forgotten,' Carman said. 'You said that Thorn told you about Peony. Did he let it slip accidentally or did he tell you?'

'Does it make a difference?'

'It makes all of the difference in the world. Where is my new body armor? Come now, I need to get clothes on. We must start this assault before any of my sisters have a chance to hatch.'

Two attendants rushed over to Queen Carman and began snapping on a corset made of silver plates sewn together with black leather. Above the corset on Carman's back a set of new wings still lay folded. The nurses were forced to gently lift the wings to tie the corset snuggly around Carman's ribs and breasts.

Carman's new adult form was taller by a head than all of her attendants. In the leather and metal corset and matching black leather boots she looked menacing. As she stroked her new stinger lovingly she began to look downright deadly.

Sister Snakegrass could not remember how Thorn had broken the news about Peony. After all, that was nearly thirty days ago. But Queen Carman had a short temper and suffered no fool gladly. In order to make her look more important to her Queen, the nurse decided to make up an answer. 'I tricked Thorn into telling me about Peony.'

'You? You tricked Thorn?' Carman's dismissive snort told Sister Snakegrass how little she believed that tale.

'I told Thorn that if he helped you there was a possibility that you would make him your drone.'

'I would never mate with a mere worker! The male must have Royal blood too. That's what sets us above the workers!' Carman argued, but she stopped talking while she thought for a moment. 'But was he interested? Did he believe?' Carman would never admit it, but she secretly worshipped Thorn. Ever since she was a young princess she adored the handsome Captain of the Guard.

'He was very flattered my Queen. Besides, I only said that you might consider making him a drone. That means nothing if he's dead.'

'Of course he was flattered. Look at me!' Queen Carman smiled at her reflection in the mirror. 'I am a Queen! Look at my long legs, my beautiful hair, my breasts, and my stinger! Who wouldn't sell their soul just for a dream of mating with me?'

'My point exactly my Queen.'

Carman considered her reflection for a moment longer. 'Did Thorn seem suspicious of us in the matter of my mother's death?'

'He showed no suspicion.'

'Maybe I give him more credit than is due to him. He is after all a mere male. They have such limited mental powers. The poor dear does the best job that he can despite the limitations that nature sets upon his sex.' Carman finally managed to tear her gaze away from her reflection. 'So, Peony is back in the running eh? I wonder if one of her nurses saw the dead guards at the vault of Royal Jelly. Well, it hardly matters. I still have a considerable jump on all of them. We will simply start with Peony first. The overall plan is still good, and any great plan is flexible. Gather my troops. We have a few social calls to pay.'

'Attendants!' Sister Snakegrass summoned all of the nurses in the chambers, a total of sixty-five females. 'Now is the time to aid our Queen as she secures her Throne and assures peace for the Hive! Take your weapons! Get into line!'

The females were ready in a short time. Each was armed with a knife and a sword as well as the last resort, her stinger.

Queen Carman and Sister Snakegrass reviewed the troops.

'Everything appears to be in order,' Carman said. She stopped in front of one of the new attendants. 'Are you prepared to defend Queen and Hive?'

'Yes Princess Carman,' the attendant stammered out.

Carman quickly turned and plunged her stinger into the worker's chest. 'Princess? I am no longer a princess. I am the Queen. Try to remember that.'

The worker sunk to the floor, paralyzed. She was dying quickly as the new Queen's venom spread through her nervous system.

Carman watched the attendant die. 'It's always good to test your weapon once before trying to use it in battle.'

'Yes my Queen,' Sister Snakegrass agreed.

'Try to have that cleaned up before I return.'

'Yes my Queen.'

Princess Peony's regular attendants knew that they had no hope of getting her hatched before Carman launched her attack. The new attendants were not let in on this little secret. The forty females were given weapons and placed near the doors of the chambers as a physical barrier between the regular attendants and the ultimate prize in the chamber, Princess Peony's sarcophagus.

Sister Snakegrass led the charge. She pushed through doors of Peony's chambers and held them open as Carman's troops advanced into the chambers. Recently recruited attendants led the first wave of the assault. They were eager to prove themselves to their new Queen.

While waged by amateurs, the first clash was violent enough to put the smell of blood into the air. Seasoned attendants waited for the new recruits to reduce the numbers on the other side before they themselves would weigh into battle.

Like most fights in cramped quarters many attendants were harmed by their own troops. Once the wall of attackers pushed through several weak spots in the defensive line no one could tell who was on which side. The rule quickly became kill anyone who was trying to kill you. Bodies began to fall.

There was no retreat. There was no back exit out of the chambers and Princess Peony's regular attendants would not allow their own troops to fall back into the princesses' personal room to regroup. Several of the new recruits turned against Peony's regular nurses.

The two-front melee raged for twelve minutes but seemed much longer. Soon pockets of fighters were forced to yield to Sister Snakegrasses' core attendants. Blood pooled into thick blots. Various body parts lay detached from their owners.

Queen Carman stepped into her sister's chambers. 'Do we have the sarcophagus yet?' She asked in a bored tone.

'Not yet my Queen. They are stubbornly refusing to yield.'

'I have no time for this! My other sisters could hatch at any moment. Has Peony hatched?'

'Not that I can tell.'

'Thorn lied to you!'

'Maybe he didn't, Queen Carman. You had quite a long head start on the others.'

'Don't chat with me. Kill the damn attendants.'

'Yes my Queen.'

Queen Carman casually walked around the room and stung the captives to death as Sister Snakegrass and her troops once again flew into battle against Peony's attendants.

This battle was much more ferocious. On either side were nurses willing to lay down their own lives in defense of their princess. But none was willing to die without taking someone from the other side into death with them. While swords and knives determined the first half of the battle in Peony's chambers, stingers were drawn for the second half.

'Wait! I want to question their head nurse! Try not to kill her!' Queen Carman demanded as Sister Snakegrass cornered the female.

'I'm not sure I can capture her. Ask her your question now!'

Carman did not care for Snakegrasses' tone, but realize that in the heat of battle niceties were easily overlooked. 'When did Peony start her transformation? Did you get Royal Jelly before hearing official word of the Queen's death?'

Princess Peony's head nurse was well aware of the situation around her. Few of her own attendants stood between Princess Peony's sarcophagus and the deadly Queen Carman. There was no saving her own princess and no saving herself, but she could try to save the Hive from Carman. 'We saw your attendants kill the guards at the vault. We knew right away that something was up, so we took Royal Jelly and gave it to Princess Peony.'

'Then why hasn't she hatched yet?' Carman demanded.

The nurse's mind raced. 'Uh, uh, well, in the olden days they lined up the princesses and fed them Royal Jelly within seconds of each other. Then they sealed them in chambers right next to each other. There was always one who hatched a long time before the others emerged.'

'Yes, the strongest one.'

'And she was the new Queen.'

'But first she had to take care of business.' Carman smiled at the golden wax sarcophagus in front of her. No defenders remained. 'Thank you for the information. I may let you live.'

The nurse threw herself against Sister Snakegrass in an effort to get herself between Carman and Peony. Sister Snakegrass stabbed her knife into the nurse's ribs. The knife sliced upward with a sickening sound as the nurse's body slid to the ground. Using her foot to push the body off of the weapon, Sister Snakegrass pulled out her bloodied knife.

'My Queen,' Sister Snakegrass gestured to the sarcophagus.

Queen Carman stepped up onto the platform underneath her sister's sarcophagus. 'No last words Peony? I thought not. You always were the quiet one.' Carman slammed her stinger repeatedly into the sarcophagus. The wax walls failed and broke apart. With a gush of amniotic fluid Queen Peony slid out onto the floor. Carman stung the body a few more times.

'It looks like our work here is finished. Who's next?'

Lily woke with a start. A flood of thoughts crammed into her brain. She was a Queen. She was successfully transformed! The next thought that came to her normally sweet and gentle brain was that she needed to make sure she was the only Queen. Pushing through the walls of her sarcophagus with both hands, Lily hatched.

Attendants were ready for her with towels and cups of nectar.

'My Queen, Carman has already hatched and is on her way to Peony's chambers. You must try to walk.'

Lily nodded mutely. Supported by loving nurses on both sides she took tentative steps. As her blood began to flow into her new legs she felt strength grow. A new Queen had to be fully physically functional in moments after her rebirth, and regaining functionality meant hard work. It hurt to walk on new feet. Every step was agony.

'What other news?' Lily grabbed a large cup of nectar and gulped it down.

'Princess Gladiola was assassinated. Thorn told us that he suspects Carman strongly in the attack. We have no news from Princess Aynia's chambers.'

Lily nodded. 'I can walk on my own now thank you my dears. Now get me dressed. It's time to go on the offensive.'

'Whom will you take on first? Carman or Aynia?'

Lily thought about the question for a time while her attendants dressed her. 'Carman is the danger to the Hive. We know that she is hatched. If I fail at least I'll have bought Aynia time to collect her defenses.'

'What if Aynia is hatched already?'

Lily laughed. 'Don't be foolish. Aynia is my younger sister. Why would my Queen Mother place her above me on the notification list?'

'An excellent point my Queen.'

Carman's forces slammed open the doors to Lily's chambers. They jumped forward, weapons drawn, but met no resistance. Confused, they looked about the chamber. It was empty.

Queen Carman stomped into the chambers. 'Where are they?'

'I do not know my Queen.'

Thorn appeared at the door of the chambers and slid into the room. 'But I do know.'

'Tell me!' Carman demanded.

Thorn casually took a seat on the arm of one of the overstuffed, dainty chairs in the front room of the chamber. 'Queen Carman, I presume?'

'Yes, I'm Carman. Can't you tell?'

'My lady is much changed since last I saw her,' Thorn commented.

'I am Queen.' Carman said proudly.

'You are a Queen, one of several in the Hive right now.'

Carman advanced on Thorn, her stinger exposed. 'Don't play games with me Thorn.'

'I wouldn't dream of it. I'm here to help you.'

'Then help me! Quit being evasive. Where is Lily?'

Thorn smiled. 'Her attendants took over Princess Gladiola's chambers. They figured that would be the last place that you would look for her. They wanted to make sure she had time to hatch before you came.'

Carman smiled. 'I thank you for your information Thorn. But why are you helping me? Isn't it forbidden?'

'I look to the future of the Hive. I want to protect the strength of the Hive.'

'I understand.' Carman purred. She thought that she did understand Thorn's motivation for helping her. For now she saw no reason to disillusion him.

Thorn stood and made a bow, kissing Carman's hand. 'My Queen.' He turned and left the chambers.

Carman looked after Thorn with new interest. 'Perhaps he is worthy to mate with royalty.' She was seeing him for the first time as an adult female. Suddenly his large brown eyes seemed to hint at a touching naiveté. 'He was so virginal,' Carman thought with an excited shiver.

'My Queen, we must go.'

Carman looked up. 'Yes, yes. How many did we lose of our own troops?'

'Not too many. We're down to fifty. A few more are wounded but will still fight.'

'Let us go visit Lily in Gladiola's chambers then. But I have an idea.'

'My Queen?'

'Follow me.'

The attendants and guards with Queen Lily knew that their hiding place had been discovered. Queen Carman's troops were coming down the hallway to the chamber and made no secret of it. The noise was unbelievable. Carman's troops slapped their metal breastplates with their knives as they marched to Princess Gladiola's old chambers.

Lily and her attendants braced themselves for the coming attack.

Suddenly the wall of the chamber near the back room where Queen Lily stood with her most loyal nurses exploded. In the ensuing dust and confusion half of Queen Carman's troops swept into the chamber.

Queen Lily and her attendants were forced to back into the main room of Gladiola's chambers, fighting each step as their most experienced troops were placed at the front of the battle line. The attendants focused on moving Lily to safety and created a tight fighting shield around her as they moved through the additional guards in the front room of the chamber.

Then the other half of Carman's forces burst into the room through the front door of the chambers. The retreating attendants stopped where they were. Caught in a classic pincher army formation they were driven against the north wall of the chamber.

The armies once again clashed. Carman's troops were already weary and Lily's attendants outnumbered them, but they had seen too much blood already in this day to be fazed by the first spill. While Lily's troops recoiled involuntarily in horror the numbed army fighting for Carman took advantage.

Lily climbed on top of her desk. 'Sting them! If we must die then we will take them with us! Attack!' She commanded her troops. Realizing that death was probably imminent and with no desire to die slowly Lily's troops took her advice and dropped their swords in favor of stingers.

Carman's attendants shrunk back. A knife wound or a sword wound was possibly survivable. A sting was not. The tide of the fight started to turn.

'Don't fall back!' Queen Carman yelled at her troops. 'You have the honor of dying for me. What else are your miserable lives for?'

The troops were too busy fighting for their own lives to respond.

'Make them go forward again!' Carman yelled at Sister Snakegrass. 'We were winning!'

'I will do what I can my Queen.'

'Do it quickly. Aynia could hatch at any moment.'

'I am doing my best my Queen.'

'If you were doing your best I would be dancing on my sister's graves right now.' Carman turned back to her attendants. 'If you do not fight back and win I will personally sting each of you to death. Now fight!'

The troops fell back into the fray with renewed enthusiasm.

Within half an hour Queen Lily was the lone survivor of her side in the chamber. Casualties were heavy on both sides. Carman's remaining forces who could continue on to fight Aynia's numbered in the low twenties. But first Carman had to kill her sister Lily.

Queen Lily stood in the center of the chamber in a fighting stance.

Carman walked around her in a circle.

Lily didn't just have to keep her eye on Carman. An attack could come from any side. Her own mother's death proved that any worker could kill a Queen. A realist, Lily knew that she would not survive this fight. But Carman would expect her to fight to win. Lily decided to fight to survive. That would give Lily an edge in the fight because her strategy would be different from the one Carman expected. That meant that the fight would be drawn out. Every extra second that Lily could buy for Aynia was precious. Every second was purchased at a great expense to Lily, but the Hive came first. And Queen Lily would not let the Hive fall into Carman's hands.

'You're not in physical shape for this fight sister. Too many sweets,' Carman taunted Lily.

Lily initiated an attack move as if she was testing Carman. Her scorpion-like stinger swung through the air.

Carman laughed mockingly. 'Is that it? Is that your best attack? Oh please!'

Lily did not respond. She was too busy keeping watch on the attendants circling around her.

'If you are going to attack you must go at it whole-heartedly. Don't do a timid little thrust with your stinger. You must commit! Lunge forward,' Carman instructed Lily as she indeed lunged forward in an attack.

Lily spun away.

'Oh, that was a nice move. Were you practicing it when you heard my troops coming down the hallway? Or were you just quaking in your boots?'

Lily saw Sister Snakegrass out of the corner of her eye and moved away from that threat, but she was now closer to Carman. Lily swung her stinger around menacingly at the troops near her. 'Are you going to have your troops kill me? Are you really going to allow a worker to kill a Queen? Oh, that's right, you already did. You let one of your common little nurses actually touch our Royal Mother. Have you no sense of what it means to be Royalty? I saw your chamber, a pathetic little model of a real Throne Room. Did you play at being Queen like other females play at dolls? But you don't have what it takes to be real royalty because you're really just a little worker yourself aren't you?' Lily taunted Carman.

'What do you mean?' Carman hissed.

'Don't you know? Didn't any of your loyal retainers ever tell you?'

'Tell me what?'

'Your father was a common…'

'No!' Carman screamed.

'Ordinary,' Lily continued.

'Shut up, shut up!'

'Dirty little worker that got very lucky. I believe that Mother enjoyed him as a novelty, a freak of nature. Of course I remember him because of the great scandal at the time. He wasn't even allowed to sit in our presence, but he went on a mating flight with Mother. She tired of him quickly as I remember.' Lily made a face as if recalling a very nasty odor. 'Aynia and I found out that he couldn't even read. And his parents worked in night soil removal.' Lily mentioned the lowest job any worker could do.

Carman screamed a primal scream of pure anger. Her face was deep red. 'Don't touch Lily! Don't touch her. I will kill her myself!'

Lily allowed herself a small cool smile. She didn't feel calm, but at least now she could concentrate all of her efforts on watching Carman. The other attendants fell back. It felt so good to heckle Carman about her lineage. Lily wanted to do it for years, but their mother the Queen would never allow it. If only the Queen had realized how dangerous Carman was.

Carman was seething. Now she was intent on destruction. Howling an animal cry she rushed Lily and began her attack in earnest.

Lily fought back solidly. She avoided Carman's feints with agility no one would have suspected that she possessed. She counter attacked with determined moves.

Carman used her sword in one hand, but kept her stinger ready in the other.

Lily launched a series of attacks concentrating on Carman's upper thighs, about the only part of Carman's body not covered in leather or metal. She managed to draw blood with her stinger, but very little of the venom went into Carman's bloodstream.

Carman looked down at the blood. It was the first strike to actually harm her. Already angry, now she was enraged. She threw herself at Lily again, never allowing Lily another chance to breathe.

Lily was no physical match for Carman. She was barely able to bring her stinger into position. When she did manage a hit on Carman her stinger was deflected easily by the tight corset of metal and leather that Carman wore.

Carman went on a vicious new attack with unrelenting speed. Lily was forced to her knees. In a useless gesture she threw her hands before her face. Carman's stinger punctured the middle of Lily's right hand and sliced on through Lily's eye.

Lily fell backward. She clutched at her bloody face as Carman's venom pumped into her brain. In a desperate move she threw herself at Carman, but Carman saw her coming. Lily lunged forward and caught herself square in the chest on Carman's stinger.

Lily convulsed and fell to the floor. Carman jumped on top of her body and began stinging her sister repeatedly with angry stabs. Again and again she stabbed her stinger into Lily.

'I'm not a worker!' She screamed at Lily. 'I am Queen!'

But Lily was beyond hearing.

Snakegrass finally stepped forward with a quiet cough. 'My Queen, we still have Aynia to contend with.'

Carman was panting from the effort of continually stinging Lily's body. Spatters of blood peppered her exposed skin. 'How many are we?'

'We are twenty three counting you my Queen.'

'How many of those left are my original attendants?'

'All but two of the remaining troops are your original attendants. We lost several of our own in this battle.' Sister Snakegrass informed Queen Carman.

'What do you think?' Carman asked as she rose from the ground. 'Do we use this surprise side attack on Aynia?'

'Coming through the wall was most effective, but splitting our forces would mean only eleven coming in from each side. Both Lily and Peony increased their number of attendants by triple. If Aynia has done the same splitting our meager numbers could mean certain defeat.'

'Then so be it. We attack her head on. Gather the troops.'

'The troops are very tired my Queen.'

'Are you tired?' Carman asked her attendants with mock concern. 'Let me tell you this, there is only rest at victory or rest at death. Until you have one or the other you will not be tired. Every second that we waste is a second that Aynia could be growing stronger. She could have hatched already. It is much easier for me to kill her while she is still in her sarcophagus. It means fewer casualties on our side, get it? Now march!'

Carman led the way out of the chambers. Her troops had no choice but to follow.

Heliotrope and Passiflora could hear the commotion in the hallway outside their chambers. 'Do you think that it's Carman?'

'I have no doubt that we are down to Carman and Aynia at this point. It was awfully nice of Carman to clear out the rest of the field for us.' Heliotrope said.

'She must be very tired about now.'

'I hope so. I wonder if she realizes that each time she stings her venom supply grows more diluted?'

'Hopefully not. Are we ready for this?' Passiflora asked. 'I think that they are here.' Passiflora sighed. 'I'm too old to die today.'

'Stations everyone. Expect the attack to come from any direction. This means above and below. Ready or not, here they come,' Heliotrope shouted.

Carman herself slammed the doors open to Aynia's chambers. She held the double doors open as her own troops slipped in underneath her outstretched arms. They went into formation just inside the door and stopped. Of the chambers they had been in this bloody morning Aynia's home was the oddest. Carman's troops looked about with an air of uncertainty. What were they up against?

All of the furniture was gone from the chamber. The wall between the front room of the chamber and the back room was gone. Now the chamber was a large open rectangle with a bare ceiling and floor. Not even a picture hung on the walls.

In the center of the room sitting on the floor was Princess Aynia's sarcophagus. Carman breathed a sigh of relief. Aynia was not hatched yet.

Around the sarcophagus was a twelve-foot diameter circle marked off in white paint on the floor. The rest of the floor was also marked in paint in squares seven feet by seven feet. There were about thirty squares. In each square stood an attendant armed with a spiked and double bladed staff.

As Queen Carman and her troops entered Aynia's chambers Aynia's attendants began twirling their staffs in figure eight patterns in front of their bodies. In a moment of complete silence Carman could hear the whoosh whoosh whoosh as the blades sliced through the air.

'Their staffs are longer than our swords my Queen,' Sister Snakegrass observed nervously. 'If we advance we will be cut to ribbons.'

'This is a gauntlet of death,' one of Carman's other attendants observed with awe.

Queen Carman was in no mood to listen to the talk of frightened females. It was time to get in and kill Aynia before she could emerge. 'Find a way to get past them,' Carman demanded.

'How my Queen?'

Carman took her knife and hurled it through the air, catching one of Aynia's attendants in the throat. That female sunk down to the ground, still within the lines of her square. The defender in the square behind her moved into the space, straddling the body. 'Do you get the picture? Attack!'

Sister Snakegrass swung into action. The death of the attendant made defeat of the opposing forces now seem possible. 'See how the come forward to fill the empty square? What we need to do is to protect each square in the grid as we win it. And we have to clear off enough squares to make it through the maze. Use the north wall as our guide. Kill everyone in the two squares to the south of that wall. That will be enough room to make a path to Aynia's sarcophagus. Go.'

The strange battle began. The defenders treated each square of the grid as its own independent entity. Not one moved out of her own square to help an adjacent square. Still, to avoid the swinging blades in the next box over Carman's troops were forced to fight one on one to take each square. By the time they had secured the twelve squares leading to the edge of the circle around Aynia's sarcophagus Carman's forces had lost another seven attendants. And in order to make sure that they did not get locked into the center of the grid of whirling blades, Carman's troops were forced to leave behind six attendants to secure their escape route. That left Carman with nine defenders to take on the circle around Aynia's sarcophagus.

Carman was suddenly very aware of how very tired she was and how overwhelming the numbers were against her. All that she had to do though was to kill Aynia. With Aynia gone she would be the only surviving Queen. At that second all fighting would stop.

Carman allowed herself a grim smile. Poor Aynia, didn't everyone believe that Aynia was the late Queen's favorite child? Obviously she was not. Poor little Aynia was about to die.

Carman pushed past her troops who were securing squares in the grid. She stepped into the open circle and prepared to sting Aynia through the walls of her sarcophagus.

Suddenly Aynia's hands pushed through the golden wax of the sarcophagus. Liquid pored onto the floor in a gush. Aynia stepped out of the sarcophagus and immediately fell to the floor gasping and panting.

'Well, if it isn't my dear sister, Aynia. You're a little late for this party hon, and you're terribly underdressed,' Carman smirked down at her wet, naked sister.

Aynia struggled to stand. None of her attendants could come to her. They were held back by Carman's troops who now ringed the outside of the circle in the center of the chamber.

Aynia's wet hair appeared to be dark. As a princess she had been a strawberry blonde. Now her hair was a deep titian red with glinting gold highlights. Her adult face had high wide cheekbones and a chin that gave her face a heart shape. Like all of the other queens her breasts were large and full. Almost by definition she was wasp-waisted, and then at her hips her body flared out again into shapely buttocks and long legs.

Aynia was the only Queen to emerge taller than Carman, but this added height was no advantage now as she stumbled about trying to get used to her new legs. Every second that Carman wasted gloating was giving Aynia a chance to grow stronger. Carman wanted to torment her sister but she also wanted for this day to end.

Carman lunged forward at Aynia.

Amazingly enough, Aynia was able to stumble out of the way at the last second. Carman failed to make contact.

Aynia slid a little on the wet floor but kept her footing. She turned again to face Carman. Her legs quivered like a newly born fawn.

Heliotrope began to move sideways across the floor towards the back of the chamber.

Carman saw movement out of the corner of her eye. 'Snakegrass get the Head Nurse! She's trying to sneak out the back!' Carman turned a little to Snakegrass and raised her hand to point in the direction of the escaping nurse.

Snakegrass quickly grabbed Heliotrope and handed her to two of Carman's attendants to guard. They forced Heliotrope to her knees.

All attention was away from Aynia. In a flash her wings expanded to their full span. With a snap she leapt up, her body twisting in midair so that her stinger swung around to her right side. Grasping it and guiding it, Aynia slammed her stinger into one of the few spots on Carman's body that was unprotected, her armpit. Aynia's stinger sliced deep into Carman's body, missing the heart by inches. Aynia pumped venom into Carman with single-minded focus.

Carman gasped and fell to the ground. She was not dead but the entire left side of her body was paralyzed. The shock was evident on her face. How had Aynia attacked her? Carman had never once thought of using her wings. She forgot that she could fly. And how could someone so freshly hatched have the strength to fly?

Snakegrass realized immediately the situation. She ordered the two attendants near her to break through the wall to the north. Then she turned to the two holding Heliotrope. 'Kill her, kill her now,' Sister Snakegrass told them. She ran to Carman.

Aynia was about to deal a deathblow to the defenseless Carman, but heard the orders from Snakegrass. Once again she launched herself into the air, coming down with her stinger to attack the two attendants holding Heliotrope.

Behind Aynia the north wall of her chambers fell apart.

Heliotrope struggled to her feet. 'Where is Carman? Where is Snakegrass?'

'Gone! Gone!' Aynia turned to her attendants. 'After them, don't let them get away. Kill them when you find them and bring me their bodies.'

'Cut their heads off before you bring them back into the presence of the Queen,' Heliotrope ordered.

'Why?' Aynia asked in a loud whisper.

'We want them dead Majesty. Who cares who kills them?'

Most of the attendants raced from the room. The rest fell on the few attendants remaining from Carman's attacking troops. Within seconds those attackers were dead.

'You should not have stopped your attack on Carman. You should not have tried to save me,' Heliotrope scolded Aynia.

'Perhaps not Heliotrope, but we can not take back what has been done.'

'There is another Queen alive. This is a bad omen.'

'I agree. We will put together a special group to hunt her and her retainers down.'

'My lady, some of your attendants are dead.' Freesia informed Aynia.

'Attend the wounded,' Aynia commanded in a clear voice that snapped everyone out of shock. 'And bring me the dead. The time of fighting has passed. It is time now for prayers.'

Thorn stepped to the door of Aynia's chamber. He was in his most formal uniform, as were the twenty guards with him. His eyes searched frantically for Aynia. She was not hard to see. She stood much taller than her attendants did. And she was gloriously nude. His heart leapt as she made eye contact with him. She was alive!

Thorn and his guards marched into Aynia's chambers as her attendants placed a black leather corset on her. Before the males came to a halt Aynia was appropriately dressed in a long deep green skirt and black leather boots that laced up the front.

Thorn dropped to his knee. 'My Queen.'

Aynia extended her hand to Thorn. 'Rise Captain Thorn. There is still a threat to the Hive. Carman is gravely wounded, but her attendants managed to spirit her away before I delivered the final sting. Send out a search party immediately. Bring me back her body.'

Thorn stood and saluted Queen Aynia. 'It will be done my Queen.' He turned to his guard. 'Queen Aynia is the last remaining Queen. She is Queen of the Hive. Long live Queen Aynia!'

'Long live Queen Aynia,' the males echoed.

They all bowed reverently to their new Queen and backed out of the chamber. Within five minutes the entire military was actively searching for Carman and Sister Snakegrass.

Sister Passiflora took Queen Aynia's hands in her own. 'I can't believe that the little princess I raised is Queen. Your Majesty,' Passiflora sunk into her lowest bow, made difficult by a rheumatic back. Tears welled up in the corners of her eyes.

One by one Aynia's attendants came to bow to her. Some hugged her; the last time that they would be allowed such a familiarity with the Queen. Others kissed her cheek or hands. All were in tears.

'Come Aynia, it is time.' Heliotrope told her quietly while pulling her gently from the chamber by the hand.

'Time for what?' Aynia asked, confused.

'It is time to meet your subjects. Everyone in the Hive has been counting the days. They know that some time today their new Queen will come to the balcony and greet them. All activity in the Hive has come to a stop. Everyone is in the Hive center awaiting your arrival.'

'I have never been to the Hive center. I've never been out of the Royal Palace, except to attend the Temple,' Aynia admitted nervously. She and Heliotrope walked past the doors of the Queen's Royal Chambers. Those would be the chambers Aynia would call home from now on. She would never see her princesses' chamber again.

'You will rarely venture beyond these safe walls my Queen. But never fear, you will be guarded closely with each step you take, and no one will let you become lost or alone.' Heliotrope stopped at the end of the hallway in an alcove. She pulled back the red velvet curtain and gently urged Aynia forward. 'You are the Mother of the Hive now, you are Queen.'

A loud shout arose from the workers of the Hive as they saw the curtains part. Slowly Aynia moved into view. Stunned by the throngs of workers, the entire population of five thousand must have been packed into the Hive center, Aynia could barely move.

'Long live the Queen!' A shout rose up. The crowd roared in approval. 'Long live Queen Aynia!'

Aynia nodded gravely to her subjects. The nobility, the only class with wings, hovered above the common crowd. On other balconies several stories below the balcony where Aynia faced the mob more nobles and a few honored workers cheered her on. Her eyes swept over the crowd with unfocused panic. Then Aynia saw a face that she knew. Her eyes met Thorn's across the way from her. He touched his hand to his heart and bowed deeply to her.

Aynia could not help but smile. She waved to her old friend. The crowd, not knowing that the greeting was meant for only one of them, went wild with cheers. Aynia smiled again and looked around at the crowd, making eye contact with many workers and nobles alike. She waved to them the stately wave she had seen her mother use. She knew instinctively how to work a crowd.

'Viva Scotia!' Aynia shouted.

The crowd cheered in a deafening roar.

'I'm Queen,' she said quietly to herself. 'I'm the Fairie Queen.'

CHAPTER 5

Carman grimaced as her attendants dragged her along their escape route. Their escape plan was formulated in the event that their assassination plot was discovered. Unfortunately it did not allow for a Queen that was half paralyzed.

The tunnel below the Royal Palace was originally built to afford the late Queen private access to certain parts of the Hive. Its presence was often rumored but never proved. Several tunnels were long since collapsed. But the main tunnel was still intact.

Carman now had only five attendants. Two dragged her by supporting her shoulders. Two others tried from time to time to lift her legs. Sister Snakegrass led the way with a torch.

'You're damaging me even more!' Carman protested.

'My Queen, I must insist that you keep quiet. Who knows how thin the walls are to this tunnel?'

Workers of the Hive who longed to expand their confined quarters were known to dig into the floors and walls of the boulder that protected two sides of the Hive. Some stone walls were by now carved down to molecular widths. The poorer sections of the Hive were becoming dangerously unsound.

'I am a Queen,' Carman grumped. 'Why am I skulking through tunnels like a goblin?'

'Sh. We're here.' Snakegrass rapped three times in succession on the wooden panel above her head. 'Draw your weapons. Our escape may have been discovered.'

The attendants put Carman down and unsheathed their swords.

As it turned out it was several hours before their knocks were heard. Snakegrass spent the time massaging Carman's leg and arm. She also had the other attendants walk Carman up and down the tunnel. It was possible, Snakegrass believed, to bring some utility back to Carman's damaged limbs.

The door finally opened.

Snakegrass looked up. 'It's safe,' she whispered. She put her sword away and indicated that the other attendants were to help her lift Carman up through the opening.

'Where is this?' Carman asked. She was looking at a large room decorated in the old style. From the looks of it not even servants had been allowed inside the room for years. Dust and cobwebs were thick on tapestry sofas and piles of pillows.

'You are in my home,' her hostess informed her.

'I can not walk or sit up. Help me!' Carman demanded.

'You're injured?' The stern, gray haired older female was clearly not pleased. Her already thin lips pursed down to tight lines.

'Damned Aynia got a lucky strike in under my arm. My entire left side is useless.'

The female silently considered this news while the attendants crawled out of the tunnel. 'I was astounded to find you here. When Aynia claimed the Throne I naturally assumed that you were dead. But when I returned from the Hive center my maid told me that there were spirits in the old harem. So I came to see.'

'Aynia claimed my Throne?' Carman asked in disbelief.

'Apparently there are no others to dispute her claim.'

'Because I cleared the way for her!'

'Majesty, I ask that you keep your voice down. We must get you moved, and quickly.'

'Why can't I stay here?'

'No one lives here,' the female said through clenched teeth. 'Besides, the military will search for you. As you can well imagine I am not eager to have them find you in my house.'

'Then where will we go? I'm tired. And I'm hungry.'

'Food and shelter will be supplied. Once the search dies down I will have you taken to a special hiding place in the valley. They will not search the same area twice, so once I know they've gone over the area in question it will be safe to take you there.'

'Where? Where will I be safe from that Captain Thorn and his males for now?'

'The one place that the military may never go and the Queen may only go by special invitation. It is a place of sanctuary for the Queen's enemies.'

Carman was in no mood for riddles. 'And where is that?'

Thane Adders-Tongue, leader of the Opposition Party, smiled her steely smile. 'Parliament.'

The hiding place in Parliament was not exactly Carman's idea of a chamber worthy of a Queen. There were no beds. She was forced to share one room that measured less than ten by ten with her attendants. During daylight hours they could not risk speech.

'I am Queen and this is where I shall live?' Carman protested the proposed living quarters as she looked into the room.

'For a short time Majesty. Patience.' Adders-Tongue said. 'Begging your pardon Majesty, but I must speak with my niece for a second. Family matters,' Adders-Tongue smiled a benign, apologetic smile. 'Snakegrass let us walk. You others try to make this room comfortable for our Queen.'

Snakegrass followed her Aunt down the hallway where they would not be overheard. 'Yes?'

Adders-Tongue wasted no time on pleasantries. 'The Queen's attendants were brought in from different Hives. Although hired separately, as it turns out they are four sisters from a noble family of the Ardcharnich Hive. I convinced the Council that we need a local female to watch out for the interests of the Hive since we did not know the attendants. I assumed, of course, that the new Queen would be Carman.' Adders-Tongue said waspishly.

Snakegrass ignored the sting. 'Whom did you place in the Queen's chambers? I assume that it was family.'

'Cobra-Lily was the only one available. I gave her some instructions as soon as I heard about Aynia. Until the Royal Chambers are settled it will be difficult to get messages to her.'

'Cobra-Lily was too dumb to pull off any plots,' Snakegrass sneered.

Adders-Tongue had to agree with that. She nodded. 'She's able to do the simple task I gave her. For now that is enough. But that's not why I wanted to speak with you.'

'It's the Queen Carman,' Snakegrass guessed.

'She's damaged!' Adders-Tongue hissed. 'I can not put a damaged Queen on the Throne! The Hive will not stand for it.'

'I know therapy for her arm and leg. I swear to you that she will walk on her own in a week or two.'

'I need her healthy as soon as possible.'

'I give you my word.' Snakegrass said solemnly.

'I expect that you will deliver. I must go now. Be quiet during the day; try not to move around too much. You may be here several weeks.'

'Yes my lady.'

Thane Adders-Tongue nodded and retreated down the hallway.

Snakegrass returned to the chamber and locked the door. She looked around their disappointing surroundings and almost let a sigh escape. 'Well, shall I bring out some wine?' She asked a little too brightly.

Carman grimaced. 'Yes, and bring out some food. I starve.'

'Yes Your Highness.' Snakegrass set about serving food to Carman.

'Tell me, what's the story with the creepy harem room?' Carman asked.

'It's a long story my Queen.'

'I don't have anything better to do with my time. Tell me.'

Snakegrass did not like to tell this story in front of the other attendants. Most of the story involved matters known only to her family. 'Your Mother was the one who had the tunnels built

82

under the Hive. It led from a secret room in her Palace, a small alcove that had a spy hole to the Queen's bedroom.'

'I am aware of how we entered the tunnel, but why does it lead to your Aunt's harem room? And why is the room empty?'

'Those questions are both answered by the same story. Thane Adders-Tongue had in her possession a certain male whose physical gifts were well remarked on by the females of the Hive.'

'What gifts?' Carman asked suspiciously.

Snakegrass blushed a deep shade.

'Oh, never mind. I can guess.'

'He was quite common and quite vain about his attribute. Even though not yet a drone there was obviously great, er, um, promise. Word got around. My Aunt purchased him from his parents. Thane Adders-Tongue was pleased at the acquisition of such a fine specimen.'

'I can imagine. How, er, big?'

'They say that once he was made drone he had to lie down when aroused, because the loss of blood to his brain often made him dizzy enough to faint.' Snakegrass then went on to gesture with her hands the approximate size.

One of the other attendants gave out a low whistle of appreciation.

Snakegrass continued, 'although members of the noble houses are educated and refined, it is the nature of the females to talk about their drones in a free manner amongst friends. Well, the Queen was a guest at Thane Adders-Tongue's estate, and Adders-Tongue had her new male brought out and displayed to amaze and astound her friends. Apparently the Queen liked all that she saw. She had the tunnel built so that she could have access to Adders-Tongue's drone. He walked through the tunnel to the Palace when summoned by the Queen. There he would entertain her, and then he would return.'

'Wasn't he missed from the harem?'

'I guess not. I wasn't there at the time, so I don't know,' Snakegrass nearly snapped. 'Anyway, at the Autumnal Equinox he flew past his own lady and mated with the Queen. Adders-Tongue was humiliated. Everyone knew. That is, they knew about the fact that he ignored Adders-Tongue and mated with the Queen. No one knew about the tunnel. The common workers leave the Hive to mate in the morning. Then they eat picnics and watch the nobles take mating flights in the afternoon. They all saw this drone fly right past Adders-Tongue and take the Queen. Adders-Tongue had him put to death for that transgression. After all, we can not allow our males to mate with other females. Their seed belongs to us. They can not decide where to sow it.'

Carman nodded. It was understood in the Hive that males paid dearly for adultery. It helped keep them well under the thumb of their mothers and wives.

'Apparently during that time Adders-Tongue somehow discovered the tunnel. Deciding that none of her harem could be trusted she turned them all out of her house. The harem was closed forever.'

'What happened to the males?' A stunned attendant asked.

'A very few were taken back by their families. The rest became prostitutes and were eventually driven out of the Hive. Society will not accept a free drone.'

'So that's why the harem is empty. No wonder Adders-Tongue is so wound up. She hasn't had...' Carman started to comment, but Snakegrass interrupted her to continue the story.

'But Thane Adders-Tongue's shame was not to end. The Queen grew big with child. Adders-Tongue was insane with the desire for revenge. She was unable to have a child. She fixated on the idea that the Queen stole her one chance to conceive. Although we all know that the size of a male's penis in no way indicates his virility, Adders-Tongue believed that he was the only male who could possibly fertilize her. So she plotted against the Queen. Thane Adders-Tongue decided to alert the Mountain King of the Queen's habit of walking alone in the wood.'

'The Mountain King! But he's our mortal enemy!' Carman said.

'True, but Adders-Tongue wanted the Queen dead. She wanted revenge.'

'What happened?' Carman was thrilled by this story. As a princess no one would have dared to tell her such a tale. But now that she was an adult apparently they felt that they could tell her everything.

'The Mountain King took up Adders-Tongue's offer. The goblins have no females of their own, so they must abduct other folk females to sire offspring. A Fairie Queen is a great catch for a goblin. Since the Queen was heavy with child it would be hard for her to escape him.'

'And?'

'The Mountain King rode up on his black stallion and was about to take the Queen away when her favorite drone, Prince Thistle, came along to save her. Prince Thistle was the father of Lily, Gladiola, and Aynia, the three eldest princesses. Unknown to anyone, he watched over his Queen while she walked in the forest, believing that it was not safe for her. As you know, once a male is a drone he is never allowed outside of the harem. Somehow Prince Thistle was able to sneak out of the harem to follow the Queen. When he saw the Mountain King Prince Thistle attacked. Prince Thistle was able to save the Queen but was mortally wounded in the fight. The Queen returned to the Hive and gave premature birth that night.'

'Did the child die?' Carman asked.

Snakegrass smiled. 'No my Queen, you did not.'

Carman slapped Snakegrass with her good hand so hard that Snakegrasses' lip bled. 'Don't ever tell me that my father was a worker.'

'Forgive me Your Highness.'

'Don't ever tell that story again.'

'I will not. But you can see in a way why Adders-Tongue allied herself with you. In a way you are the daughter that the Queen stole from her.'

'I am Royalty, not mere nobility. Don't mention this again. I mean it. Adders-Tongue allied herself with me for one reason and one reason alone - she knows that I will rule with an iron fist, that I will be the warrior Queen this Hive needs, that I will never give up fighting for my Throne no matter what. She knows that I am the true Queen.'

'May I ask a question my Queen?' Thorn asked. He and Aynia, each nervous in their own way, were pacing the antechamber of the Throne Room. Thorn knew that there would be few times when he would be alone with the Queen, so if he wanted to know he had to ask now.

'You may always ask. I might not always answer.' She smiled a little as she said this. It was frequently the answer he gave to her when he was her teacher. The memory of that made Aynia pause, why was it that Thorn seemed suddenly so young and vulnerable to her?

'Fair enough.' Suddenly he was afraid to say the words out loud. 'Earlier today when you, um, when I came to your chambers during your fight with Carman, you were wet and, um, well,' Thorn's voice faltered.

'Nude?' Aynia suddenly wanted to laugh but she dared not hurt his feelings.

'Yes,' he was relieved that she said the word for him. 'It was as if you had just hatched.'

'It did appear so.'

'But I was in your chambers over an hour before that and you were already walking on your own.'

'Yes, I was.'

'I'm confused my Queen.'

Aynia smiled. 'Remember when you taught our military strategy class?'

Thorn remembered those days well. For years Aynia was the only princess in regular attendance. Her other four sisters showed up when it pleased them, and coming to class pleased some of them very infrequently. Thorn never minded because when her sisters failed to come to class he had Aynia all to himself. Not even the attendants were there. The two of them talked for hours. Sometimes they never even got to the lecture. Thorn fell in love with Aynia over the years, as she matured mentally though never physically. He adored her quick wit. Her sense of humor was delightful. She could be sweet and sensitive but also accepted without hesitation the harsh decisions a military leader had to make. She was a student without peer. Class day was the only day Thorn ever caught himself singing. For years he denied his attraction to Aynia. Finally he accepted that he loved her. With that came acceptance that he would always have to love her from afar. He kept telling himself that was enough.

'I remember every class, every day,' Thorn admitted.

'You taught me that sometimes it is best to pretend to have a weakness.'

'In some situations, yes, it is good to fool your opponent.'

'As soon as I hatched I instructed Heliotrope and the others to construct a new sarcophagus for me. I worked on building my strength right up until the last second. Then I stepped in and they sealed me up. We used nectar for the liquid.' Aynia laughed at the memory. 'I don't think that I'll be able to drink another cup of nectar for a year.'

Thorn smiled. 'How very smart of you.'

'Thank you. From my teacher that means a lot,' her soft voice carried the depth of her feeling.

'I am impressed.'

'So when Carman attacked my chambers she thought that I was just hatched. It gave me the opening that I needed.'

'It was very dangerous of you to go against her without any body protection.' Thorn objected.

'My spies told me that she had been stinging quite a bit this morning. Her venom was pretty well diluted before she got to me.'

'Still, she could have killed you with enough stings.'

'But she didn't. I am so glad that she never thought about an attack by air.'

'I heard that you did a spiral in air. I've heard that is very hard for beginning flyers to do.'

'I love flying,' Aynia said with shinning eyes. 'It was wonderful. You should go flying with,' Aynia stopped, embarrassed. Thorn was not of the class that had wings. He would never fly. Even if he had wings most males only flew with a female during the mating flight. This was yet another impossibility for Thorn. He was not a drone. 'I am so sorry Thorn, I forgot myself. Please accept my apology.'

'My Queen, I know that you did not mean to hurt me. And truthfully you did not. I fully accept who I am and my position in the Hive. After all, the Hive needs workers as much as it needs nobility.'

Aynia walked over and kissed Thorn gently on his cheek. 'This Queen needs your friendship.'

Her words might not have hurt him but the kiss went straight to Thorn's heart, where it ached for days.

The trumpet fanfare sounded. Aynia turned to face the door of the antechamber. Thorn gave her an encouraging smile as she looked back to him.

'This is it,' Aynia said mostly to herself. She took a deep breath.

Thorn stepped around Aynia and prepared to open the door. 'On your command Your Highness.'

'Open the door Thorn.'

'Yes my Queen.'

Thorn pulled the door open.

Aynia stepped to the doorway. The six-foot train of her dress pooled at her feet. The dress was a deep green material that clung enticingly to the Queen's body. The green matched well with her red-gold hair, fair skin, and green eyes. A tartan sash of yellow and black accented by a fine line of red went from her right shoulder, diagonally crossed her torso, and ended at her waist. The v neckline of the dress revealed the Queen's now ample bosom that was supported under the dress by her ever present body armor corset. As the last Queen had died from a sting to her abdomen Thorn made sure that the current Queen was well protected in that area. Aynia's corset would deflect even knife blades.

Every step that Aynia took down the aisle of the Throne Room revealed her black leather boots as far up as her ankle. Although already taller than most of her subjects by a foot or more, the new Queen's boots sported dangerously high spiked heels. The outfit projected the image of a warrior Queen.

Aynia stepped down the aisle of her Throne Room. Thorn walked just behind her. Behind him another four guards marched in close formation. Along the sides of the aisle nobility of the Hive stood at attention. Many tried to catch Aynia's eye. She looked just past each person making eye contact with none. Further down the aisle, closer to the Throne, were diplomats from the other Tuatha de Danaan Queendoms. At first Aynia was shocked to see them here so soon. She had just seized the Throne today. Then she remembered. Her Royal Mother died over thirty days ago. The representatives from other Hives had plenty of time to get the news and make the trip to Balnacra. For Aynia her mother had only been dead for two days. The grief was still fresh. For everyone else here it was old news.

Just beyond the diplomats and representatives were the two groups that would determine most of the policy of Aynia's reign. To her left the Parliament. To her right the Priestesses. Aynia's Throne sat solidly in the middle of the two.

Aynia stopped at the Throne and turned. Slowly she sank into the chair, a simple saddle chair caved of ebon wood. As far as thrones go it was quite plain. Never the less, it was the seat of power in the Hive. Immediately after she sat a small group of attendants, not ones that she knew, arranged the train of her dress so that it lay perfectly.

The entire assembly bowed, and then those with enough rank sat down. Sitting in the Queen's presence was an honor reserved for a very few.

A Cabinet member pounded the floor twice in solemn succession with a wooden staff topped by a golden knob. 'Let it be proclaimed throughout this and all Fairie Queendoms that today Queen Aynia is crowned Queen of the Tuatha de Danaan, the Fairie, of Balnacra Hive.'

'Hail Queen Aynia!'

'She is rightful Queen by law of succession. She is Queen, Royal Mother of the Hive.'

'Long live Queen Aynia,' the crowd intoned.

The High Priestess stood in front of Aynia. 'We crown you with this crown, symbol of the Children of Danu, the Tuatha de Danaan, the Fairie Peoples.' A crown was brought out on a pillow of red velvet. The crown, like the Throne, was somewhat plain. It was a circle of gold about two inches high. In the front it rose to a peak of about five inches. There was no engraving, no stones set into the piece. But somehow it suited the new Queen well. She abhorred ornate pieces. To her surprise, the crown was quite heavy as it was placed on her head. It easily weighed five pounds. One would not have guessed to look at it.

Again there was a flutter of activity as the attendants played with rearranging Aynia's hair.

The High Priestess backed away so that the nobles could see Aynia with the crown sitting on her head. 'May the Goddesses protect the Queen and find her reign pleasing in their sight.'

'Long live Queen Aynia,' the crowd said again.

A member of the Cabinet stepped forward with another red velvet pillow. On top of this one lay a scepter of gold. This was about eighteen inches long with a four-inch bulb at the end. On top of the bulb was a single thirty-carat purple stone. 'This is Your Majesty's scepter of office. Please accept it, and in so accepting, take sovereignty over your people.'

Aynia reached out and took the scepter in her hand. It was heavy, about eight pounds. Some historians of the Hive speculated that originally it was used as a cudgel to execute enemies of the crown. Feeling the solid weight of the scepter, Aynia realized that the rumors could be true.

She wondered what to do now. Everyone was looking at her with benign smiles. Did they expect her to do something? Her eyes went to Thorn. He made a small gesture with his hand that she understood immediately.

Aynia cleared her throat.

'As your sovereign Queen I accept this scepter and crown. I will rule wisely and justly over this Hive with the help of the Goddesses, and live in peace with the other Tuatha de Danaan Hives.'

Thorn gave a small nod of approval as the nobles smiled more. But he made another gesture for her to talk more.

What to say now? She thought. 'I am proclaiming a day of national mourning for my royal sisters Princess Gladiola, Princess Lily, and Princess Peony. Today they laid down their lives in defense of the Hive against the treasonous acts of Carman. I would also like to extend recognition to the families of those who assisted my royal sisters and also lost their lives in defense of the Hive.'

The nobles stopped smiling. This was not what they expected her to say.

'After the day of mourning, however, it will be time to look forward to our future. We will accomplish this by taking a day to celebrate.'

This was what the nobles had expected. Again they were smiling. As Thane Monarda was to say later, for those among the nobility who supported other princesses than Aynia, Queen Aynia's proclamation of a day of mourning went a long way to bring their support to her side. Many of her friends agreed. The only ones in disagreement were a sizable but silent group of Princess Carman supporters. The facts about the late Queen's assassination and subsequent events having never been made public, they did not believe that Princess Carman was guilty of treason. They would not forgive the new Queen for accusing Carman of conspiracy against the Hive.

'Where are my regular attendants?' Aynia demanded to know.

'Please eat Your Highness. I have dinner prepared for you. You must eat,' Cobra-Lily lectured Aynia as she pushed the bowl up to Aynia's face.

'Where are Heliotrope, Passiflora, Freesia and Verbena?'

'Here, soup. Eat a little for me. As for your old attendants, they were merely attendants for a princess. As common workers they are not fit to attend the Queen.'

Aynia was about to lose her usually unflappable temper. This attendant with her maddening answers was the last stress that Aynia needed at the end of this very difficult day. She wanted to undress. She wanted to take a long bath. Then she wanted to sleep, and she wanted to do it in the company of the attendants who had been at her side every waking minute of her life up until now.

'Name.' Aynia snapped.

'Your Highness?'

'What is your name,' Aynia said with exaggerated slowness.

'I am Cobra-Lily my Queen. Please just take a bite of this.'

'Cobra-Lily, dear, when I ask a question I want an answer that will help me. Where are my attendants?' Aynia recognized Cobra-Lily as the attendant that had irked her almost non-stop throughout the day. She was constantly fixing, fussing, and ultimately pulling, Aynia's hair.

'We are your attendants.'

'Cobra-Lily, you're dismissed.' Aynia said with a sigh.

'For the evening?' Cobra-Lily asked.

'No, for good, for ever. Don't ever come into the Royal Chambers again.'

Cobra-Lily burst into tears. 'My Queen, did I not please you?'

'Get out,' Aynia said with gritted teeth.

'But I don't understand what I did wrong.'

'And that is why you are dismissed. Now leave.'

'But my Queen!'

Aynia sank into a chair at a table in the small private parlor off of her bedroom. A fire blazed in the fireplace. Dark wood bookcases lined the walls. Two small sofas faced each other in front of the fireplace, separated by a low table of dark wood. The table that Aynia sat at now seated eight. She had taken many meals here with her Royal Mother. These were the chambers of her Royal Mother. Even now if Aynia breathed in deeply enough she thought that she could smell her Mother's scent, but the scent was fading. Her Mother was gone. Now these were Aynia's chambers.

To Aynia's relief another one of the attendants forcibly escorted Cobra-Lily to the door of the room, down the hallway, and out the door of the Royal Chamber. When she returned Aynia tiredly looked up at the remaining four attendants. 'Shall I start over again?'

'There is no need My Queen. I can answer your questions. As you are very well aware, the Hive has a very complex social hierarchy. Unfortunately our work is so stratified that those who attend a princess do not move on with their princess when she becomes Queen. There are those who attend Queens and those who attend princesses and the two positions do not overlap. Common workers may serve a princess but nobility must serve the Queen. There is almost no way to change this. I realize that at this very difficult time in your life the ideal situation would be to have your attendants move along with you. The familiarity would bring you much needed comfort. However, knowing that this was going to happen, your Head Nurse Heliotrope took the pains to train us for the past thirty days.'

'She was that confident that I would become Queen?' Aynia asked.

'Sister Heliotrope left no question in our minds as to what the outcome of the day's events would be.'

'I bet you say that to all of the new Queens. Tell me, what is your name?'

'I'm Deidre.' The elegant Fairie with color the hair of caramel tapped her breastbone. 'This is Rose.' She indicated a very maternal looking female. 'The dour blonde is Heather. To your right is Camellia.' Deidre pointed to a willowy pale blonde in a black leather cat suit who strongly resembled the other attendant, Heather.

'So you four are to be my new attendants?'

'We sisters will serve you to the best of our abilities my Queen.'

'I'm sure that you will. But what happened to my past attendants?'

'They spent every hour of their lives in your service since you were born. Now that you are Queen they will take a well-deserved rest. I heard that Sisters Passiflora, Heliotrope, and many others joined the Priestesses at the Temple. The drones in your Mother's harem were offered as husbands to her attendants. Your attendants were all given minor titles of nobility. All now have a chamber of their own to live in and a pension. After all, raising a Queen is quite an accomplishment. The Hive owes them a great debt of gratitude.'

'I agree. Perhaps I will write a little note to each of them, personally thanking them for their hard work. It seems rude to just forget about them. Make notations in my calendar to reserve time for me to write to them.'

Deidre bowed. 'It will be done. Is there anything else My Queen commands?'

'Heather, is it?' Aynia asked the brooding female in the far corner. 'I must bathe.'

Rose stepped forward. 'I have one being prepared as we speak my Queen. My name is Rose, and I will take care of your physical needs. Dinner should be taken now. You have not eaten today. You're probably starved.'

Aynia had not eaten anything since Heliotrope pushed the Royal Jelly into her mouth over a month ago. Up until now she hadn't realized how hungry she was.

'Ah, your food,' Rose placed a bowl of soup and two pieces of bread on the table in front of Aynia. 'For the next couple of days we will watch over your food very carefully. Your stomach has not digested anything before. We must break it in gently.'

'This looks wonderful,' Aynia admitted. She sipped at the soup. Although the broth was clear it had a rich flavor.

'I'm glad that it pleases Your Majesty.'

'You've done well Rose. Thank you. Now Heather, Deidre, and Camellia, before I ask you to do something that is not in your job description, tell me what you do.'

Heather stepped forward. 'I am your liaison to the Temple. As you are the Mother of the Hive it is my duty to make sure you fulfill your duties of a ceremonial nature. Deidre deals with the Parliament, your Cabinet, diplomats, and the nobility. She specializes in politics the way that I specialize in religion. We both deal with protocol, but she keeps your calendar.'

'And Camellia?'

Camellia made a little bow. 'I'm your Mistress of the Harem. Once you have drones I will take care of their needs and act as your liaison to them.'

'That would explain all the leather.' Aynia commented on Camellia's spiked heels, cinched waist, and head to toe leather garment. 'Well, it seems that we have everything covered with the four of you. What was Cobra-Lily supposed to do for me?' Aynia pushed back the bowl of soup. Although very hungry, a few spoonfuls of the soup were enough for now. She never even tasted the bread.

'Cobra-Lily was given her position due to the rank of her relatives. Since we are not of this Hive it was decided that a member of the Hive needed to be here to oversee our work. Please let us assure you Majesty, we are all experienced and need little supervision. We know our jobs. And as for our loyalty, well, we swear service to you, and we take our word very seriously.' Heather informed Aynia. Heather could not take her eyes off of the new Queen. She was so delicate and young.

'As near I can tell, Cobra-Lily's main function was to dust the plates and silverware. That's all that I ever saw her do.' Camellia commented.

Rose seemed satisfied with the amount that Aynia ate. 'You did well my Queen. Take it gently and slow. That's the best way. Let's move you into the bathing area. If you care to continue to talk to the others they may follow us.'

'Yes, come along,' Aynia said. She stood up and followed Rose to a large room off of the bedroom. The bath was the size of a pool. While inside the Hive, the bath gave the feeling of being outside. On the south end a waterfall dropped into the water. The edges were planted with ferns and flowers as if the whole bath was part of a woodland stream. Unlike a real stream however, the water was heated and delicately perfumed.

Aynia lifted her arms as Rose pulled off her dress. Then Rose bent down and unlaced her boots and pulled them off. Aynia was used to being dressed by others so she felt no awkwardness at this. Then Rose unlaced the back of the corset. Aynia was pleased to be able to take a really deep breath.

With Rose and Camellia on either side supporting her, Aynia waded into the bath.

'This is lovely, thank you.'

Rose, Deidre, Camellia, and Heather undressed themselves and slid into the water with Aynia. Gently, reverently, they washed Aynia's body.

Aynia was growing very sleepy in the warm water. She yawned. 'I must sleep.'

'Of course my Queen. Your bed is prepared. Let us know in the morning if it was satisfactory. We can change anything that does not please you.'

Aynia walked out of the bath and into the heated towel that Rose held up for her. Rose led Aynia to the bedroom and helped her into the bed. Soft sheets covered a firm mattress. Aynia lay down on her stomach. Rose put oil on her hands and gently massaged Aynia's legs and back. Before Rose was finished Aynia was fast asleep.

Camellia blew out candles in the room as the four attendants backed out of the room quietly. Rose shut the door. They all smiled at each other and went to the dining table to hold a short meeting.

'I can't believe that she got rid of that idiot Cobra-Lily for us.' Camellia laughed at their good luck.

'Oh, I know. We're so lucky.'

'What do you think?' Deidre asked Heather.

'She's lovely,' Heather said dreamily. 'But as far as judging her ability to rule? We will see. She has a day of mourning, a day of festivities, and then the real work of being a Queen starts. In three days she will have to perform the religious rites. Then I will know.'

Deidre nodded. 'She did well at her coronation today. I could tell then that she did not like Cobra-Lily. I'm intrigued by this day of mourning. As far as I can tell no other Queen has ever honored her rivals for the Throne.'

'Is it weakness?' Heather asked anxiously.

'I don't know. I don't think so. As usual the Cabinet is withholding information about the old Queen's death. I think that there is much more going on here than meets the eye. Notice that she accused Carman of treason, and she said that the other princesses helped to defend the Hive against Carman. What is this treason that Carman committed? What happened in the fight for succession?'

'I don't think that we will ever know,' Rose said.

'I don't either. The best that we can do is to speculate, and that could lead us to some very wrong conclusions. Let us take this at face value then. Carman did something wrong. Perhaps she was tied up in the death of the old Queen,' Deidre said.

'You're speculating already,' Heather protested.

Deidre gaped at Heather for a moment, and then nodded. 'Guilty as charged. Okay, Carman committed treason and all of the other princesses fought her off. That left Aynia to take the Throne. But why did the other princesses step aside to let Aynia take the Throne? Did Aynia have to fight any of her sisters?'

Heather sighed. 'You're just trying to guess again. I thought that we weren't going to do this.'

'Camellia, what do you think of our new Queen?'

'I reserve judgment until I see how she is with her harem. I like what I see so far. She won't suffer fools and she likes to hear her news straight.'

'Amen. Rose? What do you think?' Deidre asked.

'She's very strong. I heard a rumor, of course, that she attacked Carman in the air. If she could fly in her first hours than she is physically fit to rule. I felt good muscle mass. And when she is deeper into sleep I will check to see if she is fertile.'

'Rose!' Deidre said, shocked.

'A Queen must bear princesses. She is the Royal Mother to the Hive. If she isn't fertile I say find out right away and start the Cabinet up on finding a successor from another Hive. I hope that you all remember your history? The Queen of Kinvara Hive never took a mating flight and never bore a princess. In the second century of her reign she fell down and punctured the bottom of her foot on an ornamental gate. Three days later she was dead and the Hive had no heirs. The Kinvara Parliament applied for a replacement Queen but there was an unfortunate lack of seasoned, trained princesses due to several recent fights of succession in the neighboring Hives. Finally they imported an English Princess.' Rose told them.

'They must have been desperate.' Heather observed.

'Of course they were, but that's not the point. The princess that they got was only twenty and was a poor student at that. She became Queen since she was the only one that they fed Royal Jelly to and she didn't have anyone to fight. Within three years the Hive was laid to waste.' Rose said.

'Wait a second, I remember this story. The reason the Hive went to waste is that humans moved into the area and they had anti-Fairie magic. The Hive couldn't survive after the humans plowed all the land around the Hive into farmland. It didn't go to waste because they had to bring in a foreign princess.' Deidre argued.

'She was English. Of course it was her fault.' Heather said.

'The point is,' Rose raised her voice, 'that if their Queen raised princesses of her own there would have been a fight for succession, leaving the fittest to lead. Maybe that Queen could have saved that Hive.'

'This is a ludicrous argument,' Deidre commented. 'Anti-Fairie magic isn't anything a Queen can fight.'

'Oh sure, make excuses for the English princess.' Heather said.

'Go to sleep, all of you. Tomorrow is a big day for our Queen, and we won't be of much use to her if we're half asleep.'

Rose yawned and nodded in agreement.

Camellia took out four glasses and poured a deep gold liquid into them. 'First, let us drink a toast to our new Queen. To our new Queen, long may Aynia reign.'

'Here, here,' the other three raised their glasses.

'To our new Queen, the most beautiful Queen I have ever served. Thank the Goddesses Carman didn't win.' Heather toasted Aynia.

'Amen to that!'

Rose smiled mischievously. 'To our new Queen, may her mating flights be successful.'

The four attendants clinked their glasses together.

'And to our new Queen, our deepest gratitude for getting rid of Cobra-Lily.' Deidre added.

'I'll drink to that,' Rose said.

'Me too!' Camellia nodded.

'No truer words spoken,' Heather agreed. The four drained their glasses.

'I'll clean up,' Camellia offered. 'Go do what you have to Rose.'

Rose nodded and left the room.

Heather and Deidre headed for their own private rooms in the Royal chambers. Camellia washed out the glasses and placed them back in the bar. Some of the plates and glasses were dusty, so she flicked a rag over them. She smiled a little to herself. In the next few days they would have to take on some servants for the Royal Chambers. Right now they were on minimum staff as the old Queen's staff had been pensioned off already. Once the servants started she would have them give this place a top to bottom scrubbing. Camellia was from a noble family, after all, and didn't think that washing dishes or floors was in her job description. However, she had an overwhelming need for order and was not above doing any job that needed to be done to maintain the chamber properly.

Aynia woke early in the morning. She could have slept longer. She was exhausted, but her staff pulled off her warm blankets and began making noises in her sleeping chamber until she gave up trying to stay asleep.

When she sat up her head swam. The feeling of lightheadedness nearly made her fall back onto her pillow, but Rose was by her side in a second with a supporting arm.

'Your problem is low blood sugar. You haven't eaten anything substantial in over twenty-four hours. While I don't advocate putting too much into your stomach to begin with, we should have you eating a light meal every two hours for the next day or so until your body begins to function normally.'

'I'm going to throw up.'

'Put your head between your knees Your Highness. It will help.' Rose gently bent Aynia's head down. It helped to stop the room from spinning, but her stomach was still very queasy.

'Did I have to wake so early?'

'You have many duties my lady.'

'Am I Queen or not?' Aynia asked waspishly, although she immediately regretted her tone.

'A Queen is the servant of the Hive. I'm afraid that your days of leisurely scholarship are over.'

'Forgive me for snapping Rose. It's hard to be friendly when one is ill.'

'I think a little nectar would do you good.'

'I despise nectar.'

'Never the less, a sip or two would go a long way to correct your low blood sugar. Please my lady. The sooner that you start eating the sooner you will feel better.'

If Aynia had had her full strength she would have been able to resist the cup that was placed against her lips. In order to stop the liquid from pouring down her face she had to take a sip, then another. Within minutes she no longer felt as queasy. Finally she could sit up.

'Thank you Rose. I do feel better now.' Aynia looked around the bedchamber. It was completely changed from the late Queen's interior design. As was the current rage, the room was sparsely furnished. In a corner near the bed was a collection of large pillows surrounded by sheer curtains. Swaths of richly colored silk extended from the corners of the room to the ceiling, then across the ceiling to the large chandelier in the center of the Queen's bedroom. Deep jewel-toned purple, red, blue, and green, sometimes edged in ornate gold or silver patterns, the fabric made the room look like someone's fantasy idea of a tent.

'My lady must eat a little more. This was merely enough to revive you.'

Aynia rubbed her hand over her face. 'What is my schedule?'

'In an hour you have a State Funeral for your sisters. Then you have a short meeting in your Throne Room greeting the emissaries and diplomats from the other Tuatha de Danaan Hives, not more than one hour. After that you will go to your Mother's tomb and pay your respects. That should take a little more than two hours. Lunch is back here in the Royal Chambers, alone.' Deidre told Aynia.

'Lunch alone?' Aynia couldn't believe her luck.

'It took a great deal of juggling with your schedule Highness.'

'I'm very pleased Deidre.'

'Thank you Your Majesty.' Deidre smiled to herself. That fool Cobra-Lily would have never thought to give the new Queen a moment to herself. 'After lunch you have a three-hour meeting with the Parliament. A briefing from the military follows that here in your chambers. During that meeting the Captain of the Royal Guard, Captain Thorn, will introduce your personal bodyguards. Then you will go back to the Throne Room and officially receive status reports from all of the Ministries. They've been asked to keep it short, no more than three hours.'

Aynia groaned.

'You don't have to pay a great deal of attention. You will be given the reports at the Meeting of Parliament. This will just be the official presentation. It takes place about once a year. Don't drift off or yawn. Try to ask at least one question from each Minister. For example, due to the long winter we are behind on our food gathering operation. Ask when the Minister of Food expects food production to reach sufficient levels, or some question along that line.' Deidre told Aynia.

'My Mother had me sit in on many of these presentations. I have an idea of the types of problems I am looking for. However, if you are aware of specific problems like the one that you just mentioned, please do brief me ahead of time.'

'That is my job Your Majesty.'

Rose interrupted Deidre. 'We must get the Queen into her bath, dressed, and to breakfast. The rest of you come along. You can continue talking to her while we get her ready.' Rose helped Aynia to her feet and led her to the bathing room.

The sound of the waterfall into the pool soothed Aynia's nerves. She waded into the water and swam to the far side. She let her eyes close only for a moment.

Gentle hands touched her skin. Aynia surrendered to her attendants. Pleasant massages worked between her shoulder blades, on her tense forehead, and on the balls of her feet. Another tentative hand caressed her inner thigh then slowly worked higher and higher between her legs. Aynia was too mesmerized by the touch to object to where the hand was heading.

Soft pressure accompanied the circular stroking of her clitoris. Aynia sighed and leaned her head back onto Rose's shoulder so that she could concentrate on the sensation.

Aynia's eyes opened to slits.

Lady Heather was looking intently at Aynia's face.

Aynia closed her eyes again and smiled.

'If you keep doing that I will never leave this bath,' Aynia purred.

'Heather,' Rose snapped at her sister.

The touch pulled away.

'I can't think of a better way to start the day,' Camellia said.

'We don't want the Queen to fall back asleep.'

Convinced that the bath was nearly over, and that Heather would not dare continue to stroke her, Aynia opened her eyes and tried to get her focus back. 'After the meeting in the Throne Room what am I to do?'

'You have dinner with the nobles, dignitaries, priestesses, and the Parliament. This will be a full State dinner. Expect it to go on for about four hours.' Deidre told her.

'Is that all?' Aynia asked.

Deidre realized that Aynia was joking. 'I am sorry my lady. It is unfortunate. You must expect these State Dinners at least twice a week.'

'Please tell me at that point I am allowed to come back here.'

'You are my lady, but you will have a staff meeting with Rose, Camellia, Heather, and myself.'

Aynia waded out of her bath. Rose was ready with a towel. She gently patted down Aynia's body, and then wrapped a loose kimono around her. 'Come on, you must eat,' Rose led her into the parlor and sat her down at the table.

With a nod from Rose a bowl of soup, this time with small bits of vegetables and matchstick size slivers of meat, was placed in front of Aynia. Aynia was not hungry but she ate a few sips anyway.

Rose hovered over her like a mother hen. 'Try a bite of bread.'

'No, really,' Aynia declined.

'I must insist Highness.'

'One.' Aynia took a little bite of the bread. It had honey on it, which she did not care for, but she ate it anyway.

'I hope, Deidre, that I am not expected to memorize this agenda.'

'I will be at your side all day my Queen.'

'Good, because I have already forgotten half of the schedule. What's next?' Aynia asked.

'My lady should be dressed for the day. But first,' Deidre hesitated.

'Yes?'

'I set aside time for you to write notes of thanks to your past attendants. Would you like for me to take dictation?'

'No. Thank you Deidre, but a real note of thanks must be handwritten, don't you think?'

'As my lady sees fit,' Deidre said. She was pleasantly surprised.

'Where will I find paper and a pen?' Aynia asked.

'There are supplies in the desk.'

'Leave me, all of you. Come remind me in ten minutes if I have not come back to the room to get dressed.'

'Are you going to eat more?' Rose asked anxiously.

Aynia answered by taking another miniscule bite of the bread.

'Will you eat at least half of the soup?' Rose dared to ask.

'I will try. Now go.'

Aynia paused over her thank you notes momentarily. She wanted to send a message conveying thanks, but she also wanted her old staff to know that she needed their ears in the Hive. These new attendants might be fine, but Aynia knew whom she trusted. Those who earned her trust with a lifetime of service were not about to be forgotten. Pensions were all very well but they didn't replace the feeling of being needed.

In a code developed by her chamber for secret messages, Aynia asked her nurses to keep her apprised of rumors and events in the Hive. They would understand this brief request, and they would respond.

Aynia already missed her life as a princess. Rose was right that her days as a princess had been of leisurely scholarship. Aynia enjoyed every moment of it, especially her lessons with Thorn. They both had a passion for history, for debate, for books, for learning. She thought fondly of Thorn. He was the only remaining constant in her life. Perhaps that was why since hatching as a Queen she had felt drawn to him as never before.

After Aynia finished writing her notes in less than the promised ten minutes she emerged from her private chamber and went into the bedroom. She handed Deidre the notes. 'Please see that these are delivered today.'

'Yes my Queen,' Deidre bowed out of the room to find a Royal Messenger. Usually there was some loitering around halls of the Royal Chambers.

Deidre went to the very first room in the Royal Chambers, near to the massive door. Several young males sat playing cards while they waited to be sent out on errands. These were connected males whose families would marry them off soon. They took their jobs about as seriously as a male destined to be a drone could.

'You, messenger,' Deidre called out to a young man in the Queen's livery.

'Yes Lady Deidre?'

'See that these are delivered at once.'

'Yes Lady,' the messenger took the note, but did not move.

'Yes?'

'The Lady Camellia, will she be wanting anything delivered today?' The lad blushed as he avoided Deidre's eyes.

Deidre laughed. 'What's your name?'

'Copperhead.'

'Well Copperhead, I will tell the Lady Camellia that you asked after her, and I will tell her how fine you look in your livery as you were headed out the door delivering those messages that I just handed to you.'

'Yes Lady Deidre.' Copperhead took the hint. He put the notes into his carrier and left the Royal Chamber.

Deidre was still laughing about the Royal Messenger later as she teased Camellia about him. Camellia, who had many such young males dancing in attendance, was hard put to place the name to a face.

The Royal Messenger did not exactly make a beeline to the recipients of the letters. He left the Royal Palace and crossed the Hive center. Rather than turning to his left, to the Temple and the chambers of the Priestesses, he instead went right, towards Parliament and the large hereditary chambers of the nobles.

His path took him to the outer walls of the Hive, to his own family's estate. Copperhead's Mother was the youngest sister of Thane Adders-Tongue.

Copperhead bluffed his way past the armed guards at the heavily fortified front door of the family chambers. The Royal Livery he wore could be intimidating to males who did not qualify to serve in the Royal Guard.

'What do you want nephew?' Adders-Tongue asked grumpily as she saw him over her breakfast.

'I bring you a present Auntie.'

'Don't call me that. I'm Thane Adders-Tongue to you, even if you are my sister's whelp. Seven boys. Seven! Not one female to carry on the family name. And whom do you think that she'll come to when its time to get you all married off? Me. I'll have to call in every favor owed to me to get her sons off of her hands.' Adders-Tongue paused to sip her tea, but went on speaking as she chewed toast dripping with honey and butter.

'Have you met the Queen's new attendants?' She changed the subject. 'They're sisters from Ardcharnich Hive. I hear that the eldest, Heather, is a real orthodox follower of the Goddesses. Keep an eye on her for me. Those religious conservatives are always the easiest to corrupt.'

'She doesn't seem that bad, but she's really stern.' Copperhead said. 'The Lady Camellia is very interesting.'

'I know about her, that new Mistress of the Harem, Lady Camellia. Humph! Like letting a fox watch the chicken coop. Mark my words; there will be trouble in the Queen's chamber over that one. She's got an eye for the males. But don't warn them that I said so. I want trouble for the bitch Aynia.'

Adders-Tongue gulped some tea to wash down the toast. As she talked to Copperhead she punctuated her words by jabbing the butter knife into the air. 'And don't let the Lady Camellia sweet-talk you into taking a sip of her milk! I know that you males all want to make your last transformation but mark my words boy, if you have a beard I won't be able to buy your way into any harem, even with all my money. So you stay out of her bed, keep her hands out of your pants, and keep your mouth tightly shut around her. I know the type. She'll ruin many a boy, and then leave them.'

'Yes Auntie.'

Adders-Tongue growled.

'Yes Thane Adders-Tongue.'

'You mentioned a present.'

'Yes.'

'Well, let's have it boy. Parliament starts in less then an hour. I have some news to spread around.'

Copperhead held out the letters.

'What is it?'

'The Queen Aynia asked me to deliver these.'

'Don't ever call that bitch a Queen in my house boy. We all know who the true Queen is.'

'Aynia gave these to me.'

'So?'

'They are addressed to her prior attendants.'

'Oh?' Adders-Tongue's interest was peaked. She wiped her hands and face with exaggerated delicacy on a cloth napkin. 'Bring 'em here.' She extended her hand.

Copperhead walked nervously up to his Aunt and handed over the letters. Adders-Tongue expertly unsealed the envelopes and read over the missives. She was unimpressed.

Both Copperhead and Adders-Tongue looked up as the doors to the breakfast room swung open. Copperhead's mother, Lady Snakeroot, bustled in. 'I suppose you heard that the bitch Aynia fired our niece last night,' she started in without bothering with pleasantries. 'Hello darling,' she kissed the air near Copperhead's cheek. 'Don't you look sweet in your little uniform? You should wear it a smidgen shorter in the back. Give the females a bit of a show. You've got a good bottom, just like your father.' Lady Snakeroot sighed. 'Or at least like he used to have. I made my mother draw up a marriage contract with his mother based on that alone. I didn't even know his name. But like all drones, after we had a few sons he just kept adding the weight. Don't do that when you get into a harem son. No lady likes to mate with a fat slob, and no drone is worth anything except mating.'

'Thus speaks motherly advice,' Adders-Tongue said acidly.

'Well, do I speak the truth?'

'Yes, but he's still a bit young to be hearing all of this.'

'Nonsense. A properly raised son knows his place well before he takes milk. And I want all of my sons to know what it takes to seize the position of First Consort, and how to keep it. They are only males, so they need to know how to take what power they can.'

'Shouldn't they learn that from their fathers?'

Lady Snakeroot laughed. 'Oh dear, yes, I suppose that they should. Except that I have a new First Consort every six months. None of their fathers was successful, so how can they teach their sons? Copperhead, sweetie, are you putting that extra padding down there like I told you? Don't too much padding, but you need to fill your hose out in front or no one will give you a second look.' Snakeroot turned her attention back to her sister. 'I am determined to have them all married off this year. My chambers are much too crowded. And I need the money!'

'That bridal money is supposed to insure your son's futures, not yours. And what connections do you have to place them in good homes?'

'Our sept has always looked inward for males. I'll just have a little talk with our cousins.'

'Oh no you don't! This clan is much too inbred. And it's beginning to show. More than a few idiots have appeared already,' Adders-Tongue glared meaningfully at her younger sister, but the comment went over Snakeroot's head. Adders-Tongue had just about as much of her sister's company as she could take. Her sister was far too vulgar.

'Did you hear that Aynia isn't eating well?'

'Oh my no, how delightful,' Snakeroot clapped her hands together.

'How unfortunate that our new Queen isn't seem physically fit to rule.'

'Who else knows about this?' Lady Snakeroot asked her sister slyly.

'Well, it's sort of an official secret. You know, only Members of Parliament and the like would be told.'

Lady Snakeroot, always eager to show off her insider knowledge, suddenly remembered a few social calls she needed to make. 'Oh dear, look at the time. Must run,' she kissed the air near Copperhead again and dashed out of the room.

'Do me a favor,' Adders-Tongue said to Copperhead as she watched her sister depart.

'Yes my Lady?'

'If your Mother marries you off to anyone like her, especially a blood relative, just fall on your own stinger and make it quick death.'

Copperhead smiled wanly. 'I will do my best Thane Adders-Tongue. Of course, I would prefer that someone sensible like you found a wife for me.'

'You mean someone better connected.'

'As you will.'

'Well, these notes are hardly interesting.' Adders-Tongue handed them back to her nephew. 'But if more messages flow between the Palace and the Temple, continue to bring them to me. I'd like to know if they mean to pass information.'

'I am your servant.' Copperhead began to bow his way out of the room.

'Copperhead,' Adders-Tongue recalled him. 'I mean what I say about Lady Camellia. She would ruin a boy like you without a second thought.'

'I listen and obey Thane Adders-Tongue,' but while Copperhead spoke of obedience his mind was on the fun games that he played with the Lady Camellia in her room late at night. If only he could take her milk he would be able to finish off what they started. He so wanted to finish growing up.

'Reverend Mother,' Heather made her bow to the High Priestess. 'I admit that I've wanted to meet with you, but this is a very busy time for us in the Queen's chambers.'

'I did not summon you here for a social visit,' The High Priestess snapped. She didn't offer a chair to Heather. 'This won't take long. I simply wanted a word with you.'

Heather blinked slowly. The High Priestess was clearly angry about something. Correction, she was angry with Heather. 'Go on.'

The High Priestess leaned to her side, resting an elbow on the arm of her throne. 'I must know if you are a true servant of the Goddesses.'

'I am.'

'The Reverend Mother of the Russian Hive warned me against you.'

Now Heather was very confused. She always considered her relationship with the High Priestess in Russia to be strong. 'I attended services religiously.'

'The Queen of the Russian Hive was not a true servant of the Goddess. The Queen of a Hive has one duty, to ensure the future of the Hive. The Russian Queen failed in her duty. She was warned by the Temple to breed or die.'

Heather's face drained. 'What happened to my Queen Yelena?'

'She is dead.'

Heather gave a little shudder. It had only been thirty days since she last lay in Yelena's arms. Now Yelena was dead. It seemed a lifetime ago and a world away, but Heather felt a deep pang of guilt. If only she had talked Yelena into mating with one of her drones!

'The stars bode ill for this Hive if this new Queen does not breed. The stars bode ill for you if I feel that your presence has a negative affect on our Queen's desire to breed. Do we understand each other?'

Heather gave a short bow. 'We do.'

Aynia raised her arms as her servants placed a new corset around her torso. She held her breath as they laced up the back a little tighter than she would have liked. Once again tall spiky boots were placed on her feet and laced up the front. A long, slim black leather skirt with a slit along her right thigh was pulled around her waist.

While she inspected herself in the mirror Thorn came into the room. 'I look like Camellia,' she thought to herself. All that was missing was a riding crop.

'Your Highness.' He made his bow.

Aynia gave him a bright smile and walked toward him. As she walked Thorn saw a garter on her upper right thigh with a knife in it. Aynia put her hand into Thorn's.

He pressed his lips the back of her hand. 'My lady looks well this morning.'

'I feel much better, thank you.'

'She didn't eat nearly enough,' Rose grumbled as she walked in from the parlor.

'Lady Rose,' Thorn acknowledged her. 'I hesitate to mention this, but the knife on the Queen's thigh shows as she walks. If it's visible to me it will be visible to others.'

'Then move it Captain.' Rose ordered him.

Thorn hesitated only a moment then led Aynia over to a chair. As she sat down two servants hustled over to brush Aynia's waist length hair.

Thorn dropped to his knees in front of his Queen. Aynia obligingly parted her thighs a little as Thorn slid his hands up her leg and pulled down the garter. Then she lifted her foot and allowed him to slide the garter up her other thigh, securing it in place far up above the slit.

The back of Thorn's hand accidentally brushed against the tip of her stinger, which was coiled tightly around her upper thigh twice. He swallowed. He was no drone, so why were the nerves on his fingers going crazy as he touched her skin? Did she notice that he let his fingers brush her inner thigh? Did she notice that he let his finger linger seconds beyond when he should have?

Aynia did notice, but wondered if it was her imagination. Could she still feel the warmth of his single finger as it brushed the delicate, sensitive skin of her inner thigh? Did he touch her a little longer than he should have? No, he was not a drone. He could never have any sexual thoughts. The thoughts were hers. It was all in her imagination.

Aynia silently cursed Heather for her attentions in the bath. Aynia felt an aching desire to finish what had been started.

Thorn rose and crossed the room. He leaned against the wall with a deceptively casual air as he critiqued her new outfit. The corset emphasized the two stunning features of her adult form, make that three. Aynia's bosom was now amply endowed and much in need of the support given by her corset. The other feature was an impossibly small waist, pulled in even tighter by the relentless corset.

He looked down at the floor for a moment to remember his Aynia, as she was only a month ago. Then she had been shorter than Thorn and her body had no shape. Back then she was just skinny and straight as a board from shoulders to feet. But her eyes were the same. They were still so full of questions and impatience. And her flaming gold red hair was the same although now it held a deeper hue. Except for the noticeable external features there was one other change to Aynia. Her voice had dropped nearly an octave and a half. Something about the honeyed voice went straight through to Thorn's spine and made him a shiver. He could listen to Aynia talk all day.

Aynia looked over at Thorn, a bit annoyed. Was he staring at his feet? What could be so interesting about the floor that he could not look up at her? She wanted someone to notice how good she looked. She wanted someone to say something about her new adult form.

'I'm not sure that I want to wear this,' Aynia said finally, more out of anger at Thorn's ability to ignore her than out of displeasure with her outfit. 'Did we borrow this outfit from Camellia's closet?'

Her sullen remark caused a major flurry. The two servants who were braiding black laces of leather into her hair stopped immediately and stepped away. Rose, who seemed to have been terribly busy only seconds ago, rushed over.

'Your Majesty, forgive me. I didn't realize that you were unhappy with the dress. I know that it is a bit unusual for a Queen, but we had not expected this day of mourning and it was all that we had that would fit you in black. We will of course begin a whole new wardrobe tomorrow. I can perhaps find something else?' Rose flitted about in deep concern.

Aynia looked up to see that Thorn was now staring at her. She had wanted him to notice her as an adult, but the first time she had gotten his attention was with a childish temper tantrum. She was embarrassed. She did not like the faintly amused expression on his face. Was he thinking about how childish she was?

Thorn was indeed amused by Aynia, but not for the reason that she thought. In all the years that he had known her he had only heard her snap at others a couple of times. In each case she immediately regretted her loss of temper. This time was no exception. Aynia appeared to be mortified at the commotion around her. No matter what she looked like on the outside this Queen was still the Aynia he knew so well.

Aynia was wishing that she could take back her words. The only thing to do was to mollify Rose. 'Rose, I'm sorry. I was only snapping about the clothes because I'm still so tired. I think that you were right, I didn't eat enough breakfast. Can you have a little more food brought to me?'

Rose immediately brightened. 'Of course Your Majesty. I warned you that you didn't eat enough.'

Soup was brought into the bedroom with great speed. Despite the fact that she really didn't want to eat any more, Aynia obediently sipped a bit more from her spoon. Rose was still not completely satisfied, but now she was concentrating on the soup and not the clothes. That was just fine with Aynia.

Aynia allowed herself a weak smile. Here she was, Queen, and she was letting an attendant boss her around like a Nurse with a child.

The smile did not go unnoticed. Everyone in the room visibly relaxed and returned to their work.

'You must be going Majesty,' Deidre announced.

Everyone finished working abruptly.

Aynia took as deep of a breath as her corset would allow. 'I've forgotten already. Where do I go first?'

'To the Temple. Your sisters lie in state for their memorial service.'

'Yes, I remember now. Thus the black clothes.'

'Exactly. Shall we go?' Deidre beamed benevolently at Aynia.

'I'm ready if you are.'

'We are always ready when Your Highness is.' Heather reminded her gently.

Aynia started walking out of her bedroom. Immediately her attendants fell into step just behind her on her left. Suddenly the bedroom door snapped open. Just beyond those doors Aynia's personal guard fell in step with their Captain Thorn just a step behind Aynia on her right. They continued through the hallway of the Royal Chambers to the outer door. Like the door of Aynia's bedroom these doors opened just as she reached them. She stepped out onto the red carpet in the public halls of the Palace. As her entourage walked it grew. Nobles that they passed bowed to the new Queen then fell in step behind her.

Aynia thought that they sounded like a marching army. By the time they reached the tall glass doors that separated her Palace from the rest of the Hive close to sixty Fairie walked behind her.

One in particular, Thorn, noticed how well the black leather skirt cupped her rounded bottom and how well it accented the sway of her voluptuous hips as she walked. He was almost too distracted by the sight to pay proper attention to where he was walking. Being a military man he recovered himself quickly as he missed a turn in the hallway. Within a matter of seconds he was back in step, this time with his eyes firmly focused on the hallway ahead.

'Have you finished searching the Hive?'   Thorn asked Lieutenant Sage.

Sage saluted. 'Well, we did what we could sir, but there are a few places that we have not searched.'

'Such as?'

'We didn't dare set foot inside Parliament. You know how those Members of the Opposition Party are.   They would denounce the Queen from the floor of Parliament for allowing the military to invade the Parliament building. So we never went inside.'

Thorn looked at Sage with new respect. 'You're right. That was a good call.'

Sage blushed. 'I wish that I could take credit sir.'

'Who warned you?' Thorn was curious to know.

'My mother,' Sage now dropped his gaze to the floor.

'Your Mother?'

'It was the strangest thing sir. We were debating about going into Parliament when my mother appeared on the front steps. She pulled me aside and told me that a new servant at Thane Monarda's told her that she should warn me not to go inside. The new servant has lots of friends who serve the Goddesses in the Temple, so mother thinks that one of them got a warning from the Goddesses. We went to talk to this servant, and she told us about how Parliament would blame the Queen for allowing the military to go inside. It seems that there is some law against the military going in.'

Thorn smiled. 'Did this servant have a name?'

'Verbena. She's a nice lady. She treats my mother really good. When my mother's back is hurting a lot Verbena helps her lift things and helps her on the stairs.'

'I think that I may know this servant. Thane Monarda is indeed fortunate to have someone of her abilities on staff.'

'That's kind of the funny thing. Mother says that Verbena practically ordered Thane Monarda to take her on. Thane Monarda wasn't even looking for someone.'

'Then I know that we speak of the same person. Verbena is a pushy, opinionated female who delights in pushing others around and getting her own way. She likes action.'

'Sir, I must take exception. She's very good to my mother and very good at her job.' Sage said in shock.

'I have complained about this female for years Lieutenant Sage and nothing you say will stop me.' Thorn said with a smile. 'She's my sister,' he explained.

Carman and her attendants were caught off guard when Adders-Tongue threw open the door of their room. She came in quickly and shut the door.

'Well, if Adders-Tongue was my enemy we would all be dead,' Carman complained. 'From now on at least two of you should be on guard at all times.'

'There is no time! You must leave now,' Adders-Tongue hissed.

'Now?'

'Members of the Royal Guard are gathering outside Parliament. If they search in here we will all die.' Adders-Tongue warned them. 'Get your belongings. I will show you where to go. I have my outside person coming to lead you to the hiding place. The Guards have already searched that quadrant of the valley, so it's probably safe to move now.'

Carman pulled herself up into a standing position. She walked across the room to Adders-Tongue. Her left foot dragged a little, and her left arm was still held against her body in a fixed position, but she could walk unsupported now.

'You are improving my Queen. You couldn't walk on your own when I last saw you.' Adders-Tongue observed.

'It is daylight,' Carman growled. 'How are we to cross the Hive safely and get to the outside? Last time that we went through the Hive center it was night and the Hive was safely asleep. Everyone is up now.'

'I have thought of that my Queen.' Adders-Tongue showed a bundle of the plain clothes of the working class to the females. 'The only workers who regularly leave the Hive are the food gatherers. If you are dressed like this your passage out of the Hive will not cause comment.'

'You expect me to dress as a common worker?' Carman leveled her scorpion-like stinger at Adders-Tongue's throat. 'I am not a common worker. I will not dress like a common worker. Find another plan.'

'But the Royal Guard could be entering the Parliament as we speak!'

Carman threw down the clothes with contempt. 'I will not dress this way. Do what you have to, but secure this room. We will leave the Hive tonight. Shadows will hide my clothes. Darkness will be my ally. I will never stoop to pass as a common worker.'

Adders-Tongue backed away from the deadly stinger. 'As your Majesty wishes.'

Mumbling to herself, Adders-Tongue scurried back to the front hall of the Parliament Chambers to observe the Royal Guard. As she peered around the corner she saw an amazing sight. A lowly female servant stood on the steps of Parliament. With words the servant managed to turn away the guards.

Adders-Tongue recognized the female. She served Thane Monarda. Perhaps Thane Monarda was more of an ally than she pretended to be. Still, it was a close call.

Adders-Tongue was in no small way relieved when her niece Cobra-Lily led the Queen Carman and her followers out of the Hive later that night to the hidden glen in the valley.

CHAPTER 6

'Leave me,' Aynia commanded her attendants in a quiet voice. She stood at the door to her bedchamber, her back to her attendants. She could not let them see how much her sister's memorial service had affected her.

'Majesty!' Deidre blurted out her protest.

'A Queen is never, ever left alone,' Rose said as a frown settled on her brow.

'Alone?' Aynia's voice sounded strange. 'My mother, my dear sisters, all are dead. My attendants are gone. And this happens to every Queen, not just me. A Queen is never left alone? A Queen is forever alone.' Her tone was bitter. But all it would take was one more word and they would be able to hear the pain in her voice.

Aynia was so very tired of being Queen. For the next hour she wanted to just be Aynia again, to mourn her mother and sisters, and to cry in privacy.

Before the sisters could object again she closed the door firmly behind her.

Rose wrung her hands together. 'This is not good.'

Deidre paced. 'You three have served more Queens than I,' she began.

'Advice?' Camellia growled, interrupting her. 'I refuse to give advice.'

Deidre dared to give Camellia a dirty look but continued to talk. 'Is this common behavior?' She twisted one lock of hair around her finger, a further sign of her consternation.

Heather paced opposite Deidre.

Rose stood just out of their paths. 'Every Queen is different, Deidre. I've seen Queens who were evil, smart, kind, stupid, every possible personality. But Queen Aynia is, well, she has an otherness about her, doesn't she?' Rose thought out loud.

'Otherness?' Camellia snorted. 'Is that a word?'

'You know what I mean.'

119

'As a matter of fact, I don't. You act as if the Queen is some sort of an enigma. She is simply a young Queen. And the weight of the crown rests heavily on her brow. The only difference that I see is that unlike most Queens she doesn't have a father to guide her.'

Rose gasped. 'That's it! That's it Camellia!'

Camellia shook her head no, her eyes opened wide. 'Oh no you don't! Don't start listening to what I say. I'm the one you ignore, remember? I'm here strictly for comic relief.'

Heather's face betrayed a slight smile, a rare occurrence on her normally somber visage. 'Oh, I agree with Rose. I think that you might have something there Camellia.'

Camellia's jaw dropped. 'Et tu Heather?'

Deidre, who had never seen anyone make Camellia nervous, stopped pacing and enjoyed the sight. 'Are you blushing Camellia?'

Heather leaned in for a closer look. 'I think that you might be right Deidre. Camellia's actually blushing. Who would have thought her still capable of it?'

The sisters made their sport of Camellia for a while longer, but eventually there was little else to say. Camellia glared at them from the top of a table in the hallway, her arms crossed over her chest.

Rose and Deidre resumed pacing. They grew more agitated as the minutes slipped away. Heather leaned against the table where Camellia fumed and glowered. Among the sisters only Heather understood that Camellia's temper was much more show than actual fury. Strangely enough, among the four sisters, it was the maternal Rose who possessed the deadly temper. Rose's fuse was incredibly slow to catch, but once angered she was a dangerous Fairie to cross.

Thorn emerged from the guard's chambers. He was startled for a moment, then curious. He politely made his bow. 'Lady Heather, Lady Rose, Lady Camellia, Lady Deidre,' he nodded to each one.

Deidre started to explain why they were loitering in the hallway outside of the Queen's bedchamber when Rose interrupted her. 'Tell me, Captain Thorn, which male took the place of Queen Aynia's father when he was killed?'

Thorn looked angry. 'No male could replace Prince Thistle. He was the greatest of heroes.' It was obvious that Thorn idolized the late Prince.

Rose patted Thorn's arm. 'I didn't mean to upset you Captain Thorn. We are aware of his legend. Every Fairie knows his name, a rare accomplishment for a male. What I meant to say,'

'But muffed it,' Camellia quipped, her normal good humor returned.

Rose continued, 'what I meant to ask was: 'who took over the education of the princesses that he sired?' I believe that he sired not only our Queen but two of her sisters as well.'

Thorn nodded. 'Prince Thistle sired the Princesses Lily, Gladiola, and Aynia. But they were not the only princesses without a father. Princess Carman's sire did not live to witness her birth.'

'Who protected the young Princess Carman's life? And who was responsible for educating the other orphaned Princesses?'

'That's ancient history Lady Rose. I can not fathom why it would be of interest to you,' Thorn said coldly.

Rose's lips flattened into a tight line. She did not allow males to talk back to her in this manner. 'But it is of great interest to *me* Captain Thorn. It bears on the health and well being of our Queen.' Her tone was as sharp as a slap.

'The late Queen entrusted the education of her daughters to me.' There was no hint of pride in his voice. But Thorn squared his shoulders and stood ramrod straight when he spoke.

'Praise indeed from Caesar,' Camellia mumbled to herself.

'You?' Rose asked, incredulous. It was not meant as an insult, however, and Thorn did not take it as one.

Heather circled around Thorn, newly interested. 'Are you of noble birth?'

'No. I am a common worker.'

'The late Queen thought very highly of you.' It was not a question.

'It makes sense,' Camellia commented. 'He's obviously intelligent,' she and Thorn both made small bows to each other to acknowledge the compliment, 'and who could she trust in the harem? The infant Carman would have been defenseless against the Queen's drones. So she picked a male who had no vested interest in which Princess took the throne. Very smart. I stand in awe of the late Queen of Balnacra Hive.'

'A worthy strategic move,' Rose agreed.

'I've heard that the late Queen was nobody's fool,' Deidre added.

'And yet she was assassinated by a common worker,' Camellia said dryly. Heather nodded in agreement. Deidre, deep in thought, began to pace again.

Eventually all four of the attendants paced in a tight circle around Thorn.

Rose finally screwed up her courage and peeked into the parlor. 'She still hasn't eaten. What should we do? She has to be at Parliament in less than an hour.' Her agitation showed as she wrung her hands together.

Deidre twisted a lock of her hair as she paced.

'Will Parliament wait?' Camellia asked Deidre.

'Everyone waits for the Queen, but if she's too late they will forever hold it against her.'

'But she's Queen.' Rose said.

'I repeat,' Deidre said, 'they will take it as an insult if she arrives very late.'

'Is she still sleeping?' Camellia turned to Rose.

'Was she sleeping? Do we know?' Heather asked. 'Rose, it's your job to be in there. Just go in and see.'

'Oh, thank you very much. Make me the sacrificial one. I remember a Hive in Llanbryde where an attendant startled the sleeping Queen and got stung to death for her efforts,' Rose informed her sisters.

'We'll see that you have a nice funeral,' Camellia joked.

'Very funny,' Rose frowned. She didn't think Camellia's comment was at all funny. 'Why don't you go in?'

'Not my job,' Camellia said with a wicked, smug, smile.

'Deidre? Heather?'

'No thanks,' they said.

'We have to get her dressed. We can't just do it in a couple minutes. Dressing the Queen takes time.' Rose was getting quite distressed.

'Then go on in,' Camellia urged her.

Thorn was getting quite tired of this argument. It was time to stop talking and take action. He walked boldly into the parlor and took the lunch plate from the table. 'Is this her lunch?'

Rose nodded mutely.

'Bring her drink or open the door for me.' Thorn commanded.

Rose took the flagon from the table and handed it to Thorn, then opened the door to the bedroom for him. He walked into Aynia's bedroom and to the side of her bed.

'Oh, I like him,' Rose told Deidre.

'Should we leave him alone in the bedchamber with the Queen?' Heather asked with a worried expression.

'Oh good Goddesses,' Camellia rolled her eyes. 'He's not a drone. What could he possibly do to her? None of his equipment works.'

'He could sting her.' Deidre said soberly.

'If we can't trust the Captain of the Royal Guard, the most trusted male in this Hive, then we are in deep trouble,' Heather observed.

'Besides, I don't think stinging her is what our good Captain has in mind,' Camellia mentioned, although none of her sisters paid her any attention.

'Come on then,' Rose said. She opened the door to the bedroom and followed Thorn in.

Thorn sat down on the bed next to Aynia. She was sleeping face down. He placed the plate of food and the drink on the floor next to his feet. Then he gently shook Aynia's shoulders.

'Highness, wake up.'

'Go away,' Aynia mumbled, or something that sounded very much like it.

'Queen Aynia, you have to wake up. You must go to the session at Parliament.' Thorn took a quick look around the room. The attendants had not followed him in yet. Risking much, he sharply slapped Aynia across the rump.

Aynia opened her eyes and looked up at Thorn, her expression very stern. 'What?' As soon as she realized Thorn was the one who woke her, Aynia's face softened into a smile. She rolled over on her back and stretched out like a cat after a nap.

Thorn noticed how the sheet clung to her shape just enough to entice. Soft curves invited exploration. He was tempted but did not dare. Any moment the Queen's attendants would follow him into the room.

After delicately yawning Aynia asked 'I'm sorry, did I sleep too long?' She looked around the room and was disappointed to see her attendants entering. 'Don't be afraid to join me in my bedchamber in the future,' she purred quietly to Thorn.

'Her Highness says that her attendants should not be afraid to come in and wake her in the future,' Thorn said to Rose, though he still looked at Aynia.

'Thank you Your Highness,' Rose said as she laid out Aynia's next outfit.

'That's not what I meant,' Aynia thought, but then decided not to correct Thorn.

'I have food for you,' Thorn told Aynia quietly.

'I'm not hungry, but thank you,' Aynia declined his offer.

'You must eat your Highness,' Rose said. She bustled over to the bed, followed closely by Heather.

Heather had a grim expression on her face. 'I am afraid that I too must insist Your Majesty. If you don't eat properly your milk won't come in. As your liaison to the Temple I must tell you that would be disastrous for the Hive.' Heather bent down and gently brushed away a lock of hair from Aynia's face, a gesture that she hardly realized she made.

Thorn almost glared at Heather, then resumed a mask of neutrality.

Deidre also came to the edge of the bed. 'Highness, you can't go to Parliament without eating. The leader of the Opposition Party is notorious for verbally sparing with the Queen. She would smell weakness in you a mile away.'

Aynia sat up and faced her staff. 'Well Camellia, I haven't heard from you yet.'

Camellia sauntered over to stand beside the others. 'I am afraid, Highness, my only reason for being in your service also hinges on your production of milk. I will have to take the side of my sister attendants in this matter, as much as I hate to see them treating Your Majesty in this dreadful manner.' Camellia shook her head in mock dismay. 'However, in the future I promise to side with you resolutely, wrong or right, just as a matter of principal.'

'Thank you Camellia.' Aynia said with all the gravity Camellia's comments warranted. She turned her attention to Thorn. 'I suppose that you will have your way with me.'

Thorn's expression was of shock. Up until this moment he wasn't sure if Aynia was aware of the other interpretation he could find in her words. Her expression was innocent enough. But he was certain that he saw a glimmer of amusement in her eyes.

'I will take the plate of food,' she said as she took the plate from Thorn.

Thorn was confused again. Now he didn't see what he'd thought he'd seen in her expression. Maybe it was all his imagination. Serving Aynia's mother had never been this difficult, Thorn mused.

Slowly Aynia stirred the food around the plate, a great trick she had learned as a child to avoid eating meals that she didn't like. 'Deidre, please refresh my memory as to who is in Parliament and what their alliances are. I require a full briefing.'

'But your Majesty, we only have an hour.' Deidre said in disbelief. Where would she begin to explain the complex mixture of personalities that comprised Parliament?

'Sketch out the important information. You may provide detail later.'

Deidre launched into a series of brief biographies of the most influential members of Parliament and attempted to summarize key alliances. While she talked, Thorn leaned over Aynia and whispered so that only she could hear. 'I know what you're doing. Moving food is not the same as eating it. Now eat something or I will personally hold you down and force the food in.'

Aynia's eyes went wide for a second. She wondered briefly what it would be like for Thorn to wrestle her down on the bed. Not wanting to give away her thoughts, she gave Thorn a weak smile and ate a few bites. But once he was distracted again she resumed pushing the food from one side of the plate to another.

Rose bustled into the room and took the plate away. 'Pardon Majesty. The hour grows late. We must dress you.'

Rose and her two helpers slid a deep green dress over Aynia's head. Aynia played with the sleeves for a moment, intrigued with trailing fabric that almost touched the floor. Once again the sash of the yellow and black Hive tartan crossed her chest.

Aynia looked herself over critically in the mirror. 'Do all of my clothes have to be cut this low at the neckline?'

'It is the fashion my lady. Besides, as the Mother of the Hive you are expected to display your more, er, matronly attributes.'

'But they're so, so, out there,' Aynia gestured with her hands. Indeed, her corset pushed her bosom up and out, accentuating already generous cleavage. 'Don't you think, Captain Thorn, that this dress is a bit improper?' Aynia asked, turning towards him.

Thorn was trapped. Every female in the room was now staring at him. Protocol demanded that he stand at attention when the Queen addressed him, but he knew better than the stand at attention just then. He cursed his uniform for its brevity. He simply looked up at the Queen and shrugged. 'I know nothing of fashion Majesty. Ask Lady Camellia perhaps.' He was relieved when the females in the room once again turned their attention away from him. He was no drone, but he'd taken more than one cold bath to clear his mind since Aynia became Queen. Tonight he was due for another.

'May I at least cover up a little of it? Maybe some sort of a necklace?'

'We have one for you, Your Highness. It has green stones to match the dress. Oh, and of course you will wear a crown.'

'That crown they put on me at the coronation gave me a headache,' Aynia complained.

'Oh, you won't wear that one Your Highness. The Hive Crown you only wear at state occasions,' Rose informed her.

'When you're bound to get a headache anyway,' Camellia quipped.

Rose instructed a member of the Royal Guard bring in several boxes from the Royal vaults. 'I was given a complete inventory of the Crown Jewels and I can research the journals of the late Queen's attendants if you want to know when she wore certain pieces. If your lady mother was like most queens some of these pieces she never used.' Rose gestured towards the glittering display of Royal Jewels. 'Some she would have worn all of the time. It's a matter of personal choice. Your Majesty will of course decide which ones you prefer to wear. And jewelers always stand ready to make anything the Queen desires.'

'Find me something that will stay well seated on my head without weighing too much.'

'I know just the thing. It has green stones to match the necklace.' Rose searched through boxes, but to no avail. 'That's odd. When we first arrived at Balnacra I took an inventory of the Crown Jewels with the retiring attendants. I distinctly remembered a piece that I don't see now.'

'Perhaps it's still in the vault,' Camellia commented. Her tone betrayed some concern.

'No, this is everything. How very strange,' Rose muttered to herself.

Heather peered into the boxes along with her sister. 'May I suggest a new, complete, inventory?'

Aynia picked out a very delicate crown made of curves of gold wire but no jewels. It was simple and unobtrusive.

'It's not very noticeable in your hair,' Rose commented once she had placed it on top of Aynia's head. The black leather laces and braids had been removed. Now her hair was swept up in a simple yet elegant twist.

'Well, it's not as if they wouldn't know I was Queen even without it. After all, I stand a head taller than any other Fairie in the Hive, my wings are translucent where theirs are opaque, and only I wear the Hive tartan,' Aynia said.

'True Majesty,' Rose agreed halfheartedly. Rose loved jewelry and could not fathom why the Queen would choose not to wear something more ornate. It nearly insulted Rose's sensibilities.

'Deidre, how soon must we leave?'

'We go when your Majesty is ready.'

Rose shook her head. 'No, no, no. If you leave now you'll be on time. The Queen is always half an hour late.' She never answered Heather's suggestion about taking another inventory of the Crown Jewels, but she placed it high on her priority list. Who would dare to take gold from the Queen's treasury? And who had the opportunity?

Thorn looked down at the plate on the bed. 'The Queen could eat some more food.'

Aynia wanted to avoid that issue at any cost. She walked briskly toward the door. 'Let's put the Parliament on the defensive. I'll be on time.'

The Queen's attendants had no choice but to fall in behind her as she headed out the door.

Aynia nearly collided with Lieutenant Sage as she stepped out of the Royal Chambers and into the palace hallway.

The Lieutenant went beet-red. He bowed as low as he could. 'Pardon me my Queen. It was most clumsy of me.'

Aynia felt that she was as much to blame for the near collision as he was, but decided not to point that out to him. 'You're in great haste Lieutenant. Do you have important news?'

Lieutenant Sage snapped to attention and saluted first Queen Aynia then Captain Thorn. 'Humans have been spotted near our valley.' What he did not say was that a group searching for Carman had stumbled upon the humans. Carman's escape was still known to only a very few Fairie.

Thorn turned to Aynia. 'Your orders my Queen?'

Aynia took a deep breath, not because she had to think about her response, but because this was her first real command as Queen of the Hive. 'Kill them immediately,' she told Thorn. 'See to it yourself, Captain.'

Thorn bowed low and backed away from Aynia and her entourage. He almost had a spring in his step as he went down the hallway. Aynia commanded him to personally handle the situation. That spoke highly of the faith she had in him. But more important, he was now freed from the mind-numbingly-dull duty of a member of the Royal entourage. Action, that was what made Thorn happiest.

Aynia continued on down the hallway. A member of the Royal Guard that she did not recognize filled Thorn's position at her right flank. Suddenly Aynia was not as confident as she was a second ago. Then Aynia noticed that a few members of her staff were quite pale. Heather had beads of perspiration at her top lip. Rose's expression was downright grumpy. 'So they're nervous too,' Aynia thought. For some reason that made her feel better.

The Queen and her entourage stepped out of the glass doors leading to the Hive center. Aynia felt suddenly exposed.

Waves of sound and heady scents overwhelmed her senses. The Palace was so quiet compared to the steady buzz of thousands of Fairie living and working in the confined space of the Hive.

The center of the Hive, normally a wide-open plaza of Italian design, was crowded with tables set up in anticipation of Festival. Workers and their drones enjoyed beer, food, song, and perhaps a bit more beer, also in anticipation of Festival. Under tables, on top of tables, across the plank benches, and on the floor, Fairie coupled openly. Aynia stumbled a few times as she stared and gaped at the sight of naked buttocks waving in the air. In all her life she had never seen a nude male drone.

Heather wrinkled her nose up at the sight and lightly tapped Aynia's arm to get her attention. 'Some Fairie have no self-restraint. They know that it will be another day before the festivities; still they fornicate as if drunk on the Queen's scent. They don't even acknowledge that it is their Queen who walks past them.'

Camellia laughed. 'Once a male couples with a female he can not separate himself until he climaxes. They can hardly stop nature just because the Queen is nearby, begging your pardon Majesty.'

'No offense taken,' Aynia said in a distant voice as she spied a wriggling mass of naked workers off in the distance. She could not make out clearly what any one Fairie was doing, but the entire mass seemed to be moving to a common rhythm. 'But what does this have to do with my scent?' Aynia took a surreptitious whiff of herself to see if she smelled an odor, but did not.

'Tomorrow you will bestow a gift on your people. When you release your Queen's scent into the air of the Hive all of the workers and nobles will loose all inhibitions. The desire to mate, with anything or anyone, will take over for hours. Your scent has a powerful affect on the minds of the citizens of the Hive. They can not resist it. It's like a drug to them.'

'How do I release my scent?'

'You will know.'

'And everyone will just throw off their clothes and start having sex?' Aynia asked, incredulous. She might have spent her entire youth as a student, but her real education seemed to have started the moment she became Queen.

'Oh yes,' Camellia purred.

'Did I release some of my scent early? By mistake?' Aynia asked, concerned.

'Oh no Majesty, Festival is tomorrow.'

'Then what is all of this?' Aynia wanted to watch. There was so much to see. Every Fairie seemed to be sucking or licking on some part of another Fairie. She wondered if she would be allowed to just stop and stare.

'This is just a little kick-off party to start things warming up for the main event.' Camellia told Aynia.

'If this is just a warm up, what's the real thing like?' Aynia wondered out loud.

'Breeders,' Heather snorted in contempt.

Camellia's hearty laugh soared to the heights of the Hive.

The doors to the Parliament chambers flew open before Aynia. Parliament, as predicted, was caught by surprise. Members were gathered in small groups around the room, deep in personal conversations. Real annoyance showed on more than one face as they realized that for the first time in memory the Queen was punctual for the opening session of Parliament.

The Parliament chamber was a large rectangular room with pews running the length of the room on both sides. In the center of the back of the room were small tables in rows that seated various clerks and secretaries. In front of those were desks for the Members of the Queen's Cabinet, who were, theoretically, impartial. And at the far end of the room there was a dais with a speaking podium to the extreme right. A Throne sat to the left.

Aynia strode purposefully down the center of the room as Parliament members dropped into their deepest curtseys. She met a few eyes coming down the aisle, some openly hostile, some overly friendly. When she reached the Throne she sat down carefully. Deidre pushed her scepter into her hand. Rose and Camellia artfully arranged the long train of her dress. Aynia placed one elbow elegantly on the arm of the Throne and waited for Parliament to come to order.

It wasn't a usual occurrence for the Queen to attend Parliament. She was in fact only there at the express invitation of Parliament. It was the only place in her Hive that she was not legally allowed to go without invitation. She supposed that this was so members of Parliament could feel free to vilify her behind her back. In truth, with Parliament sessions open to the public there would always be a member of the Royal Staff spying on the proceedings. Members of Parliament insulted the Queen at their own risk.

The late Queen frequently told her daughters that the only reason for Parliament to exist was to give the common workers a feeling of having a voice in government. In reality the late Queen thought that Parliament was nothing more than a tool to make public decisions already made in private by the Queen and her Cabinet. Aynia never said it out loud but she felt that her Mother was very cynical about the process of government. Then again, when one reigns for over three hundred years one is bound to become jaded. Besides, what did Aynia know? Perhaps her Mother had revealed a truth about the government of the Hive.

Aynia spent three dull hours hearing speeches by practically every Member of Parliament. From time to time if it appeared that Aynia was about to yawn Deidre would step in front of her to hand her a fan, a glass of water, or to rearrange the train of Aynia's skirt. Aynia realized that she was completely bored when she began to fake yawns in order to watch what new method Deidre would use to cover for her.

Time crept by alarmingly slow. The chamber was a little too warm, and the air was far from fresh. Despite her best efforts

Aynia's eyes began to droop into slits. She looked up hopefully when Deidre nudged her. Deidre nodded to her right, where Heather was standing. Aynia looked over to Heather, who slipped a note into Aynia's hand. Casually and without showing any emotion Aynia read over the document. Then she rolled it closed and laid it on her lap.

Moments later Deidre coughed discretely. Aynia looked over at her with an inquiring glance but Deidre simply looked back out at the podium as another Member of Parliament stepped up to speak.

'Your Majesty,' the female's voiced boomed out.

Aynia controlled her urge to flinch. Instead she looked over at the Member of Parliament with veiled interest. Who was this female? And why was she shouting?

'I hope that we have not bored you with our humble, though heartfelt, welcome.'

Aynia did not comment. Was she supposed to? She didn't let her expression change.

'Beware,' Deidre whispered like a sigh. 'It is the Honorable Thane Adders-Tongue, leader of the Opposition Party.'

'Honorable?' Camellia snickered quietly.

Aynia barely nodded her head in acknowledgement of Deidre's brief introduction. But Aynia needed no introduction. Thane Adders-Tongue and the rest of her clan were well known to members of the Royal household. The late Queen and Thane Adders-Tongue were long time enemies.

'I realize that you haven't been Queen for long. Two days. I'm sure that you have found these days to be quite exciting? It was commendable to set aside a day of mourning for your sisters. Unusual, to say the least, but showing a certain sentimentality for those who were unfit to rule our Hive.'

Aynia waited for this viper to get to her point, which was bound to be painfully sharp.

'You've spent the last two days enjoying the benefits of being Queen, but it is now time to take on the responsibilities of the position you hold by the grace of the Goddesses.'

Aynia wondered for a moment what this female thought was enjoyable about her last two days. Was it the battle to the death with Carman? Maybe it was the senseless slaughter of over a hundred faithful attendants? Or was it the complete abandonment by her old attendants? Perhaps it was the constant nagging pains in her digestive track.

Adders-Tongue raised her voice higher so that she could be heard clearly by the spectators in the upper tier of the balcony of the room. 'Humans! Queen Aynia, it has come to my attention that there are humans in our valley at this very moment! And you are completely unaware of this important fact! A Queen, a good Queen, is always aware of anything that impacts our Hive!'

As Thane Adders-Tongue expected there was a loud buzz from not only the other members of Parliament but from the crowd of nobles above.

Aynia raised her hand only slightly, but the gesture was enough to quiet all other voices. 'Members of the Cabinet, members of Parliament, nobles, workers, it is a little known bylaw of these chambers that no member of the military, save my own personal body guards, may enter this chamber where Parliament convenes. This is to avoid the undue influence of the military and their weapons upon the processes of this Parliament. It is out of respect for these laws that I've held back my Captain of the Royal Guard from reporting directly to me the results of his operation against the human intruders. With your permission, though, I will read this message from Captain Thorn.' Aynia did not wait for permission. She simply unrolled the report and scanned it briefly before reading it out loud.

'Your most Royal Majesty, I am pleased to report that in reference to the mission assigned to my troops this afternoon, the human intruders have been eradicated. Three humans were spotted six miles south west of the Hive. Two were killed immediately by drowning in the Loch. The third was questioned thoroughly about the presence of other humans. He did not survive the questioning. However, we are satisfied that the three humans encountered were alone and no longer represent a threat to the Hive.' Aynia let her voice trail off. 'We will of course allow Parliament to have copies of this report. It goes into further detail of the torture and the deaths, which We have no doubt the members will find satisfying reading. We thank the Member of Parliament for bringing this to Our attention, and to the military's attention. We trust that you notified the military of the threat?'

Adders-Tongue made a face but recovered herself quickly. 'Of course Your Majesty. I am but a humble servant of the Hive.'

This set off the members of the majority party in a round of disparaging coughs and under-the-breath attacks on Adders-Tongue's sincerity.

Aynia did not allow herself to smile. She did meet Adders-Tongue's gaze briefly. If Adders-Tongue was expecting to see some look of triumph she missed it. Aynia looked vaguely bored and coolly detached. And that unnerved the Thane more than she would have liked to admit.

By the time Aynia was whisked off to her Royal chambers for yet another change of clothing to attend the State dinner she was exhausted. No one would have guessed it though. She had her late Mother's ability to summon up reserves of strength seemingly from nowhere.

It was a long day for the Queen's staff too, and Aynia noticed that her attendants were starting to droop as they prepared for the State dinner.

Before the staff left the Royal Chambers they sat around the dining table to eat dinner. It was the first meal that they all took together. They were discussing the guests at the State dinner and the formalities that would have to be observed.

Thorn entered the room, made his bow, and then stood at attention behind Aynia's chair. He leaned over and whispered into her ear. Aynia nodded and took several notes from him. She slit open the seals and read the contents. Except for a small frown she made no comment. When done she touched each note to the flame of a candle and let the paper burn. Deidre and Heather exchanged a glance. Whatever was in those letters was a secret now.

'Sit down and join us Thorn. I dislike having you hover behind me. It makes talking to you impossible.' Aynia told him irritably as she watched the last of the notes turn to ash. In truth what she disliked was the warmth of Thorn's breath on the nape of her neck as he whispered to her. No, she didn't dislike it, but she found it to be very distracting. She wondered very briefly how his soft full lips would feel pressed against her neck, or the generous swell of her breasts. That thought almost made her blush.

Thorn bowed and took the remaining empty seat at the end of the table across from Aynia.

'Do you care for a plate Captain?' Rose asked. 'I can have the staff send up another plate.'

'He has already eaten,' Aynia answered quickly for Thorn.

It was true. Thorn had taken dinner with his men, as was his custom, but he was surprised that Aynia answered for him. He should have expected it though, he thought privately. Eventually all females ended up speaking for the males around them as if the males were incapable of thinking and speaking for themselves. Somehow he thought that Aynia would be different though.

'Apparently the Queen is still declining food.' Heather commented. She did not want to stare, but she found it difficult to tear her eyes away from the new Queen.

Rose turned her attention to Aynia and frowned. 'Really Majesty, I must protest. You do not eat.'

'You yourself warned me against taxing my system with too much food.' Aynia gave Rose a serene half smile that Thorn recognized as her stubborn expression. The only thing that worried him was the fact that when Aynia grew stubborn she usually had a very good reason. He frowned and leaned forward, ready to hear what she had to say. To his surprise she simply said, 'I will eat at the State Dinner.'

This caused great upset along the table.

'Highness, no!'

Aynia raised one eyebrow. 'No? Why not?' A small smile pulled at the corner of her lips.

'It is impossible to eat at a State Dinner.'

Aynia laughed. 'What is so difficult? You sit down, they place food in front of you, and you eat. It sounds rather simple to me.'

'Majesty, few Fairie actually eat at a State Dinner.'

'Well, that certainly of defeats the purpose of serving food.'

Deidre felt that she needed to weigh in here with her opinion. She thought that she had some influence on the new Queen. She was wrong. 'Majesty, important Fairie will be seated around you. Many of them will want to talk to you. This will be their first chance to get your ear. They will expect you to take part in conversation.'

Heather nodded. 'For the first three courses you will speak with the person on your right. Then the next three you will turn to the person on your left. That is what everyone will expect.'

'And I will do that, but I will also eat.'

'When?'

'I'll eat when they're talking. I will eat and listen at the same time. I can do that. It's one of my many talents,' she said a bit sarcastically.

Deidre shook her head. 'This isn't going to work.'

But somehow it did.

With apparent, though feigned, regret Aynia arose from her seat at the head table well after one o'clock and bade her dinner companions goodnight. All down the sixty-foot long table guests rose from their chairs and bowed while Aynia left the room. Her entourage followed her out of the palace's formal dining hall.

'How did I do?' Aynia asked Deidre when they were well away from the dining hall.

'Very well my lady. Your conversation was light, pleasant, and displayed an understanding of all topics. In all I would say that many of your dinner companions were pleasantly surprised.' Deidre struggled to keep up with Aynia as she walked quickly for the Royal chambers.

'And I managed to eat a little from each course.'

'Amazingly enough, yes you did eat a full meal tonight. I was surprised at your appetite considering how little you eat in the Chambers.'

'So do you think that I ate enough to dispel that nasty rumor currently floating around the Hive that I am ill and not taking food?' Aynia commented waspishly. She suddenly stopped and turned to Deidre. She caught the eyes of each of her staff members in turn. Each looked very worried and unhappy.

'You know about that rumor?' Deidre asked in shock.

'Yes I do,' Aynia said, sounding more than a little annoyed. 'As my staff I expect you to be the first to tell me about rumors circulating through my Hive. Why did I have to learn about it from other sources? How did word get out that I have no appetite? Do you have any idea what would happen if the Hive were to decide that I was physically unfit to rule? I would be executed in hours, and a foreign Queen placed on my Throne. This is extremely serious. In the future don't try to protect me from rumors. Let me know immediately. Do you understand?'

'Yes my Queen,' Deidre said quietly.

'Heather?' Aynia demanded.

'Um, no my lady, I mean,' Heather stopped walking and wavered for a moment. Her face was ashen.

Thorn looked up and down the hallway nervously. There were too many places where an assassin could hide along this route. They were pausing too long, and this was exposing Aynia to needless danger. 'I beg your pardon Majesty,' he tried to interrupt.

Aynia held her hand up and looked at Thorn with an expression that he couldn't read. Suddenly Rose doubled over and vomited on the floor of the Palace hallway.

Aynia and Thorn were of one mind. 'Poison!'

Without hesitating a moment Thorn swept Aynia off of her feet and ran down the hallway to the Royal chambers, carrying her the entire way. His other guards followed, leaving Aynia's staff to fend for themselves in the hallway.

Thorn kicked open the door to Aynia's bedroom and rushed in. As gently as he could in haste, he placed Aynia down on her bed. Immediately he jumped up and gave orders to his guards. 'Lock all of the doors. Search the chambers for intruders. Send for the Royal Physician.'

'What about my staff?' Aynia asked. She had to admit to herself that being swept away into her bed by Thorn was surprisingly arousing. She fought the urge to grab his tunic and pull him onto the bed with her.

'I'm sorry my Queen, but your safety must come first. Besides,' Thorn's voice grew gentler, 'odds are very slim that your staff will be attacked. The attack would be on you.'

He turned back to his guards. 'Have all of the food and serving dishes used at the banquet held. I need a seating diagram of the guests and notify me immediately if any other guests fall ill. Isolate the serving staff and the cooking staff. Make them each tell you what dishes they prepared and who they saw working with what.'

Within seconds Thorn and Aynia were left alone in her room. Outside of the bedroom doors a contingent of guards was gathered, ready in case of an attack.

'With all due respect Thorn,' Aynia began, 'I think that perhaps you are looking in the wrong place.'

'What do you mean Majesty?'

Aynia rose from her bed and walked to her dining room. She paused at the door and motioned for Thorn to follow her. Thorn strode over to the door and held it close with his hand. 'That room has not been searched yet. I can't allow you to go in there.'

Aynia was standing very close to Thorn now. With her new height she was looking down at him. His line of sight, had he not been looking up at her face, would have been just below the hollow of her throat. This put his lips just about at the swell of her bosom.

Aynia allowed herself the pleasantly distracting thought of his lips pressed there. But she saw the deep concern in Thorn's eyes and felt ashamed of her wayward thoughts. 'I will wait here while you search the room.'

'I cannot leave you unprotected Majesty.'

Aynia allowed herself a small smile. 'I'm a big girl now. I can protect myself for a few seconds.'

Thorn did not like this but he went into the parlor anyway. The room was small with few pieces of furniture. There was really no place for an assassin to hide. He returned and opened the door for Aynia. 'The room appears to be safe my Queen.'

Aynia walked into her parlor. She stopped at the dining table where the dishes from the staff's dinner remained. 'I believe that we have the scene of the crime.' She walked over to the side pantry of dishes used for meals eaten within the Royal Chambers. 'And these are the suspects.'

'You think that your plates and glasses are poisoned? Not the food?' Thorn caught onto her meaning right away.

'I thought at first that I was feeling ill because my stomach was not used to food. But I felt better when I was starving than I did just after I ate. At first I wondered if it was the food but I have tasters and they are well. I did notice this afternoon, although it did not dawn on me at the time, that every member of my staff looked ill. The sisters share these plates and glasses with me. Forgive me for speaking for you this evening when Rose offered you food, but I was beginning to suspect these plates and I could not risk letting you become ill too.'

'So it is poison.'

Aynia ran a finger over the dishes stacked in the cabinet and held it up for Thorn to see. There was a white powdery residue on the tip of her index finger. 'There is just enough poison here lightly coating the plates to make me sick to my stomach. Not enough to kill. I think that perhaps the idea was to weaken me so that I appeared to be too ill to rule. Hives historically have not reacted well to the idea of a physically weak Queen. I would appreciate it if you took all of these plates away and destroyed them.'

Thorn looked down at the plates for a moment. 'I think we have only one person with opportunity. Cobra-Lily.'

'But she was dismissed from my service and escorted from the Royal Chambers immediately. She might have a motive for revenge but she didn't have opportunity.'

'You assume, my Queen, that she wanted revenge for being dismissed. It could be that she was planted here on your staff to do just this bit of sabotage. She is, after, all related to Snakegrass.'

'And Adders-Tongue.'

'And Adders-Tongue,' Thorn agreed. 'And that entire family was supporters of Carman.'

'Are supporters. Until I see a body I refuse to believe Carman dead.'

Thorn nodded. 'I feel the same way. And I would be very interested to know if that rumor about you being ill originated in the chambers of that clan.'

Aynia sighed. She was extremely tired. 'Let my staff into the Royal Chambers. We need to have a meeting. Oh, and have the kitchen send up some food for me. I'm starved.'

'Right now?' Thorn asked in disbelief. 'You want to meet with your staff now?'

Aynia looked at him with one eyebrow raised. 'My enemies had thirty days to put their plots together. We must make up for lost time.'

'I want to know several things.' Aynia told her assembled staff. Out of respect for their upset systems she ate in her own room before joining them in the parlor. While still pale and tired, the attendants were much improved over the last hour. 'One, did Adders-Tongue inform the military that there were humans near the Hive. Two, did someone in the military tell her? Three, if she knew without being told by the military, where did she get her information?'

'It's not against the law for nobles or workers to leave the Hive Highness,' Thorn informed Aynia.

'I'm aware of that. Even I am allowed to leave the Hive.'

'But the entire adult population of the Hive would follow you out, so what would be the point?' Camellia observed.

'My point is, find out if she has a spy in the military. And find out if she or someone in her family is in the habit of leaving the Hive. I'm not saying that its illegal, but it is highly unusual.'

'Amen to that,' Rose said. 'Unless it's a solstice or harvest I can't think of a reason why someone would want to venture outside of the Hive.' The rigors of Rose's trek to Balnacra from Wales were still fresh in her mind. She personally never wanted to leave the comfort of a Hive again.

'And as a citizen of the Hive it should be her duty to report any sightings of humans directly and immediately to the military. It was pure political posturing to save that bombshell for my first visit to Parliament.'

'She was definitely out to embarrass you.' Deidre agreed.

'At least she let me know that she's an enemy. There are many others who won't be so bold. There are workers and nobles waiting on the sidelines to support my enemies.' Aynia said.

'They are waiting on the sidelines for what? Do you suspect another Hive of plotting against us?' Heather asked.

Thorn and Aynia exchanged a glance. His expression said nothing. He did not want to influence her decision.

Aynia already knew what her decision was. Heather, Rose, Deidre, and Camellia would be her closest advisors for the rest of her life. It would hamper their ability to make good decisions if she withheld important information from them.

'There is another Queen,' Aynia admitted.

To a female each attendant displayed shock. 'How can this be?' Heather demanded. She looked deeply offended.

'I stung Carman. She was paralyzed, but my attention was diverted across my chambers before I could deliver the deathblow. During that fraction of a second Snakegrass and a couple of the remaining attendants broke through the wall of my chamber and dragged Carman out. They escaped. I sent Thorn after them immediately but we have not found them yet. We feel that it is best to assume that they are alive and dangerous until we have definitive proof otherwise,' Aynia confessed.

For a long moment the parlor was silent.

'They must have had an escape plan in place,' Thorn observed, 'in case they were charged with treason in the assassination of the Queen.'

'They had help,' Camellia said.

'Probably,' Thorn admitted.

'Do you continue to search for her?' Deidre asked.

'Yes. Our biggest problem comes from those who know that another Queen exists. It could be that whoever helped her to escape knows that she didn't make it out alive, but is using the rumor that there is another Queen to help build a rebellion.'

'Civil war!' Deidre breathed the dreaded words.

'Few Hives can survive when there are two Queens,' Rose said. 'I seem to remember hearing about a Hive in Telavag, in Norway, that was split apart by civil war. The winning side slaughtered every worker who was not clearly with them. Then there was a split between factions of the rebels. Soon there was another war and another part of the Hive was put to death. Finally the Hive was down to a small core of two hundred rebels. No wait! I misremember. It wasn't the Norwegians. It was the French! It was the Hive at Coclois. How silly of me! As if the Norwegians would descend into a mess of counter rebellions! Of course it was the French.'

'The French Hives have close ties to the Scottish ones,' Deidre reminded Rose archly. 'I beg that you remember that!'

'I do remember. It's just that the whole thing was sort of a Frenchy way to go about things. They made a terrible mess of it,' Rose confided to Camellia.

'I'm surprised that it wasn't an English Hive,' Heather weighed into the argument.

'Will you three please?' Deidre raised her voice. 'Sorry my lady. My sisters often get carried away with their prejudices.'

Aynia laughed. 'As much as I would love to hear your views on our neighbors and allies, we must get through this meeting. You are all ill. Tomorrow is another important day. But before you retire, make me this pledge: No word of Carman leaves these chambers.'

Camellia nodded. 'I think that I heard an important bit of news, not related to the prior topic, but just as important. I was seated at the dinner next to an emissary from Lanark Hive. She said that the humans are at war. The English have invaded Scotland again and are turning the people off their lands.'

Rose nodded. 'I can attest to the fact that the English Armies were on the move north. I had a time keeping from their path.'

'Who cares if the humans slaughter each other? I say the more dead the better.' Deidre displayed a lack of concern for human well being that was a hallmark of the Fairie. In fact the Fairie people held a malicious hatred for humans. They felt threatened by humans. Humans took Fairie lands and made farms out of the wilderness. Hives could not survive on land settled by humans. Humans, for their part, seemed stupidly oblivious to the harm that they inflicted on Fairies. At some point near the dawn of time Fairies had taken a murderous dislike to humans. The Fairie didn't just want humans dead; they wanted humans to die in agonizing pain. Fairie schools held classes in human torture. Every Fairie child knew how to kill a human at least a hundred ways.

'When humans are thrown off of their land they look for new land to farm. The next thing we know they'll be in our valley cutting down trees,' Camellia warned.

'The nymphs won't stand for it.'

'The nymphs will be dead,' Camellia told Deidre flatly.

'Humans have little magic of their own so they don't understand how much they harm magical folk with their actions,' Rose said.

'Every time I hear someone say something like that I wonder how much pro-human sentiment is creeping into our workers. Next thing you'll tell us is that they don't mean to do harm,' Heather sneered.

'Humans are too stupid to understand what harm is,' Camellia said with disdain.

'Ladies!' Aynia knocked in the table to get their attention. 'I can assure you that I don't care what the human's intentions are. If I hear of a human within five miles of Balnacra I will have them killed.'

'That's all very well and good Highness,' Camellia said, 'but if the humans are at war and thousands of them are being displaced from their farms they will probably come to the north. They might come to Balnacra, and they might come in such numbers that we have no way to fight back. Their magicians may have limited powers, but they have figured out anti-Fairie magic. Where there are enough humans, enough humans desperate to farm new land, there will be a magician in their employ.'

Aynia yawned slowly. 'This isn't a comment on our discussion. I find it interesting. However, we all need sleep. I want you all to get as much rest as you can. Especially you, Rose. You seem to have ingested the most poison.'

'I must help Your Majesty to undress,' Rose started to rise, but she was still very weak and had to sit down again.

Aynia looked around the room at her tired staff. 'Thorn can help me,' she said brightly. 'He's the only one in this room who didn't eat off the tainted plates. Now go on, I command you. Go to sleep.'

Aynia walked into her bedroom. Thorn followed her a bit reluctantly.

'Just help pull the dress off. The servants can worry about putting it away properly in the morning.' Aynia started pulling her dress up over her head.

Thorn hurried over to help her. 'Wait a second. I think that it has buttons.' He was right. When he looked at the back of the dress he groaned. 'Oh Goddesses, there must be a million of them, and they're tiny!' Thorn observed with dismay. He carefully unbuttoned her dress one miniscule button at a time despite the temptation to simply rip the dress off of her.

The work put Thorn close to Aynia where once again she could feel the warmth of his breath on her skin. Too soon he was done and the dress slipped off.

Aynia sat down on the edge of her bed. Thorn bent down on his knees before her and removed her shoes. He looked up only once and found himself facing into the sharp tip of the Queen's stinger which was wrapped once across her hips, then twice down her right thigh. Staring straight into the font of death was a bit much even for Thorn. He kept his eyes down.

Barefoot, Aynia stood up again. 'Only the corset to go.' She turned her back to Thorn.

Thorn took a deep breath. This was almost too much to ask, but how could he refuse? He began unlacing the back of the corset. As he released the laces off of each hook the gap at the back of the corset grew wider. Finally the corset dropped to Aynia's waist.

Aynia pushed the corset down over her hips and thighs. She bent over inches from Thorn and wriggled it down to her feet. With a little hop she stepped out of the garment and stood back up again, depriving Thorn of a view of her shapely buttocks. Thorn fought down the urge he had to cup her buttocks in the palm of his hand, and worse, the urge to slide her skimpy panties down.

Aynia turned around to face Thorn and to give him the full frontal view of her breasts. For the first time ever Aynia noticed that Thorn was not looking at her face. He seemed enraptured by the sight of her naked flesh.

Aynia took off her crown. She handed it to Thorn with a smile. He held the crown, wondering what he was supposed to do with it. His usually keen mind was suddenly refusing to function.

Aynia reached up with her hands and let her hair fall down from the twist so that it cascaded down loose to her waist.

Thorn took a deep breath. He had dreams about this, but he could never follow through with what he did in his dreams.

'I won't ask you to tuck me.'

'Pardon?' Thorn sputtered out.

'I won't ask you to tuck me in,' Aynia told him. 'You look so tired. For a second there I thought that you were dreaming. You had this odd look on your face.' She caressed his cheek lightly with her hand then moved away.

'I must confess Your Highness, I was dreaming.'

'It's too bad that your chambers are so very far away from mine. It would make it so much more convenient for the both of us to have bedrooms closer to each other.' Aynia's softly purring husky voice made everything she said sound very suggestive.

'It's quite all right your Majesty. Good night.' Thorn stammered. He could swear that she was doing this to him on purpose. Perhaps it was payback for ordering her around at lunchtime.

'Good night Thorn. Pleasant dreams. Oh, and Thorn, why don't you drop the crown into one of the jewelry cases on your way out?'

Thorn nodded. So that's what he was supposed to do with the crown. 'I'll just blow the candles out on my way to the door Your Highness.'

'Thanks,' Aynia sighed as she nestled into her bed.

By the time Thorn had blown out the last candle his Queen was fast asleep.

Thane Adders-Tongue despised festival days. When the Queen released her scent it permeated every corner of the Hive so that no one could escape the mating madness. With her own harem discharged years ago there were no males around to satisfy Adders-Tongue once the madness got into her brain.

Determined not to suffer through Festival, Adders-Tongue left the Hive in the early morning and planned to spend the entire day outside.

The High Priestess almost bounced as she walked from her cell to the common dining room in the Temple. She adored Festival. The only problem was her lack of a personal harem. Normally she didn't care much for male company. If she wanted a male to pleasure her there were always the rogue drones for hire. She used their services from time to time, but had not thought to secure herself several for the day of the Festival. By the time she remembered there was not a single drone available for the day. Tulip, the proprietress of the Hive's most popular brothel, confided in the High Priestess that she was getting more than ten times her usual fees on her males.

The communal nature of the Temple offered a solution to the needs of the High Priestess. Priestesses who had harems were asked to share their males with the other females of the Priesthood for Festival. Those who balked at the idea were threatened with the wrath of the Goddesses. As usual that threat worked miracles, suddenly entire harems were being freely shared among all the Sisters at the Temple.

The previous evening the High Priestess asserted her power and picked two males from one of the sister's harems for her personal use. They were taken into her cell and chained to the walls. After morning prayers Festival would begin. The High Priestess planned on starting out in the common room with all the Sisters and their procured males. Then she would return to her room and make use of the two males waiting for her. By the time she got to the two she had set aside they would be crazy for a female.

With her plan for the day well in place, the High Priestess hummed a happy little tune.

Tulip woke her sleeping males. They all shared a bed that filled her small sleeping quarters wall to wall. She liked the feeling of all those firm bodies cuddled against her. There was no privacy, but what did she care? Only the males new to her brothel stared as she enjoyed a romp with one or two of her favorites. All of the others slept.

Tulip was mightily tempted to keep all of her males to herself today. Looking over at the small dark haired drone to her right, she stroked his buttocks with loving caresses. In her own way she adored them all. Their sad stories of abuse, betrayal, and abandonment were all so similar, yet so individual. Tulip had yet to turn down a male looking for shelter. Some males eventually self-destructed and disappeared, a very few were taken into the homes of long time customers, and others stayed on for years in Tulip's employ.

Despite her kind nature, Tulip demanded that her rules be followed, never let a male get the upper hand, and never cheated a rogue drone out of his money. She held affection for each male in her care, but she loved money more. So she rented them all out to regular customers for the Festival at impossibly high fees. She could have sex with any of her males any day that she wanted to, but she couldn't get money like that until the next Festival came around, so the choice was clear.

'Wake up boys. We've got a long day ahead.' Tulip nudged the drones on each side of her. 'Come on, it's Festival today. It's time for you lazy drones to earn your keep.'

With a great show of groans and yawns the group of males climbed off of the bed and went to the communal bath. Tulip followed them into the water.

'Give the customers their money's worth lads.' Tulip lectured while she floated in the steaming water. 'Don't let me hear of you spending time sleeping or talking together. Most of all our clients pay for your undivided attention.'

'And a good hard shag,' one of the males shouted out.

Many of the other males laughed in agreement.

'Aye, that too,' Tulip agreed. 'So take them once and while you rest up wait on 'em hand and foot. Get her something to drink. Massage her feet; brush her hair, whatever it takes to stay in constant physical contact with her. Don't rush into your second or third time with her. You've got all day so take your time and make sure that you're really ready to go again. You're all used to doing your trick and then rushing back to serve drinks. Today you'll have to think more like a drone in a harem than a prostitute in a brothel. I'm charging good money for each of you to be rented out all day. Festivals only last one day though, and at the end of the week I want that customer back in my place. Do you hear me boys?'

'Yes Tulip,' the males answered her.

'So who have you set aside for yourself?' The small dark haired male asked.

Tulip sighed. 'Well, I meant to spend the day with one of you, but demand was high and the money was so good.......'

The male closest to Tulip groaned. 'You took the money over having one of us? Damn you're a cold hearted pimp.'

Tulip sputtered a little. 'Well now, you know that I meant to set one of you aside, but while I was thinking on my selection I had so many valued customers ask to rent you all out, and before I realized it I had no one left.'

'Don't worry Tulip, if I can manage a fourth today I'll save the last dance for you,' the male offered, referring to the house rule that each male had to service three customers a day. A fourth sexual encounter in twenty-four hours was beyond the physical stamina of most drones. But sometimes one would rise to the occasion.

'Me too.'

'And me.'

Tulip pinched her nose to hide the sniffle forming. She blinked back a tear. 'I love you all too boys. Now get your fat asses out of the water and go downstairs. We have a lot of cleaning to do before we open our doors today.'

Aynia walked around the cage that sat in her bedchamber. 'This is new. What can it be for?' She asked. It took up about a third of the space in the chamber.

'Today is Festival.' Heather said as if that explained everything.

'And?'

'You will be releasing your Queen's scent today.'

'So I have been told. Heather, you fail to give me enough information. Do I have to beg for each small bit of detail from you?'

Camellia lounged on a pile of pillows in the corner of the room near Aynia's bed. She propped herself up on one elbow. 'My sister is much too puritanical to go into details. I, on the other hand, am all too happy to discuss the entire matter in lurid detail.'

'I'm listening.'

'Queen's scent has an effect on the brains of the workers of the Hive. It's like an intoxicant. As soon as you release your scent it will begin to fill the air of the Hive. The workers will breathe it in, it will seep into their pores, and it will possess their minds. Within an hour every adult worker in this Hive will shed their clothes and begin to have sexual relations with every other worker and object that they can reach.'

'But what's the cage for?'

'You're still a young Queen, and as yet unmated. Until you can handle the madness that is Festival we feel that you will be safest, and most comfortable, inside this cage. Ordinary workers will begin an orgy in their own chambers and in the Hive center, but the nobles will tear down the very walls of the Palace unless we allow them some access to you. Your scent has the strongest effect on the nobles.'

'Why?'

'For the most part they're all related to you. Workers of a Hive are usually all linked, however distantly, by blood, but the nobles are frequently very close blood relatives. When your scent fills the air it calls them to you. It is a call that they can not resist.'

'How can I be safe in the cage if everyone is mad to reach me?'

Heather stepped forward. 'Since we, my sisters and I, are not of this Hive, your scent will not affect us as strongly as it will the natives of the Hive.'

'I will feel safer yet if I am the only one holding the key.' Aynia said.

Heather frowned. 'I am perfectly trustworthy to hold it Your Majesty.'

'Don't be insulted. Lock me in and hand me the key. When the day ends I will hand it out to you and you can unlock the door.'

'I don't like this plan Majesty.'

Aynia shrugged. 'I don't believe that I asked if you liked it.' She turned away from Heather and went to her bath chamber to prepare for the day.

Camellia watched her glowering sister. 'The Queen has the right of it. Of all of us you should be the last to be trusted with the key to that cell.'

Heather snorted. 'I will not fall under the spell of the Queen's scent.'

'That's theory, not proven fact. For all we know in several hours we'll be copulating mindlessly with the masses. Besides, you've already fallen under the Queen's spell. Or was that little scene in her bath just an innocent mistake? Your hand just accidentally floated up and stroked her clit again and again, and again?'

'What do you mean by that?'

'It's always red heads, isn't it?'

Heather pulled Camellia up off of the floor by the throat and held her by the black leather collar around her neck. 'What you think you know and what you do know are two very different things little sister. Do you doubt that I have enough moral strength to overcome the intoxication of the Queen's scent?'

'No, I don't,' Camellia said. She didn't mean a word of it, but she knew that arguing with Heather was useless. Besides, Heather was strong enough to lift Camellia off of the floor if so inclined. And Camellia desperately wanted to breathe.

Aynia returned from her bath.

'That was very quick Majesty,' Camellia said.

'Rose said that I had better get started soon. Apparently workers have been waiting since the stroke of midnight. Now tell me,' Aynia asked as she walked into the cage and pulled the door shut behind her, 'just how do I release my scent?'

'We are not Queens so we can only tell you what we've heard from others we served,' Camellia told Aynia. 'Close your eyes. Now imagine that somewhere in the Hive is someone that you want to come to you. Without using words or gestures, call out to that Fairie.'

'Lock the cage first,' Heather cried out. She turned the key in the lock and reluctantly handed over the key to Aynia. 'Place it somewhere where no one could reach in and grab it.'

Aynia placed the key along the back wall of the cage where the cage was welded to iron rings embedded in the stone walls of the bedchamber. Then she sat down on the single chair provided and closed her eyes. Taking a deep breath, she mentally called out for Thorn.

She opened one eye and looked at her attendants. 'Is anything happening?'

'Not yet. It is something physical Majesty, a release.'

Aynia frowned and concentrated. Somewhere in this new adult form was a scent that she could release. She wondered how she would do it. She took in a deep breath and exhaled slowly. Closing her eyes, Aynia tried using her body, not her mind, to call out for Thorn.

A scent, not sweet, but faintly exotic, like spices, filled the air.

'She's doing it!'

'That's it my lady.'

Aynia shut out the voices of her attendants and pictured Thorn crawling to her, begging for her to let him touch her. A smile played across her lips. The room was growing warm. Aynia stood and pulled off her skirt.

The Queen's scent affected the Queen too.

From a distance she could hear a low rumbling sound.

One of the Royal Guards ran into the room. 'You should see the Hive center! Fairie are throwing their clothes off!' The guard stopped. He could see his Queen in a cage. Her eyes were closed as if she was in a trance. She swayed a little then began to unfasten her corset. Hook by hook the black leather parted, promising a tantalizing view of her chest.

Aynia opened her eyes. She saw the male in front of her. His eyes were wide. She smiled at him and licked her lips. Then she slowly slid the straps of the corset off of her shoulder, enjoying the expression on his face.

Unable to stop himself, the Guard stumbled closer to the cage.

The sound of the mob grew louder every second.

Aynia half turned away as she finished unhooking the corset. With a wriggle it fell to the bottom of the cage. She turned back to the Guard, giving him a full frontal view.

The Guard's mouth flew open. He was no drone, but he liked what he saw.

Aynia laughed gently.

'Okay lover boy, you've had your look. Now it's time to go,' Camellia told the Guard. She firmly escorted him to the door of the Queen's bedchamber. When she opened the door there was sudden chaos.

'The Queen's chamber is open!'

Nearly eighty noble females and over a hundred drones rushed into Aynia's bedchamber.

'Don't worry my Queen, you are safe,' Heather warned Aynia. 'If the Hive smells fear it will throw them into a panic. And if the Hive panics there will be death.'

Aynia retreated to the far wall of the cage. Soon she was surrounded. On each side Fairie pressed themselves against the bars of the cage. Some tried to crawl between the bars. Arms, hands, and feet reached out in an effort to touch Aynia.

Aynia felt something brush against her hair. She looked up. Fairie were on the top of the cage reaching down for her. She saw how this scene could cause a young Queen to panic. But she felt no fear.

'Undress,' she commanded the nobles before her.

They were happy to comply.

Aynia walked near to the outstretched fingers. She let fingertips just graze her thigh.

'Touch me Majesty!' Someone pleaded.

Aynia closed her eyes and began to dance to the song only she heard. She let her long red hair tumble out of its neatly arraigned twist. Her hands went to massage her breasts. As she twirled hands grasped at the ends of her hair. Then she stopped twirling and let her hands slip inside of her panties. Aynia felt her dampness and stroked it with the ends of her fingers.

The nobles threw themselves at the cage with renewed vigor.

Aynia's eyes opened to lazy slits. She went to the edge of the cage and placed her fingers into the mouths of the nobles. They greedily sucked her juices off of her fingers.

Across the Royal bedchamber drones and their Mistresses writhed together. Drones sucked on toes, on nipples, and on lips. Aynia watched with fascination as one lady of a particularly old and distinguished clan displayed skills best described as acrobatic.

'You see sister, the Queen's scent has no affect on me,' Heather told Camellia proudly.

'Perhaps not.'

Rose stood by her sisters and watched the nobles enjoy their orgy. 'I'm getting plenty of ideas to take home though. Look at her,' Rose pointed to a couple near the fireplace.

The male was standing with his legs slightly apart. Using both hands he held onto the hips of his female. The female was using her wings to levitate herself horizontally at the level of his pelvis. She held onto the back of a chair while he made deep thrusts. Closing her eyes, the female began to grind her hips. The male pulled out of her and slid three fingers into her vagina.

'Don't stop,' she cried out.

'Beg me for it,' the drone said as he slapped her ass hard with his free hand.

'I'm so close,' the female moaned.

'You're so tight,' the drone told her.

The female's whole body convulsed.

The drone plunged deep into her and came.

The female turned and wrapped her legs around the male as they embraced. 'I've been dreaming of this for years. I love it when you get rough.'

Heather snorted. 'No good comes of letting a male have the upper hand.'

Rose rolled her eyes, but Camellia nodded in agreement. 'Males need strong discipline. A male who is tightly bound to his place is happier.'

Rose nodded to another couple. 'Then he must be deliriously happy.'

The drone in question was completely nude except for a black leather hood and a pair of nipple clamps. There were eyeholes in the mask, and a hole for his tongue. The drone was attempting to pleasure his mistress by suckling on her nipples but apparently was failing as she delivered repeated blows from a cat 'o nine tails. Occasionally she would tug at his nipple clamps.

It was Camellia's turn to roll her eyes. 'Oh please, how very theatrical. You don't punish males for failing to please; you punish them for breaking rules. They find comfort in knowing the limits set for them will be enforced. But sex, well, sex should be about pleasure,' she practically purred.

'Are you saying that you've never found a male who enjoyed that?' Heather asked incredulously.

'Oh sure, many get sexually aroused by discipline. Some even like a little rough sexual play. Many like being tied. But that drone isn't even near being hard, so how much can he be enjoying the session? She's just trying to show off how much control she has over him.'

Rose winked at Camellia. 'So, do you get sexually aroused by disciplining the harem?'

'I enjoy my job,' Camellia said with a dignified tone, her expression slightly insulted.

'How much?' Rose probed. She always wondered if the black leather clothes were just a prop of Camellia's position or if Camellia really was a dominatrix.

Camellia pointed over the Aynia in the cage. 'How's the Queen doing?' She changed the subject.

The sisters turned to see Aynia in a trance where she danced in sinuous grace as she ran her hands over her body.

'She seems to be doing fine,' Rose said.

'Yes, she is,' Heather said disapprovingly. She wanted to go clear the nobles away from the cage. Actually, she wanted to get into the cage with Aynia. Camellia and Rose were right about Heather's weakness for red heads.

Aynia stroked her self again. Before long her knees went weak and she needed to sit on the chair in her cage. Time after time she dipped her fingers into her own juices and languidly allowed the nobles surrounding the cage to lick her fingers while she enjoyed the show before her.

Trapped in his Mother's chambers, Thorn shouted at his sister, Verbena. 'You can't do this to me.'

'We will do what is best for you. You may be the Captain of the Guard, but you are still an unattached male. We will not let you go out today.'

'I have to see my Queen.'

'No Thorn,' Verbena said with quiet finality.

Thorn struggled against the chains. 'She's calling to me!' He sniffed the air and closed his eyes. 'Can't you smell it? She wants me to come to her.'

Verbena pulled her Mother out of the room. 'Mama, Thorn isn't a drone. Why is the Queen's scent affecting him like this?'

Their Mother shrugged. 'There are stories about males spontaneously becoming drone, but I never really believed it. I thought it was myth. I do know that Thorn is very attached to this Queen. Maybe he wants to become her drone so badly that he is imagining that the scent affects him.'

'I can't imagine Thorn as a drone,' Verbena shook her head. 'I don't think that he'd be very happy confined to a harem.'

'I can't imagine it either dear, but it seems that his heart is in conflict with his mind. But would it be so bad, really, for him to be the Queen's stud?'

'Yes it would,' Verbena snapped. She had little patience left for practical thoughts today. It took every once of strength for her to ignore the lure of the Queen's scent.

Their mother sighed. 'We could certainly use the money.'

'Would you sell your son into a harem? Even the Queen's?'

'Sweetheart, it is the destiny of males. Now don't be angry with me. I've been offered fine bridal prices for him before, and I've never said yes. But I wouldn't protest either if he made the decision to lie in the Queen's bed.'

They went to the doorway and looked in on Thorn. He was still fighting the chains. When he looked up and saw his sister a deep, angry, growl emitted from his throat.

'Poor boy. Is there anything we can do for him now?' Verbena was quite worried about her brother. Never in her life would she have imagined the calm, cool Captain Thorn succumbing to the mating madness of the Festival. In a day he would probably look back at this moment and be horribly embarrassed. What was worse, he lacked the ability to release the sexual frustration that was growing in his body.

'Before we chained him I gave him a powerful sleeping drought.' Their mother told Verbena. 'It was a miracle that you managed to bring him here.'

'He put up quite a fight,' Verbena said, displaying scratches on her upper arm. 'And I'll be bruised tomorrow, that's for sure.

It was pure dumb luck that I was passing by the entrance to the Hive when he came in like this. Apparently he was on a mission outside. I would hate to think what would happen to him if he were out loose in the Hive in this condition.'

'Some female would have him take milk and he would have been ruined, or abducted into a harem. Poor boy. He must love the Queen more than even he knows.'

Thorn wailed in pure frustration as he fought against the chains. He was sure that Aynia wanted him, and who was he to deny his Queen? He thought about her lovely naked form, and he knew exactly what he wanted to do with her. If only he could pull the chains out of the wall.

'He'll fall asleep soon. See, his head is drooping and he's losing strength.'

'Good. Then we can stop watching over him and go have our own fun.'

'Amen to that. But you won't believe the prices Tulip is charging!'

'How kind of you to visit me in my exile Thane Adders-Tongue,' Carman said grumpily. She reclined on a bed of moss and heather.

'Oh, don't rise on my account Majesty,' Adders-Tongue said although Carman made no effort to rise. 'And how is Your Majesty's health?'

'What brings you out here Adders-Tongue?' Carman dismissed the pleasantries.

Adders-Tongue sat down, much to the consternation of Carman's attendants, and removed her gloves with exaggerated care. 'It is Festival today in the Hive. I have no desire to watch the nobility copulating for the pleasure of that bitch Aynia.'

'It's Festival?' One of the attendants asked wistfully. One look from Adders-Tongue was enough to silence that attendant for the rest of the day.

'You dare sit in my presence?' Carman managed to move past her stuttering outrage. 'No one sits in the presence of the Queen!'

'Actually, many of us nobles do have the right to sit in the presence of the Queen. Besides, I made you Queen. At least I handed you the throne on a platter. How you managed to muck it up is beyond my understanding.'

'We had bad luck.'

'Bad luck? I told you to kill Aynia first! She was the only threat to you. She was the only Princess capable of ruling the Hive.'

'Peony took the Royal Jelly early. We had to take her out first.'

'Peony? Who told you that?' Adders-Tongue looked from Carman to Snakegrass.

Snakegrass made a bow to her clansman. 'Thane Adders-Tongue, it was I who ascertained that Princess Peony took Royal Jelly before official notification came of the Queen's death.'

'You personally checked this fact? I would hope so. Because if I were to hear a little rumor that the Captain of the Royal Guard told you this, and that you believed him without checking up in it yourself, I would be most displeased.' Adders-Tongue's stinger suddenly rose above Snakegrass where it wove like a cobra assessing its prey.

Snakegrass swallowed. 'I would never trust Thorn's word. I checked out everything myself.'

'I would hope so. Now Carman, how is your recovery coming?'

'I will remind you to address me as Your Majesty or Your Highness. I am Queen. I am no longer your pupil.'

'On the contrary child. You still seem to have much to learn.'

Carman stumbled to her feet. She whipped out her stinger and leveled it at Thane Adders-Tongue.

Adders-Tongue's steely smile slid off of her face. Her stinger moved from Snakegrass to Carman. Both females stared at each other with naked hostility, their stingers bobbing and weaving around in the air.

'Just try it Adders-Tongue. But remember that your stinger is only good once,' Carman warned.

Adders-Tongue thought the better of the situation and lowered her stinger. Picking up her gloves, she made it clear that her visit was over. Snakegrass handed Adders-Tongue a list. 'What is this?' Adders-Tongue asked coolly.

'This is our provisions list. See that these things are brought to us soon. I can not recover fully if I don't have adequate clothes, food, and shelter,' Carman said.

'But my dear, you have this lovely badger barrow.'

'Send the provisions, or I will go home to the Hive. I wonder what Captain Thorn or my sister would say if they knew that you planed the assassination of the late Queen?'

Adders-Tongue stomped away from Carman's hovel, not answering Carman's threat.

Snakegrass followed Adders-Tongue out into the glen. 'Forget the fancy things, but we do need food and medicine. Please. She cannot recover without adequate food and medicine.'

Adders-Tongue looked around the glen. 'Is she really recovering?'

'Yes! You saw yourself. She can walk now with only a little limp. But her arm is still heavily damaged.'

'Can she fly?'

'Not yet,' Snakegrass admitted, 'but there is hope.'

'If she can't fly she can't breed. The Hive won't accept her as Queen if she can't fly. Have her flying in three weeks. If she can't by then either you terminate her or I will let Thorn know where this hiding place is. Understand?'

'I understand Aunt Adders-Tongue.' Snakegrass said as she bowed and retreated.

CHAPTER 7

Copperhead fell into step with his cousin Cobra-Lily. He saw her across the Hive center as he came from the Royal Palace. Now every message that he delivered went to Thane Adders-Tongue first. So far nothing of interest was contained in the notes between the Queen and her old attendants, but both Copperhead and Adders-Tongue suspected that there were messages encoded somehow into the seemingly banal correspondence.

'Where are you going?' Copperhead asked.

'None of your beeswax,' Cobra-Lily snapped.

'What's in your purse?'

'Never you mind, male.' Cobra-Lily used the one insult that she could think of.

'I still work for the Queen.' Copperhead baited her.

'So what? She won't be Queen for long.'

'Sh! Don't talk so loud about you-know-who.' Copperhead warned her.

'What? Oh no, I wasn't even thinking about her. Really, I couldn't care less about revenge for some guy that I never met. I mean really, that was years ago, get over it already! Besides, that all worked out for the best as far as I'm concerned.'

'How so?'

'Since our Aunt never had any children of her own I'm in line to become the next Thane.'

'No you're not.'

'Yes I am.' Cobra-Lily insisted.

'What about my mother, your mother, our Aunts, and our cousins? They're all in line ahead of you to inherit the title and estate.' Copperhead reminded his cousin.

Cobra-Lily shrugged. 'As if I'd let them get in my way just because they're family. I remember, you know. I remember every single mean thing they ever said to me. I know that they all call me dumb, and some day they'll get theirs.' Her fist tightened around the purse that she carried.

'What were you saying about letting things go?'

'Shut up. I'm busy. I have a little payback of my own to put together. I'm not stupid. I can figure out how to get back at someone who humiliates me.'

'Where are you going?' Copperhead was truly curious now.

'I'm not going to tell some lowly male my business. Go away.'

'Fine, I'll go away,' Copperhead appeared to capitulate, but he only fell back far enough into the crowd that she couldn't see him.

Copperhead followed Cobra-Lily to the artisan's section of the Hive. There he saw Cobra-Lily enter a small shop with a dishonest looking proprietress. A smudged sign in the window proclaimed it to be a metal smith's, Magnolia the Metal smith. Presumably the female inside was Magnolia.

Peering into the shop from a hiding spot Copperhead saw the rough looking Magnolia weigh out the contents of the bag. He needn't have bothered. The windows were coated with so much filth that he could have stood openly in front of the window and his cousin would not have been able to tell it was he.

Inside the shop, Magnolia looked inside the bag for a second, and then she tried to thrust the bag back into Cobra-Lily's hands.

Cobra-Lily and Magnolia talked for a short time. Stingers were drawn. Copperhead grimaced. Should he go in and assist his cousin? She might be family, but Copperhead had plenty of other family that he was fonder of.

Before he made his decision, Magnolia made hers. Grudgingly she counted out coins for Cobra-Lily. It was more coins that Copperhead had ever seen in one place, but Cobra-Lily seemed displeased with the payout. After another short argument Cobra-Lily took her stack of coins and headed for the door of the establishment.

Copperhead withdrew deep into a shadow. When Cobra-Lily was a safe distance away he again followed her. She went into a jeweler's shop. Copperhead thought about alerting his Aunt Adders-Tongue to his cousin's strange behavior, but decided to keep the secret to himself. Maybe he could wheedle information out of Cobra-Lily at a later date. Besides, the hour was growing late, and unaccompanied males were not supposed to roam around the Hive past daylight.

Aynia awoke as Rose gently nudged her. 'Forgive me my lady, you looked so peacefully asleep, but today is the most important day of Your Majesty's reign.'

Aynia was confused. 'I've had a coronation, I've attended a session of Parliament, and I've presided over the celebration of my coronation. What more is there?'

Deidre, who was also standing beside the bed, chuckled. 'Your Majesty, there is always something for you to do. Your calendar is full already for this year, and would be for next year too if we allowed it to be booked that far ahead. I believe that you have at least one official function every day.'

'Oh very well,' Aynia grumbled. She sat up in the bed, and then placed her hands supportively across her chest. 'What is this? Has someone placed iron weights in my breasts?'

Rose actually giggled a little. 'No Majesty. I guess that I should have warned you, but I thought that you knew.'

'We did mention this a few times,' Heather added, her face also betraying a smile.

'Even I said something,' Camellia added.

'Told me what? That while I slept my breasts would explode?'

Rose tried to wipe her smile off of her face. She grew serious. 'Your milk has come in Majesty, that's all. It will be uncomfortable for a couple of days, and then you'll grow used to it. On the positive side, the corsets that you wear offer excellent support and will relieve some of the discomfort.'

'My milk?'

'The Queen's milk. The Hive could not exist without it.'

'I thought it as a figure of speech!' Aynia protested.

'You are the Mother of the Hive.'

'Do you really mean to say that I supply milk for the Hive, the entire Hive?' Aynia was incredulous, thinking of the thousands of Fairie Folk that she saw in the Hive center her first day as Queen.

'Your milk will be used three ways. One is for religious ceremonies, like the one today.' Heather informed the Queen. This was her area of expertise. 'This is the reason why the new Queen visits the Temple on the third day of her reign. That's when the milk comes in. At the Temple the Priestesses will relieve you of some of your milk which will be taken to make Royal Jelly for the next Princesses. The Priestesses will use the rest for other ceremonies.'

'Why didn't my Mother warn me about this?' Aynia wondered.

'She was very used to it by the time you were born. She probably didn't even think about it.' Rose said as she led Aynia to the bath. The other attendants followed as Aynia waded into the warm water. The added buoyancy of the water, and its warmth, relieved some of Aynia's pain.

'The second use of your milk,' Heather continued lecturing despite the fact that no one was listening to her, 'will be to nurse your own children, like any mother in the Hive.'

'Do all females produce milk, even when they have no children?'

'Yes Majesty, every adult female produces milk, though not of the quantity or quality that you do.'

'So what makes me so special?' Aynia asked. 'Is it the Royal Jelly I ate?'

Heather paused for a moment. 'Well, not exactly. You see, it was the Royal Jelly that started you going.'

'Primed the pump, so to speak,' Camellia quipped.

'But in order for you to continue to produce the milk that the Hive needs for religious ceremonies you will need to continue to stimulate the production of milk.' Heather said with caution that made Aynia suspicious.

'And this means, in plain Fairy speak?'

Camellia could not miss this chance. 'This is where the harem comes in my lady.' She laughed heartily at her Queen's expression. 'That's the other Royal duty you must perform today. All of the emissaries from the other Tuatha de Danaan Hives will be presenting you with their noblest sons this afternoon as tokens of friendship. The ones that you choose as your drones will nurse to stimulate your production of milk. It makes them virile.' Camellia laughed again roguishly. 'And then I'll have a harem to manage finally.'

'I can't believe this.' Aynia sighed. 'By this afternoon I'll have a harem? And I have never even met any of the males. How many husbands am I going to take on?'

Camellia shrugged. 'Not more than forty I would think.'

'Forty?'

'Well, it should be more, but the Fairie Hives of England apparently couldn't be bothered to send representatives. Three of the French Hives managed to cross the channel. So did the Irish and the Belgians and the Norwegians. We even have a representative from a Hive in Alesd, Romania, but could the English cross a simple border? No,' Heather grumbled.

'If it's true that the humans are at war it could be that the border is very dangerous to cross right now.' Deidre said.

'Dangerous if you're are an innocent Scot, not so dangerous if you're one of those filthy English swine.' Heather protested.

'So speaks a true daughter of the Hive of Ardcharnich. Do you realize, sister, that you are defending humans?' Deidre chided Heather.

Heather would not be put down. She sniffed. 'Aye, but they're Scots. If there must be humans at least let them wear tartan.'

Aynia started to wade out of her bath. With all of her sisters dead or dangerously missing she felt odd eavesdropping on these four and their familiar conversations. It made her miss, however briefly, those days when she was a Princess, she had a clan of her own, her Mother was Queen, and she held similar arguments with her sisters Lily, Gladiola, and Peony. However, Aynia was not one to dwell on a past that was forever gone. She was alive, she was Queen, and there was a lot to be said for both of those facts.

The attendants jumped up to assist Aynia as she waded out of the bath. They toweled down their Queen gently, applied lotion to her skin, and then powdered her lightly with scented talc before bringing over the corset she was to wear to the Temple. For the first time since she had acquired that piece of clothing Aynia was relieved when the corset was laced up. The support that it gave to her full breasts did relieve a lot of her discomfort, as predicted by Rose.

While two servants carefully brushed her hair Aynia looked at herself critically in the mirror. 'Rose, how do they, um...'Aynia almost could not finish her sentence.

Camellia was the one to answer for her. Walking over to Aynia, she said, 'with your permission Highness?' After Aynia nodded Camellia showed Aynia a clever hidden hook that disconnected the cup of the corset, exposing her breast without having to disrobe entirely.

'Aha!' Aynia said with obvious relief. 'I was worried for a second there. But how do they?' She also let this question trail off into silence.

Camellia smiled. 'This is getting very personal, but again, with your permission?' She stood behind her Queen, massaging Aynia's breast, kneading the sensitive organ firmly. Finally, separating her fingers so that her thumb and index finger were on top of Aynia's areola and her other fingers below it, Camellia gently pressed against Aynia's breast. Aynia watched in fascination as some of her milk sprayed out of her nipple and onto the mirror in front of her.

Aynia laughed. 'Oh my Goddesses it works. Okay, so the Priestesses are going to milk me?'

'Basically, yes.' Camellia admitted.

'They're going to do it in front of everyone?'

'Not everyone, just the hundred of nobles who can fit into the Temple.'

'Oh, well as long as it's just a few hundred Fairie, no problem,' Aynia sighed. Apparently all of the wealth in her treasury could not buy for her that most precious luxury, privacy.

Heather took exception to this discussion. She felt that any questions about the Temple should be directed to her, not her sacrilegious sister Camellia. 'It is not done exactly like that,' Heather snapped. 'It's a beautiful ceremony, thousands of years old, with deep meanings that are beyond the understanding of my silly sister. And don't waste the Queen's milk in that fashion. She doesn't have much now and they need all that they can get for the ceremony. Besides, the Queen's milk is sacred and shouldn't be treated like this.' Heather went to find an appropriately distinguished cloth to wipe the milk off of the mirror.

As soon as Heather disappeared from the room Camellia and Aynia looked back at each other and burst out in gales of laughter.

Thorn strode into the bedroom. 'I hear my Queen laughing. She must be feeling better today.' He hoped that Aynia did not suspect his behavior from the Festival day. It was difficult enough this morning to face his mother and sister.

Aynia hastily reattached the cup of her corset while Camellia shielded her from Thorn's view. As soon as Camellia knew that Aynia was presentable she stepped away from Aynia with a bow and a big smile.

Thorn dropped to his knee and kissed Aynia's extended hand. 'My Queen.'

Aynia beamed down at Thorn. When he walked into a room it always seemed to Aynia as if a thousand candles were just lit. The very sight of him made her heart grow lighter. 'Thorn. Have you eaten? We were just about to go into the parlor and have a quick breakfast before the ceremonies at the Temple begin.'

'I have eaten Majesty. Thank you. You look in excellent health. It appears that food and sleep agree with you. Laughter does too.' He looked up into her shinning eyes and saw how much happiness improved her countenance. There was usually radiance to her face that had been missing since she became Queen.

'I am gratified that you find my looks pleasing Captain.'

Thorn cleared his throat. Yesterday all he could think about was her naked flesh. Glancing away from her with only the barest hint of a blush on his high cheekbones, Thorn rose. 'Shall I escort you to the parlor?'

Aynia stood and took Thorn's arm. He walked her to the parlor, pulled out a chair for Aynia, and then seated her.

Rose stood and stared after the two as they walked out of the bedroom.

'What do you look at Rose?' Heather asked. 'You have the oddest expression on your face.'

'Sometimes, well, I'm not accusing anybody of anything, but do you ever get the idea that those two only have eyes for each other? Everything that they say in conversation between them seems to have deeper meaning.'

Heather looked over into the parlor where Aynia was now eating her breakfast while Thorn sat and talked with her. Her eyes narrowed suspiciously. 'Our Captain does seem especially devoted.'

'Oh don't get so worked up,' Camellia said with a laugh at her sisters. 'What can he do? He's no drone. And what if they did? She would hardly be the first Queen to take a soldier as a lover.'

'I remember a story about a Hive in Tandragee, an Irish Hive. The Queen there took on a military man as a drone. He hated it. He hated what it made him. Soldiers don't like being turned into lazy drones. Soon he fell out of the Queen's favor. Before you knew it his head was on a post at the palace gates. The military took exception. They staged a coup and executed the Queen.' Rose informed them.

'They haven't shown any signs of anything like that,' Camellia said with a little impatience. 'Good Goddesses, you and your deeper meanings. So what if they talk in double entendres? So what if she wants to bed him and he wants to become a drone? It's not a big deal. It's none of our business. Her own Mother actually allowed a worker to sire a Princess after all.'

'Look how well that turned out,' Rose reminded them. 'Princess Carman had her mother killed and tried to take over the Throne.'

'What do you mean tried? As far as we know she's still trying.'

'You can't really believe that a half paralyzed Queen would survive outside of the Hive this long?'

'What if she's here in the Hive, but hidden from sight?'

'Now you're seeing bogeymen everywhere.'

'Don't get complacent. You can bet that our Captain isn't. He still thinks that Carman is a threat. Maybe that's why he sticks so close to the new Queen. After all, it's really quite embarrassing how easily he lost the last one.'

The High Priestess waited for breakfast to be served. Usually she ate with all of the Priestesses who served in the Temple at a morning breakfast meeting, but today, due to the importance of the occasion, she met only with the Senior Priestesses.

'A historic day,' Priestess Cerridwen mentioned.

'Indeed. Do you even begin to realize how momentous this day is for us? The late Queen, may her soul join the Goddesses,' the head Priestess intoned the usual prayer for the dead without any of the feeling she would have used for a religious service.

'Amen,' the other Priestesses answered out of habit and with as little feeling as the High Priestess used.

'The late Queen barely tolerated the Temple. The last year, when she came for the Ceremony of the Milk, she refused to allow me to touch her. This Queen however, she is a true

believer. She used to attend services regularly with her father
and even after he died. Her attendants, with a few exceptions,
were also devoted to the Goddesses. Do you realize that at least
three of her closest attendants from when she was a Princess are
now serving in the Temple? And all of them are still in constant
contact with the Queen via notes?'

'Really?'

'Oh yes. I've read them all. Truly dull stuff, but it is a
connection never the less.'

'And we have Lady Heather,' Cerridwen reminded the High
Priestess.

'I had my doubts about her when she first came here. I even
spoke against her in Parliament. She came to this Hive with
quite a bad reputation. They were very unhappy with her at her
former post in Russia. But as it turns out Lady Heather is as
orthodox as they come. She serves the Goddesses first, then the
Queen,' the High Priestess said.

'Which means that she serves us,' Cerridwen noted.

'She can be bent to our needs. For instance, I informed her
that the stars bode ill for the Hive if the Queen does not mate this
coming Vernal Equinox.'

'Do they?' Cerridwen asked with concern.

'Oh good Goddesses, you didn't make it this far in the clergy
by maintaining your faith did you? The stars only say what I
want them to say.'

'Why are we so determined to have the Queen mate?'

'Because a Queen with a Princess is far more likely to look
to the future of the Hive than a Queen with no children. We like
our Queens pregnant and we like for their milk to flow. That's
all that we ask.'

'Especially the milk,' Cerridwen dared to say while looking
up at the High Priestess.

The High Priestess winked at her current favorite.
Cerridwen started off as downright puritanistic, but lately she
was showing signs of becoming delightfully sensualist.

Only the Priestesses knew the spells to convert Queen's milk into Royal Jelly. The Priestesses relied on the Queen for milk, and the Hive relied on the Priestesses for Royal Jelly. It was a symbiotic relationship that kept both the Queen and Parliament in check. But that did not mean that the Temple couldn't suffer from a lack of favor. The late Queen sent very little gold to the Temple and rarely attended services. Thus nobles rarely attended. Patronage was dangerously low. The new Queen might turn that around.

'Let us offer up a prayer to the Goddess for our new Queen. Long live Queen Aynia.' Of all the powerful Fairie in the Hive repeating this mantra, the High Priestess was one of the few who actually meant it.

The Temple was much too small to hold all of the nobility, their children, and harems. While everyday services were attended by only a few of the faithful, any day that the Queen set foot inside the Temple was a day to see and be seen. The two hundred seats inside were filled early, and the screened off portion in the back for males was also filled to overflowing.

The inside of the Temple was done entirely in black marble. The original architect had thought to create a sensation of staring into a deep pool of water or the night sky in order to facilitate contemplation. Indeed, most days, for a Fairie who knew the Temple well, it was one of the few places in the Hive that offered the peace and solitude required for meditation.

However, for those unacquainted with the basic floor plan of the main sanctuary, stepping inside the Temple was at best disorienting. The black marble pews, floor, walls, and steps all blended together so that their shapes were indiscernible to the untrained eye. Many a Fairie bumped into pews or tripped on stairs that she never guessed were right in front of her.

Regular attendees and priestesses found this to be very amusing.

The Temple was sadly in need of a major overhaul but without regular Royal patronage it was financially unfeasible to renovate the interior.

Aynia was led into the Temple through a back entrance. After the service began one of the Priestesses took her gently by the elbow and led her out to the dais that rose about chest high to the nobles who stood when the Queen entered.

Aynia sat on the Throne before the main altar, her tight black leather corset creaking as she sank into the marble seat. Camellia, Heather, Deidre, and Rose adjusted the purple velvet skirt she was wearing then took their places standing behind the Throne.

Aynia scanned the audience, hoping to see the one face she always looked to for reassurance, but he was not there. At first she was unhappy, but as she contemplated the possible humiliations about to take place, she decided that she was glad Thorn was not present.

Thorn would have been in attendance, but as he marched behind the Queen through the Palace hallways a messenger slipped him a message from his guards. More humans were spotted near Balnacra. He fell out of the Queen's entourage and took his troops to exterminate the human encroachers.

As the service wore on Aynia was aware of an uncomfortable feeling. Her breasts were already tender. Now they seemed to be getting heavier and heavier and even the corset was failing to support them enough.

Once worried about the personal aspect of the ceremony, Aynia was relieved when at last the High Priestess motioned to her to stand. When the Queen stands everyone rises to his or her feet, so the entire congregation noisily woke up and struggled to stand. The Priestess motioned to the acolytes to bring a golden chalice over. The acolyte kneeled in front of the Priestess who said a prayer over the chalice. Then the acolyte stood and brought the bowl just under Aynias' right breast.

Aynia noticed that the acolyte looked down to the floor.

Muttering prayers to the Goddesses, the Priestess unlatched the right cup of Aynia's corset. She took Aynia's right breast in a cool, soft hand and massaged in tightening circles from the outside towards her nipple. Suddenly the Priestess applied pressure. And as her breasts had done for Camellia, Aynias' breast began to flow with milk.

The acolyte caught each drop of the fine spray. For five minutes the Priestess worked the right breast over. Every time it seemed to stop giving milk she found a new place to apply pressure. Still, for the amount of time it took, Aynia was shocked to see only a few ounces of her milk in the bottom of the chalice. Then there was no more milk, and the Priestess fastened the cup of the corset up.

Aynia expected the Priestess to begin to work on her other breast right away, but she had Aynia sit while she and the other Priestesses murmured prayers over the chalice. Then they sprinkled drops of the milk onto small altars about the Temple dedicated to individual goddesses.

Camellia leaned forward. 'So, are you going for accuracy or distance with the left nipple?' She whispered. 'I'll give you a thousand gold coins if you hit the front pew.'

Deidre conveniently had a coughing fit to cover Aynia's laughter. Then Deidre shot her sister a nasty look.

Camellia would not be cowed by such looks. She winked at Aynia. This time Heather was forced to drop her prayer book to cover the giggles from their Queen.

'I'm curious,' Aynia told the High Priestess over a modest lunch in the Temple's private chambers, 'what is my milk used for? You don't seem to have gotten much.'

'A little goes a very long way My Queen.'

'But how do you use it?'

'There are, of course, the offerings to the Goddesses. Some is used in a ceremony for members of the nobility when they are ready to transform into adults. Females receive it in their twentieth year. Males receive it on the first day of their wedding ceremonies.'

'All females and males?' Aynia asked.

'Oh no, not all, only nobility. Only Queen's milk has the power to bring out wings. After all, we can't have common workers with wings.'

'Why not?'

'Majesty! What a question,' the High Priestess was shocked. The High Priestess was born a common worker, but like most who manage to rise above their station in a highly stratified society, she was a horrible snob.

Conversation all down the table stopped.

'It's a simple question. Would it be so terrible if the common workers had wings?' Aynia asked.

'Wings are a sign of the nobility. If you took that away how would we be able to distinguish the common from the noble?'

'By clothing, by wealth, by education, many other features separate the nobility from the workers.'

'But none so markedly as the wings.' The High Priestess said in a tone that suggested she would discuss the matter no further.

'What else is my milk used for?' Aynia asked.

'We process it into Royal Jelly Highness.'

'Which is used for what?'

'The Royal Jelly is used to transform Princesses into Queens.'

'I'm aware of that, of course. But I believe that in my studies I read that Royal Jelly has another use.'

'Quite so. That is a fact not well known outside of this Temple. While Royal Jelly brings life to our Queens it is a powerful poison bringing death to the other Sidhe, magic folk. The smallest drop kills gnomes, pixies, and nymphs,' the High Priestess said.

'And the Mountain King?'

A murmur went around the table. The Mountain King was a powerful foe of the Fairie. His skin was impervious to their stingers. He alone among the Sidhe could shrug off an attack by the Fairie. This made it simple for him to abduct Fairie brides.

Aynia did not see the reason for such alarm at the mere mention of the Mountain King. He did not currently threaten the Hive at Balnacra. The Queen and High Priestesses knew what weapon to use against him. Being frightened of the mere mention of their enemy was ludicrous in the extreme.

Aynia decided to change the subject. There was a question that puzzled her. 'How do you transform my milk into Royal Jelly?'

The High Priestess smiled slowly. Other Priestesses around the room exchanged glances across the table. Some used table linens to hide smiles.

'I seem to have asked a question with an interesting answer.'

'What do you mean Majesty?' The High Priestess acted as if she did not hear the quiet laughter.

'I mean that Priestess Cerridwen is blushing deep red, the others here are stifling giggles, and there is a distinct twinkle in your eye. What could I have said that they find so amusing?'

'I really don't know Your Majesty.'

'How is Royal Jelly made?'

'We take your milk and say a few prayers, spells if you will, to the Goddesses.'

Aynia was beginning to lose patience. 'But how exactly is the transformation made?'

'I can not tell you Majesty. It is a secret of the Temple.'

'It's my milk.' Aynia's tone took on a hard edge.

'No,' the High Priestess said with finality. 'It is not your milk. It is the Hive's milk.'

Before Aynia could make her angry retort, Camellia stepped forward and cleared her throat. 'Majesty, I am terribly sorry to interrupt, but you have a very important function in the Throne Room to attend.'

Aynia slowly placed her napkin on the table. As civilly as she could following the prior exchange she said, 'I'm sorry to leave you. This has been a most interesting lunch.'

'We must be going too My Queen. After all, today is the day you receive your tribute. We must be present to bless your new harem of males.'

Thorn met Aynia and her entourage outside the Priestesses' chambers. Aynia motioned to the others to stay back as she beckoned Thorn to her side.

'Your news Captain?' Aynia asked. She was pleased to see that he was unhurt. It was foolish to worry so much about him when he ventured outside of the Hive. Indeed of all the workers of the Hive he was probably the most able to take care of himself. Besides, if the Fairie went seeking humans, it was the humans who were endangered, not the Fairie.

'More humans Your Highness. Many more. Families. They had all of their belongings with them.'

'I don't like this Thorn. It's only spring. The English army could continue to advance through to autumn. What chance of peace?'

'I know nothing of the human politics. For the English side of it, I can not tell. What do they want? Obviously Scottish soil is far superior to that muck that the English wallow in, so I can see that they would want to conquer this fair land, but they can not take the land back with them and if they stay here eventually the Scots will find a way to kill them. There is little for the English pigs to steal here, so I don't see the profit in the war from the English side. As for the Scots, well, I know that if the English Hives came to war against our Scottish Hives, we wouldn't stop fighting the English Hives until our last worker was dead. If the human Scots are near the same they will continue to retreat into the highlands with their families to find secluded valleys such as ours. They will hide their families where they think that they'll be safe. Then the men will leave to fight the English, and the war will continue until there isn't a Scot left alive.'

'So we must keep an eye on the English. I don't suppose that the Hives in the lowlands could work to scare the English army away?'

'Aid the humans?' Thorn looked shocked at the very idea.

'I am picking my enemies. If we help the Scots we keep them out of the highlands.' Aynia turned and motioned for the rest of her entourage to resume walking with her.

'We would have to negotiate with the southern Hives.'

'I am about to meet my new harem. The southern Hives will all have brought tribute. Let us see how much they wish to please me. If their gifts are generous then I will think about approaching them with this idea.'

'Your enemies in Parliament will say that you have gone soft on the humans, they will use this against you.'

'My enemies in parliament will twist everything I do, and everything that I do not do, to suit their own ends. I can not let a fear of censure paralyze my ability to act.' Aynia turned away from Thorn, signaling that she was through with the conversation. Thorn felt a bit of sting in her tone. Aynia was displeased with him. She had not attempted to make any part of the end of their conversation private; neither had Thorn, but he wondered just how safe it was to let the Priestesses hear her plans.

Thorn thought that he had the stomach for anything. He was, after all, a soldier. But no scene he witnessed as a soldier made him want to turn away as much as the session of Royal Court on this day. Emissaries from Hives in Ireland, Scotland, France, Belgium, Norway, Sweden, Prussia, and even Romania brought forth tribute to lie at the foot of the new Queen of Balnacra Hive. Jewelry, gold, statues, rare spices, gemstones, cloth, tapestries, dresses, pearls, wines, all were placed before her in boxes that were treasures by themselves. The assembled court, clergy, and government officials ogled the riches with excitement and joy.

But the tribute and gifts were not the main reason for the gathering today. On this day the new Queen would be presented with males that would eventually become the Queen's drones.

The first males to be presented to the Queen were sons of common workers from Balnacra Hive that wished to gain favor with the Queen. Of course, no worker family would send a merely ordinary son to the Queen. These males were either extremely handsome, exceptionally smart, or they possessed physical attributes meant to stimulate the sexual appetite of the Queen. Although not drones yet and not fully physically developed, these males possessed enough raw material to leave females with a good guess about the finished product.

'My Gracious Queen Aynia,' an official presenter started her practiced speech. Families of too low of a birth often hired these professionals to represent them in Parliament, in Court, and in front of the Queen. 'May I present a gift from the Alcae Clan?' The official presenter brought forth a male in his mid twenties. As the male made his bow to Aynia the presenter started unwinding the length of white chiffon that wrapped the male until the male was left standing before the Queen and Court completely nude.

Females in the court surged forward for a closer look. Aynia was not sure where to rest her eyes. The presenter moved the male closer to the throne, taking a red ribbon and wrapping it around the male's flaccid penis. Until he became a drone the male would never be able to reach a stage beyond semi-hard.

'Note the circumference Majesty. And the length! Swinging between his legs is a cudgel guaranteed to satisfy any female.' The presenter then took a square plate and slipped it under the male's testicles. Using the red ribbon she lifted the penis so that it did not block the view of the plated up testicles. 'And the scrotum. Note the nearly hairless character. And feel his skin, how smooth it is.'

Aynia let her finger pass over the skin of the male's testicles. It was indeed soft. She took her hand and caressed the balls some more. Aynia looked up at the male's face. He had a curious expression, like a cat about to purr. Suddenly the presenter removed the plate so that the entire weight of the male's testicles was in her hands. Aynia cupped them gently again then slowly moved her hand away.

The presenter looked on with an inquiring expression. 'Do you care to keep him Majesty? He's a fine specimen, very obedient.'

Aynia was not aware that she could turn down any gift offered to her and did not know what the ramifications of turning down an offered male was, so she nodded her head. She glanced up at Heather, who nodded in approval.

Across the room Camellia winked at Aynia and then lifted her eyebrows in a roguish expression.

Thorn stood across the room near the door. Aynia could see that he was frowning. 'I have no power over this,' Aynia told herself. 'If Captain Thorn has a problem with the idea of my harem, well...' she mused pleasantly about the thought that he might be jealous of the other males.

Male after male was presented to her. Most were nude. Some sported body piercings in the most uncomfortable places. A male named Wheat took a cherry stem into his mouth and spit it out tied in a knot several seconds later. Aynia had no idea what that was supposed to mean, but the females in the Royal Court exclaimed excitedly over the dexterity of his tongue. She supposed one day she would find out just why his talent was so impressive.

After the sons from the common workers had been presented next came the sons of nobility. None of them was presented completely nude, as befitted their rank, and the dignity of their families. Each wore a modest leather thong. Aynia had now seen the gamut of male shapes. She was beginning to think that none would really excite her interest.

Camellia, a true admirer of male flesh, was in rapturous delight as she saw the harem that she was to manage for the Queen.

Deidre nudged her sister. 'You do realize that these are for Queen Aynia, not for you.'

Camellia frowned. 'There's no sin in enjoying the view.'

'Our Queen does not seem to enjoy the view.'

'Indeed. Have you ever seen someone look so bored?'

Aynia was not bored. She was mortified. Her body was beginning to react to the males displayed for her. And there was this strange feeling of jealousy as the other noble females openly ogled the males being presented. Territorial fights over mating males was largely avoided in civilized society by confining the males to harems, but thousands of years of instinct were difficult to ignore.

She glanced over at Thorn. He looked tense and angry. She wondered idly what he would look like with a red ribbon tied around his penis, and nothing else on.

Heather nudged Aynia. 'Majesty, the Emissary is waiting for your approval.'

Aynia tore her eyes off of Thorn and focused her attention back onto the crowd in front of her.

Rose leaned over to whisper to Heather. 'Am I mistaken, or is that Cobra-Lily trying to hide herself in the crowd?'

Heather looked casually in the direction that Rose indicated. Then she looked away and pretended to admire a bolt of wool woven in the Hive's distinctive yellow and black tartan. 'It is indeed her.'

'How did she get in here?'

'I presume that she came with her Aunt, Adders-Tongue. However, since she has never shown any interest in the Royal Court prior to today, and since she is obviously trying to hide herself, I think that she bears watching.'

Heather waited several minutes then wandered off of the dais to go find a spot with an unimpeded view of Cobra-Lily.

Heather was not the only person to notice Cobra-Lily's presence in the room. Something about her overly casual actions made Aynia focus on her former attendant. 'Rose, Cobra-Lily is in the audience.'

'We are aware of her presence Majesty. Heather has gone to watch her.'

'Let me know is she shows any unusual interest in any male or any gift presented to me,' Aynia said.

'How shall I let you know?'

'Say something about how much it merits extra attention, how special it is, whatever, then resume watching Cobra-Lily for me.'

'As you command, my Queen.' Rose stepped back to her position behind the Throne.

Twenty minutes later Aynia got the signal from Rose.

'Who has given me this fine gift?' Aynia peered closely at a gold lace collar that was encrusted with tiny pearls and sapphires.

'There was no note Majesty.'

'Oh, it is beautiful,' Rose enthused. 'Majesty, have you ever seen a collar that merited such interest?'

Aynia gave Rose a look that was interpreted as a signal for her to keep quiet by the crowd. Rose knew the Queen's real meaning. Her eyes went back to Cobra-Lily.

'It is a fine gift. Very fine. Perhaps the message was lost? Who in this hall will claim to have given Us this fine gift?' Aynia asked. 'It pleases Us well, so do not be afraid to admit to it.'

The temptation was great, but no one stepped forward.

Aynia sighed with seeming sadness. 'We can not accept such a fine gift without knowing who gave it. We guess that We shall have Thorn destroy it.'

Rose watched Cobra-Lily's face. She was staring with rapt attention as the gift was presented, before the box was even opened. Now that the Queen was refusing the gift she seemed greatly agitated. Rose stepped forward. 'Perhaps, Majesty, such an act would be hasty. It seems a shame to destroy such a fine piece of workmanship.'

Aynia peered at the gold lace collar again. A small tug of war with her conscious played out across her face. 'Very well, have it added to Our tribute. We are sure that the donor will make herself known before too long.'

As more tribute was offered Aynia took the opportunity to talk again with Heather and Rose. 'Have the collar put aside carefully.'

'It most assuredly poisoned.'

'I agree.'

Aynia nodded. 'Mark it so that none of our staff touches it in error. That could be disastrous.'

'But why keep the thing?' Rose asked.

'Because this is Cobra-Lily's second attempt to poison me and I may need this as evidence when I bring her to trial. And be sure to find the jeweler who fashioned it for her.'

'As you wish Majesty.'

Across the room Deidre and Camellia were unaware of the events taking place near the Throne. They opted to blend with the crowds of nobles rather than stand behind the Throne. Normally Aynia would not allow her attendants to desert her, but as the day took on the air of a holiday she was inclined to release them from duty.

'The Queen, she whispers so long with my sisters. You'd think that she'd be more interested in the bounty of male flesh in this room. We've seen the sons of nobility and the lookers, and the gifts and the tributes, so I am guessing that the next males brought in will be the Princes. Oh look, a golden bier. And look at those four drones carrying him! They have the curtains closed to build the suspense. Either that or he's really ugly.'

'Camellia, please be quiet. You are giving me a headache,' Deidre complained.

Camellia sucked in her breath sharply. 'He's not ugly. Hold me back, I'm in total lust.'

'He belongs to the Queen.' Deidre reminded her sister again, but one look at the very tan, blonde haired, brown-eyed

Prince from a Swedish Hive was enough to make her take a deep breath too. 'He's a god,' she finally sputtered.

'Oh yes he is, and I'd like to worship his body on a horizontal altar.' Camellia added.

Behind the sisters Thane Adders-Tongue allowed herself a tight smile. Then she faded back into the rest of the crowd. Already her mind was working on a way to use this overheard piece of conversation against the Queen and her attendants.

Thorn was also moving out of the crowd. He knew what upset him. Males were born to this position in life and fated to this treatment. There was no getting around it, but did they have to enjoy showing off their bodies so much? And did Aynia have to caress them in front of everyone? The room seemed too crowded with too little air. Thorn needed space to wrestle his jealousy.

He was almost out of the room when an expectant hush settled over the crowd. Two Princes were being presented at the same time. He had heard of these two. One was from an Irish Hive; the blonde haired blue eyed one named Moss. Moss's best friend, a Prince from a Hive in Romania, stood next to him. This Prince, Sarkany, had black curls, thick black eye brows, and high cheekbones. They were an excellently matched pair of contrasts and similarities. While their coloring was polar opposites, they were both tall, thin, and held themselves like males who had served in the military. It was not the sight of this pair that excited the crowd's interest however. Queen Aynia had motioned for the two to come sit beside her. After giving her hand a quick kiss Moss sat down by her feet on her left. But Sarkany lingered over her hand and turned it over, kissing her palm while he met her eyes.

The crowd gasped at this gesture. It was familiar, as if he was already First Consort, and brazen. All eyes looked to the Queen.

Aynia was a little aghast at what this strange male did to her hand. His eyes seemed to challenge her. Would she react to him? Would she refuse him now? There was a question there in the deep brown eyes.

And there was something else, a mystery that she longed to explore. Something about his air, or the air around him, excited her very blood.

Aynia smiled. 'Your friend is quite the rogue Prince Moss. Shall We turn him away?' Aynia knew that she should be angry with the Romanian Prince, but she still felt the warmth of his kiss on her palm, and his touch seemed to have traveled from her hand to her heart to her loins. Even now she fought the temptation to reach out and wrap the curls of his hair around her fingers.

'His manners are different from ours Majesty.' Moss apologized.

'Yes, Ours are excellent and his are much in need of improvement. Explain to him the need to follow our customs now. This will be his home.' Aynia stood up, still allowing Sarkany to retain her hand. 'We retire now. Moss, you may take Our other arm.' Aynia swept out of the Throne Room as her court bowed.

Thorn fell into Aynia's entourage as it left the room, but as he followed the harem his place in the parade came quite near the end now, far from the Queen's ear. He was still fuming when his replacement came for the watch three hours later.

CHAPTER 8

Thane Monarda returned to her less than palatial family chambers in the Hive. A staunch supporter of the late Princess Lily, and a determined gossip, she attended Royal Court every day. Once the Queen retired Thane Monarda would gather with her cronies to discuss everything that they saw, all that they did not see, and all that they wished would happen.

Thane Monarda was a little surprised to see Lady Snakeroot in her parlor. Not noted for having many friends outside of her own family, Lady Snakeroot was the most sociable of the entire Adders-Tongue sept. Lately though Snakeroot was becoming a frequent visitor. Not that Monarda liked having her visit. Snakeroot refused to chat with the other guests and never stayed long. Still, Thane Monarda thought, a female with seven sons to marry off couldn't afford to be too standoffish with the other noble ladies of the Hive.

'To what do I owe the pleasure of this visit?' Thane Monarda asked. Thane Monarda prided herself on her flawless manners. Snakeroot would never detect how very little she was welcome.

Snakeroot slowly pulled off her gloves. She was scowling. Did this female have to have tea with her inane friends every day? Snakeroot could hear those titled ladies arriving for tea now. 'I am afraid that I can not stay for tea today.'

'Oh, what a pity.'

'I just came to discuss how poorly our new Queen is protecting our Hive from the humans.'

Monarda was not sure that this was a just a friendly chat. She felt that she was being told what to discuss with her friends. Well, she would be damned if she'd fall into this trap again. Snakeroot had convinced her that the new Queen was deathly ill. Monarda gossiped openly of the supposed illness with her friends. Then at the Royal banquet the Queen ate a healthy meal and kept up a lively conversation until the wee hours of the morning. A red faced Monarda was scorned publicly for passing around such blatantly false information by the same friends who helped pass the gossip along.

Monarda was not wealthy enough to buy back a position in society if she continued to make such mistakes. However, she was willing to allow Snakeroot to believe that she'd pass along any gossip that she heard. That would keep Snakeroot coming back to supply gossip. Then maybe Monarda could figure out the game she was playing at.

Pretending compete agreement with Snakeroot, Monarda nodded her head vigorously. 'Oh, those horrible humans.'

'Don't you think that we need a strong Queen who will help to protect us from the human threat?' Snakeroot asked.

'Oh, absolutely.'

Snakeroot stood. 'Well, I have taken enough of your time, and your friends are here. Please excuse me.'

'Must you go?'

'I apologize, but I have, er, plans.'

'Stop by anytime dear. We have the most interesting discussions.' Monarda waved goodbye to Snakeroot. She then closed the door to her parlor and turned to her new social secretary. 'Verbena, what do you know of this Lady Snakegrass? She is certainly no friend of our new Queen. Every time she comes she spreads ill news about Queen Aynia.'

'It is not my place to judge the nobility my lady.' Verbena said diplomatically.

'Well, it suits me for now to pretend to believe her. But please, don't let me catch you passing on what you hear from her. I think that her news may be false. I don't want it getting around that my house is the source of those rumors. I may not have been a staunch supporter of Princess Aynia, but I do support Queen Aynia.'

'I promise, Thane Monarda, that I will not breathe a word of this to any living soul.'

'That's what I like so much about you Verbena. You take your job so seriously. I guess they taught you that when you served in the Royal Palace.'

Verbena only bowed to acknowledge the compliment. In her mind she was already working out the exact wording for her next note to Aynia. The wording had to hide in plain sight in the banal text of the message. They knew that Copperhead was taking their notes to Adders-Tongue to read. Thane Adders-Tongue didn't even bother to properly reseal the wax.

Verbena pondered for a moment how long the Queen would allow the Royal Messenger to betray the trust placed on him before she decided to punish him, but the other gossips were arriving for tea, and she had to go help the noble ladies.

It was true that all of the Queen's former attendants were given minor titles of nobility and reasonable pensions. Verbena, however, found the idea of spending the rest of her life in genteel idleness distasteful. The Temple did not tempt her as an occupation as it did many of her friends. Verbena was used to more sumptuous surroundings than the private chamber she was given at her retirement. So she returned to service. When she tried of waiting on others she would move on to her waiting title and pension.

Verbena was very picky about whom she worked for. Picking the biggest gossip in the Hive was a natural. By influencing Monarda's attitude of Queen Aynia in her own way Verbena could remain in service to her Queen. Besides, working for Monarda had another benefit. Verbena never knew how dull life was in the Royal Palace until she got a view of life amongst the nobility. There was nothing quiet or staid about Thane Monarda or her friends. They openly discussed their harems, their friends, and their children in most intimate detail. These raucous discussions gave Verbena a wide-open window into the way the rest of the Hive lived. She found it most enlightening.

'Oh, I've invited that Ambassador Cowslip from the Norfolk Hive.'

Verbena eyed Thane Monarda coldly. 'Oh?'

188

'Don't get high and mighty Verbena. She may be English, but she knows a great deal of important news.'

Verbena knew that by news the Thane meant gossip. There was something about the Ambassador that Verbena didn't like. There was slyness there, as if the Ambassador thought that she was smarter than the Scottish Fairie, and as if she was up to something very unpleasant.

Aynia shifted again in her chair as her staff meeting wore on. It was late and they all showed signs of fatigue. Camellia's presence was missed, but understandable as she was still working on settling the fifty males into the harem rooms.

'Did we find the jeweler who fashioned the gold lace collar?'

'Yes, and no,' Deidre admitted.

'Explain.'

'There is a jeweler missing. Her family is worried, as well they should be. No one goes missing in the Hive for more than a couple hours. We live in close quarters here.'

'Thank the Goddess that we all have rooms in the Royal Palace.'

Aynia tried moving to another position, but found no comfort in it either. 'Do they have any idea if she was working on a collar?'

'The daughter took us to her bench where she plies her trade. There are no sketches, none at all. Someone was not particular about how much evidence they took away. The daughter swears that there should be sketches of the next commission that the jeweler was to work on. She was gifted and had regular work.'

'Does the daughter know anything?'

'Yes. Her mother just paid off all of her debts in gold coin.'

'That's no proof. I can not take this to trial.'

'Many a Queen has taken the law into her own hands.' Heather said ominously.

Aynia tried sitting up straight, then tried slouching. Nothing worked. She was losing her focus. 'I don't want to resort to that now. Eventually Cobra-Lily will die by my hand. She must be put to death for her attempts on my life. But for now, let us wait. Perhaps we can catch her in another plot.'

Rose and Deidre noticed their Queen's discomfort and exchanged knowing smiles across the table.

'If you two smirk at each other one more time I will throw something at you. What is it that amuses you so much?' Aynia demanded.

'Nothing Majesty,' Deidre protested innocence.

Rose could not help herself. A giggle burst out. She tried to stop, but tears ran out of the corners of her eyes. Deidre tried to hold back, but she too started laughing so hard that she soon could not catch her breath.

'Forgive me Your Highness,' Rose said in a moment of barely controlled sobriety, but soon collapsed into giggles again as Aynia once again shifted around in her chair.

'I take it that there is something about me that you find funny?' Aynia was not really offended, but she was tired and uncomfortable.

Heather looked with sour displeasure on her two sisters. 'If Camellia was here she would have sense to speak clearly to Your Highness while these two revel in juvenile behavior. Your Majesty is uncomfortable because your breasts are now swelling with milk. You should relieve yourself of the burden at least four times a day. Unfortunately your schedule did not permit today. You must call for one of your harem to nurse or you will continue to be in pain. If you do not properly drain your breasts of milk your milk will dry up and that would be a disaster for the Hive. Please let me call for a male for you. Rose can take you into your chamber and prepare you to receive him, or at least I hope that my sister can bring herself to perform her duties. I would have thought that since Rose has a harem she would not be so easily amused by the idea of you entertaining a member of your own.' She looked back at her sisters and shook her head gravely.

'I am sorry Rose. I did not realize that you had your own family. How thoughtless of me not to ask,' Aynia said.

Heather gritted her teeth. 'Highness, you have been sequestered in the Palace your entire life. You only knew those who served you and your immediate family. Some matters of public manners are beyond your experience. As Queen others will have to allow you to make faux pas without inciting a duel, but let me warn you before you make this mistake in public: never discuss a female's harem. Once males are taken into your harem they become yours alone. It does not dignify their position to be discussed in public as if they were common, well, prostitutes.' Heather snapped.

'I have offended you Heather. I apologize.'

'It is Rose's harem that you asked after. She is the one who should be offended.'

'But I am not offended,' Rose assured Aynia.

'Never the less, she should be more careful. If I had a harem I would be quite upset.'

'As if Heather would ever take on a male,' Deidre said in an aside to Rose.

Heather pretended that she did not hear. 'I am too well trained to let the Queen know how such casual questions can offend. I am grateful to have been able to clear up this matter in a private manner. Now Highness, we are avoiding the subject at hand. I will notify Camellia that she should send one of the harem to your bedchamber. Which male do you desire this night?'

Aynia shrugged. 'I have no real desire to, well, is there any other way of, what I mean is,' she tried to find the words.

'You can not avoid this Majesty. Like everything else, it is your duty.'

'The Priestesses don't want more milk?'

'They desire for the flow to continue. The best way to insure it is to take a male to suckle.' Heather's growing impatience with Aynia's reluctance was showing.

'Very well. Tell Camellia to send me a Prince, that interesting dark haired one.'

Heather bowed. 'I will inform my sister of your decision.'

Rose started out the door to prepare the Queen's bedchamber, but turned back. 'Highness, it can be a most pleasurable experience. Take a flagon of wine and relax. He will know what he is to do. You literally only have to lie back and enjoy.'

Aynia nodded to Rose. 'I guess that I could sip some wine, and let's go get this corset off.'

Rose and Deidre, mortified at Heather's admonishment in front of the Queen, were no longer in a laughing mood. They jumped up and hurried to assist their Queen.

Heather was shocked to see just how organized the harem rooms were. In a matter of only five hours Camellia managed to assign Princes to separate rooms in the chambers, assign each of them a personal servant, and get their personal belongings stashed away. In the shared chambers sons of nobility chatted amicably with their new roommates. Beyond those rooms, and past a large parlor where the harem shared meals and spent their days, was a wide-open room with a number of beds. This was where the sons of common workers lived. It was possible for the common workers to move up all the way to a private chamber if they found favor with the Queen, but such occurrences were more legend than fact.

Camellia looked surprised to see Heather. 'She actually sent for a male tonight? I didn't think that she had it in her.'

'I made it clear that she had little choice.'

'You didn't offer to do it for her?' Camellia asked sarcastically.

'What do you mean?' Heather's eyebrows arched.

'I know you very well Heather. I see how you look at the Queen. I see how you touch her when we bathe her. Given her inexperience, a dose of Rose's special wine might be all that it would take for you to talk her into letting you suckle from her breasts tonight. Then as she learned to take pleasure from you it would be oh so easy for you to take the affair much further. If you want a shot at the Queen now is the time to do it, before she knows any males.'

'I don't know what you're talking about.'

'It's always the redheads that get you.'

'Speak no more of this sister,' Heather growled. 'The Queen must learn to be with her males. If in the future, once she has borne a princess, she finds that her males don't serve all of her needs she may turn elsewhere for satisfaction. Until then I want her to think that her drones are the only source of such relief.'

'That's fairly sneaky and underhanded for such a pious person. Are you getting soft Heather?'

'I'm trying to stop her from self-destructing. She's got to realize that it's her duty to breed. And she has to realize that it's her duty to provide milk for the Hive. The males will stimulate her milk flow. That in turn will stimulate her desire to mate. I will make her understand that she must submit her body to the good of the Hive.'

'You've served several Queens in different Hives, so I guess that you know best,' Camellia said. Privately she thought that Heather seemed almost scared. But of who or what? This was not the same Heather that Camellia was used to.

'I've never seen a Queen this frigid though, and that damn Captain Thorn isn't helping matters. She's in love with him,' Heather admitted, 'and part of the attraction is probably the fact that he can't touch her sexually.'

'Pure love.'

'Exactly. Romantic love, the stupidest idea ever invented. It's a human philosophy, of course.' Heather was beginning to pace around her sister.

Camellia, well aware of her sister's mood, stood still.

'I don't think that it's all romantic love between them. I've seen plenty of lust there in her eyes, and in his.' Camellia told Heather.

'But he can't do a damn thing! I swear to you, I will get her to send him away, or I will have him transformed to drone, but one way or another I will have my Queen mated this Vernal Equinox.'

'Would you be sending him away for the good of the Hive, or out of jealousy?'

'I already asked you not to talk of this anymore.'

'Thorn isn't the only Fairie lusting mightily after the Queen.'

Heather gritted he teeth. 'I think only of the Hive. Queen Aynia must breed and bear a Princess. The stars omen disaster for us if she does not.'

Camellia snorted. 'You actually believe that hogwash? What have the Priestesses told you?'

'Somehow it doesn't surprise me that you're an unbeliever.'

'It shouldn't. I'm not the type to trust a priestess to read the stars for me when I can see clearly with my own two eyes.'

Heather noticed the inquisitive glances of the males in the harem. She shook her head. 'Now is not the time for this discussion. These gossiping hens will chatter themselves to distraction if we talk openly in front of them. Back to the business at hand, I was commanded to bring a Prince to the Queen's bed.'

Camellia walked over to a small gong and struck it with a mallet three times. Within seconds all of the Princes were lined up for her inspection. Camellia smiled at Heather. 'I already have my boys trained. Do you see?'

'I'm always impressed by your ability to manage. Harems can get so chaotic.'

'You mean Rose's. I will gladly come over and help her to get her delicious drones under control again.' Camellia offered.

Heather laughed. 'Let you into her harem? Our sister knows better than to let you near a male like the ones she keeps.'

'And yet the Queen trusts me with hers.'

'Well, she didn't know any better.'

'I came highly recommended.'

The two sisters exchanged a friendly smile. Heather, the eldest of the four sisters, was closely bonded to Camellia, the next to the youngest. Despite their opposite outward demeanors both were very similar in many ways.

'So, who shall it be?' Camellia asked as she walked down the row of princes as all the males stood lined up for inspection. 'How about this one?' She paused in front of the Swedish Prince, Noisi. She walked back over to Heather. 'He's gorgeous. I can't keep my eyes off of him.'

'Better keep even your eyes off of him. He belongs to the Queen. Don't forget that.'

Camellia looked offended, as she well was. 'I'm not the direction that kind of trouble will be coming from. I have a few Royal Messengers to play with that please me quite well for the time being. Besides, to use a gross Anglo-Saxonism, I don't shit where I eat.'

'See that you don't, or it will be your head, and his.'

'I won't,' Camellia said, exasperated.

'I know. But please, just don't.'

Camellia growled. 'I can't believe that my own sisters know me so little.'

'Or we know you too well?'

'I can't believe that I have to defend myself. I swear by and at your damn Goddesses that I have never, ever, so much as improperly leered at a drone in a harem that I managed.'

Heather laughed. 'Just don't.......'

'I know,' Camellia snapped. 'Did you come here for a reason or just to torment me?'

'Like I told you, I came for a male, but the Queen asked for a certain one. She wants,' Heather started to say, but was interrupted by Camellia.

'She wants the Romanian Prince! I knew I saw a little sparkle in her eye. Tell Rose that she owes me five pieces of gold. Well, he's not my type, but he's obviously hers.'

'No male in this harem is your type.'

'Sure, right, I understand. Quit fussing over me. I promise to behave and keep my hands to myself. If you didn't think I was trustworthy Deidre wouldn't have seen to it that I got this position.'

'I trust you. I just worry that your loose tongue will be misunderstood. The enemies of the Queen will try to get at her any way they can. That means even using us. If we are very careful they won't find an opening.'

Camellia nodded agreement though privately she thought Heather was paranoid. 'Prince Sarkany, front and center. The Queen has chosen to honor you.'

Sarkany stepped forward with reluctance. 'Pardon Lady Camellia, but Prince Moss and I go everywhere together.'

Camellia and Heather both showed their surprise and annoyance. 'You forget yourself sir. Step back in line,' Camellia snapped.

'I will tell the Queen that he isn't available tonight.' Heather went to the Prince from Sweden and pointed at him. 'You, follow me.'

Prince Noisi stepped out of the line and followed Heather who was marching quickly from the harem. He looked back only long enough to flash a triumphant smile at the other fifty males in the harem.

Camellia turned with blazing eyes to Sarkany. 'Don't ever do that again boyo.'

'Servant! Bring me my lashes. You two,' she indicated two Princes near to her 'strip Prince Sarkany and tie him to the post near my chamber door. It's unusual that we have someone to use as an example on the first day in the harem, but there's always the exception. I'm so glad that the entire harem is already assembled here to witness this. Prince or common worker, I will be obeyed.'

Prince Sarkany dared to meet Camellia's glare with an insolent gaze. Slowly he began to undress himself. The other Princes stood ready to grab him if he tried to run or protest, but they weren't sure how to handle the cool, aloof, dark Prince.

As Prince Sarkany sauntered casually over to the whipping post Camellia saw proof on his back that this was not the first time he had been punished. She frowned. She condoned a tight tether for males, but permanent scarring was unprofessional.

Camellia tried not to let anger influence her as she began to methodically work her lash across his back. It would never do to let a male see that he could anger her. But when she found herself cringing every time the lash touched one of the old scars on his back she decided to bring his punishment to a more personal level.

'Bend over my lap Prince.' Camellia raised her hand high and slapped it sharply across his buttocks in the first of many blows. Despite his bravado Sarkany learned that the Lady Camellia was a tough mistress who did not allow her authority over the harem to be challenged.

The other males were commanded to watch the high born prince humbled in front of them. Sarkany grunted but did not cry out each time Camellia's hand met his flesh. The sight held a kind of terrible fascination for them. This was a lesson they and the prince would not quickly forget. For the next week as Sarkany walked stiffly through the harem the other males cringed, and when he slowly lowered himself into a chair to sit many held their breath in sympathy.

Aynia lay upon her bed in a gauzy gown spun from silk and threads of silver. Where the fabric touched her skin it seemed transparent, but artful draping kept some of her shape a secret.

Aynia would only allow Rose to give her a small glass of wine. Rose countered by giving the Queen a very strong fortified wine that quickly left Aynia in a very relaxed state. She was so relaxed that she didn't notice that the Prince who entered her chambers wasn't the one she sent for.

The Prince from Sweden, Noisi, was more than a little nervous. When he entered the room he saw the Queen waiting for him in her bed. She merely watched him. He had no idea that she was unaware that he expected her to say something. He stopped about six feet away from the edge of her bed and glanced nervously around.

'We are alone,' Aynia finally spoke to reassure him.

'Yes Your Majesty. I was just wondering if I should undress now, or later?' The Prince asked.

Aynia smiled a slow, lazy smile. 'Come to me now. I want so much to sleep, but I can't until you suckle.' She moved aside one side of the gown she wore, revealing her breast.

The Prince nodded and walked to the bed. If he bounded onto the mattress with too much enthusiasm she did not admonish him for it. Laying beside the Queen he gently and hesitantly took her breast into his hand. Massaging it slightly he saw a drop of milk form at her nipple.

Common belief, which was not entirely wrong, held that Queen's milk made a male virile, and that the more he drank the more virile he would be. The truth was that once a male had milk from his female he would become a virile drone, but no amount of milk that he took after his transformation to drone was complete would change his virility beyond that. However, myth was a strong factor among uneducated males and none would let a drop of milk be wasted.

The Prince latched onto her breast and began to suckle firmly. Aynia placed her hand on his shoulder. 'Not quite so hard,' she said gently.

Nodding, but not releasing her, the Prince nursed with a little less gusto.

The release of the pressure in her breast was an improvement, but Aynia felt another sensation growing. As Rose had counseled the sensation was not unpleasant. It was actually quite nice.

Hidden in the spy hole last used by Heliotrope, Thorn peered into the Queen's chambers through the slit in the wall. From his perch that gave a full view of her bed and the room around it, Thorn watched the scene between the Prince and Aynia with growing jealousy. He was unaware of Aynia's inebriated condition. And he was very surprised to see her with a male from her harem so soon.

Thorn's idea was to simply look in on Aynia as she slept. Since his watch was over there was no legitimate reason for him to be in her chambers. He had this brilliant idea to look over his sleeping beloved from the alcove before he retired for the evening. Finding her with a male was a shock. Finding her with a male and behaving so seductively was maddening.

When had her voice ever sounded so husky and alluring? Not when she spoke to Thorn. She openly dressed and undressed in front of him, as if Thorn was just another piece of furniture. For this Prince though she unveiled her nude form with practiced skill. She showed only enough to tempt. And the Prince restrained himself no more.

In a mighty leap he was on the bed with Aynia. Accosting her eagerly he took her nipple into his mouth and suckled. Thorn could not look away, and he could not calm his temper. Aynia was his. She was not here for this blonde, pampered Prince. Thorn would not let her be taken while he stood by impotent.

That word stopped him: impotent. The word described him, impotent and hopeless. Unless he became a drone he would never be more than that. As much as Thorn wanted Aynia he was not ready to stoop to becoming drone to have her.

Thorn looked on as the Prince moved to Aynia's other breast. After a time she suddenly sat up. Pleading fatigue she sent the Prince away. The Prince would have been insulted had he been able to take their tête-à-tête to the next step, but until his transformation to drone was complete, about three days, he was as unable as Thorn to perform other, more interesting, duties.

After the prince left her chambers Aynia lay in her bed. She now knew why Rose said that the experience of being suckled could be pleasurable. As Noisi nursed she began to feel pleasant contractions move through her vagina. They began as subtle but grew in strength. Aynia found herself looking forward to each one as wave upon wave of sensations built. Surely Noisi had been schooled in what to do to bring her to orgasm, but she could not admit to herself that she wanted him to do it. So she dismissed him. Now she lay alone in her bed fighting the urges, but to no avail.

Finally Aynia slipped her hand between her legs. Except for Festival, a day that she was blessedly unable to remember with much clarity, she had never touched herself there before, but she knew that she'd never be able to sleep until her body was given the release it craved.

She was surprised at how wet she was between her legs already. She spread her thighs further apart. For once she was alone. Now she could take the time to explore her new body.

Aynia put her hands lightly on her abdomen then started to slide her hands across her warm, pale skin. Her hipbones jutted out a little just under the lower edge of her corset. She brought her hands up to her breasts. The nipples were still hard after the prince suckled, and slightly tender, but at least now she could massage her breasts without the touch causing pain.

She latched the cups of her corset closed, as Rose had warned her not to fall asleep with them open. Then Aynia slid her hands down between her legs to feel the tuft of pubic hair. The transformation of her body into this adult form was amazing. So many things had changed, like the pubic hair, and desire she felt now, the wicked thoughts that seemed to fill her mind, and even the fact that just down the hallway there were over fifty males whose only purpose in life was to service her sexual needs.

Aynia slipped her fingers into her wet pussy. She liked that, but moved her hand around to explore other sensations that felt wonderful. She found her clitoris and realized instantly that this was where her fingers needed to be.

Thorn heard Aynia whisper something. He concentrated all of his efforts on hearing what she was saying. Finally he caught the single word. It was his name.

As Aynia touched herself Thorn felt an urge to take Aynia into his arms and mate with her. Males who were not drones weren't supposed to have such feelings. But Thorn remembered the smell of her scent from Festival and craved inhaling that perfume from the source. Sometimes when he entered the Royal Chambers her scent would wash over him and he would have to stop, close his eyes, and regain his composure.

A kind of madness tortured him at night. He would dream simply at first of events during the day, but suddenly at some point in his dream he would grab Aynia, pin her to a wall, or her bed, or even over a chair, and share urgent kisses with her. In his dreams he undressed her and they lay together, their bare skin touching, and he would bury his face into her hair and smell the scent that enticed him like an addict. Trembling and dripping from sweat he'd wake and groan in the urgent need he had for her, an urge he had that could never be released unless he was a drone.

Eventually Thorn would resort to an ice-cold bath to be able to sleep again.

As Thorn watched Aynia stroke herself he touched his own penis. He was semi-hard, as hard as he could get unless he was a drone. He stroked himself, matching the rhythm of his hand to the thrust of her hips. It would lead to nothing but more frustration, but it felt good.

With her right hand massaging her clitoris Aynia slipped the fingers of her left hand in and out of her vagina. The heat of her body made even the sheer silk draped over her too much. She pushed it away. Bracing with her heels, she lifted her hips again and again to her own hand as she countered the thrust into herself. In a short time she felt the wave of pleasure grew into a climax. Her back arched, her muscles went stiff, and then sweet release coursed through her body.

Thorn could smell the faint scent released into the air. Fighting back with every reserve of his self-restraint he turned away from the alcove. Another second breathing in her scent and he would have destroyed the wall that separated them with his bare hands.

The following day Thorn ordered his guards to permanently seal the hidden alcove.

Panting and exhausted, but feeling physically better than she ever had in her life, Aynia lay on the bed and enjoyed the afterglow of her orgasm.

'It's been a long time since we've had fresh Queen's milk,' Priestess Cerridwen commented to the High Priestess as they carefully poured the precious liquid into several small golden cups.

The High Priestess nodded. 'Thirty-three days since the death of the late Queen,' she spat on the floor. 'May the Goddesses curse her. She refused to give us her milk in the last months of her life.'

'She was growing older,' Priestess Cerridwen admitted. 'Maybe her flow was diminishing.'

'She flowed with plenty. That horny old bitch had her males suckling seven times a day, and sometimes once during the night. She wasted milk creating new drones that she couldn't possibly have had time to mate with. She refused out of spite against the Temple.'

'What spite?'

'The late Queen held nothing but contempt for the old ways, for our religion. Luckily for us Queen Aynia's father, Prince Thistle, was a religious male and he brought his daughters to services regularly. Queen Aynia learned her dedication to the Temple from him,' the High Priestess told Cerridwen, who was not old enough to have known the great Prince Thistle as anything but a legend.

'We're quite lucky that she became Queen.'

'Indeed. Our future looked dim if Princess Carman ascended the Throne. She was as full of contempt for us as Thane Adders-Tongue is.'

'But there would never be any new Queens if it wasn't for us, so they can't forget the Temple entirely.' Cerridwen observed as she lit candles all around the room where the ceremony was to take place.

'No, but they can take away our funds and take away our space in the Hive. Power in this Hive is displayed by the amount of space you're allowed to occupy. That's why the poor live in cramped quarters, some in one-room chambers. That's why the estate cells of the nobles are separated by wide avenues, but in the poorer quarters there are only narrow twisted alleys barely wide enough in some sections for a single Fairie to pass. That's why the poor carve out the very walls of their hovels to try to get more precious space.'

'Is that why the Royal Palace is larger than our entire Temple and the Parliament combined?'

'Yes. Despite the lip service to the Temple and Parliament, most of the power in the Hive lies in the hands of the Queen,' the High Priestess lectured. 'Can you imagine all of that space devoted to just one Fairie? The population of the Hive hovers at about five thousand. Yet the Queen alone occupies a space big enough to house another four thousand.'

'The Queen and her family and her staff and servants,' Cerridwen pointed out that the Queen did not occupy the Royal Palace alone. But even with twenty nurses assigned to each princess it was rare that the population inside the Royal Palace exceeded two hundred.

'My point is that the Palace occupies more space in this Hive than any other structure. That's where all of the power is,' the High Priestess said more bitterly than she meant to. She was glad that the new Queen was faithful to the Temple, but something about Aynia irritated the Priestess. More accurately, it was the power that Aynia obtained merely by birthright that irritated the High Priestess. She herself was from a common family and had to fight every day of her life for the power she held so precariously now.

'You can't be saying that the Queen doesn't deserve her Palace.'

'No Cerridwen dear. What I am saying is that this Hive is dangerously cramped and overcrowded. There is nowhere for the Hive to grow. Parliament refuses to budge, and that's the only direction we can grow since the other two sides are against the boulder that provides the Hive's structure. The Hive is populated well beyond capacity. At some point the Queen is going to have to take drastic measures to stop this Hive from disintegrating.'

'Like what?'

'If she gives birth to a Princess it's possible for the Queen to swarm part of the Hive to a new location and to allow her daughter to remain here and rule. That's why I press Lady Heather to make sure that the Queen mates. I told her that the stars omen disaster if the Queen does not mate this coming Equinox. I'm sorry to admit that it isn't the stars that bode ill. It's the living conditions of the poor and the threat of revolution if nothing is done to ease the plight of the common worker.'

Cerridwen laughed. 'I got the impression today that you didn't think very highly of our common workers.'

'I don't, but I respect their ability to form an angry mob.'

'I see.'

The High Priestess sighed again. She was feeling maudlin today, and that just wouldn't do. 'Enough heavy discussion for today. We have reason to rejoice tonight. Tell the other Priestesses to come join the ceremony.'

'Yes Your Grace.' Cerridwen bowed and went to fetch the five other Priestesses who were to take part in the ceremony. She didn't have to go far. They were eagerly awaiting the evening's events right outside the chamber doors.

'Come in Sisters,' Cerridwen motioned for the other females to follow her inside. She didn't have to ask twice.

The Priestesses hurried inside the chamber. Cerridwen closed the heavy oak door and threw the iron bolts across it. No one would disturb them but they preferred the sense of safety the bolted door gave them.

Once a Priestess and committed to life in the Temple no female ever cut her hair, so many wore tresses down past their knees. Tonight their locks of hair would be all that the Priestess wore. Without being told they all slipped off their Temple robes. Excitement and the chill of the late winter air made them shiver.

'It is time to start the ceremony of the Royal Jelly,' the High Priestess intoned. 'Come; take your cup of Queen's milk.'

The other Priestesses came to the table and took a cup each. Above them, in the roof of the chamber, a small skylight was opened to the night sky. Moonlight shone brightly into the room through the open ceiling. It was the night of the full moon.

The Priestesses raised their cups to the moon and began to chant the words of the spell. Then they took their goblets and drank the Queen's Milk. All seven chanted the words of the prayers as they began to dance about the room in a wild dance. Twirling, chanting, singing, they worked themselves into frenzy.

One by one as they exhausted themselves the Priestess fell back onto piles of pillows about the room. Cerridwen cuddled next to the High Priestess. 'It's cold tonight Your Grace.'

The High Priestess bent over and licked Cerridwen's lips. Cerridwen responded by kissing the High Priestess.

'Then we must think of a way to keep warm,' The High Priestess said.

'Shall I taste your milk?' Cerridwen began to suckle from the High Priestess's breast.

The High Priestess cupped Cerridwen's breast in her own hand. Looking about the room she saw the other Priestesses in two groups, one a threesome, the other another couple.

Cerridwen bent down further and parted the High Priestess's legs. 'I want to taste you.' Parting the curly black pubic hair of the High Priestess, Cerridwen started to suckle and tease the older female's labia.

The High Priestess smiled down at her protégée. 'Some days I have my doubts about you my dear.'

'You do?' Cerridwen said, letting just enough of her teeth scrape across the sensitive flesh of the High Priestess.

'Yes, but not now. You remind me of myself. I too was eager to taste my High Priestess.'

'And how did she taste Your Grace?'

'Like sweet honey.'

Cerridwen worked her fingers in and out of the High Priestess's vagina as she continued to lick and suck. Soon the High Priestess was working her own hips in rhythm with Cerridwen's fingers.

A low moan escaped from the High Priestess. Cerridwen knew that she would come any second. Grasping the offering cup, Cerridwen worked with renewed vigor. She knew when the High Priestess came her juices would turn sweet. Cerridwen longed to lap up those juices that she earned all for herself, but it was forbidden. The juices, by now a concentrated form of Queen's milk, were what made the precious Royal Jelly.

The High Priestess arched her back and thrust her pelvis into Cerridwen's face. Cerridwen took one last well-earned taste, and then put the cup in place to catch the small flow of Royal Jelly.

Cerridwen carefully placed the cup on a table. As she lay down next to the High Priestess the High Priestess pulled her close for a kiss.

'I love the smell of my juices on your face,' the High Priestess murmured to Cerridwen. 'Now, be a good girl and let me have my turn with you.'

'As you command Your Grace,' Cerridwen said happily. She lay back on the pillows and looked up at the bright stars overhead. She no longer felt the chill of the night air.

Carman's Throne Room was, by generous comparison, much larger than the stifling chamber where Aynia held Royal Court. With no roof but the sky and no walls save the steep canyon walls of the valley it appeared that she ruled over a large domain indeed. In truth, Thorn's guards made constant sweeps through the valley, confining Carman and her few attendants to a small, well-hidden glen.

An old badger's barrow with a ledge of rocks over it served as the chamber where Carman and her attendants slept. The place smelled of musty old animal, and the proximity of the barrow to the mountain that defined the back wall of the valley made the Fairie nervous with thoughts of the Mountain King.

Daylight hours were mostly spent in the glade where sunlight penetrated the pines overhead. The ground was still damp and gave off the smell of rich loam, earth bursting with fertility. As spring approached the sun penetrating into the hiding place would dry out the forest floor. But for now it was a cold, wet, and miserable place to live.

Carman sat on her makeshift Throne now. She was uncomfortable and very unhappy. 'I feel like there is a weight on my chest.'

Carman's five attendants stood at attention, as did Cobra-Lily, who had come with provisions Adders-Tongue stole from the Hive's food storage. Adders-Tongue should not have had access to the Hive's food, but Adders-Tongue knew too well how easy it was to corrupt low level officials.

'It is your milk my Queen.' Snakegrass informed Carman.

'I know that it's my milk,' Carman shouted. 'How many times today have you been told me that it's my milk? But knowing that it's my milk does nothing to lessen the pain,' Carman said waspishly.

Cobra-Lily yawned openly. She hated Aynia, but she didn't care much for this pretender to the Throne either.

'You can express it Majesty.' Snakegrass offered a suggestion. 'Most females do keep their own flow managed by massaging the breast and expressing the milk by hand.'

'That's not a solution. It takes too much time and doesn't do enough. My breasts are growing hard and my flow is drying up. It's very painful. What are you going to do about it?'

'If you had males they would suckle and relieve you of the burden Majesty.'

'I don't seem to have any males. Have you looked around yourself lately Snakegrass? Are there any males here? Any drones?' Carman threw her arms open wide and looked around the glen with a sarcastic expression on her face.

'No Majesty,' Snakegrass almost bit her own tongue to avoid matching Carman's tone.

'Of course not, because my bitch of a sister stole those males that were rightfully mine.'

'Might I make a suggestion? Ask my Aunt Adders-Tongue to send you a male.' Cobra-Lily offered.

'That will take days. I want this taken care of now!' Carman shouted. 'If I do not have males I will do what I must. Snakegrass! Come here and suckle.' Carman unlatched the right cup of her shiny steel corset.

Snakegrass shook her head. 'Oh no, Majesty, no.'

'I command you.'

Snakegrass continued to shake her head no and to back away. 'I, I just can't possibly do it Your Highness.'

Carman strode over to Snakegrass and leveled her stinger at Snakegrasses' neck. 'I think that you can.'

Gulping, Snakegrass let Carman lean over her and bring her nipple close to her mouth. Opening her mouth just a little, Snakegrass closed her eyes tightly and stuck out the pink tip of her tongue.

'So here you are!' Copperhead called out as he spotted Cobra-Lily on the edge of the clearing. He had been following her for days, wondering what she was up to. When she left the Hive his curiosity got the better of him. With the Queen's letters to her old attendants stuffed carefully into his tunic he followed Cobra-Lily from a safe distance. That safe distance turned out to be dangerous as he got lost in the thick undergrowth of the forest. A playful nymph led him further astray. Finally, following Carman's voice, he stumbled upon their hiding place.

Several attendants who had their swords drawn immediately surrounded Copperhead. 'Oh, hello,' He tried to smile charmingly.

He was hauled up into the glen.

Snakegrass breathed a sigh of relief. 'The Goddesses provide!'

Carman strode over to Copperhead and leveled her stinger at him. 'Who are you and why are you here?'

Copperhead looked over at Cobra-Lily. 'I'm Copperhead, Cobra-Lily's cousin, and Snakegrasses' cousin. I followed Cobra-Lily here.'

Suddenly Copperhead was very sorry that he followed his mother's advice about shortening his tunic. The females surrounding him were openly leering. Someone boldly squeezed his buttocks with a firm hand.

'Cobra-Lily?' Copperhead pleaded pathetically for help from his disgusted cousin.

'He's a spy my Queen, kill him now,' one of the attendants urged Carman.

'No!' Snakegrass stepped in front of her foolish cousin. 'He's my blood too, Majesty, and loyal to you.' She was embarrassed to admit the family connection, but one stood by one's clan no matter what.

'Then what is he doing in the Palace uniform?'

'I spy on the Queen for my Aunt,' Copperhead tried a convenient lie.

Carman put her stinger away. She stepped back and regarded Copperhead with an appraising look. Then she leaned forward and pushed his cheeks so that his lips puckered out. 'Looks like your prayers have been answered Snakegrass. He's such a pretty boy.' She looked over to her other attendants. 'Strip him, bring him to my room.'

'Majesty, you'll ruin him.' Snakegrass protested.

Carman answered by slapping Snakegrass hard enough to toss Snakegrass to the ground. 'It's him or you. Besides, he's just a male.'

Snakegrass and Cobra-Lily exchanged a glance. Lowly males were not worth risking their own lives for. Angering Carman would not bring them favor in Adders-Tongue's eyes, but this shame on their family was difficult to stand by and watch.

'My work here is done,' Cobra-Lily said as she started to back away from the scene.

'Oh no you don't. You brought him here; you can take him back to the Hive when she's through with him.' Snakegrass caught her cousin by the arm.

'I'm not going to be seen with a shamed male. Someone will think that I did it to him. Forget it, forget him. He's no longer our blood.' Cobra-Lily tried to shake off the tightening grip of her elder cousin.

Snakegrass drew her sword. 'Listen; once Carman falls asleep we will lure him out of there. You will take him back to the Hive. No one will know right away that he's been shamed. It takes a day for the first signs to become visible. Get him back safely and hide him,' she hissed. 'Promise me this or I will kill you.'

'All right,' Cobra-Lily grumbled. 'Stand down. I'll take the little whore back to the Hive. Maybe Thane Adders-Tongue will hide him. She has that huge empty harem. After all he did lose his virginity in service to Carman. Hey, maybe Carman will take him on as a drone. After all, she'll need a drone in just a few weeks.'

'Don't count on it. I've never seen anyone so obsessed with her own Royalty. She wouldn't stoop to mate with mere nobility.'

'Can this be? Is the great and loyal Snakegrass actually rebuking her beloved Queen?'

'Shut up Cobra-Lily, or I'll tell Adders-Tongue that you're the one who transformed Copperhead into a drone. How do you feel about a forced marriage cousin?' Snakegrass hissed menacingly. 'Fancy a stinger pressed against your back while trading vows in the Temple? Fancy being stuck with a male some other female made drone? Want a used husband?'

While Copperhead knew that he was supposed to be frightened and unwilling to allow Carman to transform him while he was still a free male, he was in truth not opposed to the idea. He wanted to be a drone. Frequently he spied on the drones in his mother's harem either mating with his mother or with each other, and he desired the experience. Besides, he liked the danger involved in taking milk outside of the harem. It was supposed to be a very wicked thing to do.

Carman lay down on her cot and beckoned for Copperhead to come closer. Her right breast lay exposed, while her left breast remained hidden.

Copperhead was a little embarrassed. As per his mother's instructions he had padded the front of his hose. Now with no clothes on there was no faking the truth of his size. But Carman didn't seem to care.

'Come suckle.' Carman commanded.

Copperhead didn't hesitate. He went to her breast and hungrily took what she offered.

'Sh,' Snakegrass whispered to Copperhead as she shook him awake. 'Don't talk. Come with me.'

'I don't want to go.'

'Don't fight me boy.'

'I'm a drone,' he said proudly.

'Sh!' Snakegrass decided to take no more chances. She shoved a towel dosed with ether over Copperhead's nose. He struggled for a moment then collapsed in her arms. Dragging him out of Carman's bedchamber, Snakegrass brought her cousin to Cobra-Lily.

Cobra-Lily was furious. 'What the hell am I supposed to do with him now? He can't walk back on his own.'

'Quiet.'

'Quiet yourself,' Cobra-Lily hissed.

'I'll rouse the Queen and tell her that you're trying to steal her drone,' Snakegrass warned.

'Liar!'

'She'll believe me before she'll believe you. Did you know that she likes to sting her enemies over and over again until the body is a pulpy, bloody mess?'

'What about clothes? He's naked.'

'No time. Get him out of here,' Snakegrass whispered urgently. One of the other attendants muttered in her sleep, and then rolled over. Next time they might not be as lucky.

'I can't fly with him over my shoulder,' Cobra-Lily protested.

'Your problem, not mine.'

'Come on; help me to fly him to the entrance of the Hive.' Cobra-Lily whined.

'Fine, you take his head, I'll get the legs.' Snakegrass capitulated. Together it took them over an hour to fly the three miles to the Hive. It took Cobra-Lily another hour to drag the nude and unconscious Copperhead to her Aunt's estate.

Copperhead awoke as his Aunt brandished a cat o' nine tails against his naked buttocks. Screaming in pain, he twisted off of the bed and jumped up. His head throbbed in pain, but nothing like the pain searing into his flesh.

Thane Adders-Tongue loomed over him. 'I told you not to take milk! I warned you boy.' She easily grabbed him and pulled him over her knees.

Copperhead tried to struggle away, but suddenly a stinger appeared in front of his face. He decided to hold still.

Adder-Tongue smacked her open palm repeatedly against his buttocks until they warmed and glowed pink. 'I ought to put you up for sale to a brothel. I should shave your head and drive you naked through the passages of the Hive.'

Copperhead began to cry. 'The Queen Carman ordered me to take her milk.'

'What were you doing out of the Hive anyway?'

'I was following Cobra-Lily.'

'You idiot, you could have exposed Carman's position to Thorn's guards.'

'I was careful.'

Adders-Tongue answered this by bringing out a thick strap of leather and slapping Copperhead's sensitive inner thighs hard. Occasionally the strap would slap his testicles. Copperhead screamed and squirmed to get away.

'I have a plan! I have a plan!' He yelled.

Adders-Tongue gave one last lash across his back. 'I'm listening. If I don't like your little plan I will take you to your Aunt's harem and leave you tied up spread-eagle on the floor for her entire harem to use as they see fit. Do you get the picture boy?'

'Yes Auntie.'

Adders-Tongue slapped his bottom again. 'Don't call me that.'

'Yes Thane Adders-Tongue. Since it isn't apparent yet that I'm a drone, why don't I slip into Lady Camellia's room and suckle from her in her sleep. When she wakes up she's think that she made me a drone, and then she'll have to keep me.'

'More likely she'll toss you out like I should.'

'I'll make her feel guilty. And I'll try to stay in the Royal Chambers and spy on the Queen for you.'

'Now that is a worthy idea.' Adders-Tongue thought aloud. 'There's a Prince in the Queen's harem that I want you to befriend. He's Prince Noisi. Your Lady Camellia has her eye on him. Once he's a drone convince him to work his way into her bed. Shouldn't be hard. I can tell just looking at her what type of female she is, a real slut. I can't think why so many Hives still seem eager to hire her. Do you know that she earns nearly twice what any of her sisters do? And all for doing something that she'd probably do for free.'

'Prince Noisi is already a drone. He was the first one that Aynia took into her bed.'

'Good. That saves time. I know that Camellia has her eye on him. Do whatever it takes to get him into your confidence. Get down on your knees for him, bend over for him, do anything that he wants. Then start luring him into committing adultery. Once he's a regular lover of Camellia's let me know when they will be together. I'll give you a powerful sleeping potion that will incapacitate them. Then I'll arrange a little surprise for the lovers.'

'Then will you forgive me?'

'Perhaps,' Adders-Tongue purred.

'What can I do to please you?'

Adders-Tongue smiled. 'Talk the Prince into committing adultery.'

'I will, I swear it.'

'Good. However, that does not mean that our little session here is over.'

Copperhead gulped. 'What do you mean?'

Adders-Tongue picked out a thick leather strap from the wall and tested it against her hand. 'Lay down on the bed face down boy, and put a pillow under your hips to raise your ass up for me.'

Copperhead began to cry. 'I don't want this.'

'You should have thought about that before you took milk. Do you have any idea of how unclean you are? You're a free drone now. Any female who wants to can use you any way she wants, and you won't be able to stop her, because free drones are there for everyone to use. That's why we protected you. That's why we warned you. But you wouldn't listen, and now you pay the price.' Adders-Tongue raised her arm up and began a methodical attack on Copperhead's buttocks.

CHAPTER 9

'Another incursion by humans?' Aynia read the report that Thorn handed her as she sat in the Throne Room at Royal Court. Angered she thrust the report down on the ground. 'We will not stand by and allow our lands to be polluted. Captain Thorn, send out your guards and kill these humans!'

'Majesty,' Adders-Tongue made a small bow, 'Captain Thorn has gone to battle against the humans again and again. He kills them only to see more return. Perhaps he is ineffective?'

Aynia noticed that the members of the military took deep exception to this insult. Thorn, as usual, betrayed no emotion.

In her full court dress with the ever present Hive tartan worn in a sash across her breast, Aynia looked remarkably like her Mother. Even her mannerisms reminded many of the late Queen, but where the late Queen was verbally very expressive Aynia was silent. Where her mother would have raged Aynia sat impassive. While some admired her regal bearing others found this new Queen cold. But if they had known to watch her eyes they would have seen a hint of the emotions that boiled beneath the surface.

Aynia leaned on one hand and murmured to Heather who sat on her left. Heather nodded once.

'We have full confidence in our Captain, Thane Adders-Tongue. However, perhaps now is the time to seek help from the lowland Hives near the point of conflict between the English and Scottish humans? If we work against the English army perhaps we can turn the tide of this war.'

'You seek to aid humans? Are you a Fairie Queen? The Fairie do not help the humans. We are mortal enemies. You betray us,' Adders-Tongue quickly took advantage of an opportunity to question Aynia's actions.

'We seek to end the war between the humans. If the war ends the human Scots will stay in the lowlands. If it continues they will come to the highlands. More and more humans will come until we can no longer hold back the tide. We are fighting off raindrops now. If a deluge comes it will sweep this Hive away in a river of blood,' Aynia said with cold reason. She kept her voice low and calm so that Adders-Tongue's yelling would seem overly loud and unreasonable.

Aynia turned to Thorn. 'Send more troops to slay the humans, but stay with us Captain Thorn. We wish to hear your council on this matter.'

Thorn bowed. He preferred to lead his troops into battle, but there was a battle of words raging in the Throne Room that demanded his full attention. His primary duty was, after all, to protect the Queen. With a nod the orders were given to launch the attack.

Adders-Tongue stood up again to harangue Aynia, but was interrupted by Deidre.

'The nymphs of the valley beg an audience, my Queen,' Deidre said. Her tone betrayed her own puzzlement.

'The nymphs? They actually organized themselves long enough to come to court?' Someone among the nobles joked. Others laughed along.

Aynia also gave a little smile. 'Tell the nymphs that We are pleased to grant them an audience.'

The nymphs were of two varieties. Many were tree nymphs as the end of the valley that backed into the hills was deeply wooded. Then there was the lone water nymph that lived in a deep pool hidden amongst those trees where an artesian well burbled up from the granite depths of the mountain.

The water nymph, possessing depths beyond that of the tree nymphs, was the chosen spokesman for the group. She made her curtsy before Aynia.

Aynia nodded in acknowledgement. She was curious as to what would lure the nymphs into the Hive. The nymphs and the Fairie lived in reasonable harmony, but they did not socialize.

'Your most Royal Highness, Queen of Balnacra Hive, ruler of the valley, we Nymphs of the Valley come to you in an hour of dire need. As you may know, humans have been invading the woods around the valley. It is only a matter of time before they come into our valley. We nymphs can not live in contact with the humans. They will cut down our trees; they will befoul my waters with their animals and their own wastes. This is a matter that requires action now. We have a plan to secure the valley against these invaders once and for all, but we need your help.' The water nymph turned deep blue eyes on Aynia, pleading as much with those bonnie orbs as with her words.

Aynia was impressed. For a nymph the female stated her case well. 'We share your concern nymph,' Aynia told her gently. 'The Fairie also can not share land with the humans. We sent guards to kill those who come close to Our valley.'

'We are most grateful for your protection Majesty. But word has spread among the wild folk that many humans are on the move north as the human war wages deeper into Scotland. It is only a matter of time now. We can not continue to simply attack them as they come. We need a permanent solution.' The nymph's voice wavered. Aynia could not tell if it was nervousness at approaching the Fairie Queen or emotion over the situation that caused the nymph's voice to falter.

'The nymph echoes my words Majesty!' Adders-Tongue piped up.

'Echo was a nymph,' a tree nymph agreed, proud that she knew her own history. The tree nymphs were very concerned about the human problem but lacked the capacity to stay focused on the issue for long.

'What is your proposed solution?' Aynia asked with great hesitation. This was bound to be a nonsense idea. Nymphs lacked practical thoughts.

'We, with the help of the Fairie, should dislodge the boulders from the tops of the mountains. As the boulders crash down they will roll to the front of the valley and seal it off. We will make the valley disappear from all human sight.'

Aynia sighed. It was as bad of a plan as she feared. 'Do you realize how many tons those boulders weigh? We don't think that the combined strength of two Hives could move even the smallest one. And once the boulders land on the valley floor it will be near impossible to move them to the entrance of the valley. Plus they will crush everything in their path as we roll them. And then, even if we were to accomplish this great feat, do you know what we will have built?'

'No, Your Majesty.'

'We will have built a great wall resembling a human fortress. Rather than repelling the beasts it would attract them in droves as a safe place to house their families.'

'But they won't be able to get inside!' The water nymph protested.

'Do you think that they'll let a little stone wall stop them? They'll just climb over the boulders. And besides, if we were to completely seal off the valley, where would your water flow? There would be no outlet. Soon your waters would start pooling at the end of the valley. In two years this valley would become a loch!' Aynia didn't know why, but these females mere presence in her Court was irritating her.

'But Your Majesty!' The nymphs wailed, realizing that their great plan was not going to be accepted.

'Silence nymphs,' Aynia said. 'We give you Our solemn word that even now We work to find a solution to the human problem. Spread word among the wild folk that the key to preserving Balnacra may be to end the war among the humans. If we help to foil the English army they may go away. Once they return to England the Scots will return to their homes in the lowlands.'

'We don't help humans!' The nymphs shouted.

'But you sure as hell mate with them,' a noble in the court couldn't help but accuse the shapely females.

'Even nymphs see the flaw in Your Majesty's plan,' Adders-Tongue piped up.

The water nymph looked at Adders-Tongue for a second, and then another idea dawned upon her. 'If Your Majesty doesn't care about the fate of the valley and won't help us, perhaps there is another great one who can,' she said slyly.

Aynia knew immediately that the nymph referred to Carman. It appeared that Carman was still alive, and somewhere in the valley. If the nymphs knew that she was alive they might soon tell others. A look at Adders-Tongue showed that she too knew of this, but when Adders-Tongue looked at the Queen she only saw the same expression of mild boredom. As far as Adders-Tongue knew, Aynia was unaware that another Queen lived.

Aynia waved her hand in a bored gesture as if to wipe the nymphs out of her sight. 'Then go seek your other power. See if there is assistance there. But We doubt it. Be gone.'

Angry, the nymphs backed out of the Throne Room.

'What other power did they refer to Majesty?' One of the nobles asked at the urging of Adders-Tongue.

Aynia sighed. She had to summon up a believable lie. 'We fear that our friends have decided to seek the Mountain King.'

A gasp went through the audience.

'Can't you stop them Majesty?'

'It is madness!'

'We can not and will not stop them if they foolishly decided to seek his help. We can not protect all the wild folk. We are Queen of the Fairie, and We protect our own kind.'

Aynia leaned over and motioned to Thorn to come near her. She whispered quietly, 'Have the nymphs followed. They may lead to an elusive enemy.'

'Yes My Queen.' Thorn bowed and backed his way down the aisle of the Throne Room. Halfway across the room he turned and marched out of the door.

'I wonder where the valiant Captain Thorn goes to.' Adders-Tongue commented in acid tones to her friends and cronies who surrounded her. 'I think that I shall go see,' but as Adders-Tongue stated to make her bow to leave Aynia motioned for her to stand in front of the Throne.

Adders-Tongue was surprised. It was no secret that she despised the new Queen. It was assumed that the Queen knew of Adders-Tongue's constant verbal attacks in Parliament against her policies. It was an unusual move to confront such an enemy face to face in the Throne Room where nobles, members of Parliament, and dignitaries from other Tuatha de Danaan Hives could witness it.

Aynia murmured for a moment into Deidre's ear. Deidre laughed a little and bowed to her Majesty. Adders-Tongue began to fume.

'In our many encounters, Thane Adders-Tongue, We have been impressed with your deep concern for the future of the Hive.'

Adders-Tongue was flattered, but deeply suspicious. 'I'm grateful that my meager efforts have pleased Your Majesty.'

'We are coming out of a very harsh winter, and food stores, We are informed, are falling behind the required levels. We will replace our current Minister of Food Harvest and name you to the position.'

The position of Minister of Food Harvest was a thankless job. While it carried much power it was also the source of misery for the holders of the office. Many political careers had been destroyed by an appointment to the post. Still, no one would ever turn such an important appointment down. Refusing to serve was as sure a political death as accepting the post.

'Your Majesty honors me,' Adders-Tongue said through gritted teeth.

'My old Minister of Food Harvest, Thane Cornflower, has accepted a new position as Chief Engineer for the Hive. As you may be aware, our Hive is bursting at the seams. We are in desperate need of new space and perhaps should consider reallocating the existing space. Thane Cornflower has agreed to chair a study on proposals for the Hive.'

'We will need more food storage space,' Adders-Tongue piped in.

'Of course Minister Adders-Tongue, We will gladly supply all of the space you need, as soon as our current storage space is full.'

The eldest Priestess stepped forward. 'If we are thinking of reallocating space in the existing Hive structures, I would deem it a personal favor if you were to include plans for expansion of the Temple. We are unable to house all of the faithful, as our Majesty has witnessed.'

'We agree that the Temple is too small for current needs,' Aynia said before Deidre was able to signal to her not to speak on the subject.

All hell broke loose in the Throne Room.

Adders-Tongue was in rapture. Finally this Queen had said something foolish. 'Our Queen, she sides with the Priestesses! She has spoken, and her word is against the workers!'

Even members of the ruling party threw their voices into the fray. 'Parliament is the center of the Hive! If you allow the Temple to expand it will be at the expense of Parliament!'

The Priestesses, not willing to give in on a fight that had been brewing since the original Hive structure was built seven hundred years ago, came out swinging verbally. 'The Temple is the center of the Hive! The Queen recognizes our need to expand!'

'She will give up the Parliament floor to the Temple, throwing the power of the Priestesses over the power of the people. Workers! Hear me, protest this attack on Parliament!'

When the Balnacra Hive was first designed the Master Builder sought to create a Hive center that was anchored on three sides by the three powers that governed the Hive. On one side was the Royal Palace, on another Parliament, and on the third, short side, of the triangle, the Temple. Unfortunately the geography of the Hive restricted building additional floors either up or down as two of the three outer walls of the Hive were carved out of a single, though massive, granite boulder. The third wall, the only one that would give, was to Parliament's back. Parliament staunchly refused to be moved despite the fact that it was the only solution for Hive expansion.

Reason had no place in this argument.

Aynia looked over at Deidre. Deidre shrugged. She would have saved her Queen from this if she could have. The words slipped out before she could stop them. Now the Queen had to take her public beating.

Although Adders-Tongue tried to whip up mob fury over the idea of Parliament being moved she was unable to get much enthusiasm. There were several reasons for this. One was that most of the Fairie in the Throne Room were nobles who thought of Parliament as a place only for common workers. Since the nobles were the ones most likely to be harmed if a riot broke out in the Hive they were unwilling to contribute to a mob atmosphere. Another reason was that the workers were still unsure of their feelings for the new Queen and thus were not about to turn on her yet. Besides, the common workers viewed Parliament as a club for the powerful nobles to play at government. Common workers felt that any reference to their needs was lip service. They were not going to riot for the preservation of a club that would not have them as members. The third reason covered Priestesses, nobility, and common workers alike. Adders-Tongue was not popular with any of those groups. Her arrogance and constant harsh criticisms of the Queen left her without much popular support.

Thorn entered the Throne Room again. Whatever melee was about to break out would have to wait. He rushed to Aynia and made a quick bow. 'Majesty,' he said in his commanding voice. Instantly the crowd fell silent.

'You have urgent news Captain?' Aynia asked. The worried expression on Thorn's face spoke volumes.

'My troops, the ones we dispatched to attack the newest human invasion, they have returned Majesty.'

'We are concerned. Tell us.'

'The humans had Anti-Fairie magic. Only two of the entire legion returned alive.' Thorn fought back betraying emotion, but Aynia, who knew him well, saw how deeply the news affected him.

Since they were in public she could not comfort him as she wished. But she did place a hand on top of his shoulder as he knelt before her. 'We are distressed to hear this news Thorn. How far away is the enemy?'

'They are over five miles away. The troops were not pursued. As far as we can tell the humans weren't even aware of the attack. They simply set the magic to protect their encampment.'

'This must be new and more powerful magic than they had before. Their mages are growing wise in the use of magic.'

'We must fight the humans. Send more troops!' Adders-Tongue yelled.

Aynia leveled a calm stare at Adders-Tongue. She waited a moment as the Throne Room quieted. 'We will not send Our military to senseless death. This is not a war but a slaughter. We must study this problem and act with caution. Captain Thorn will meet with his advisors and present options to Us in, shall we say, four hours?'

The members of the military nodded their agreement with this plan.

Aynia stood up. She was heartily tired of the Throne Room today. The assembly bowed as she swept out of the room.

'A word with you Captain, before you go into your meeting,' Aynia said to Thorn as he walked slightly behind her on her right side.

Thorn leaned in closer.

'Your timing was impeccable,' she whispered so that only he heard her. Out loud she said, 'Our condolences on the loss of your guards. We know how troubled you are by such senseless bloodshed. Please convey to the families of your guards that We vow vengeance against the humans responsible.'

'Thank you my Queen.' Thorn bowed, as did the many Nobles assembled in the hallway, as the Queen continued towards her Royal Chambers.

'Rose, we will need dinner brought to my parlor. This will be a long session.'

'Yes My Queen.' Rose disappeared.

Camellia sat on the sofa in front of the fire. Her nodding head betrayed her exhaustion.

'Camellia, you may go to sleep if you wish. We can brief you later.'

'You're generous My Queen, but I feel like I need to catch up on current events. I've been too busy to attend the Royal Court the past few days. However, I did hear that I missed all of the excitement in the Throne Room today. Apparently you stepped into a hornet's nest.'

Aynia sank into the sofa opposite Camellia. 'I think that I played right into Adders-Tongue's hands.' She sighed. 'The scrutiny that female puts me under is making me miserable.'

'Just a question, why appoint her to a ministry post? Now you'll have to deal with her at every cabinet meeting. Your majesty,' Camellia added quickly. She realized how tired she must be to address the Queen as an equal.

'If Thane Adders-Tongue fails as Food Minister she's through politically. It's an easy post to fail at. If by a miracle she succeeds then we win by having adequate food for the coming year. Besides, her influence in Parliament grows. I want her where I can see her and I want her too busy to cause trouble.'

'Amen to that.'

'Now I have a question for you.' Aynia looked across at Camellia.

'Yes?'

'I believe that I sent for the Romanian Prince last night. You sent me Noisi instead. At the time I was a little too inebriated to care. That wine Rose brews packs a powerful punch. However, now as my bosom grows heavy again the matter returns to my thoughts.'

Camellia sat forward. 'It was a question of discipline Majesty. He wanted to bring along his friend, the Prince Moss. I have found that the only way to keep control in a harem is to assert dominance from the beginning. I couldn't let him get away with questioning my authority in front of the other Princes.'

'I understand. I respect your expertise in the area. Would you go into a frenzy of panic if I were to walk over to the harem now to check on him? Because if you are going to rise from your comfortable seat on my account I won't go.'

'That's a conflicting order my lady. If you want to go I wouldn't allow my actions to stop you. However, I feel that I should accompany you. I'm not worried about what you'll find there. I'm confident in my abilities. Then again, if my rising would stop you from going.......'

'Oh be still Camellia. I command you to stay here while I go inspect my harem.'

'I'm most happy to obey my Queen,' Camellia replied with a grin. She rested her head on the arm of the sofa.

Aynia stepped into the harem. Deidre followed her and was looking around the rooms with keen interest. Many males, none of whom Aynia recognized, lounged around the common room playing cards, reading, and talking. As she stood at the door every male jumped to his feet and bowed. They remained bowing as she walked through the room. None dared to look up her.

'Where is Noisi, the Prince from Sweden?' Aynia asked.

More than a few of the males immediately gestured towards one of the private rooms. 'Shall we?' Aynia indicated that Deidre was to follow her. 'You are all dismissed,' she told the males.

The males started to move back to their pursuits but still none would meet her gaze.

The private rooms had no doors, only a curtain to separate them from the common chamber. Aynia pulled aside the heavy purple velvet curtain to look inside at the Prince Noisi. He struggled to rise.

'No, no, do not rise. I'm aware of the pain of transformation to adult form. How are your wings?' Aynia asked.

A servant beside the bed answered. 'They haven't yet broken through the skin Majesty.' As proof he pulled back the

Prince's tunic and revealed an angry red welt between Noisi's shoulder blades. 'Perhaps another day.'

Aynia sat on the edge of the bed and placed her cool hand on Noisi's fevered brow. 'I'm no authority on drones, but I've heard that the first day is the worst. Once your wings break through the skin on your back the pain will subside.'

Noisi smiled weakly. 'I thank my Queen for her kind interest.'

Aynia bent down and kissed him on his forehead. 'Sleep now.' She rose.

'If Your Majesty does not mind, I will stay behind and help to tend Prince Noisi.' Deidre offered.

'As you wish.' Aynia didn't really want to have Deidre along as she made her next stop. Addressing the servant she said, 'see that Prince Noisi gets something for the pain. The mistress of the harem will supply you. And point me in the direction of Prince Sarkany's chamber.'

The servant bowed. 'If Your Majesty will follow me.'

Aynia would never think to question Camellia's management of the harem, but one look at Sarkany gave her cause to reconsider. His back and buttocks told a story of harsh punishment. Prince Moss sat beside Sarkany's bed, helpless to do anything.

Moss rose and bowed. 'My Queen. Please forgive Prince Sarkany for not rising.'

'Not at all,' Aynia mumbled as she knelt on the floor by Sarkany's bed. 'I see that you have learned the wages of disobedience.' She was scolding him, but her tone was soft and full of concern. What was it about this male that made her every sense tingle near him? She took a deep breath, trying to find his scent in the air of the room.

'My Queen, I wasn't trying to disobey. It was just that Moss and I wanted so badly to talk to you about our ideas for the harem. In my enthusiasm I forgot myself.'

'Ideas about the harem?'

'We both served in the military, so we know what it means to lead an active and useful life,' Moss explained. 'We both know the bad reputation of the harem, that drones are lazy and do nothing to contribute to the Hive. We wanted to ask you if we could add some physical activities so that we can stay in shape. We'd like to play sports, go outside, and exercise.'

'Drones can't wander around the Hive. Their place is in the harem.' Aynia said, scandalized.

'Then we need to change the inside of the harem.'

'Your idea might have merit. I will think on it. This is not a promise.' Aynia was already thinking of how much Thorn despised the drones for their inactivity. If she made them stay fit maybe he would drop his objections to joining her harem. That was not, however, a matter to address today.

'Moss, if you will excuse us.'

'Majesty,' Moss bowed and left the chamber. He was perplexed by his dismissal, although the Queen did not appear to be angered by their ideas. Still wondering, he joined the other males in the common room.

The servant followed Moss out of the private chamber then went in search of a healing salve for Prince Noisi's back. Having a gift for medicinal herbs, Moss showed the servant what herbs were best to use.

Aynia gently turned Sarkany onto his side. 'I'm sorry if this hurts but you can't remain lying on your stomach.' She lay down on the bed next to him.

Sarkany dared not speak as the Queen at first gently brushed a lock of hair from his forehead. Her generous lips pulled down a little at the corners as if she was frowning at some private thought. But rather that making her look angry the frown pushed her bottom lip out in the faintest of pouts.

Her hand slid away from his hair, down the side of his face, until her fingers traced the outline of his mouth. She gave him a light kiss. Finally she looked into his deep brown eyes.

'I've come to allow you to suckle.' Aynia used the hidden hook to release the cup on her corset.

He was greatly surprised. 'This is a great favor, Queen of my heart.' His hand reverently caressed her breast.

Aynia laughed. 'Don't be so sure. With the state that your back is in, when your wings come in you'll be in agony.' But of all the males in her harem this one she wanted to be a drone. She wasn't willing to wait for him to heal first.

'I'll be in heaven. Can you imagine, to fly!' His dark eyes sparkled.

'Flying is wonderful. It's so freeing.' Aynia matched his enthusiasm.

'I would like to fly with you,' Sarkany said. He drew Aynia closer with his arm so that their bodies touched from knee to stomach. It was a pity that the Queen was dressed. But no matter, in several days he would be drone. Then he would have her undressed as often as he wished. Females had a hard time resisting the Romanian Prince when he wanted their attention.

Aynia gave a sigh of delight as his full soft lips gently took in her nipple and areola. As Sarkany suckled her eyes closed and once again she felt the sensations cursing through her body that she had been looking forward to all day.

Camellia returned to her own chamber to find Copperhead lying in a feverish state on her bed. 'What are you doing here?' She asked with obvious anger. 'You disappeared. Everyone was looking for you. Where are the letters that you were supposed to deliver?'

Copperhead turned teary eyes to Camellia. 'I had to get away. I went to my Mother's house, but she turned me out. I had nowhere else to go.' Copperhead started to sob.

Camellia was suspicious and confused. 'Why did you need to get away, and why did your mother turn you out?'

'She wouldn't take a shamed male into her house.'

Camellia drew away from Copperhead as if he were a leper. 'Shamed?'

'Yes, shamed.'

'By who?' She demanded.

'Don't talk to me like this. You're acting as if it didn't happen. That's what my mother warned me about, but I wouldn't listen. She told me that one day you would lead me astray and then you would forget me, but I thought that you loved me.'

Camellia laughed. 'I don't. We were just playing. I didn't think that you'd take it so seriously.' A new thought dawned on her. 'And just how were you shamed? Nothing we did was beyond touching and stroking.'

'Yes it was. You gave me your milk.' Copperhead burst into another convincing flow of tears.

'Like hell I did. I may do a lot with young males that their mothers wouldn't approve of, but I have yet to let a male suckle from my teat.' Camellia's voice was rising as she tried to squirm out of the neat little trap laid for her.

'I suckled on your milk,' Copperhead insisted.

'How, when?'

'I came in while you slept, the night that you were setting up the harem. You were so tired that you never woke up.'

'Well see, I didn't allow you to take my milk. You stole it. There's not a jury in the world that would convict me for that.' Camellia suddenly realized that her own reputation was enough to condemn her in the public's eye. After all, it would be hard to explain exactly what she did with the young males in her chambers without it sounding as if she was a first class corrupter of innocent boys. 'How do I know that you really took milk?'

There was no denying the evidence. Copperhead turned and showed her his back. The skin where his wings were erupting was red and warm to the touch.

Camellia sunk down on her bed near to Copperhead. She inspected his back with as much detachment as she could despite the enormity of problems he represented. She had absolutely no desire to take on a harem of her own. Despite her physical attraction to Copperhead she really had no feelings for him. If she was indeed guilty of corrupting him, a charge she was still suspicious of, she was responsible for him. The question was what to do with him? His mother already refused him, so he couldn't be sent back home. And despite her reputation, Camellia would not, could not, turn any male out into the Hive to sink into a life of degradation.

'Lay down on your stomach. I'll go get a salve for your back. It looks as if a little infection could be setting in. And I'll get you a tisane that will bring down your fever.' She shook her head and sighed. At least the physical problems were something that she could deal with. 'I don't suppose that you've eaten.'

'I didn't feel much like it.' Copperhead was still sniffling.

'Fine. I'll find you something. But stop crying. I really hate that. I have to listen to the Queen's harem complain day and night. I hardly want to hear it in my own chamber when I come home at the end of a day.'

'What's going to happen to me?' Copperhead asked.

'I have no idea. I really don't.'

'You're going to send me away?' The panic rose again in Copperhead's voice.

'No. I won't. But I have little use for you.'

'Once I am a full drone I can at least be your mate.'

'I don't need one and I don't want one. I get what satisfaction I want from my other male friends.'

'But they aren't drones, they can't mate with you,' Copperhead offered slyly.

'I have no intention of mating with anyone!' Camellia roared. 'I will not be tied down to any one male! Moreover, I sure as hell won't be breeding any of your whelp, so get that thought right out of your mind. I'll be dammed if anyone is going to call me Mommy!'

Copperhead shuddered. 'I have an idea. Why can't I be a servant in the harem? That way I'll have a place to live. And you can keep an eye on me. If you feel like you want me to visit one night, I can.'

Camellia shook her head. 'This is all too much too soon. I must discuss this with the Queen.'

'Do you have to tell her about me?'

'Yes, I do. I can just imagine what your mother will be saying about me. Since I serve the Queen I have to warn her about the trouble that will be coming to her doorstep because of me. Wait here. I'm going to get your tea and ointment for your back.' Camellia stood up and walked to the door. She almost stepped out, but paused and looked back in again at Copperhead. 'Just for the record, I'm not going to marry you. What you did you did on your own. I would have never allowed it. Do you understand?'

Copperhead nodded silently.

'To important business,' Aynia brought her meeting to order. Aynia gave Camellia a smile. 'It's good to have Lady Camellia back with us. We've all missed your advice, and wit.'

Camellia nodded at Aynia to acknowledge the compliment. Apparently the Queen wasn't angry with her about the situation with Copperhead. But she would have to bring to the Queen's attention another matter of some concern. Prince Sarkany, since taking the Queen's milk, seemed strangely ill. It was true that his wings emerged with more pain than most drones endured simply due to the punishment he received. But once his wings broke through the skin the pain should have eased. Instead his fever soared as if his body was fighting off an infection. It was a stroke of luck, Camellia mused, that Sarkany's devoted friend, Prince Moss, was quite the herbalist. He alone seemed able to brew teas that brought relief. Sarkany was healing. But the situation could turn critical at any time.

In all her years as Mistress of the Harem, this Prince's reaction to the Queen's milk was a first.

'I'm sure that you're all aware of the situation, but let me sum it all up and bring Camellia up to date. Humans have been appearing near Balnacra in increasing numbers. I would like to enlist the aid of the lowland Hives in an attempt to turn back the English army but so far I have little support from either the military or Parliament on this idea. The emissaries from the Tuatha de Danaan have indicated some interest in the plan as long as we supply most of the troops needed. Those Hives are under increased pressure from both sides in the conflict and human populations in general. They would appreciate some help in relocating, possibly to the highlands. Since even our remote location doesn't seem to be safe anymore I'm not sure how much help we can offer. The Hive at Ardcharnich, your home Hive, refuses to assist any Fairie who help humans, Scot or no. Our own Hive simply can't support a refugee population. We're far too overcrowded as it is, and we have no extra food supplies.'

Aynia took a sip of wine and continued. 'This afternoon distressing news reached us that a substantial human encroachment is happening five miles south and east of here on the north shore of the loch. As predicted in this very room, they have a mage in their group and they have invoked powerful Anti-Fairie magic not seen before by our military. The losses on our side were substantial. I hear that one of the two survivors is now not expected to live through the night.'

Camellia gasped. 'I didn't realize things had gotten so bad.'

'It gets worse,' Heather grumped.

'In addition, the nymphs of the valley actually came to court to plead with me to help them in a ludicrous plan to fortify the valley against humans. I, of course, pointed out that their plan was untenable. They then told me that they would go to another person of power in the valley to apply for aid.'

'The Mountain King?'

'I have the feeling that they meant Carman. I told Thorn to follow them. Hopefully he will return with Carman's head on a plate.'

Camellia sighed with relief. 'I guess that even the nymphs are smart enough to avoid the Mountain King.'

'What I need are ideas. We're under attack from every direction. Parliament will not allow the Hive to be enlarged. Humans are about to farm our valley. Carman is out there somewhere lurking in the dark. Adders-Tongue is assassinating my character from the floor of Parliament. What am I going to do?'

The room was silent as Rose, Deidre, Heather, Camellia, and Aynia really thought to find a solution.

'I hesitate to mention this Majesty,' Heather finally said.

'Mention it. If I hate your idea I can always tell you so.'

'Actually, the idea is from an emissary from the lowland Hives. Lanark is in great danger.'

'Lanark Hive is in danger? It is the greatest of all Hives!'

'It lies too near the human battlefields. Already their land is poisoned by human blood spilt in conflict. She told me that their Queen was weighing a heavy decision.'

'And?' Aynia asked impatiently.

'Relocate the Hive.'

Everyone gasped.

'Where? Where can Lanark Hive go? Where would Balnacra Hive go?' Aynia demanded to know. 'Do you know of a place where humans will not go? They are like a fog, a fog infested with plague. Every nook and cranny of the highlands will fall under their foot eventually. Even if the war ends there will always be some humans that remain here. We must admit that Balnacra is a fair spot to live.'

Aynia didn't like the idea of moving the Hive, but despite her outburst she didn't completely reject it. If her Aunt, the Queen of Lanark Hive, a very experienced Queen, was seriously considering moving, then there had to be some merit to the idea.

'May I suggest a small island in a loch or off the coast? There are many small islands that could support Fairie without supporting humans. And there are many with coastlines so treacherous that even seals will not come upon their rocks.'

'But to move,' Rose said unhappily. 'It's a huge undertaking.'

'Better to move than to die,' Heather snapped.

'You obviously haven't had to move a harem,' Rose snapped back waspishly. She liked her cozy personal cell in the Royal Palace. And the thought of moving again made her tired beyond measure.

'There are ways of doing it that are less strenuous than moving a single Fairie family,' Camellia said. 'Besides, I'm sure that you have a nice story about moving a Hive to share with us.'

'I do not,' Rose frowned and folded her arms across her chest.

'It's not an idea that I consider lightly,' Aynia informed the sisters. She paced the room in silence for a time. Suddenly she realized that she knew in her heart that it was the right decision to make. The only question was how long could she avoid making the actual decision?

'The Hive would not take news of relocation well,' Deidre finally spoke.

'The Hive is not this place; the Hive is the Queen, the nobles, and the citizens.' Heather observed.

Aynia thought about this for awhile, but then, slowly, she smiled. 'I like that. The Hive is not a physical place. Perhaps we need to start pushing that message.'

'I will talk to the Priestesses. They will start to incorporate it into the sermons.' Heather offered.

'No. I don't want them to know about my plan to move yet.'

'They don't have to know about the relocation. We can tell them that it's a plan to build better cooperation among the workers to help with the harvest.'

'Agreed. Remember, I want no news of my plans to spread beyond this chamber.'

'But who will go find a place for us to relocate to? This is a very delicate matter. It must be kept private.' Rose asked. She hated the thought of any Fairie being far from the safety of the Hive.

Heather again was the one to answer. 'Captain Thorn is our obvious choice. He's brave, he's resourceful, and he serves the Queen without hesitation.'

Deidre and Camellia cast suspicious glances at Heather. Was this an attempt of hers to get rid of a rival for the Queen's bed?

'Thorn.' Aynia said. She felt a heavy weight of dread move onto her heart, but she knew that Heather was right. Thorn was the one Fairie who could handle this mission.

'Are we agreed?' Heather asked.

Aynia sighed. Of course she would not have to make a real decision about moving the Hive until a suitable sight was found for the new construction. Until then this entire conversation was merely an academic debate. But to send Thorn away? That was an action she didn't want to take. Of course, the needs of the Hive came first. 'I can not say no.'

Thorn, always one to show up at a door just at the right time, presented himself in the parlor with a bow to Aynia and a nod of his head to Rose, Deidre, Heather, and Camellia. 'Your Majesty.'

'Did you find Carman?' Aynia asked.

'No. I failed you my Queen,' Thorn confessed. 'If we could fly we could have kept up with them, but we lack wings. The nymphs excel at eluding males. They knew that we were following them and they led us on a merry chase.' Thorn's shoulders sagged with disappointment. It seemed such an easy thing to find Carman, but somehow she still managed to hide from the Royal Guard. It was a failure that Thorn felt deeply.

'You have a chance to redeem yourself Thorn,' Heather told him.

'I will do whatever it takes.' He replied.

'Leave us.' Aynia commanded. Heather and Deidre exchanged surprised looks, but Camellia and Rose quickly moved from their seats and pulled their sisters out of the parlor.

Aynia walked from her seat at the table to one of the sofas in front of the fire. 'We must talk.'

'My Queen?'

'Sit beside me Thorn.'

'I would prefer to stand.'

'Then stand,' Aynia said with some irritation. She clasped her hands in her lap. It was a gesture that Thorn knew well from when she was a Princess. Aynia always clasped her hands together in her lap when she reached a difficult decision. 'You know as well as I do the pressures that the Hive is under. It is sad that a more experienced Queen is not here to deal with this crisis. However fate, or the Goddesses, placed me here at this time and this will perhaps be the defining test of my reign.'

When a speech starts out in this ominous tone, the news to follow is bound to be worse. Thorn had been dealt several bad blows this day. He was not sure that he could withstand another. He sank to his knees and peered up into Aynia's eyes. 'What can I do for you?' He asked softly.

'My idea of aiding the Scots in their fight against the English army is not being taken seriously.'

'It has some merit,' Thorn said cautiously.

'You tone betrays your misgivings.'

'In theory it is a sound idea, but in practice I don't think that the Sidhe, the magic folk, have enough power to drive out an entire human army. Not to mention that the Scots are just as likely to invoke Anti-Fairie magic against us as the English are. They could harm us because they won't understand that we're trying to help.'

'Then we must move on to a plan that will work. Thorn, I hate to admit defeat before my Throne has a chance to grow warm, but I think that the Hive may have to relocate. I'm seriously considering moving the Hive away from Balnacra.'

Thorn looked shocked, but he saw the seriousness in her eyes. She truly believed this to be the best course for the Hive. 'If this is the decision you have reached.'

'It is an option that I must leave open. Thorn, I rely on you very much. You are the best Captain of the Royal Guard in history. You are a close and dear friend. But I must ask you to go and find a new location for the Hive.'

'Where?'

'Perhaps a small island in one of the nearby lochs, somewhere where humans will not follow us.'

Thorn recognized the merit of the idea. He didn't like it, but he understood that it might be the last hope for the Hive. 'I will go immediately.'

Aynia placed her hand tentatively on Thorn's cheek. She knew that a single Fairie out in the world stood a small chance of surviving. This might be the last time that she saw him. She trembled. 'Thorn, I ask you this not as your Queen, but as Aynia. Promise me that you will come back home to me.'

Thorn took Aynia's hand. He turned her palm up and pressed her hand to his lips. He could taste a slight trace of her scent.

'Promise me,' Aynia demanded in a whisper. She placed her hand under his chin so that he could not avoid looking into her eyes.

'I will come back to you.'

Aynia leaned forward and lightly kissed Thorn on the lips. Unable to stop herself, she kissed him again with crushing intensity.

Thorn wrapped his arm around Aynia's waist and pulled her down to the floor with him. As he rolled on top of her, Thorn kissed Aynia like he'd dreamed of doing many nights. He was hungry to taste her lips.

Aynia placed a hand deep into Thorn's hair, keeping his lips pressed against hers. She was determined to make this brief moment last.

Thorn pulled her dress down from her shoulders. He kissed the space between her breasts as he unhooked her corset. His hands trembled a little, but he fought the urge to simply rip the fabric away.

Finally there was nothing between their skin.

Aynia kneaded his buttocks with her hands, pushing his pelvis into hers.

Thorn's hand slipped down to her breasts and massaged them roughly with his hand. This was unlike the tentative touch of the harem males. Milk began to bead up at Aynia's nipples.

Thorn watched the whitish fluid drip onto his hand as Aynia wriggled in interesting rhythms underneath him.

'I will let nothing stop me from coming back to you,' he promised, whispering into her ear.

'You can touch me without danger to yourself.' Aynia pushed Thorn's hand between her legs.

'I don't want to touch you,' Thorn withdrew his hand.

Aynia misunderstood. 'I have asked you to do something you don't want? I thought that you wanted me as much as I wanted you.'

'I said that I don't want to touch.' Thorn kissed Aynia again hard against her lips before he slid down between her thighs. 'I want to taste.'

Aynia smiled, relieved.

Thorn pushed her dress up above her waist. Slowly, almost reverently, he pulled down her panties. They were already damp at the crotch.

He realized with a touch of panic that as his mother did not maintain a harem he was never brought up around males who could teach him how to please a female. He was aware of the general layout of her anatomy. But he had no idea of what to do.

Aynia used light pressure with her thighs to push his face closer between her legs.

Thorn took a deep breath. The Queen's scent was here. He remembered the things he wanted to do to Aynia on Festival day. He buried his tongue inside of her.

Aynia wriggled obligingly. She slid her hand between her legs and pointed. 'Lick me here,' she told him.

Thorn was grateful for the suggestion. He suckled where she indicated.

Aynia moaned. The mere thought of Thorn being here with her was enough to get her wet. It was a fantasy come true.

He hungrily lapped the juices that flowed from her.

Aynia pulled her skirts higher around her waist so that she could see his head between her legs.

Thorn used his tongue to explore Aynia's vagina. He licked and sucked her clitoris with such intensity that Aynia didn't know if she wanted to scream at him to stop or to continue.

Aynia's scent was growing stronger. Thorn felt the rush of blood to his penis. He wet his finger in her juices and stroked himself. 'Goddesses let me get hard,' he prayed urgently, but his prayer was not answered.

Thorn realized from the way Aynia was starting to push her pelvis into his face that she was about to climax. Taking a cue from when he had spied on her, he plunged his fingers into her vagina.

Aynia slammed against Thorn and came in hard waves that almost caused her muscles to spasm. The line between pain and pleasure disappeared.

'I can feel that,' Thorn told her. 'I can feel you coming. It must be incredible to be inside of you when that happens.'

'I would love for you to be inside of me,' Aynia admitted 'I dream of you being inside of me.'

There was a discrete knock on the door.

Like guilty illicit lovers, Aynia and Thorn scrambled to hide their indiscretion. Aynia climbed back up onto the sofa. She hooked up her corset and covered her breasts. Then she carefully rearranged her skirt.

Thorn threw on his tunic then stood up, back at attention. Unfortunately his tunic was too short to hide the bulge of his remaining semi-hard-on. He clasped his hands in front rather than at his side, which was the correct way to stand at attention.

'Come in.' Aynia said with that instant calm detachment she was able to summon up at any occasion.

Heather came into the room. The smell of sex hung deliciously in the air. From Thorn's shiny face and barely covered arousal to Aynia's disheveled hair there was no question what had happened. Heather glowered at Thorn. 'If you have finished briefing Captain Thorn, Majesty, I have taken the liberty of preparing his pack for travel. It is best that he leaves now. No one will see him.'

'But!' Aynia protested.

'I agree,' Thorn said.

Heather pretended not to notice as Thorn picked up the pair of the Queen's panties and put them into a pocket in his tunic.

Thorn bowed deeply to Aynia. 'My Queen, I will find your haven.' He dared to take her hand one last time and kiss it, but this time on the back of her hand, not the palm. He took the pack Heather handed to him and headed out of the Royal Chambers.

Thorn realized that it had been a close call. If Heather had not come to the door when she did he might have forgotten himself and taken Queen's milk. He could admit to himself that the temptation was strong. Tersely, Thorn reminded himself that he didn't want to be a drone. He wanted to be a soldier. But in following nights when he woke from dreams of mating with Aynia, and he smelled her scent on the pair of panties he carried near his heart, his resolve wavered.

Carman sat on her makeshift Throne. 'What do you nymphs want?' She demanded in a haughty tone.

'Most gracious Majesty, true Queen of Balnacra Hive, we humbly ask you to hear our pleas.'

Carman was well flattered and inclined to listen. She nodded her head slightly to indicate that the nymph was to continue.

'More humans have been spotted making camp near our valley. You know as well as we that humans mean death for Sidhe. We have a plan to help hide this valley from human sight forever and to preserve for the magic folk.'

'I am listening.' The fact that Carman was examining her fingernails belied that statement, but the nymph wasn't going to leave without asking for help.

They were not prepared for Carman's response.

'That's the stupidest idea I have ever heard. You nymphs are just as dumb as legend has it. No wonder the male humans try to mate with you. They figure that you're the only beings dumber than them.' Carman and her attendants laughed loudly.

The nymphs were angered. They knew that they were as smart as the Fairie, but to be compared less than favorably with humans was an insult that even a nymph could understand. 'Laugh if you will. We have another great one that we can appeal to.'

'If you mean my sister, go ahead. She'll laugh in your face too.'

'At least she is not contorted and ugly like you!' And angry tree nymph shouted.

'I'm not ugly, I am a Queen!' Carman screamed back.

'I don't mean to ask your sister,' the water nymph said with steaming ire. She didn't want to get into a shouting match with the Fairie, so she hushed the other nymph. 'We will appeal to the Mountain King. He has the power to move the very stones! With his voice he commanded the rocks to dance and form Stonehenge where we once worshipped the Goddesses beside the Fairie and other Sidhe, in the time before the humans. If the Mountain King can command the rock at Stonehenge he can do the same for us here.'

'Did it ever occur to you that by walling the valley you would be creating a perfect haven for the humans? They would see it as a natural fort.'

Having heard this same reasoning from Aynia, normal Sidhe would perhaps rethink their plan. But not the nymphs, 'The Mountain King will do it for us!' they cried.

CHAPTER 10

Copperhead sat playing cards with Prince Noisi. Moss and Sarkany, the only other drones in the harem, were enthusiastically fencing up and over every table, chair, and pile of pillows in the main room of the harem. The other males kept apart. They were in awe of the drones.

Copperhead lazily threw in his losing hand. 'I'm so bored.' He looked around the harem with a jaded air.

Prince Noisi was similarly slumped in his own chair. 'I'm also quite bored.'

Copperhead motioned towards Moss and Sarkany, 'look at those two fools. Shirts off, sweating everywhere. They practice fencing as if they'll ever have use of their swords again.'

Moss and Sarkany heard Copperhead but ignored him. They were well aware of how he came to be a drone. In their home Hives no Prince would be forced to live with such a shamed male in his presence, but this was not their home Hive and they both understood their Queen's reasons for not throwing Copperhead out of the Royal Palace. The fact that Prince Noisi didn't mind associating with such a person was no business of theirs.

Copperhead leaned forward so that only Prince Noisi could hear him. 'Speaking of swords, have you, er, used yours yet?' He made an unmistakable motion to indicate that he did not mean a sword of steel.

Noisi gave a disgusted snort. 'I have yet to unsheathe mine. What good is being a drone if your female does not allow you to make love to her?'

'Do you mean that you haven't even unsheathed it? Haven't you grown hard yet?'

'Of course, many times a day since taking milk.'

'Well, what do you do?'

'What do you mean?' Noisi whispered.

'Haven't you used it yet? Relieved a little of the pressure?' Copperhead asked conspiratorially.

'I did once.'

'Well?'

'It felt wonderful. I never felt so good, but then Camellia saw the stain on the sheet and had me whipped in front of the entire harem for spilling seed that belongs to the Queen. It was very embarrassing.'

'Why? I think that every male in this harem has been whipped twice already.'

'Yes, only I got hard in front of all of them while I was being whipped. They were all staring at it,' Noisi indicated his crotch.

'Jealousy.'

'Of course, but I was still embarrassed. When I tried to cover it from their eyes with my hands Lady Camellia put me over her knee and spanked me. Of course, while she was spanking me I was rubbing against her thigh, and I almost came.'

'You like Lady Camellia that much?'

Prince Noisi went red. 'No. I was thinking about the Lady Deidre. When my wings were coming through she rubbed ointment into my back. She came back the next day and did it again, but since Lady Camellia was not there,' Prince Noisi made sure that no one was near enough to hear, but with Moss and Sarkany pulling over furniture across the room from them no one could hear what they said. 'Lady Deidre sat on my ass while she rubbed the ointment into my back. That's when I got my first hard on.'

'No! What did you do?'

'She went away, and I turned over and stroked it until I came. That's when I got caught.'

'So you like Lady Deidre?'

Noisi looked about the room with a guilty glance. 'This could get me stung to death for treason.'

'Do you think that the Queen cares what you do? She has so many males that she doesn't even know most of them by name.

She's only interested in those two clowns over there.' He nodded at Moss and Sarkany.

'I know,' Prince Noisi agreed unhappily.

'Lady Deidre likes you, a lot.' Copperhead was smart enough to adapt his plan instantly to the new information. He would have to let Adders-Tongue know, but that was no problem. Since Camellia did not consider him to be her drone she paid very little attention to his whereabouts during the day. One harrowing incident in the Hive center made it clear that as a drone he couldn't freely go where he wished anymore, but he had access to the Royal Messengers and had no qualms about using them to deliver his personal messages to his aunt.

'Don't even talk about Lady Deidre,' Noisi said miserably. 'She's so beautiful,' he added wistfully.

'I could take her a little note from you. Something innocent wouldn't get you two into trouble. Just thank her for healing your back.'

'I don't know,' Prince Noisi said slowly.

'Of course, Camellia will keep even her own sisters out of the harem now that there are drones here. As drones we're trapped in the harem. We've lost all of our freedom. Well, you have. I can still pretty much go where I want to.'

Prince Noisi's face showed the great temptation that he felt.

Before he could answer, Moss jumped in the middle of their card table. Sarkany flew across the room, brandishing his sword. They fought until the table turned over.

'Oops, sorry,' Moss called over his shoulder as he went in pursuit of Sarkany.

'You don't have to answer me now,' Copperhead whispered to Noisi. 'Just think about it.'

Camellia blocked the door of the harem. Deidre tried to look over her sister's shoulder, but could see nothing of the males in the room.

'What do you want Deidre?' Camellia asked. She couldn't decide if she was annoyed or amused by her sister's actions.

This was hardly the first time in Camellia's career that a member of the Queen's staff tried to catch a glimpse of the Queen's drones. But this was the first time Camellia had worked with her sisters.

Camellia's usual response to this type of thing was to give the attendant a good thrashing. Occasionally she went so far as to procure males for the attendant. Nothing got a female's mind out of the Queen's harem like a harem of her own. But in this case Camellia was a bit at a loss. She had no desire to punish her sister, and would never saddle her ambitious sister with a harem against her will, but she couldn't allow Deidre to become infatuated with the Queen's males either.

Perhaps, Camellia mused, she could give Copperhead to Deidre to use for a night, or a week, or for forever. The idea of passing off the free drone was quite tempting. And it was perfectly acceptable in the eyes of society.

'What are you doing?' Deidre asked petulantly.

'Blocking off the door to the harem,' Camellia told Deidre calmly, as if it were not evident.

'I used to be able to go inside.'

'There are drones in here now. What's your business little sister? You can't possibly want to talk to one of the Queen's males.' Camellia's stern expression brought Deidre to her senses.

'No. I don't. I just came here to tell you that the Queen is ready for our staff meeting,' Deidre gave up her futile attempt to see into the harem past her sister.

'Very well, let's go.' Camellia closed the door of the harem behind her and locked the door.

Deidre sighed but could do nothing. She felt a little silly anyway. All that she could think about every day was catching a glimpse of Prince Noisi. Ever since the day she stole into the harem and massaged his back she was obsessed with the thought of touching him again. While rubbing his back that day she rubbed her crotch against his firm buttocks as she straddled him. Now each night before going to sleep she fantasized about him. She dreamed that she ordered him to turn over, and when he did she saw his swollen cock. In her fantasy she lowered herself on him and they rocked together to a decadent rhythm.

The previous day when Camellia told the Queen about spanking Noisi for hiding his hard on from the rest of the harem, Deidre had to excuse herself from the room in a hurry to go masturbate in her own chamber.

Where Deidre once felt smug superiority over the females of the Hive de Chambord for their ridiculous obsessions with romantic love and the pursuit of males, she now found herself giddily swept up in thoughts of sex, love, romance, courtship, and perhaps even more sex.

Despite Camellia's insistence that Deidre stay out of the harem, Heather was allowed into the rooms with the males. It was a sign of Camellia's trust in her eldest sister, or perhaps her belief that Heather would never willingly touch a male, that Heather went through the harem unescorted. The males grew silent as they watched her make a beeline for Prince Sarkany.

'Come, we will talk.'

Sarkany looked over at Prince Moss, who only shrugged. Lady Heather was an unknown to the males, but if possible she was more intimidating to them than the Mistress of the Harem. However, they all knew that she represented the Queen. No male would dare cross her.

'You have a private room?' Heather asked.

Sarkany silently led the Lady Heather to the room he shared with Moss. Once the curtain fell and closed off the room Heather sat down on one of the chairs before the fireplace. 'Sit,' she indicated the chair opposite her.

Sarkany grimaced. 'I'd rather stand Lady.' He still couldn't sit without pain.

'Suit yourself.' Heather snapped. 'I've made some inquiries about you Prince.'

'Oh?' Sarkany replied cautiously.

'Princes don't usually leave their home Hives until offered in marriage to a Queen. But your Mother sent you away from her Hive without a marriage contract.'

Sarkany shrugged. 'Eastern customs differ.'

'Not that much.'

'What do you want from me Lady Heather?' Sarkany asked impatiently. His past was questionable, but not quite shady enough to be used against him. Blackmail, he mused, seemed out of character for Lady Heather. She was more likely to physically force someone to do as she wished than to try something subtle like extortion.

'Your mother was shocked when she heard that you were here instead of in Ireland. Prince Moss's mother offered a bridal price for you, which your mother had already accepted. You've caused a little international incident with this stunt of yours. Apparently Prince Moss's mother really wanted you for her bed. I hear that you were quite popular with the females in your mother's Hive too.'

Sarkany said nothing. His recent punishment for a smart retort to Camellia was enough of a deterrent to stop him from speaking. The fact that Heather appeared to be even stronger than the Mistress of the Harem was added incentive to hold his tongue.

'Our Queen also seems very fond of you. Tell me Prince, what is it about you that makes you so irresistible to the ladies?'

With a slight look of disgust on his face, Sarkany took Heather's hand in his and turned it over so that her palm was up. Pressing his lips to her palm, then her wrist, he waited for a moment to meet her eyes.

Heather was staring at her hand as if it had betrayed her. Never in her life had she reacted to a male like this. She fought the desire to push his head between her thighs. She took another deep breath of his scent, and then her mind went hazy.

Suddenly Heather realized that her corset was open and she had the Prince's hair entwined in her fingers as she was forcing him to her exposed breast. 'No!' She pushed him away, horrified and mystified at her actions.

Sarkany smiled up at her with an insolent grin. 'My father had this ability too. He was a great favorite of my Mother the Queen until he met his unfortunate demise. There's something in my scent that affects females. If I can press my lips to a pulse point it enters their blood. When I was young and foolish I was careless about attracting females. I enjoyed using my powers without thinking of the consequences. I almost got myself into serious trouble with a number of noble ladies in my Mother's Hive. Now it appears that I have myself in serious trouble with you.'

'Why?' Heather asked.

'Perhaps you should look to where your stinger is.'

Heather saw that her stinger was indeed unsheathed, and was pressed against Sarkany's scrotum. 'When did that happen?' She asked, bewildered.

'Right after I kissed your wrist. You told me to take milk from you and then pleasure you, or you would use your stinger on my tender parts.' Sarkany pointedly moved Heather's stinger away. 'I don't mean to complain Lady, but I prefer not to be threatened.'

Heather hastily closed the cup of her corset. 'I wanted to discuss the Queen with you.' She felt that the power in the room was crazily out of balance. She was supposed to have the upper hand here. He was supposed to fear her. But she felt oddly vulnerable to him.

'My favorite subject.'

'It is very important that the Queen breed at the Equinox.'

'I'm more than willing to breed with her.'

'It's not you I'm worried about,' Heather snapped. 'The Queen seems reluctant.'

'What do you want me to do?' Sarkany asked.

'Seduce her, entice her, use your powers, whatever, but get her to mate.' Heather gripped Sarkany's wrist perhaps a little too tightly. 'Let me make this clear. If you have this power over females then I expect you to get the Queen to mate or I will have you killed, understand?'

'It's not that easy,' Sarkany tried to get Heather to release her grip by pulling back his arm. She clung on tenaciously.

'What do you mean?'

'I mean that I have suckled from her breasts, kissed her lips, hands, and neck, and she has never once threatened to kill me if I didn't mate with her instantly.' Sarkany decided to add insult to injury. 'Not all females are as susceptible as you are.'

Heather backhanded Sarkany across the face. 'I am not under your power you nasty little drone.'

'Do you want me to couple with the Queen or not?'

Heather struggled with her desire to storm out of the room and her knowledge that of all the drones this impertinent one was the only one Aynia was likely to mate with. 'You would mate with the Queen even if I didn't want you to.'

'I don't take your wishes into account on such matters Lady.'

'Filthy drone.'

'Jealous? You would take the Queen into your own bed if you dared. Don't look so surprised Lady Heather. Russia is not that far from Romania. News travels fast in our little corner of the world.'

'What is it that you want?' Heather asked as she stood to leave. She was feeling queasy.

'Want? What could I possibly want? I've just about reached the height of power and position for a male. Although,' Sarkany paused for a second, 'it pales in comparison to my ambitions.'

Heather laughed a short bark of surprise. 'The only proper ambition a male should have is to sire a princess.'

'I'm not what you'd call a proper Fairie,' Sarkany growled suggestively as he took a menacing step towards Heather.

Heather backed away from Sarkany then stomped out of the Prince's chamber. The conversation had not gone well, not at all. When she got to her private chamber she sat down with a large glass and reached for the decanter of whiskey.

Moss stuck his head into the room. 'I was wondering if I was going to find you lying dead on the floor. Lady Heather was blazingly angry when she left.'

Sarkany laughed. 'Yes, I suppose that she was.'

'What did she want?'

'She wanted me to suckle from her breasts, like this,' Sarkany pulled up Moss's tunic and roughly licked Moss's nipples. Moss pulled his tunic off.

'I can see why she wanted that. What else did she want?' Moss asked, a little breathless.

Sarkany roughly pulled Moss close. His hands slid down the Prince's back, into the back of his tights, and rested on his buttocks. Sarkany's lips crushed against Moss's for a lingering kiss.

'She wanted me to behave like a proper little whore.'

'What is this?' Deidre asked as Copperhead dropped a note into her hand in the hallway of the Royal Chambers.

'It's a letter.' Copperhead whispered.

'Why do you give this to me?'

Copperhead made a face. 'Listen to me. You don't want to be seen taking this note from me. So if I were you I wouldn't bring attention to the fact that I gave it to you.' Copperhead leaned down close to Deidre's ear. 'It comes from a prisoner of the harem, one who wishes to thank you for helping him.' Copperhead continued on down the hallway.

Deidre looked at the note with fascination. Was this really what she thought that it was? Hearing a noise down the hallway, she placed the note in her pocket and ran to her room. Once safely inside, she took the note out again and stared at it.

'I should destroy it,' she told herself. It was the right thing to do. She could not betray her Queen by accepting notes from one of her drones.

With hands shaking, Deidre lit a candle and placed it on her desk. She watched the flame rise. With resolve in her heart she touched the tip of the letter to the flame. At first the paper only smoked. Then the flame jumped to the paper and it began to burn. The paper turned to black and curled the edges where the flame was glowing orange. Then unaccountably the flame died.

The paper was too heavy to burn well. Deidre sighed and unfolded the letter. Despite the temptation to read it Deidre placed the note in her fireplace and turned away. After a reasonable amount of time she turned back to see if the note was ash. Unfortunately it was not. Deidre picked up the poker and pushed the note back into the flames. Finally it caught. She tried not to see, but could not help but read the phrases 'think of you day and night', and 'love to you'.

Despite her resolve, her heart felt the delicious agony of infatuation.

The nymphs milled around a clearing in the forest. Forceful decision was not their forte. They had been so sure that the Fairie Queen Aynia would vow to kill off the humans, but she didn't. Even after they threatened to go to Carman Aynia refused to aid them. Then Carman laughed at them too. The nymphs were used to derision from the Fairie, but they were also used to living a carefree existence. With humans invading their lands they could not live as nymphs should. Something had to be done.

'We will go to the Mountain King!' The tree nymphs from the far edge of the forest rallied.

'No! We shouldn't do that.' The nymphs from the deep forest argued.

'Why not?'

'Even the Fairie fear the Mountain King. If they fear him he must be bad.'

'I've seen him! He's quite handsome.'

The nymphs giggled.

'Stay focused,' the water nymph begged her sisters.

'Maybe the Fairie fear the Mountain King because he is powerful.'

'Yes, he is powerful!' This cry echoed through the glen.

'Then we should go to the powerful Mountain King and ask him to help us against the humans.'

'Yes, let's go to the Mountain King!'

The nymphs cheered their plan and began the hike to the hidden entrance to the Hall of the Mountain King. The entrance was deep in the valley, up on the slope of the eastern wall, protected by a great granite boulder. Rapping three times on the stone, the water nymph caused the entrance to be revealed. As the earth rumbled and the boulder moved the water nymph was bugged by a niggling concern at the back of her mind. There was some reason why this was a bad idea. She just couldn't remember why.

The Hall where the goblins lived was a stone cavern with stalactites and stalagmites that were carved into columns. The massive, dark room was bare of any furnishings except the Mountain King's Throne and a dull red carpet that flowed from under the Throne like a pool of old blood. The nymphs grew increasingly nervous as their steps echoed loudly through the hall.

With flesh hard as stone and fingers that ended in talons, the Mountain King, King Liderc, was an imposing figure. He sat very still on his Throne. Even his pure black eyes didn't flicker as he watched the nymphs draw near.

The nymphs were right about one thing. King Liderc was in his own sinister way an attractive male. Bearing a remote resemblance to the Fairie Prince Sarkany, he had curly, thick black hair and a narrow black beard that defined the edge of his jawbone, met at his chin, and came to a point that curled up just the slightest bit. There was an undeniable scent that emitted from him. Masculine, earthy, it was the kind of scent that made the nymphs breathe deeply through their noses to catch a better whiff, but that they couldn't decide if they liked it or not.

King Liderc maintained a stony silence.

The nymphs nervously pushed their leader ahead of them. 'Ask him,' they all urged her.

'Great Mountain King, King of the underworld, Dread Lord of Darkness, we, the nymphs of Balnacra, come to ask Your Highness a favor.'

'What favor can I do for overworlders?' The cool rumbling voice of the Mountain King echoed off of the stalagmite columns with a strange hollow sound.

'There are humans coming to Balnacra. We want to hide the valley from them so that they will pass us by.' The water nymph quickly outlined their plan. Her nervousness showed.

'Humans? Isn't killing humans more in the expertise of the Fairie?'

'We asked the Fairie.'

'You asked them?' King Liderc only slightly raised one eyebrow.

'Yes Dread Lord. We asked Carman, and Aynia.' The water nymph explained.

'I do not know these names.'

'There is a new Queen of the Fairie at Balnacra Hive. Queen Aynia rules the Hive after the death of the old Queen.'

'Then who is Carman?'

'She is another Queen, but she has no Hive.'

'There are two Fairie Queens in our little valley? An embarrassment of riches.' King Liderc said in droll humor, but his interest was piqued. 'Tell me about them.'

'Well, Carman is damaged. She limps badly and her left arm doesn't work well. Her left breast is also shriveled, but she's still kind of pretty, if you look at her right side.' The water nymph stumbled along her words. She was growing uneasy again.

'And the other, Queen Aynia?'

'She has hair of red, like fire and skin like snow. She is tall, very tall. She is as curvaceous as a nymph is. She is quite lovely, but her heart is cold. She didn't care about our plight. Tell us, will you help us?'

'I think not.'

'But we need your help,' the nymphs whined.

'I said that I would not help drive the humans away, female. What do I care? They only affect you overworlders. They can not touch me.'

The nymph stomped her foot. 'If you won't help us then we will be going.'

'I don't think so.' King Liderc told her, amusement in his voice.

'Why not?'

Suddenly the Hall was filled with goblins. The nymphs screamed and tried to run, but the entrance of the hall was closed. Panicked, they ran in circles.

With surprising smoothness and speed, King Liderc rose from his Throne and grabbed the wrist of the water nymph. 'You're mine now,' he said while looking deep into her eyes.

The nymph took a deep breath of the intoxicating scent of King Liderc. She stopped struggling. 'My Lord,' the nymph kissed the Mountain King on his cold lips. He touched her and her body responded as it never had to other males. King Liderc whispered into the nymph's ear. 'Give yourself to me.'

'Yes, I will.' The nymph dropped her gauzy dress on the floor.

King Liderc placed his fingers between the nymph's legs and rubbed her clitoris. She closed her eyes and breathed in deeply of his exotic scent. 'I like to watch you get yourself off,' he murmured.

The nymph fairly quivered. She looked around the bare room. The only place to sit was the nearby throne. The nymph climbed on the arm of the throne and rubbed her clitoris against the knobby protrusions carved into the arms. The rough sensation was exciting to her. She began to grind herself against the arm of the chair.

King Liderc reached over and pinched both of her nipples hard.

'I am close my Lord.' The nymph sighed.

'That's good enough for me.' He pulled her off of the throne and dipped his fingers into her wet pussy. 'Very well.'

Beaming with pride that she pleased King Liderc, the nymph bent over his throne and spread her legs. 'Take me now my King!'

The other nymphs stopped running long enough to witness how their sister begged King Liderc to take her.

He complied. The nymphs were fascinated. They ran from males, not to them. What had King Liderc done that their sister behaved this way? Why was their sister moaning in ecstasy? Then his scent filled the air. Suddenly all of the nymphs wanted to mate with King Liderc. As goblins looked on from the dark recesses of the Hall the nymphs shed their clothes and began to dance around King Liderc.

'Take me next!' They cried out.

'Don't worry ladies,' King Liderc assured them in his calm, silky tones, 'there is plenty of my seed for all of you.' Moments after coming into the water nymph, the Mountain King grabbed another nymph and bent her over the arm of his stone Throne.

The goblins watched from the darkness as their King took each of the nymphs in turn. All the while the goblins hooted eerie sounds of celebration.

Copperhead paused in the hallway of the Royal Chambers as Deidre passed by. 'My Lady Deidre,' he made his bow. 'I'm going into the harem now to play cards with my good friend Prince Noisi. Do you perhaps have something for me to pass on?'

Deidre frowned. 'I do not.'

Copperhead's mouth dropped open. 'My lady, is there no reply to the Prince's note? How can you fail to reply to such a moving letter?'

'I burned the note without reading it. Tell Prince Noisi that I will not accept any more messages from him. I am loyal to my Queen.'

Copperhead bowed. 'Of course I will tell him. He will love you all the more for your devotion.' He left Deidre and went into the harem.

For a second Copperhead paused at the door. Getting those two together was going to be hard. Prince Noisi refused to write notes to Lady Deidre. Copperhead forged the first one. Now Lady Deidre refused to read or respond to any notes. Copperhead chewed on his thumb. There had to be an answer.

'Copperhead, don't hover at the door,' Camellia chastised him.

'Sorry my lady,' Copperhead moved over to Camellia's side. 'May I visit my lady's chambers tonight?'

'No.'

'Please?'

'No.' Camellia repeated with irritation.

'But we can play games. I know what you like, and I can do more.' Copperhead made a vee of his fingers and fluttered his tongue crudely between them as an example of what he proposed.

'I'm warning you Copperhead,' Camellia tried to sound irritated, but she couldn't hide the hint of a smile in her eyes.

Copperhead smiled with false contrition. 'Or what? Am I being a bad boy? Perhaps I could come to your chamber, and you could put me over our knee. Then you could slide my hose down just past my buttocks. Since I'm such a bad boy I guess that you'd have to spank me. Maybe with your hand? Or perhaps with a lash? And then when my ass is all nice and pink I could beg your forgiveness on my knees, between your thighs?'

Despite any denials from Camellia that she derived any sexual stimulation from punishing the harem, what Copperhead proposed sounded interesting enough to bring a familiar tingle between her legs. And Copperhead was able to go beyond the usual games she liked to play with the young males that she seduced. Besides, she did feel that he needed some discipline.

'Come with me.' Camellia grabbed Copperhead's arm.

'Now?' Copperhead asked hopefully.

'No.' Camellia took him to her office. 'Pull down your hose.'

Copperhead was more than willing. He yanked down his hose, unleashing a very hard penis.

Camellia took a heavily padded thong out of her supply cabinet. 'Here,' she quickly and expertly strapped Copperhead in.

'What is this for?'

'It stops you from playing with yourself. When I have problems with a male who can not remember to save his seed for the Queen I strap him into one of these. It makes it impossible to feel any sensations, no matter how hard you try.'

'But I'm hard right now.' Copperhead whined.

'I could see that.'

'Please? I'm going to go crazy if I'm like this all day.'

'That's the idea. By the time I take you into my chamber tonight you should be quite ripe for action.'

'But I am so hard that it hurts.'

'I could keep you hard for days and not let you come, so don't complain about a few hours. Now, be a good boy and pull up your hose. You can go visit your friend. Play cards, talk, take your mind off of it for awhile.'

Copperhead sullenly pulled the hose up over the contraption. When Camellia seemed to be looking away he gave himself an experimental rub, but he felt nothing.

'That's going to cost you.'

'What?'

'I saw that. You're not supposed to touch yourself. Just for that I'm going to wait for after dinner to let you out of it. I will be watching you. If I see you try anything else, even bumping into a table, I will keep putting you off by half of an hour. Understand?'

'Yes.' Copperhead finished dressing and walked stiffly out of Camellia's office.

Camellia sighed as she watched Copperhead walk away. He was in need of a lot of discipline. Luckily, she was just the female to do the job.

'What's the matter with you? You're walking strange.' Prince Noisi mentioned to Copperhead.

'That damn Camellia, she put me into this underwear where I can't feel anything. It's very bulky.'

'What did she catch you doing?' The Prince asked in alarm.

'Nothing. She just wants me to be really ready to go tonight. She's going to take me to her chamber.'

Prince Noisi groaned. 'Great, even the shamed male gets to have sex before me.'

'Perhaps not.'

'But you just told me that you were going to tonight.'

'Listen, while I'm in Camellia's chamber the Queen will probably be with those two jokers again,' Copperhead indicated Moss and Sarkany, who were involved in a spirited shinty match that raged through the harem. It took some doing, but Moss and Sarkany finally convinced the other males not to stand in such awe of the drones. Once they were friends it was easy to recruit teams for sports. Today the game was shinty. Regardless of furniture, spectators, or personal safety, the teams of seven treated the main room of the harem, the only available space for them, as a playing field.

'Yes. So?'

'I heard that Lady Rose is taking a night off to spend with her own harem.'

'And? Get to the point. And deal the cards.'

Copperhead took up the deck and dealt out two hands. 'I talked to Lady Deidre about you.'

'No! I told you no letters. I refuse to write one.' Price Noisi hissed even though his normal speaking voice would have been drowned out by the game being played around them.

'I told her that. She was very touched. She agreed that it was best that you two deny your love for each other and remain loyal to the Queen.'

'She said that she loved me?'

Copperhead made a great show of examining his cards.

'Well?'

258

'I told you what she said. Do you want another card?'

'What do you think that she meant by that?'

'I don't know. Do you want a card or not?'

Prince Noisi tried to focus on his cards but was too distracted. 'I wish that I could ask her.'

'I told you that you could. You'll have your chance tonight.'

Prince Noisi shook his head. 'No. I can't. It isn't right. And besides, we'd get caught.'

'By whom? Listen, it's none of my business, 'cause I'll be too busy learning the art of love from the Mistress of the Harem. I'll know what it's like to slide into her hot, wet pussy. And you, well, don't even fantasize about it, because Camellia will catch you with stained sheets. Besides, who said anything about sex? You'd just talk to Deidre, right?'

'Right,' Noisi agreed slowly. But even as he said it another, more sinful, thought came to mind.

'You know what to do?' Adders-Tongue asked her niece, Cobra-Lily.

'Yes, for the hundredth time. We go down the tunnel and come up through the hidden alcove in the Royal Palace. Then we go into Deidre's room and catch her with the Queen's drone. We arrest them, they go on trial, and then you get to embarrass the Queen.' Cobra-Lily secretly thought that this was a stupid plan. She preferred direct things, like poison, although she had to admit that her poisoned gold lace necklace had failed to work its magic yet. Cobra-Lily wondered if she failed to file the points on it sharp enough to prick skin, and she wondered if the poison would fade in lethalness over time. She knew from experience that the trick clasp tightened the collar around the wearer's neck until a secret hinge was released. Cobra-Lily actually got the gold lace to go tight enough around the metal smith's thick neck to strangle her, and the jeweler had provided a convenient, if not very willing, test for the poison, so Cobra-Lily knew that it would work. The hard part was placing the two bodies into the fire at the metal smith's workshop. It involved a lot of cutting to finish the job.

Adders-Tongue clasped her hands together. 'This is so sweet. I'll get rid of Deidre. Then I'll think of a way to get rid of that religious fanatic Heather. And finally, I'll allow Copperhead to kill that tramp Camellia.'

'You're forgetting Rose.'

'Rose doesn't interest me. She has no power and she doesn't council the Queen. The others have obvious flaws that I can exploit. And they're stronger advisors. My plan is to strip Aynia of all of her quality advisors. Then I will place my own followers into advisory positions for her. After that it will be easy to lead her into mistakes. How nice of Captain Thorn to take a leave of absence just as the pieces of my plan fall together. The Queen won't have her precious Royal Guard to save her at the last second. That new Captain Sage is inexperienced, and frankly not very good at his job. He seems to think that if the outside of the Palace is protected the Queen is safe.'

Cobra-Lily stifled a yawn. Why did her Aunt take every chance to soliloquize? Perhaps it was a habit picked up on the floor of Parliament where members were speechifying at every possible opportunity. 'Can we go now?'

'Another ten minutes. We want the happy couple to get comfortable.'

Copperhead poked his head into Prince Noisi's chamber. 'Well, I'm off to my assignation. I'll be sure to fill you in on all the details tomorrow morning.' Copperhead crudely mimicked the motion of thrusting into a female.

'Don't,' Prince Noisi groaned. 'I'm jealous enough already and I don't even know what I'm missing.'

Copperhead turned away, and then came back. 'By the way, thought you might like to know, I gave all the other lads in the harem a sleeping drought. And I told Lady Deidre to expect you.'

'No! I told you no.'

'She seemed very pleased. Of course she'll hate you forever if you don't even bother to show up and explain your reasons for not coming.'

'Tell her that I'm not coming.' Prince Noisi demanded.

'Copperhead?' Camellia's voice could be heard from her chambers.

'Do you think I'd dare be late for this tonight? I've had a hard on all day. And besides, my lady punishes with a heavy hand. Sorry.' Copperhead closed the curtain and scurried over to Lady Camellia's chambers. 'You called, my love?'

'You're late,' Camellia observed without humor.

Copperhead smiled. 'I know. I really am a bad drone. Now, can we take off this thing that you put on me? I've been hard so long that it's beginning to hurt.'

Camellia took out a small cat-o'-nine tails and a riding crop from the impressive display of whips and straps in the cabinet behind her desk. 'Later. First we have a small matter of discipline. Take off your tunic, then get down on your knees and crawl to my feet.'

Copperhead took off his tunic as he was told. Then he sank down to his knees and crawled over to Camellia's feet. As he looked down at the floor he offered up a small plea to the Goddesses that Adders-Tongue's guards would wait until after he had sex to invade the Royal Chambers.

Prince Noisi sat for a time and considered his options. He did not want to betray the Queen, but he also didn't want Lady Deidre to hate him. Tonight was clearly his only chance. Creeping over to Camellia's closed door, he listened. There was the sound of an open palm smacking against naked flesh. No male lived in a harem managed by Camellia more than week without hearing that noise. He also heard Copperhead moaning. If it was in pleasure or pain he didn't know, and quite frankly he didn't want to know.

The Prince looked around the harem. It looked as if there had been a drunken revelry at dinner. Everyone was asleep, or passed out, on the couches or at tables. The sleeping drug that Copperhead administered worked well.

Noisi went to the door of the harem. It was just a threshold, but one that he was forbidden to pass except at the express direction of his Queen or the Mistress of the Harem. Until he became a drone he had freer access in and out of the room. Since taking Queen's milk he was a virtual prisoner.

He opened the door.

There was no one in the hallway. Lady Rose was gone that afternoon to be with her own family. Lady Heather had at the last moment decided to accompany her sister. Unlike during Thorn's watch, there were no Royal Guardsmen actually inside the Royal Chamber. Lady Camellia was enjoying a dalliance with Copperhead. The entire harem was asleep. Only Deidre and Noisi were awake.

'I'll just tell her that I can't see her anymore,' Noisi told himself. 'Then I will return to the harem.'

He stepped out, and crossed the threshold.

Deidre looked up when she heard the soft scratching on the door. She wondered who it could possibly be. She went to see. 'Yes?'

'I must see you,' Prince Noisi said. 'Can I come in? It isn't safe in the hallway.'

Deidre grabbed his arm and pulled him into her chamber. 'What are you doing here? Do you want to be arrested?' She took a quick look down the hallway and then shut her door.

'No, I don't want to be arrested. That's why I came to tell you that I can't see you anymore.'

'I know that. Noisi, you're in real danger here. We both are. What on earth possessed you to come see me?'

'I can't stop thinking about you Lady Deidre,' Noisi admitted.

'Be that as it may, you belong to the Queen, and I serve her faithfully. I refuse to commit treason.'

'That's what I came to tell you. Copperhead said that you expected me tonight. I just wanted to tell you that I won't be coming.'

'But you did! You did come. And I was not expecting you. I think that Copperhead is trying his hand at mischief.'

'No. He's a friend. He just knows how much I think about you and he wanted me to have a chance to be with you.'

Deidre doubted this, but there was no reason to argue the point with the naive Prince. 'We need to get you out of here.' She opened the door of her chamber, but pulled back immediately and shut the door. 'It's Heather; she's come back from Rose's. I thought that she was going to stay the night.'

'She'll be out of the hallway soon,' Prince Noisi said hopefully.

'Maybe she will, but they won't,' Deidre showed him a quick glimpse of two servants with buckets and scrub brushes. 'Of all the stupid times to be cleaning the chamber.'

Deidre knew full well that as soon as the Queen left the Royal Chamber or when she went to sleep, the servants of the Royal Chambers went into action. The idea was that the Queen would never see her rooms in anything but spotless order. In theory it was a fine idea. Right now it was most inconvenient.

'Have a seat Noisi. We are well trapped. Try not to speak. I don't want for you to be overheard.'

Despite what she knew to be a mistake, Deidre took Noisi by the hand and led him to a chair by the fire. When he sat he did not let go. Deidre sat down opposite him, still holding his hand, and let silence settle in the room.

'How do we know which tunnel?' Cobra-Lily asked.

'Thane Adders-Tongue said to use the biggest tunnel. She said that all of the others eventually dead-ended.'

'Then why go to the trouble to have them dug?' Cobra-Lily asked.

'I believe that all of the others tunnels were misdirection for the tunnel builders so that they wouldn't understand what the past Queen's true aim was,' the member of Thane Adders-Tongue's guards answered.

'What I want to know is how did she keep it a secret? It must have taken lots of workers to dig all of this,' another guard asked. 'And yet no one else in the Hive seems to know about the presence of these tunnels.'

'If it was me I would have planned a convenient tunnel collapse on the workers when they were done with the real tunnel.' Cobra-Lily remarked.

'Is that what she did?'

'I said that was I would do. I have no idea how she kept it quiet.'

'Oh look, the trap door.' The small group was almost at the end of the tunnel. As promised, a trap door was over their heads.

'We must be at the Palace,' Cobra-Lily hissed. She took a torch and climbed the old ladder to the trap door above them. She pushed against it, but nothing happened. 'Is there a lock on it?'

'No one said anything about a lock. Shall I try?'

'Yes.' Cobra-Lily traded places with the guard. But the guard could not budge the door either. 'I think that it has been locked. It feels like there's something resting on it.'

As part of the floor to the hidden alcove near the Queen's chambers, the trap door was blocked. Weeks ago Thorn instructed his guards to pour hundreds of pounds of rocks into the alcove. Then the alcove was sealed with an iron door and a lock that Thorn destroyed the key to. It was a trap door destined to never be used again.

'Now what?' Cobra-Lily asked, defeat announcing itself in the sag of her shoulders.

'We go back and tell Thane Adders-Tongue about the door being sealed. Maybe we can get into the Palace another way.'

'At this time of night? No way. We can't get into the Palace again until the Queen holds court. Come on. I want my dinner.' Cobra-Lily stomped down the tunnel with the torch. Her guards followed hastily. No Fairie liked being underground in the dark.

Copperhead lay in Camellia's bed, waiting to hear the commotion that was sure to take place any moment, but the Royal Chambers remained quiet. Obviously somehow the plan to trap Deidre with Noisi had failed. While Copperhead thought he suckled at one of Camellia's breasts. There was little else for him to do. He didn't even want to think about the punishment Thane Adders-Tongue would mete out to him for failing.

Camellia was asleep, finally, after a very long session of discipline that was sure to leave a mark on Copperhead's buttocks. Every time Copperhead did not follow her script to the letter Camellia would find a new patch of tender flesh to torture. When Camellia finally slipped her hand around to grab Copperhead's penis the pleasure ended much too soon. He was unable to delay ejaculation after just a few strokes. He tried to get hard again, but couldn't before Camellia drifted off into sleep.

Copperhead quietly and carefully got out of bed. He dressed, wincing as his hose rubbed against still sensitive areas on his bottom and upper thighs. Then he slowly opened the door of Camellia's room. There was no sound. Under Lady Deidre's door, which was just across the hall, he could see light.

He tiptoed across the hall and put his ear to the door. He heard Lady Deidre's voice, but was Noisi still with her? The floor was damp, but showed no footprints leading back to the harem. Then he heard a male's voice. Smiling to himself, Copperhead thought quickly of another plan. What if the Queen caught them together? Copperhead went down to the door of the Queen's chamber and pounded as loudly as he could on it. Then he ran like hell for his bed in the harem.

Deidre placed a warning finger on Noisi's lips. 'Sh. Do you hear that?'

Noisi nodded.

'I wonder what it is. Who is pounding on the doors?'

Aynia woke up to the sound of someone pounding on her bedroom door. She realized that Moss and Sarkany had fallen asleep in her bed after taking her milk. It was a bad habit. They were supposed to return to the harem.

'Go get the door.' Aynia pushed lightly against Sarkany's shoulder.

Sarkany looked up, still in the haze of sleep. His facial hair was coming in now. And although Aynia was not especially fond of it, she let him keep the thick black moustache he was growing. All signs of his boyish looks were gone. A strong jawbone and high cheekbones framed full lips and deep set dark brown eyes. Still slim and leggy, his newly broadened shoulders were the only features that betrayed his physical strength. His voice had dropped at least an octave so that now when he spoke his accent rumbled pleasingly off his tongue. Sarkany had become a very masculine drone.

Aynia realized that Sarkany was still asleep. She turned to Moss, but he was impossible to rouse. The drug Copperhead had used would keep them unconscious until dawn. 'Where are my attendants? Where are my servants? And where is my Guard?' Aynia grumbled as she crossed the floor. She opened her door but no one was there.

She started to close her door but saw motion out of the corner of her eye. She waited with the door open only a crack. She heard whispering voices, male and female. But who knocked on her door? Did they mean to wake her? Fearing a possible trap, Aynia chose not to investigate. She closed the door and returned to her bed. She lay down but did not relax her guard.

'Goddesses I wish my Thorn was here.'

Every sound in the Royal Chambers seemed magnified. For the first time ever in her life Aynia felt alone and that was not a good feeling. She went about the chamber and lit candles. But even that did not ease her fears.

Many hours later when Moss and Sarkany finally awoke they found her sitting on a chair next to the bed with a sword in her hand and her stinger poised for action.

'Shall I return to the harem?'

'Yes, go now.'

'Do you think that she suspects?'

'If she did we would be in prison. Now listen to me carefully. No matter what anyone else tells you, I am never going to send for you. Don't ever risk coming here again.'

'I understand.' Prince Noisi dared a quick kiss on Deidre's lips then slipped back into the harem.

Camellia, roused by the sound of someone knocking on a door somewhere in the Royal Chambers, awoke. It took a second for her to come to her senses. When she did she realized that Copperhead was gone. She was glad. She despised cuddling and sharing a bed all night. She did wish that he would learn to close her corset after suckling though. Her poor nipples were getting very sensitive with the excessive nursing that he was indulging in lately. Being exposed to cold air didn't help matters. While she liked the sensations she felt as he suckled, she found that because of it her milk supply was increasing beyond the point of comfort. Her favorite corset simply would not hook across her chest anymore. But that was the least of her complaints with Copperhead. The Queen disliked him, he was a bad influence on the Queen's drones, his ideas on sex were tediously self-centered and worst of all he was a distraction from her job. One way or another she would have to find a way to be rid of the stupid little drone.

One matter was certain, she hadn't made Copperhead drone, because only a dose of Queen's milk brought wings. And Copperhead certainly had wings. She wondered how and where Copperhead got hold of the Queen's milk. But at least Camellia now knew that she truly wasn't responsible for Copperhead's transformation, and thus his future.

Still half asleep, Camellia just barely opened her door. It took a second to sink in. A drone was out of the harem! Actually, he had been out of the harem, but now he was sneaking back in, and he was coming out of Deidre's room. Camellia fumed. How dare one of her sisters commit treason? How dare one of them make a mockery of her management of the harem! Too angry to trust a confrontation with either the Prince or her sister, Camellia quietly shut her door and began to pace her room, a rare rage settling into her heart.

When Aynia entered the parlor for breakfast the following morning her back was stiff from sleeping in the chair by her bed all night. She wanted to cross-examine her staff about the incident the night before, but realized that there was something very wrong in her staff's demeanor. To her surprise, Camellia and Deidre seemed ready to come to blows. Heather was holding Camellia back, but not with any conviction, and Rose was standing across the room wringing her hands. Writing it off as a sisterly argument, Aynia took her place at the table and pretended to be oblivious to the tension in the air.

'How did everyone sleep?' Aynia asked.

She received only mumbled responses.

'I didn't sleep well either.' When no one responded to this statement Aynia decided to let the matter pass. At some point someone would confess to knocking on her door, or they would mention hearing it, but right now her staff was apparently too preoccupied to discuss the previous night. 'We have a full day today. I believe that we inspect the food stores today with Minister Adders-Tongue.'

'This should be interesting,' Deidre said, but without much conviction.

'Yes. Deidre, what is the status of our food collection effort?' Aynia asked, hoping to bring her staff's attention to more important matters than a family squabble.

Her faith was quickly rewarded. Camellia stomped off to the harem, Rose fussed over breakfast, and Deidre started to recite a detailed report on the current state of the Hive's food supplies.

'I wanted those two arrested last night!' Thane Adders-Tongue yelled, stabbing her fork deep into the heavy wooden table before her.

Cobra-Lily blanched, imagining the tines of the fork embedded in her flesh. 'The trap door was blocked off.'

'Impossible. Carman came through it not long ago.'

'Maybe they found it.'

'Why didn't you go into the Royal Chambers some other way?'

'If you have a suggestion I'd like to hear it. You're talking about raiding the Royal Palace at night with armed guards. The Royal Guard would've slaughtered us.' Cobra-Lily defended herself at the top of her voice. Everyone was always expecting the impossible from her. She was getting pretty damn tired of it.

'I needed for that arrest to happen before the Queen inspected the food stores.'

'Why? You've been working the food collectors like slaves since you became Minister. Heck, I even heard a rumor that you made the poorest workers bring their drones out to help with collection.'

'That wasn't a rumor.'

Cobra-Lily gasped. 'What kind of lowly worker would allow her drones to be exposed to other females?'

'Well, we are talking about common workers, and they lack the refined dignity of the upper classes.' Adders-Tongue observed. 'However, it doesn't make a difference, because no matter how much food we collect those damn storage chambers never fill up.'

'I guess that you're in for trouble today then,' Cobra-Lily observed without any apparent care.

'If you would have done your job last night no one would care about the bloody food today!' Adders-Tongue screeched.

'We can try again, but it'll have to be during the day. The Palace is locked up tight at night.'

'Do you not understand?' Adders-Tongue rose from her chair and advanced on Cobra-Lily. 'Does your tiny brain fail to comprehend plain Fairie speak? You were supposed to arrest the drone and Lady Deidre last night. Another day does me no good.'

'What was I supposed to do? Charge the Royal Palace and attack the Royal Guard?' Cobra-Lily demanded to know, her voice rising as high as Thane Adders-Tongue's. 'That would be suicide.'

'Not with Sage in command. If Thorn were here I would say that you acted correctly. However, Sage is inexperienced and frankly not very good at his job. If you had told him that you knew of treason being committed in the Queen's Royal Chambers the fool probably would have thrown open the doors for you and followed you in.' Adders-Tongue threw her cloth napkin on the table. 'Why do I attempt to teach you? In this entire clan there seems to be only one besides me capable of scheming to bring down the Queen, and he is a mere male. But all of this is beside the point. Today the Queen comes to inspect the food stores and today I will fail publicly. I'll be out of power by sundown.'

'I can't understand why we're doing this,' the Priestess Cerridwen questioned the High Priestess. 'We went to all of the trouble to take food stores out of the chamber on the sly. Now we place them back. What is the reasoning?'

The High Priestess looked at Cerridwen with haughty disdain. 'Are you so poorly trained that you believe you actually have a right to question me?'

Cerridwen wavered. Every night as she helped to move the day's collection of food from the food storage chambers into the Temple's hidden vaults she felt like she was betraying her Hive and her Queen. And every night she chastised herself for not protesting the actions of the Temple. Now that they were

270

placing food back where it belonged she still wondered at the correctness of their actions. This time she was determined not to feel guilt for not asking for some sort of justification.

'Your Worship, I understand that this jeopardizes any future that I might have in the Temple, but I must protest. I don't feel that this is right. I can't face my Goddesses or my Queen knowing what I've done.'

The High Priestess sighed. She knew that this one would be a problem. How someone managed to be promoted this far in the Temple and not become a cynic was beyond her. Then again, the High Priestess had never in her life, not for one moment, actually believed in the Goddesses. She went into service in the Temple because it was the only route to power for one of her low birth.

The real reason for the food manipulation was simple. The High Priestess had initiated the campaign to remove food from the official food storage vaults simply in order to destroy Adders-Tongue politically. It had nothing to do with the constant feuding between the Queen and the leader of the Opposition Party. This was a fight going back many years between the Temple and the Opposition Party and in particular Thane Adders-Tongue, who harangued the Temple from the floor of Parliament as often as she denounced the Queen.

'I shouldn't have to justify myself to you Cerridwen, but I can see that you're a Fairie of good conscience, a good example to us all. No Fairie should ever blindly follow orders.' The High Priestess fought the urge to roll her eyes. 'The reason why we took the food was to prepare for an emergency evacuation of the Hive.' The High Priestess knew that the Temple's secret storage was built to insure the survival of the Temple in times of crisis. There had never been an emergency evacuation of the Hive, but Cerridwen was ignorant of that historical fact.

Cerridwen's eyes went wide. 'Is there a threat to the Hive?'

'Yes. Haven't you heard about the human problem?'

'Well, yes, I did hear news, but I didn't really think that things were all that serious.'

271

'And its precisely thinking like that which will leave the Hive unprepared to deal with real emergency! Do you think that emergencies send advance warning?'

'But why put it all back?' Cerridwen was not going to back down now. She was in deep enough trouble that one more question wouldn't change her fate.

'Because I failed to realize the depths to which Adders-Tongue would stoop,' the High Priestess admitted. 'The common workers are extremely angry right now. Adders-Tongue forced them to bring their males out of their harems to assist with harvest.'

Cerridwen's sharp intake of breath was enough to show how she felt about the matter.

'Yes, you can imagine! The entire Hive is growing angrier by the day. As you and I both know, an angry Hive is a rebellious Hive. We've all heard the stories. Once the workers decide to revolt against the Food Minister they usually take over the Temple, destroy Parliament, execute the nobility, and kill the Queen too. This Hive is abuzz with resentment. Many of the food collectors are coming today to witness the inspection of the vaults first hand. If they see that all of their hard work has been in vain, and that they will have to continue to utilize their drones in the harvest, and that there still isn't enough food for the Hive to survive the next winter, well, may the Goddesses have mercy on our souls.'

'Amen,' Cerridwen intoned with true feeling. 'I beg your pardon Your Grace. I didn't understand the situation. I will of course lend my full support.'

'Very well. And Cerridwen, don't question my orders again. I will not always feel like wasting my time teaching you about real life.'

'Yes Your Grace.' Cerridwen bowed and returned to her work. But even with the explanation she felt that there was something very wrong about what the Priestesses were doing. The High Priestess often ridiculed her ethics. But Cerridwen thought that leaders, more than commoners, needed to hold themselves up to high moral standards. For the first time since going into service to the Temple and becoming the High Priestess's lover, Cerridwen refused to accept what the High Priestess told her to believe.

For the first and perhaps last time in her life Thane Adders-Tongue offered up a genuine prayer to the Goddesses. She stood to the right of the Queen as the High Priestess went through the ritual prayers before the first food vault was opened.

The Queen, as usual, wore an expression of determined detachment.

'She knows, she knows,' Adders-Tongue couldn't stop her mind from saying over and over again.

Below the dais, in the center of the Hive, an unruly mob of Hive workers was also assembled to witness this inspection. While the Ruling Party in Parliament represented the Queen and Seelie Court; the nobility, and the Opposition Party theoretically championed the common workers, it was Thane Adders-Tongue that had the crowd's ire, not the Queen. Adders-Tongue was uncomfortably aware of that fact.

Once the prayers were complete the High Priestess made a great show of turning the combination lock on the front of the vault. The sound of the pins falling into place resonated through the inner walls of the Hive. Slowly the massive door was pulled open.

Queen Aynia looked into the vault. It wasn't as full as it should be, but it wasn't empty either.

Adders-Tongue blinked her eyes. She had no idea where all the food came from, but right now she felt like falling to the floor and kissing the sacks of stored food. Her political life was spared, for now. Recovering quickly, she turned to Aynia. 'Your Highness, are you satisfied? Did you think to find the vaults empty?'

Aynia was notified that the vaults were empty, but she expected some sort of grandstand play by Adders-Tongue this morning, so she was well prepared to find exactly what she saw.

'Actually Thane Adders-Tongue, We did expect to find this on Our inspection, because it has come to Our ears that you actually forced our workers to expose their drones to help with the harvest.'

The crowd began to murmur. If the Queen hadn't mentioned the subject of the drones the workers would have, and the workers weren't planning to discuss the matter quietly over tea and cakes.

Aynia raised her voice so that it could be heard by the entire crowd. 'We command that the use of drones cease immediately! It's obvious that our food stores are not what they should be, but the situation isn't dire enough to warrant the use of drones. This intolerable attack on the sanctity of the worker's harems must stop!'

If Aynia planned to say any more her words would not have been heard. The workers of the Hive burst into wild cheers. The roar was deafening. 'Long Live the Queen!'

Adders-Tongue held her hand up for silence. 'I was going to propose the same course of action. It was the Queen who…. 'Adders-Tongue's speech was drowned out by loud boos.

Queen Aynia turned and waved once more to the crowd, then left the dais with the High Priestess and the Royal Guard. Adders-Tongue, realizing that she was left alone with a crowd of a thousand workers who hated her, quickly retreated up the stairs of Parliament. As the door slammed shut behind her she sighed in relief. Parliament, at least she was safe from having to deal with the common workers there.

CHAPTER 11

Thorn thanked the Goddesses that he had one of the Royal Steeds to ride. He would have been able to cover at most ten miles in a day walking. If he had wings he could have searched over even grater distances than he could on the miniature gray stallion, but the price of wings was too high.

Thorn's first move was to ride south. He needed an accurate picture of just how many humans were fleeing north along the coast. Within a week he had a grim count. There were thousands. They were all on the move and they all carried their household possessions. The humans were looking to make permanent farmsteads in the highlands.

After a week of scouting he turned to the west and began to search with renewed vigor for a safe haven for the Hive. He could see with his own eyes the urgent need to move the Hive to safety.

Thorn rode for days in solitude. He missed the steady busy hum of Hive life but he also found that he loved this freedom. While his heart ached to be near Aynia he thought that this quest was the greatest gift that his Queen could have bestowed upon him. He was a soldier, built for action. This was action. He enjoyed an element of danger. This journey was fraught with peril. Most of all he enjoyed being free of the court intrigue and political games played out in the Palace and in Parliament.

The countryside was beautiful this time of year. With winter just past the rivers and streams flowed fast with cold, pure water. The hillsides were lush green with new growth, and everywhere the world was waiting with impatience to bloom. As he traveled he could feel the vibrations of energy from the earth as she prepared to rise from her winter's nap.

Thorn rode from one land-bound loch to another, but found no island in those waters that matched the Hive's needs. Once, amid the mist-shrouded waters of Loch Awe, he thought that he sighted the perfect island. Fashioning a raft from logs on the shore of the loch, Thorn crossed the waters to inspect the island.

It was not meant to be. The island showed signs of humans, a fire ring here, a rusted metal tool there. While there was no permanent settlement on the island, which was far too small to support a single human family farm, in this time of danger a single man hiding from the English Army might take refuge in such a place as this. Despite his desire to return to Aynia's side, and his oft changing decision to remain as he was or to become her drone, Thorn would not go home without succeeding. He would never place his own needs ahead of the Hive. Turning his horse south and towards Ireland, Thorn's quest stretched into a third week.

At Kilmartin he ran into a band of traveling Irish Fairie folk. He took refuge with them with some relief. Fairie were seldom alone. He missed the singing, the tales, and the close companionship of the Hive on cold evenings after dinner. Thorn was surprised that Irish Fairie knew his name. They even seemed honored to have him in their company.

'We travel quite a bit between Scotland and Ireland,' the lead female informed him. 'Our Hive was destroyed quite awhile ago. Now we rove in these small bands. Occasionally we all meet up and have ourselves a grand party, but mostly we live in small groups.'

'Our own Hive is in danger from the humans. I'm seeking a place to move the Hive.' Thorn explained his reason for being out in the elements.

'The humans have a far reach.' The elder female agreed.

'I'm looking for an island, something that would not interest a human, but big enough for the Hive.'

'There are small islands north of the Island of Skye, in the sounds. You should search there.'

'But those are in the sea.'

The Irish Fairie shrugged. 'This earth was not designed to our wishes. You must take refuge where you can. Take my word Captain Thorn; do not try to fight the humans.'

'You speak from experience?'

'Bitter experience,' The Fairie turned her eyes to their fire and began to speak. 'I know now that we should have moved our Hive, but we would not. We were stubborn, stiff necked, and proud. Now we have no Hive, and will never have a home again.'

Thorn was too shocked to comment, but he nodded his head and answered 'I will mark your words and go north.'

'Good. Now, let's have a song, and a tale or two. Then when you've paid for your supper our Priestess will look to your signs and tell you of your future.'

Thorn possessed a good enough voice, not a great one, but pleasant. He sang two songs while standing in front of the fire. Then he drank a quantity of beer to help his throat. For the small children in the group who peered at him from the shadows with wide eyes, Thorn told the story of the Mountain King, and how Queen Aynia's brave father fought off the Mountain King in order to save his Queen's life. He described the valiant death of Prince Thistle from Lanark Hive in moving prose that set his audience to tears. It was an oft-told story, a favorite Fairie Tale, but familiarity with the story did not stop his audience from enjoying it.

'Is the Mountain King going to kill all the Fairie?' A wide-eyed boy asked.

'He would if he could,' Thorn admitted.

'Is there no way to defeat him?' A girl in her middle years asked solemnly.

'There is a way, but only the Queen knows the weapon.'

'Tell another story, tell us another!' The children cried out, but their fathers took them to bed so that the females and Thorn could discuss important matters.

'We promised you a reward for your song and story,' the lead female said once the children and males were gone. 'Mother, tell this male his future.'

'If you are by, come to the Hive at Balnacra. The Queen would welcome you.' Thorn extended an invitation. He understood that the biggest problem that Aynia faced was convincing the workers of the Hive that the move was necessary. If these Fairie told the history of their own Hive to groups of workers in the pubs back home in Balnacra it might help to convince the masses to accept the idea of moving the Hive.

'We travel to Balnacra now. Our seer tells us that our services will be in demand by the new Queen.'

'How so?' Thorn asked, worried. These were Bean Sidhe, professional wailers. They did not bring death, but they followed it like a dog on its master's heels.

'As story tellers, of course. That's what we do. We tell stories.'

Thorn laughed with relief. 'The Queen has a story teller named Lady Rose. She tells more stories than the Queen cares to hear.' But he was surprised that his own thoughts mirrored those of this odd Fairie Band.

The female Fairie were dead serious. 'Telling stories is a great art. It is an important role. How else do you impart news to the common workers? Allegorical tales have a long and noble history.'

'We will not be telling allegorics.' An old female said in her whispery voice.

'No, we will not. We will be telling a history,' the lead female agreed.

'Aye,' the other females echoed sadly.

Thorn didn't know what to make of these mystics, who seemed to know already about the needs of the Hive at Balnacra, so he nodded politely. 'Well, I'm sure that our good Queen will welcome you to the Hive.'

'She must hear of Lanark!' The old female cried out and began the keening wail of the banshee.

'Lanark? What of Lanark Hive?'

'It brought us to this shore.' And they began to tell Thorn of the fate of Lanark. As the fire died down and each Fairie sat in silent contemplation, the lead female decided to change the subject.

'I'd like to have a look at this new Fairie Queen. I hear that she has hair like a flame and skin like pearls. Is it true?' she asked.

Thorn thought for a moment on Aynia's coloring. 'It is true that she has reddish hair and pale skin,' he admitted cautiously, 'but I wouldn't call her hair fire or liken her skin to pearls. How do these stories get so exaggerated?'

'I hear that Queen Aynia is devout to the old ways. I hear that her milk flows sweet and true for the Hive.'

Thorn thought for a second on the sweetness of Aynia's juices, not her milk. Around these mystic he needed to guard his thoughts. Sometimes they seemed to read his mind.

Before Thorn could answer the elderly female sat by him and took his hand. She peered at his palm and muttered to herself.

'What do you see?' The lead female asked.

The Priestess looked up. 'I see that his Queen will accuse him of betraying her.'

Thorn withdrew his hand. 'No!'

The Priestess raised a warning finger to Thorn. 'What is written is not yet done, but try as you might the Queen of your heart will accuse you of betrayal.'

'My hand does not tell this lie,' Thorn protested in despair.

'My eyes read what you will not see! You will never lie with the Queen who makes you drone, Captain Thorn. You will despise her for the gift of milk, and in the end you will part ways.'

'I will never be a drone,' Thorn snapped, and as he said it he knew that it was true. He wanted Aynia but could never bring himself to be a drone.

'You can not deny the fates Thorn.'

'I would never betray my Queen.'

'You will, or at least she will accuse you of it.'

Thorn took his pack and went to his horse. He was angry and embarrassed. How could he be accused of betraying Aynia?

'Don't take umbrage to our words Thorn. Stay and share our camp for the rest of the night.'

'I will not betray her!'

The females didn't speak, but they knew that their Priestess had true sight, a gift from the Goddesses. Thorn might fight his fate, but his Queen would accuse him of betrayal.

Aynia one again heard knocking on her chamber door in the middle of the night. She got up out of bed and flew down the hallway so that her steps would make no sound. Through a slit in the bottom of a door she saw light from a chamber. Suddenly the light was extinguished. Hovering for a short time, Aynia took a torch from the wall and landed softly in front of the door. It was Camellia's room.

Aynia opened the door as noiselessly as she could. Camellia lay in her bed, deeply asleep. Copperhead, the shamed Royal Messenger, the one who let his Aunt Adders-Tongue see Aynia's letters to her old attendants, lay next to Camellia in the bed. Aynia had all but ordered Camellia to throw him out of the Royal Chambers. She was not pleased to see him still here.

Aynia peered down at the couple. This lad was not Camellia's drone. Technically this was a violation worthy of a public flogging for the both of them, but the females in these cases were never actually flogged. The males frequently were punished severely as a warning to other males. As Copperhead was related to Adders-Tongue Aynia wouldn't mind seeing him and his family publicly humiliated. However, Aynia was not inclined to bring this matter out to the public. It would only reflect badly on Camellia.

Thinking on the knocking on her chamber door, Aynia knew that someone wanted her to wake and see something. Was this what she was meant to see? This scene was hardly a secret. Aynia knew about the drone Copperhead and Camellia. Perhaps she was meant to witness something else, but had instead come to this wrong chamber. Aynia wondered for a moment. Then she noticed. Camellia was fast asleep, but Copperhead was not. He was pretending to sleep. His breath was uneven and too shallow for a sleeper. There was much to think on here. Aynia took her torch and left the room, silently closing the door behind her.

Across the hallway Deidre held her breath. 'Do not speak, do not speak,' she whispered into Noisi's ear.

'We do nothing but talk. There is nothing to be ashamed of.'

'There is everything to be ashamed of. I can barely stop myself from touching you. You're so beautiful. I dream of you every night.'

Prince Noisi stopped Deidre from talking by kissing her. Deidre knew that she should stop him, but somehow she let herself continue to kiss the beautiful Prince.

'This is wrong, it is so wrong.'

'If we are already condemned, let us a least have a reason to die,' Prince Noisi said. He lifted Deidre and carried her to her bed. Lying down beside her he started to unhook the front of her corset.

Deidre pushed away his hand 'No! If I die I want to face the Goddesses with a clear conscience. Go. Return to the harem and stay there.'

Noisi rose from the bed. 'Okay. I'll go. But remember, you sent me away before, and then you called me back again. Next time you send for me I will not stop myself, no matter what you say.'

'I will not send for you again.'

'That's what you say now. I can see desire in your eyes. I can see your resolve melting.'

'Go away.' Deidre hissed.

'As you wish,' Noisi smiled and slipped out of the room. Once back in the harem he lay down on his cot and thought about the evening. It went exactly as Copperhead predicted. Deidre still denied sending for him. As Copperhead explained, this was a game that the females played to make sure that their males were wild with desire before making love. And, as Copperhead explained, next time she called for Noisi, Noisi should not take no for an answer. Males were stronger than females. He could easily overpower Deidre and force her onto the bed. Tonight proved that point, and she didn't really fight back when he picked her up. Copperhead swore that even the dominatrix Camellia liked to be held down and entered roughly, sometimes even allowing herself to be gagged while they played the mating game.

Noisi was thankful that Copperhead was willing to impart all of this wisdom. Noisi wanted to mate with Deidre. He thought of nothing else. Some days he walked around the harem hard from sunrise to sunset. Next time Lady Deidre sent for him he wouldn't take no for an answer. After all, according to Copperhead, that was the way the game was played.

The following day while taking her daily stroll through the harem Aynia noticed that Noisi and Copperhead were seated in an alcove of the common room. They were talking to each other with such seriousness that they didn't notice that the Queen was in the room.

'Lady Camellia.' Aynia caught the attention of the Mistress of the Harem.

'Yes my Queen?'

'I don't like seeing one of his ilk in my harem. He's a bad influence.'

Camellia knew that Aynia meant Copperhead. If only she could think up some way to get rid of him without his family causing a huge scene over it.

'He doesn't pay me proper respect and he influences my drone with his poor behavior.'

'They are great friends Majesty.' Camellia acknowledged.

'See that he never crosses my sight again.'

'Yes my Queen,' Camellia bowed. There were poor females who couldn't afford a bride price, but even the poor were too proud to take a shamed drone. After all, once a male was used he lost all his value. Perhaps one of the brothels would take him on. But this wasn't the time to think about Copperhead. The Queen was angry. 'Shall I punish the drone?'

'Yes. He mustn't forget his place. But Camellia, use a lighter hand than you did on Sarkany. I want Noisi punished, not scarred.'

'Don't worry my Queen. The first punishment meted out in the harem is always the harshest. After that there is little need to apply the whip hard enough to draw blood.'

'I have a meeting with my Cabinet. Please attend to your duties.' Aynia turned and left her harem. Before she was seated in her parlor Copperhead was banned from the harem and Prince Noisi was learning that being a drone did not necessarily mean protection from the Mistress of the Harem.

He would never again fail to rise for his Queen.

Adders-Tongue, miraculously saved from almost certain political death, was not about to let another chance pass to bring down the Queen. Not that she currently had any weapons to use against the Queen. They were still trying to catch Deidre and Noisi together.

However, if political life taught Adders-Tongue one thing, it was that a lie, no matter how grossly unfair, took on a life well after the truth was proved. It was the fault of the common workers. They liked the lies more than the truth. They held on with fascination to rumors long disproved, spreading them back and forth through their pubs. Having no true rumors with which to bring down the Queen, Adders-Tongue was now quite willing to start a lie circulating. The problem was how to do it. Thane Monarda for some reason no longer seemed to be such a determined gossip. Or at least, the stories that she spread were not the ones that Adders-Tongue's sister, Lady Snakeroot, leaked to Thane Monarda.

The idea of frequenting a pub with common workers being beneath Thane Adders-Tongue, she was left with only one great public forum in which to spread lies. With great malice in her heart Adders-Tongue prepared to take on the Queen on the very floor of Parliament.

'Where is Thorn?' Aynia asked with irritation. 'He's been gone over three weeks.'

'He won't return until he's found a new location for the Hive,' Heather counseled. While Aynia was impatient for Thorn to return Heather was more than grateful that he was still away. The Vernal Equinox was only nine days away. With Thorn gone there was good reason to believe that Aynia would agree to mate with one of her drones. If he returned to the Hive before that, who knew what the foolish young Queen would do?

'Where is Deidre? She should be here.'

'She is, um, indisposed Majesty.'

'She can not be indisposed for me. I'm aware that she's involved in some disagreement with Camellia.'

'Actually, Your Highness, we are all at odds with our sister these days.' Rose admitted.

Aynia sighed. 'I don't care what has come between you four, but I expect none of you to let it interfere with serving me. If Deidre can not bring herself to face me then she should leave my service immediately.'

'I will tell her Majesty,' Rose said quietly.

'See that you do. I expect her to be present at our next meeting.'

'She will,' Heather promised grimly.

'There is much being said about me from the floor of Parliament right now. I must have her ears there. I understand that I am under daily attack from Thane Adders-Tongue.'

'Not just you Majesty. She is also attacking the Temple.

'What have they done to raise her ire?'

Adders-Tongue protested that last week's sermon was somehow a reference to the idea of enlarging the Temple at the expense of Parliament. She said that you were clearly in collusion with the High Priestess in a bid to destroy Parliament.'

'Good Goddesses, will that mistake haunt me to my grave?'

Heather smiled. 'Actually, the High Priestess gave her solemn word in services yesterday that the Temple would never again broach the subject of enlarging its space. She announced the addition of two new services each day to accommodate the worshippers.'

'How can this be?' Aynia couldn't believe her good luck.

'I have no idea, but I don't trust that High Priestess any more than I trust Thane Adders-Tongue. They are both very powerful females and they don't have your best interests at heart,' Rose said.

Aynia laughed out loud. 'Agreed.'

'I must protest Rose, how can you say that about the High Priestess?' Heather was indignant.

'I know what I see, and hear what I hear.'

'You're as bad as Camellia,' Heather snorted. 'But it's true that Adders-Tongue is always up to no good. To believe otherwise is to live in a fool's paradise.'

'Welcome to the dark side Rose,' Camellia quipped. 'Now I believe that our next order of business is a report from our new Captain of the Guard, Sage.'

'Bring him in.'

'Should he be attending the full meetings?' Rose asked. 'Captain Thorn did.'

Everyone looked to Aynia.

'I'm aware that Captain Thorn has been gone much longer than I expected. Until I feel comfortable with this temporary Captain in his role I prefer that he not take part in these discussions. Captain Thorn earned his place at this table. Sage is still unproven.'

The sisters didn't comment. Each day that passed without Thorn's return was a cause for concern. The Queen flatly refused to discuss the growing possibility that Thorn would never return. Despite her inability to confess her fears to her attendants, the Queen was showing signs of distress. She was refusing to attend many state functions. Her appetite was diminished. Worst of all, Aynia seemed disinterested in the Hive.

'Bitch! That fucking bitch!' The High Priestess screamed.
Cerridwen cowered.

'How dare she refuse to give us milk?'

'Her attendants say that she is too busy today,' Cerridwen attempted to mollify the High Priestess.

'Oh no, I don't believe a word of it. She's just like her damned mother! Fucking royalty!'

'Your Grace!' Cerridwen was shocked to the core.

'What do you know? You're nobility aren't you?' The High Priestess pointed an accusatory finger at Cerridwen.

'Only a minor title,' Cerridwen admitted timidly.

'But you're still of the Seelie Court. So you don't know what it's like. I was born a common worker. My position isn't an accident of birth. No one simply ceded power to me. Every bit of power I wield I paid for in a hard school. But as much power as I have it's a poor shadow of the power of Parliament, the power of the Seelie Court, the power of the Queen. I'm like a dog begging for scraps from their banquet. I'm reduced to bargaining for the Queen's milk. I'm sick of it. I thought that I could use the faith of this Queen to seize more power. But already she denies me my proper due.'

'Your Grace, please,' Cerridwen begged.

The High Priestess shook her head. 'No more, I tell you, no more. I will never beg for scraps again. Queen Aynia has shown her true face. And I am not pleased.'

Prince Noisi woke up with a start. Someone was in his private room, sitting on the bed with him. That someone placed their hand over his mouth. Struggling against the hands that held him down, the Prince tried to break free.

'Sh! It's me, Copperhead.'

'What are you doing?' Noisi demanded. 'Why did you wake me up?'

'Everyone is asleep.'

'Yes, so was I,' the Prince said grumpily.

'So we have to be quiet.'

'What for?'

'Well,' Copperhead admitted, 'I was lying in bed, and Lady Camellia is asleep. I couldn't seem to fall asleep, so I suckled from her breasts.'

'Thanks for the update. Can I go back to sleep now?'

'But suckling always gets me hard.'

'Me too,' Noisi sighed, although he was rarely called in to suckle from the Queen.

'But I get punished for masturbating,' Copperhead pouted.

'Me too.'

'I had a great idea. Why is it that they know we've been playing with ourselves? The stain. I swear no matter how hard you hide it, Lady Camellia finds it. So I had this great idea.'

Prince Noisi was waking up, and was growing interested in what Copperhead was saying. 'What is it?'

'I'd rather show you then tell you. Your bed is too narrow. Come here to the floor over by your fireplace, on the rug.' Copperhead pulled Prince Noisi over to the plush Persian rug in front of the fireplace. The fire lived only inside the logs now. Behind white ash the fire glowed deep orange, giving off little light to the room.

'Take off your clothes.'

'Aren't you banned from the harem?'

'Sh. If I'm caught in here you'll be in big trouble.'

Copperhead and Noisi knelt down facing each other on the rug.

'Now what?'

Copperhead looked at the handsome Prince in front of him. Noisi was the perfection of male beauty. He had broad shoulders, a narrow waist, long legs, and a nicely rounded ass. Copperhead was shorter, and smaller overall. While better than average on looks, Copperhead knew that his plain brown features did not possess the same stunning looks of the Swedish Prince. 'Have you ever wondered what it feels like for the Queen when you suckle on her breast?'

'I guess I didn't think about it too much.'

Copperhead leaned over and sucked on Noisi's right nipple.

Noisi sighed. 'That's nice.'

Copperhead licked and sucked the left nipple, then pulled back. 'Now do mine.'

'Okay.' Noisi complied. 'Now what?'

Copperhead kissed Noisi on the lips at first with hesitation, then with more force until he was able to slide his tongue into the Prince's mouth. As they kissed he slid his hands down along Noisi's muscled abdomen and to his crotch to check if Noisi was getting hard.

'You know, this would be much nicer if we lay down,' Copperhead suggested.

Copperhead lay on top of Noisi. This time he aggressively kissed the Prince while using his hands to feel Noisi's body. Grasping the Prince's penis in one hand, Copperhead gave it a couple of strokes. 'You're so hard already.'

'Yes, but I don't see how this is different from masturbating.'

'Turn over.'

'I can't.'

'Then put this pillow under your hips.' Noisi did as he was told, but he wondered what Copperhead had in mind. 'Now what?'

Copperhead slowly parted Noisi's ass cheeks and bent down to flick his tongue over Noisi's anus. 'Do you like that?' Copperhead whispered.

'Oh Goddesses yes.'

'Let me taste you some more. Spread your legs a little more for me.'

Noisi perched himself up on his knees. He was moaning as Copperhead's tongue flicked expertly over his anus, then as Copperhead stiffened his tongue and darted it deeper into Noisi. 'Don't stop,' Noisi begged as Copperhead pulled back for a moment.

'Turn back over.'

'But I like that.'

'Turn over,' Copperhead swatted the Prince's buttocks once, then again much harder so that the sharp sound resonated in the chamber.

'Don't do that,' Prince Noisi muttered, but he was completely at Copperhead's mercy.

Copperhead saw a drop of salty moisture at the tip of Noisi's penis. He tasted it, running his tongue down the shaft of Noisi's penis until he came to the Prince's balls. Copperhead took first one testicle, then another, into his mouth and sucked on them. The soft skin had a musky odor, not unpleasant, that filled Copperhead's nose.

'I swear, I'm going to come,' Noisi warned Copperhead.

Copperhead hesitated only a second before taking Noisi's penis into his mouth. Using his tongue to lubricate, Copperhead kept his lips tight around the shaft. He worked up and down, flicking his tongue around the head while moving his lips in a stroking pattern.

Noisi moaned louder and louder. Suddenly he jerked his hips up, grabbing Copperhead's head and pumping into Copperhead's mouth as he exploded.

Copperhead licked the head of Noisi's penis until there was nothing left. 'You see, I swallow, and no evidence is left.'

Noisi smiled while enjoying the euphoria. 'That was great.'

'I'm glad that you enjoyed it.'

'Wonderful.'

Copperhead moved up beside Noisi and kissed him again, long and slow. 'But of course, I'm still very hard.'

'Oh, yes you are.' Noisi felt Copperhead's stiff penis against his thigh. 'Should I do for you what you did for me?'

'We can start out that way. First I'm going to lie down, and I want you to lick my ass like I did for you.' Copperhead turned over and spread his legs.

'I'm not so sure about this.'

'Listen, if you expect me to ever suck your cock again you had better get used to the idea of sucking mine too. This works both ways Prince.'

'Fine. I'll do it. But I won't like it.'

Copperhead didn't care. He closed his eyes as Prince Noisi licked his anus. Copperhead could have spent all night in that position, but he turned over. 'Wait a second; I want to sit in a chair.' Copperhead pulled himself up into a chair. 'Crawl across the floor to me on your hands and knees.'

'Why?' Noisi asked.

'Because tonight I'm your master, and I tell you what to do. Crawl to me.'

Prince Noisi crawled over to Copperhead.

Spreading his legs, Copperhead pointed down to his crotch. 'Now suck my balls.' Copperhead took a riding crop he borrowed from Camellia's cabinet and flicked it across Noisi's ass. 'Good boy,' Copperhead crooned. 'That's a good Prince. Now take my penis into your mouth and lick the whole shaft. You can take in more.'

'I'll gag,' Noisi complained.

Copperhead smacked the riding crop against Noisi. 'No you won't. I told you to take it in. Open you mouth and suck my dick. Take it deeper, or I'll use this little whip against your balls.'

'Okay. I'll do it,' Noisi grumbled as he took Copperhead's penis into his mouth.

Copperhead planned on teaching the Prince a few other new tricks during the evening, but the sight of the beautiful male's mouth on his penis was too much for Copperhead.

Copperhead pulled out of Noisi's mouth and jerked off the last few strokes. He came on the Prince's face.

'Why did you do that?'

'Lick it off of your face. You did pretty well for a first timer,' Copperhead admitted. 'We'll work on your technique in later sessions.'

'But you came.'

'That isn't enough Prince Noisi. You have to learn how to keep me hard as long as possible. You have to learn all the different ways to pleasure your partner.'

'There's more?'

'Haven't you ever sneaked a peek into Moss and Sarkany's chamber?'

'No,' Noisi admitted. 'Do you mean that they do this?'

Copperhead rolled his eyes. 'This would just be a warm up for them. Spy on them, and learn. Then you can show me next time that I visit.'

'Come tomorrow night,' Noisi pleaded with Copperhead.

'Maybe I will, maybe I won't. I have to be very careful about coming into the harem. When I come here to teach you these lessons I want you to remember one thing. I'm in charge. You must do everything I tell you to. If I ask you to lick my anus, you do it for as long as I tell you to. If I tell you to suck on my balls, suck on them. Don't ever say no to me or I will turn you in to Camellia. Do you know how she punishes drones that spill seed that belongs to the Queen?'

'No,' Noisi admitted.

'I would tell you, but you'd die of fright,' Copperhead bluffed. 'Now, come kiss me goodnight, and make it good so that I'll want to come back again.'

Noisi dutifully kissed Copperhead. Copperhead grasped Noisi's buttocks and kneaded them, grinding his pelvis into Noisi's. 'I'll be back in a couple of nights. Don't touch yourself between now and then. I want you to be so hard that you nearly come at the sight of me.'

'Our Queen,' Adders-Tongue began her speech in Parliament, 'seems bored. Have you noticed lately her complete lack of interest in the business of running the Hive? But is it actually boredom? Or is she ill?'

'I object!' The Leader of the Ruling Party stood up, as did many of her brethren on the right side of the aisle. 'You pass along another rumor of the Queen's illness. Does this game of spreading falsehoods not tire you? Our Queen is in robust health.'

'Then why does she refuse to bed her own harem?' Adders-Tongue asked in her booming voice.

Again the Ruling Party's benches came alive with loud objections.

'And how would you know something so intimate about our Queen? More lies from the Opposition!'

Adders-Tongue smiled her smug little smile. 'We shall see. I doubt that the Queen will mate this Vernal Equinox. If she doesn't fly you will all know the truth of my words!'

At this point Adders-Tongue didn't care if anyone believed her. What was important was to get rumors spreading through the hive. Before long the workers would believe that their Queen was refusing to give them a Princess.

'She is the Ice Queen, and she's letting her hard heart jeopardize the future of this Hive!' Content that she had done some damage today, Adders-Tongue took her seat.

The workers in the Hive didn't believe that their Queen was ill, but the remark about her emotional detachment hit home. Her ability to maintain a calm demeanor in any situation struck many as a little odd. Expecting, for some strange reason, that Aynia's red hair indicated a fiery temperament, workers were frequently disappointed by their Queen's lack of interest in displaying a temper. They well remembered the late Queen, who often stood at her Throne shouting commands in a Royal fit of pique. The new Queen was not nearly as entertaining.

'Let me go play cards,' Copperhead pouted.

'The Queen told me to keep you out of the harem. She thinks that you're a bad influence on Prince Noisi.' Camellia said sternly to Copperhead.

'But I'm so bored!'

'Play solitaire then.'

'I have a better idea.' Copperhead got on his knees and crawled under the desk where Camellia was working. He butted his head between her knees until she spread her legs apart. He pulled her panties to the side and began sucking on her labia.

'I don't have time for this.' Camellia said a bit grumpily, but she didn't push his head away. The sight of his head between her legs under the table was enough to excite her. Idly she thought about placing a mirror across from her desk so that she could watch him from another angle.

Camellia wondered at Copperhead's need to constantly taste her juices. Every morning and night he nuzzled his way between her thighs. For some reason she just let him do it. She had to admit that he was getting quite good. Even now she felt a tingle of pleasure building as he used his tongue to roughly lick at her.

'Can I nurse?' Copperhead asked.

'No,' Camellia said with a tone that usually made drones shiver. Once he'd become drone she saw no need to keep him away from her breasts. But every time he suckled she wondered how she'd gotten herself into this mess in the first place. Then she remembered. He'd gotten her into this mess.

'Come on. I need to. It's been all day. Aren't your breasts getting heavy with milk?' Copperhead whined.

Camellia knew that they were. In fact, as Copperhead began to work between her legs both of her nipples began leaking milk. She hated the feeling of wet leather, so she unhooked the cups of her corset. 'I really don't have time for this.'

Copperhead knew that the battle was won. He climbed out from under the desk. 'You can work while I suckle.' To prove this he got on his knees and began to take her nipple in to his mouth.

'No. You know the rules.' Camellia pulled her breast away.

'Come on. What could I have possible done? I'm locked in this room all day by myself. I couldn't have broken any rules.'

'Males are always breaking rules. Merely arguing with me is breaking a rule. Go get the strap.'

Copperhead stood up and walked over to the cabinet of whips. 'Which one do you want?' He asked over his shoulder.

Camellia came up behind Copperhead and reached down into his hose, cupping his balls in her hand. He felt her breasts pressing against his back, with a few drops of milk wetting his skin. 'Which one would you like?' She asked in a low voice.

Copperhead turned around to face his mistress. 'What I would like?' He asked in confusion.

'You're already getting hard, but I notice that you get harder when I punish you. Since you enjoy it, tell me what would give you the most pleasure.' Camellia kissed Copperhead, pushing her tongue into his mouth. Her hand slipped back down inside his hose and kneaded his buttocks.

'What I would really like,' Copperhead started to confess, but suddenly got shy.

'Come here,' Camellia pulled Copperhead over to her bed and put him over her knees. She pulled down his hose so that his bottom was bared. 'You can tell me, and you must tell me,' she told him as she smacked his buttocks smartly with her open hand.

'It's embarrassing.'

'We share the most intimate moments of our lives. You must be willing to tell me what I ask you.' Camellia pushed apart his legs while he was still over her knees. Spreading his ass cheeks with her thumb and ring fingers, she stroked his anus with her index finger.

Copperhead gasped and wriggled.

'Is this it? Do you want me to strap on one of my dildos and take you? Does that feel good when I stroke you with my finger? Do you want me to fill you up?' Camellia loved this part of her job, when the males finally surrendered to her. She loved caressing the hot cheeks of their buttocks after she got them a dark pink, but most of all she loved to watch the sensitive skin of the anus react to her every touch.

Copperhead struggled and got up out of Camellia's lap. His hose, gathered at his knees, stopped him from taking anything but small steps. His very hard penis stood at full attention, pointing right at Camellia. 'No. Don't do that.'

'You like it.'

'No! I want to do that to you! I want to wrestle you down to the floor and force your legs apart. I want for you to fight me, scratch me, and bite me. I want to turn you over and take you so hard up the ass that you scream for me to stop.'

Camellia burst into laughter. 'Is that what you think that you want? It isn't. You love to be dominated. You get hard watching me discipline the harem. Do you think that I don't know about how you watch from the window and masturbate while I have the other males tied to my whipping post? And every day we play this stupid game where you break rules right in front of me just so that I'll punish you. So I thought that we'd skip the rule breaking and just get to the discipline. I know what you need, and what you want. Admit it; you really love it when I make your ass go red.' Camellia walked over to Copperhead and slapped at his penis. 'You're dying for me to strap one of those on and spread your cheeks apart.'

'No!' Copperhead protested as he backed away into the desk. Turning around, he fell face forward across the tabletop.

Camellia wordlessly picked a dildo and slipped it into the crotch of her corset. She took her time lubricating the tip and most of the length. Copperhead didn't move.

'Well, now you're going to have to beg me for it.' Camellia told him.

Copperhead used his hands to pull apart his buttocks. 'Tell me I'm a dirty little drone, and use the riding crop.'

Camellia carefully slid the tip of the dildo into Copperhead's ass. 'Is that nice? Is that good? Am I filling you up?' She crooned to him.

'Oh Goddesses, yes,' Copperhead sighed.

Camellia slid her hand around Copperhead so that she held the head of his penis in a firm grip. The lubrication on her hand helped it to slide over his penis.

'We're going to do this together. Let me know when you're getting close to ejaculating. You're not allowed to do it without my permission. Do you understand?'

Copperhead nodded.

'Good boy.' Camellia started stroking into Copperhead, matching her own rhythm with hand strokes on his penis. She loved listening to the sharp intake of his breath as she plunged deep into his anus. With each stroke she went a little deeper inside of him.

Copperhead moaned with pleasure, and tried very hard not to come right away.

'Are you a bad drone?'

'Yes.'

'Are you a dirty little drone who took milk without permission?'

'Yes,' Copperhead whispered.

Camellia took her riding crop and smacked it down on Copperhead's ass while she rode him. She was getting wetter and wetter herself, but with one hand stroking Copperhead's penis and another using the riding crop, she had no free hand for herself.

Camellia pulled out of Copperhead. 'Take off your hose and go lay on my bed.'

Copperhead pulled off his tights and stumbled over to the bed.

'Face up.' Camellia ordered. She took the dildo out of her corset and walked over to the bed. 'First, suckle my milk.'

'But I'm so close,' Copperhead complained.

'Do as I say, or I'll put you in that padded chastity belt every day for a month.'

Copperhead knew that she gave no idle threats, so he suckled greedily from her breasts. When he finished he frowned. 'I'm not hard anymore.'

'You will be in a second. Don't complain.' Camellia took out another dildo, a much longer one. She stood over Copperhead and slid the tip between his lips. 'Get it wet,' she ordered.

As promised, Copperhead began to get hard. He closed his eyes and licked the phallus.

Camellia climbed onto the bed with Copperhead. She straddled his face. 'Lick me, taste me.'

Copperhead put his hands on her hips and guided her closer to his face.

Camellia leaned over Copperhead's body and had him bring his legs up into the air so that she could slide the dildo into his ass again. As she slid it in and out of him she took his penis into her mouth.

Copperhead pushed his face into Camellia's pelvis with renewed enthusiasm. He didn't know which sensation he wanted to concentrate on more, the smell and taste of Camellia, the dildo sliding in and out of his anus or Camellia's hot, wet mouth on his penis. He was suddenly so hard that it was nearly painful.

'I'm going to come,' Copperhead warned.

'So am I,' Camellia said in almost a whisper.

Copperhead grabbed her hips and began thrusting his tongue into Camellia as she ground herself against his face. They both came in furious force.

Thane Monarda allowed Verbena to brush her hair out. Usually a maid would do such a personal task, but Thane Monarda liked to take this quiet time in the morning to talk with her new Major Domo.

'You're very quiet this morning Verbena. Is something on your mind?'

'I beg your pardon my Lady. I guess that I'm a little preoccupied.'

'With what?' Thane Monarda closed her eyes. There was something so relaxing about the gentle stroking of her hair.

Verbena paused. Lately her employer had been too busy planning a series of weddings for her eldest daughter to hold her usual salon. Without the usual flow of gossip into the household chamber Verbena was unable to supply the Queen with the latest buzz in the Hive. But asking for information was going to be tricky. 'What do you think of our new Queen?' Verbena finally asked.

Thane Monarda opened her eyes and looked at Verbena's reflection in the mirror. Verbena did not meet her gaze. 'That's an unusual question, and one I would be careful of answering.'

Verbena sighed. 'It is perhaps not the right wording.'

'What do you want to know?'

'Well, since I have never been to see the Royal Court, and since you attend daily, I was wondering just what impression Queen Aynia makes on one. I served her as a Princess. I am simply curious how much she's changed.'

'I would have never pegged you as a Royal watcher,' Thane Monarda teased Verbena.

'Well, I…'

'No need to apologize dear, anyone who tells you that they don't get a little thrill when they see the Queen is a liar.' Thane Monarda, a devoted Royalist, was pleased to know that her severe attendant was Fairie after all. 'My impression of the Queen, well, she is a beauty. She has her Mother's coloring, but I think her features take after her father. Certainly the full-blooded sisters among the Princesses bore a strong resemblance to each other. It's that heart-shaped face, and the long thin fingers.'

Verbena thought about Princess Lily, Princess Gladiola, and Queen Aynia, and nodded in agreement with Thane Monarda. They all shared their mother's ginger coloring. Without exception the princesses had the nose, eyes, and delicate features of their father, the late Prince Consort Thistle.

'Certainly this Queen doesn't act like her Mother. The old Queen,' Thane Monarda chuckled, 'well, she did have a temper! Do you know why they refurbished the Throne Room? The Queen threw a flagon of berry nectar across the room, trying to hit Thane Plumeria in the head. Of course Plumeria ducked, and the flagon hit Thane Adders-Tongue square in the forehead. Adders-Tongue complained, but the Queen told her that it was her own fault for talking to the person in the seat next to her and not paying attention to the Queen. Adders-Tongue was wearing an ivory frock of course. It was ruined. So was every other surface that the berry nectar touched.'

Verbena laughed. 'I think I remember hearing about that. I heard that Thane Adders-Tongue was quite angry about the whole thing.'

'Oh, I don't think that she ever forgave the Queen. There has certainly been plenty of bad blood between those houses.'

'Oh?' Verbena asked with an arched eyebrow.

'Enough, enough of old history. You asked about Queen Aynia. She seems to rule well enough. She always manages to wriggle out of the traps that Adders-Tongue lays for her, so she must be quite sharp. I had the pleasure of being seating near to Her Majesty at a State Dinner last week. She seems to speak pleasantly enough with those seated near her.'

'But?' Verbena asked, recognizing from her tone that Thane Monarda had some additional thoughts on the matter.

'Well, she doesn't really seem to mix with the nobility of the Seelie Court,' Thane Monarda said hesitantly. She watched Verbena's reflection in the mirror, but when Verbena merely nodded she went on. 'The late Queen had many friends, and enemies, among the nobility. Queen Aynia holds herself distant. Except for the members of the Cabinet she doesn't meet any member of the Seelie Court on a personal basis. We never see anything of her personality. I have never seen someone with such an ability to hide her thoughts. You never know if she's happy or mad. I've never even heard the Queen laugh. I mean, that's all well and good when Thane Adders-Tongue is trying to make the Queen a fool, but not everyone is out to get her. She should look to the Nobility for companionship, for friends.'

'So you agree with Thane Adders-Tongue description of the Queen?'

'What do you mean?'

'Thane Adders-Tongue has taken to calling Queen Aynia the Ice Queen on the floor of Parliament.'

Thane Monarda thought for a moment then shrugged. 'It's perhaps a bit harsh, but on the hand, it's not far from accurate.'

Verbena nodded. She would report this conversation to the Queen.

'Have you thought about the matter that we discussed earlier my Queen?' Heather asked Aynia.

'I haven't had time to reflect.'

'I must know your plans My Lady.'

'You'll know when I've reached a decision,' Aynia snapped.

'About what?' Camellia asked drowsily.

'The Queen won't tell me if she plans to fly at the Vernal Equinox.'

'Well, she has very few drones to fly with even if she does. We're only up to five.' Camellia observed.

'There are still enough days to transform other males in the harem, if she will make her decision,' Heather emphasized.

'I tire of this conversation.' Aynia warned them.

'Thorn will not be back in time.' Rose said quietly.

'What did you say?' Aynia was shocked. Was her heart so transparent to these attendants? Her face began to flush red in a mixture of anger and embarrassment.

'I said that Captain Thorn wouldn't be back in time to transform into a drone even if he wants to. My lady, I know that you wait for him, but even if he's still alive the odds of him returning before your first mating flight are slim.'

Aynia literally trembled with rage. 'Out! Out! All of you get out of my chambers! Get out!' She yelled.

Heather and Camellia exchanged a glance as they scrambled out of the room. 'I begin to see the resemblance to her Mother,' Camellia commented.

'I'm so glad that you find this amusing. The entire future of the Hive is in peril and you want to make jokes. The High Priestess herself warned me that if the Queen does not take flight on this Vernal Equinox a great tragedy will befall the Hive.'

'Do you mean a great tragedy like having to abandon the Hive? Or perhaps an invasion of humans?'

Heather fastened her gray fur lined cloak around her throat. 'You keep laughing. This is a very serious matter.'

'I know that it is.' Camellia admitted.

'Then I suggest that you do something.'

'Like what Heather? Go pray to the Goddesses? That's your department. I have no idea of how to break the Queen out of this stupor that she's fallen into. Perhaps I should go in search of our valiant Captain Thorn myself and drag him home? Should I latch him onto her breast and force him into becoming one of her drones? What do you suggest that I do?'

'For one thing, get her to transform more of her males into drones.'

'She only wants the Princes Sarkany and Moss.'

'Then make them unavailable.'

'It only takes one drone to mate with her. If you have something against Sarkany I suggest that you get over it, because Sarkany has her spellbound.'

'Then you see it too!'

'Yes I do,' Camellia admitted.

'Then why don't you do something about it?'

'Like what? I don't know the magic he uses. I wouldn't know where to begin to break the charm. Besides, no female likes someone getting between her and her favorite stud.'

'That's all very well, but she's a Queen, not an individual. The needs of the Hive rule her as much as she rules the Hive. If she does not mate Parliament will destroy her.' Heather shook off Camellia's hand and strode out of the Royal Chamber.

'Where are you going Heather?' Camellia called out after her.

'To Temple.'

'But the Queen will be headed to court in less than an hour.'

'I will be back.'

Camellia stood in the hallway of the Royal Chamber, undecided as to what she should do. After a time the door to the Queen's bedchamber opened and Aynia peered out.

301

'Bring Moss or Sarkany to my chamber. It is time for them to suckle.'

Camellia straightened her spine and turned to face Aynia. 'My humblest apologies My Queen, but the Princes are currently unavailable.'

'I have them brought to me three times a day, every day, at the same time. How can they suddenly be unavailable?' Aynia demanded to know.

'My apologies again My Lady, but all of your drones are currently being punished. I can not release them early. It would set a bad example.'

Aynia frowned. 'Oh, very well. Send another Prince to me, quickly. I have to be at court soon.'

Camellia bowed. 'Of course,' Camellia wasn't happy. She didn't like having to choose between her sister and her Queen. She vowed that this would be the last time she'd let Heather put her into a situation where that kind of decision had to be made.

'I worry that the Queen will not take flight on the Equinox.' Heather told the High Priestess.

'So she really is the Ice Queen, as Thane Adders-Tongue calls her?' The High Priestess asked with concern.

'No. She's not cold. She's just headstrong and private about her feelings.'

'Have you corrupted her as you did your Russian Queen? I warned you once about this.'

'I didn't corrupt the Queen Yelena,' Heather protested with exasperation. That was a stigma she didn't want following her for the rest of her life. 'Queen Yelena ruled over four hundred years and never mated before I came along. Why am I blamed for her failure?'

'Because Queens don't fail! Only their attendants fail.'

'I haven't failed Queen Aynia either. I'm working as hard as I can to get her to mate. You must believe me! It's that damned Captain Thorn. She's in love with that male.'

'Force him to become a drone and get it over with then.'

Heather paused. Her loyalties were torn. 'That won't be possible,' she said slowly.

'Why not?' The High Priestess demanded.

'He isn't here. He's gone from the Hive.'

The High Priestess considered this for a moment in silence. 'Tell me all. Why was he sent away?'

Heather closed her eyes. Was she betraying the Queen by telling this to the High Priestess? 'The Queen feels that relocating the Hive best solves the problems threatening us. She sent Captain Thorn on a mission to find a place to relocate the Hive. He's been gone quite some time and we all worry that he won't return.'

'Move the Hive?' The High Priestess frowned. She was distracted for only a moment, and then turned her attention back to Heather. 'Thank you Lady Heather. You have shown yourself to be a true daughter of the Goddess.'

'But what do I do about the Queen?'

'Use your persuasion,' the High Priestess counseled.

'I'm trying.'

'Not hard enough. If the Queen is indecisive you must be willing to step forward and make your voice heard. It is your destiny to have a hand in making policy for this Hive.'

'Is it really my destiny?'

'It's written in the stars.' The High Priestess took Heather's palm and pretended to inspect it. 'Absolutely. You were placed at the Queen's side for a reason. Now, you must return to your post. I believe that Royal Court is about to start. You must remain at the side of the Queen.'

'I will go,' Heather headed back to the Royal Palace, newly determined to bring the Queen to her senses.

The High Priestess leaned back in her throne. She had much to think about. If the Queen moved the Hive there was great danger that the delicate balance between the Palace, Parliament, and the Temple, would be altered. This young Queen was not the tool the Temple had hoped for. Yes she was observant, but she never sought the advice of the High Priestess. The Queen kept her own council and followed only her own agenda.

'Your Reverence?' Cerridwen said quietly to get the attention of the High Priestess. 'The Ambassador Cowslip from Norfolk Hive is here to pay her respects.'

Aynia allowed her servants to remove every piece of her clothing. The male in front of her gasped, watching in fascination. He was about to see the Queen naked.

Aynia opened her eyes. 'Remove your own clothes.'

'Of course Majesty.' He struggled to pull his hose off without removing his eyes from the Queen.

'I haven't seen you since you were presented as tribute. I remember your face, but not your name,' Aynia admitted.

'I'm not a Prince, Majesty. It is unusual that you would remember someone from such humble roots.'

'I thought that I sent for a Prince.'

The male frowned. He was sure that the Queen was going to send him away, just as things were getting very naked, er, interesting. 'Lady Camellia ordered me to come to you. Shall I go away?'

Aynia smiled as sweetly as she could. She was beginning to get annoyed that her staff could not obey the least of her wishes. Lately she was beginning to feel that they ruled her, not the other way around. She supposed that it was her own fault for not taking charge sooner. This was all getting out of hand. Still, the male was innocent in all of this, and he was part of the tribute for a good reason. He was absolutely adorable. Some poor family sent him to their Queen in hopes that he would be able to find her favor. Aynia found that she couldn't be unkind, especially with his large brown eyes staring so wistfully at her.

Aynia extended her hand. 'Come, let us bathe together.' She waded into the water still holding the male's hand. 'You never did tell me your name.'

'I'm Wheat.'

'Well Wheat, I need for you to suckle milk from my breasts.'

'An honor My Queen.'

Wheat looked at the Queen's breasts. Buoyed by the water, they floated enticingly in front of him. He didn't want to anger the Queen so he placed one hand reverently under the royal cleavage and lifted the nipple just above the water and hesitantly took her into his mouth.

Wheat began suckling gently, unlike the rough way that Sarkany would clamp on. He tried to look up at the Queen while he took her milk, but finally closed his eyes and massaged Aynia's breasts.

Aynia began to nibble lightly on Wheat's earlobe. 'Wrap you legs around my waist. I will take us to the waterfall at the end of my bath where the water is deeper.' She whispered into his ear.

Wheat obeyed.

There was something about the gentle steady manner in which Wheat nursed that was driving Aynia crazy. When he finished with the one breast he looked up almost sleepily at Aynia then moved over to her other breast.

Aynia took him behind the waterfall where the servants waiting on the edge of the bath could not see them.

'Are you finished?' Aynia asked.

'Almost my Queen.' Wheat continued to massage Aynia's breast. As milk beaded up on her nipple he opened his mouth and allowed the drops to fall into his mouth. As the flow slowed he massaged with a little more pressure, working his hand in circles, until her breast was drained of milk. 'Is my Queen pleased?'

'Very much so Wheat,' she traced around his pouty lips with her finger. 'In fact, I like your work so well that I ask you to do another thing for me.'

'Anything my lady.'

There was a small grotto behind the waterfall in the bath. Here the water was about waist high. Across the back wall of the grotto was a ledge just big enough for Aynia to lie down on. The edge dipped into the water then rose and flattened out above the water. Aynia sat on the edge of the ledge while Wheat remained standing in the water.

Aynia wondered why she felt so odd asking a male to do this for her, but she parted her legs. 'There is another place where you might suckle,' she suggested, suddenly blushing pink.

'I am honored Majesty.' Wheat placed his hand against the red pubic hair on her pelvis and leaned over to kiss Aynia. He worked two fingers around, feeling how wet she was already. 'I can't wait to taste you. Your pussy is like fire.'

Aynia laughed. Either it was sheer nerves or his words struck her as silly, or both, but the laugh bubbled out of her.

Wheat didn't hear though. He pushed Aynia's knees far apart so that there was no hiding in modesty. He got down on his knees and kissed the inside of Aynia's thighs, growing closer and closer to her clitoris. As he teased her with kisses he worked her with his thumb. Then he finally reached the middle and set to work pleasing the Queen with his very talented tongue. The combined action of his fingers and tongue were throwing Aynia into a wild state. Every muscle was contracting from her neck down to her toes. Her back was arching high into the air and she had her knees drawn back almost to her own ears. Aynia fought the urge, but finally screamed with the pleasure.

Wheat smiled. He would forever have his father to thank for instructing him so diligently on the art of bringing a female to climax. While he had never taken milk, Wheat was not exactly new to this oral exercise.

Aynia came with shuddering, explosive force.

Wheat felt hands pulling him away. He tried to protest, but Rose gave him a stern look and a light slap on his ass. He frowned, but swam back across the bath to the far side where Lady Camellia awaited the new drone.

Aynia turned her head so that she could look at Rose. 'Tell me, will my toes ever relax?'

Rose smiled indulgently. 'The better the orgasm the longer it takes the toes to uncurl. Don't sit up yet Majesty. Give the blood time to get back to your head.'

'I remember now,' Aynia said in triumph. 'Wheat was the one who tied the cherry stem into a knot.'

'Yes My Queen.' Rose admitted.

Aynia thought back to the tribute. No wonder the females of the nobility were so excited when they saw how dexterous this one was with his tongue. 'Send his family a nice gift, and tell them that their Queen is well pleased, very well pleased.'

Racing up the stairs of the Royal Palace, Heather should have noticed the group of personal guards wearing Thane Adders-Tongue's livery loitering near the doors of the Palace. But she did not.

'Kind of you to join Us,' Aynia commented caustically as Heather made her bow to the Queen.

'Forgive me Majesty, I was detained.'

Aynia made a face and turned away.

'My Lady's face is flushed, is she well?' Heather whispered to Camellia.

'For a while there she was better than well,' Camellia commented. 'My Lady finally let a male take her juices. She was in a great mood until the Royal tailor showed her the latest fashion in dresses. It seems that she doesn't want to wear a court dress weighing fifty pounds.'

Heather had never mentioned the scene she'd witnessed between Thorn and Aynia to her sister. Now didn't seem like the time either. Heather looked over at the new style of court dress and snorted. 'She won't be able to move in that. It's ridiculous.'

'She ordered similar dresses for each of us. She said that if she has to suffer so do we.'

Heather groaned.

Aynia impatiently waited as she was placed into a magnificent dress of pale gray raw silk with a bodice encrusted with small pearls and garnets. Rose had all of the Royal Jewels gathered in the room. She was looking for just the right pieces to set off the Queen's dress. Boxes of jewels were scattered all over the room, opened to display their contents.

Camellia lounged comfortably on a pile of plump pillows piled in an oriental manner on the floor near the fireplace. Heather sat down in a particularly torturous wooden chair near the Queen's bed, her back as rigid as the chair's.

'It needs a lace collar. Something in gold would be nice.' Rose went to the collection of necklaces.

Remembering the possible lethal qualities of the only gold lace collar in the Queen's collection, Heather objected hastily to that idea. 'No. Just use a white lace collar ruff.'

Rose raised her eyebrow. 'Fashion advice? From you?'

Heather took great offense. 'What do you mean by that?'

'You dress like a dowdy old mother of ten.'

'I am not dowdy. And I'm not a breeder, thank you.'

'Ladies,' Aynia raised her voice, 'really, this dress must weigh fifty pounds. If I have to stand here wearing this damned torture device at least make your conversation interesting and take my mind off of my discomfort. I have had enough of your sisterly spats.'

'Yes My Lady.' Rose returned to her quest for the perfect jeweled accessories. 'Perhaps my sister is correct after all. You need a white lace ruff for the neck, something simple, maybe with the seed pearls, to match the dress. And a pearl crown! Very nice.'

'Don't forget a pearl necklace,' Camellia quipped. 'The drones in the harem have been dying to give one to the Queen.'

Ignoring her sister, Rose went on. 'And you need nice strand of pearls. I think that we have two ropes about seventy inches long.'

'I don't give a damn about the bloody accessories! Who decided that fashions have to change anyway?' Aynia demanded to know.

Camellia looked at Heather. 'Really, she was in a great mood half an hour ago. Too bad you missed it. Now she's showing her resemblance to her mother again,' Camellia whispered.

'Where were you Lady Heather?'

'At Temple. I had an important meeting with the High Priestess.'

'We can not think what would be more important to you than accompanying your Queen to Royal Court. We are growing worried about the persistence of attacks on Our Royal Name from the floor of Parliament. Adders-Tongue is up to something. Unfortunately I have no idea this time what she is up to.'

'If I hear I will tell Your Majesty immediately,' Heather said.

'Of course you will. And next time I want to see all of you dressed in the new fashion. Your dresses should be complete soon, right?' Aynia eyed the tailor with a malevolent gleam in her eye.

The tailor nodded then ducked out of the room.

'Well, lets get this over with.' The Queen swept down the hallway with Captain Sage at her right flank. Heather fell in on the left. Behind them marched nearly the entire Royal Guard.

Deidre peered out the door to her chambers. The only person in the hall was Copperhead. 'Are they gone?'

'Yes lady.' Copperhead whispered back. 'We are quite alone.'

'Then go to the harem and send Prince Noisi to me. You did explain to him that this is the last time that we will meet? I was offered a position at the Hive de Chambord. I intend to offer my resignation to the Queen tomorrow. After that the Prince will never see me again.'

'I told him.'

'You are a true friend,' Deidre whispered.

Copperhead gave her a weak smile and went to the harem door.

Prince Noisi was waiting just at the other side. 'Well?'

'The Queen and all of her attendants are gone. I told Captain Sage that the Queen was in danger and that he should take all of the Royal Guard with him to Court today. So you don't have to worry about them.'

'Thanks.' Prince Noisi clasped Copperhead's arm.

'Remember what I told you?'

'Yes, but are you sure?'

'Who gives his lady what she wants several times a day, you or I? Trust me. Don't even bother to speak. Just pick her up, throw her on the bed, spread her legs and enter paradise. She'll fight you back for all that she's worth, that's the way that they like it. Remember, we males are stronger.'

'Sure. Thanks again.'

'Now go. She's waiting for you in her chamber.' Copperhead watched Prince Noisi creep across the hallway and open Deidre's door. After the door was shut he went across the hallway and listened. He expected to hear screams, but did not.

'I'm so glad that you came,' Deidre said, rushing to Prince Noisi's side. She kissed him on the cheek. 'I need to tell you why I am leaving.'

'What? You're leaving?' Prince Noisi was confused.

'Didn't Copperhead tell you that I'm leaving for France tomorrow?'

'No, he didn't.'

'He promised me that he would tell you, but I guess that it's more honest to tell you to your face. Prince Noisi, you are the only male I have ever desired. I always thought that other females were silly to obsess on a male. I disdained courtly love. But now I have to admit that I can think of little but you. I guess that I too am a fool for love. I dream every night of that cleft in your chin, of your brown eyes. Do you have any idea how beautiful you are? I thought you desirable when you were first presented to the Queen. Now that you are a drone you are even more handsome, more perfect.'

'I want to be with you too,' Noisi confessed.

'I've tried to forget my desire for you. I prayed for guidance. I even risked both of our lives for stolen moments with you. I know that it's wrong and that we can't continue to meet. You belong to the Queen. I will not betray her.' Deidre began to pace. 'Just by thinking about you I betray my Queen. So I decided to leave my position here and go far away. I accepted a position in the Hive de Chambord, in France.'

'You're going away?' Prince Noisi repeated. 'Copperhead said nothing of this. He said that you wanted me to come here tonight and take you by force.'

'No female wants that.' Deidre frowned. 'Copperhead shouldn't be saying such things to you.'

'He tells me many things about females. He tells me all kinds of things that I should say to you, and he tells me things that you say to him about me.'

Deidre thought for a moment. 'I don't talk to Copperhead about you.'

'He swears that you do.'

'Noisi, I never once sent for you. I never told Copperhead to bring you to my chambers. Did he tell you that I sent for you?' Deidre's face was concentrated in a frown. Alarms were going off in her brain.

'Yes. Every time that I came to you it was because he told me that you sent for me. He arraigned for the Royal Chambers to be as empty as possible so that I could cross the hallway.'

Deidre's hands clasped together. She saw clearly what was happening. 'It is a trap, a terrible trap. Copperhead told you to rape me so that we could be caught committing treason. He arraigned these meetings so that they could arrest us together.'

'No,' Prince Noisi shook his head. 'Copperhead wouldn't do this to me. He and I, we, we have a physical connection. I made love to him.'

'You must go. You must leave these chambers immediately.' Deidre was pushing Noisi to the door.

Prince Noisi nodded. 'Lady Deidre, I do love you, and I will hold you in my heart forever. Goodbye.' He gave her a quick kiss then went to the door of Deidre's chamber.

It was too late.

Adders-Tongue's guards broke through the door.

'Going somewhere?' Cobra-Lily asked.

'Cobra-Lily! What are you doing in the Royal Chambers! And with armed guards! The Queen will have your head.' Deidre yelled as her arms were pinned behind her back. The guards placed heavy iron cuffs on her wrists that threatened to cut off the circulation to her hands.

'Of all the heads in this room Lady Deidre, I'd be most concerned about yours,' Cobra-Lily sneered.

Prince Noisi struggled against the guards but was soon overwhelmed by numbers. As he was cuffed he looked up to see Copperhead leaning against the doorjamb. 'I thought that you were my friend.'

'Nope.' Copperhead said with a shrug.

'I thought that you said they'd be caught in bed together,' Cobra-Lily complained.

'Well I certainly thought they would be.' Copperhead gave Prince Noisi a disdainful look.

'No one is going to care if we arrested them for talking together.' Cora-Lily complained.

Copperhead sighed and rolled his eyes. 'Use your imagination. Obviously these two are going to deny anything that you charge them with. So make it look like you caught them doing something wrong.' Copperhead walked over to Deidre and unhooked each hook on the front of her corset. Then he pulled the corset off and yanked down her skirt. Kneeling before her, he pulled off her shoes, her stockings, and her panties. Finally, he unpinned her hair so that it fell loose over her shoulders. 'Very nice,' Copperhead muttered as he pinched Deidre's nipple.

'And as for the Prince, well,' Copperhead went over to Prince Noisi and pulled his hose down to his knees. 'I think that this shows a certain haste in love making. It's very convincing, don't you think?'

Cobra-Lily smiled. 'We'll take them to the Royal Court like this. Everyone will see them naked.'

'Everyone will believe that you caught them in the act.'

'You won't get away with this,' Deidre yelled.

'Oh yes we will. Don't take it so personally Lady Deidre. This is all just for the benefit of the Queen,' Copperhead sneered.

'Yeah,' Cobra-Lily echoed.

'Cobra-Lily, cousin dear, are you pleased with my work?' Copperhead asked.

Cobra-Lily nodded. 'You did okay.'

'Could I come home now? I don't think that it'll be safe here for me anymore.'

'You're probably right about that.'

'So I can come home?' Copperhead asked hopefully.

Cobra-Lily shook her head. 'You're a shamed male. You'll never be allowed to take refuge with the clan. You're unclean. As far as the family is concerned, you're dead.'

'But where can I go?' Copperhead asked.

Cobra-Lily shrugged. 'I hear that they always need free drones to work in the pubs. Nice looking boy like you should find a position easy.'

'You expect me to become a prostitute?' Copperhead was dumbfounded.

'Become? You already are. Just because they treated you better than that here doesn't make you anything more than an unclean free drone.'

Copperhead watched the departing guards and prisoners with an open mouth. Suddenly he realized that he made a huge mistake.

CHAPTER 12

'Adders-Tongue seems to be enjoying herself today,' Aynia mentioned to Heather. 'I didn't know that she could smile.'

'What horrible thought is making her smile?' Camellia gave a pretend shiver.

'Exactly. I shudder to think what's going on in the evil mind of hers.'

'With good reason Majesty. She makes no attempt to hide her hatred of you.'

'And yet I have done her no wrong.'

'You fired her niece Cobra-Lily,' Camellia reminded Aynia.

'Cobra-Lily was trying to poison me. In my book that's grounds for immediate dismissal even from the most understanding employer.'

'Your Majesty was not aware that Cobra-Lily was trying to poison you when you fired her.'

'I named Adders-Tongue to a Ministry post. Surely the two even out.'

'Don't try to win this war Majesty. Just try not to loose it,' Camellia counseled.

The court began to grow impatient with this whispered aside between Queen Aynia and her attendants, but Aynia was in no mood to care.

'Where's Deidre? You promised me she would be at my side today,' Aynia complained to Heather.

'I'm as surprised as you are Majesty. Rose, Camellia, and I had a long talk with her yesterday and she agreed to desist in the behavior that was causing the rift between us. She promised me that she would be here today. She just wanted to tie up loose ends. I can't think where she might be.' Heather informed Aynia.

'Find her and bring her to me,' Aynia hissed.

'As Your Majesty commands,' Heather replied. Bowing, she left for the Royal chambers. Heather was by now quite

314

angry with her sister Deidre. Deidre had been given every warning and every chance to mend her ways. This final insult to the Queen was enough to test Heather's patience. Heather went to Camellia's office and grabbed a leather whip. If Deidre would show no remorse then Heather would whip her until pleas for forgiveness fell from Deidre's lips. Heather would not allow Deidre to debase the family name in this manner.

Heather stomped into Deidre's room. The door was wide open. Inside it was evident that a great struggle had taken place. Anger was taken over by fear. Something was terribly wrong.

Heather ran to the harem. The males of the harem were evidently already alarmed. They did not lounge in the common room. As Heather swept into the harem some of the Princes dared to peer from their rooms.

Heather addressed Wheat. 'Where is the Prince Noisi?'

'He isn't here Lady.'

'I didn't ask if he was here. I asked where he was,' Heather yelled.

'He left here soon after the Queen left the chambers for the Royal Court. I haven't seen him since. However, the personal guard of Thane Adders-Tongue came here half an hour ago.'

Heather paled. 'They dared to come into the Queen's harem? Did they touch any of you?'

'Prince Moss and Prince Sarkany tried to defend the door to the harem with their swords, but there were too many guards. When the guards broke through the door they captured Moss and Sarkany and took them into one of the other rooms.'

'Did they touch them?'

'I don't know. The guards held us in here while a great altercation took place down the hall. I fear that Lady Deidre has been taken prisoner.'

'Damn!' Heather yelled. 'Damn her and her sentimental good-byes. Tell me; was there any member of the Thane Adders-Tongue's family with the guard?'

'I saw no one. They held us in here. I think that I heard Copperhead's voice. I don't know if he was a prisoner or if he was helping them though.'

'Bloody hell! Dark days lay ahead. Go find the Princes Moss and Sarkany. Get medical attention for them if needed. Then take the harem to the Queen's chapel and offer up sacrifices to the Goddesses. We'll need divine intervention today'

'As you command Lady Heather,' Wheat made his bow and jumped to action. Within moments he rallied the males and set about securing the Royal Chambers.

Heather sprinted down the hallways of the palace to return to the Throne Room. She had to warn the Queen.

Two members of Thane Adders-Tongue's personal guard blocked Heather's way when she got to the Throne Room. They stood in front of the door and wouldn't allow her to pass. 'Stand down!' Heather ordered the males.

Both males drew their swords.

'You would draw your swords in the Royal Palace, against a member of the Queen's personal staff?'

'We have orders Lady Heather.'

'Drawing your sword against me is the same as drawing it against the Queen. Stand down I say!'

Members of the Royal Guard came running down the hallway led by Captain Sage. Heather breathed a sigh of relief as she heard twenty swords drawn in unison. The odds were now decidedly in her favor.

'Stand down or perish!' Captain Sage ordered dramatically.

Adders-Tongue's guards were not well trained enough, or fond enough of the clan that they served, to fight against the Royal Guard. They both dropped their swords.

'Adders-Tongue's guards took Lady Deidre hostage, and I believe that they took Prince Noisi from the harem too.' Heather quickly brought Captain Sage up to date.

'Adders-Tongue walks a fine line there. She could be charged with treason for sending armed guards into the Royal Chambers,' Captain Sage observed.

'Where the hell were you? You should have been guarding those chambers. You should be at the Queen's side. You're a poor substitute for Captain Thorn. This never would have happened if he were here.' Heather yelled at Sage.

'And Captain Thorn would be here if you hadn't plotted to be rid of him!' Sage blurted out.

Heather's eyes narrowed. 'How dare you!'

'Anger is a cheap way to hide embarrassment.'

'So is blaming others for your shortcomings. From now on Sage I expect the guard around the Queen and the Royal Chambers to be doubled. Oh, wait a second, if you double nothing you still get nothing. Better make it triple protection!' Heather said sarcastically.

'I've been fighting the human encroachers!'

'Congratulations. You held one rock in place while the rest of the wall crumbled!'

Sage stood and fumed while he tried to bring his anger under control. His hero Thorn would have never failed so publicly, and he never would have allowed himself to get into a shouting match outside of the Throne Room with Lady Heather. 'I stand corrected Lady Heather,' Sage said through gritted teeth. 'Now we must work together for our Queen.'

'Agreed.'

'Shall we enter the Throne Room?'

'Follow me.' Heather opened the doors and strode into the room. But she was too late to warn the Queen.

Adders-Tongue was standing triumphantly over the nude bound figures of Deidre and Prince Noisi. When Heather and Sage came into the Throne Room Thane Adders-Tongue turned around. She had a very dangerous smile on her face.

'Ah, the Captain of the Royal Guard. Captain Sage, you're just in time to bind these two traitors over for trial.'

Sage and Heather looked up at Queen Aynia. Heather wandered just what Aynia's nerves were made of. The Queen looked as calm and coolly detached as she always did. Was there nothing that would shake that icy façade?

'Majesty,' Heather started to say something, and then realized that she had nothing to say.

Rose was nearly in tears. Camellia's jaw was clenched tight, and her hand flexed compulsively at the hilt of her sword as if she would draw it at any moment and run someone through.

'They were caught in each other's arms. Apparently this wasn't the only time that they betrayed Your Majesty. My nephew, Copperhead, heard confessions from Prince Noisi that Noisi and Lady Deidre shared her bed on several occasions after he became a drone. We could torture a confession out of them, but we have witnesses. I don't think that I need to remind Your Majesty of the penalty for treason?'

Deidre tried to explain, but when her pleading eyes met the Queen's she saw an expression that terrified her. Queen Aynia was regal and distant. Her eyes looked right through Deidre.

Aynia finally spoke. 'If the two confess spare them the trial. If they refuse to confess do not torture them but bind them over for trial. Once you have a confession or verdicts of guilt bring them before Us for execution.' Aynia slowly pulled herself up to her full height. 'Until that moment We will not look upon these faces again, nor will We suffer to hear their names spoken in front of Us.'

Aynia stepped down from her Throne and walked slowly out of the room. If Adders-Tongue meant to make a fool of the Queen in public or if she thought that the Queen would bend the law, thus opening herself to further censure in Parliament, then Adders-Tongue was much mistaken. The Throne Room was silent. Everyone was too stunned to speak.

Thane Adders-Tongue knew the depth of public humiliation an unfaithful drone could cause a female. She dreamed of seeing that same humiliation written across Aynia's face. It was not to be so. The Queen acted as if she didn't care.

'The Queen is made of ice,' someone finally commented. 'I wouldn't dare cross her.'

'Remember how her mother would throw things across the room when she got mad? I miss that,' a Lady sighed wistfully. 'At least with her you knew where you stood, and after the yelling was over, well, the calm wasn't the frightening part.'

Aynia walked out of the Throne Room alone. When the door of the room closed behind her Heather, Rose, and Camellia remembered their place behind her. They hurried out of the Throne Room to follow the Queen. But they did not dare walk close.

'Why wasn't I warned about this?' Aynia yelled in full voice at her attendants and Captain Sage once they were in her parlor. Those who thought that she was made of ice would have changed their minds now. She was in a fury.

'I tried to get to you in time Majesty, but Adders-Tongue's personal guards blocked the door of the Throne Room.' Heather tried to explain.

Aynia slammed her fist down on the tabletop. Forks and plates rattled. 'I don't mean today! How long was this going on behind my back? How long did you all know that she was sleeping with Noisi? I understand now that this was the argument between the three of you and her. What made you think that I had no right to know about it?'

'We wanted to protect her Majesty.'

'And thus exposed me to danger! Don't you think that I would have put a stop to it without putting her life on trial? One word from me probably would have stopped the whole affair back before it became a political tool for my enemies. That's when I should have been told.'

'Please forgive us.'

'And you, Captain!' Aynia turned her anger on the terrified Sage. 'How could you allow a troop of armed guards to enter my chambers without a single Royal Guardsman between my chamber and their swords? If I had been here, and if this was a coup, I would have been dead before any of you could protect me.'

'I have set a permanent shift of guards around the Royal chamber Majesty.'

'Too late! You all apologize and act too late!' Aynia paced the parlor. Her anger was still growing. She turned to the cowering attendants. 'Have Adders-Tongue's guard arrested and taken to the prison. Act quickly, but try to keep your actions as quiet as possible. Replace her people with my own.'

'Yes your Majesty,' Sage bowed and turned for the door. He would have run away if he could have trusted his legs.

'As for you three,' Aynia turned back to Heather, Rose, and Camellia, 'I warned you once about withholding information from me. I have enemies surrounding me. I have to worry about other Hives who might decide to invade us. I have daily news of more humans coming north and permanently settling less than two miles away from the entrance to the valley. I have political enemies like Thane Adders-Tongue who seek to render me powerless over my own Hive. And now I have the three of you who play into the hands of all of my enemies. I have lost my faith in your ability to serve me. You put your sister ahead of me. Perhaps I need to find attendants who I know will always put their Queen first. Go now, right now, and bring me Heliotrope, Freesia, and Verbena.'

'Majesty?'

'I need attendants that I can trust. Bring them to me now. You are all dismissed.' Aynia turned and stormed into her bedchamber, slamming the door closed behind her.

Heliotrope came quietly to Aynia's side. 'Majesty, you are in great distress.'

Aynia looked up. She had been sitting with her face buried in her hands. Her voice was raspy from shouting at her attendants. In a hoarse whisper she said 'they touched my drones Heliotrope.' Aynia rested her head on Heliotrope's shoulder.

'I heard Majesty. Lady Camellia is tending to them now.'

'Don't speak her name,' Aynia growled.

'As you wish,' Heliotrope agreed in a soothing voice. 'Majesty, the females tied up most of your drones, stripped them, and fondled them, but they didn't rape them. It's a small comfort, I know.' She stroked the back of Aynia's hair gently.

Rage welled in Aynia's heart. 'The drones are mine! How dare they even set their eyes on my harem?' The ancient territorial instinct over mating males boiled in her blood.

'It is your right to seek vengeance,' Heliotrope commented. She had little help to offer to her Queen at this time. So much of Aynia's life was now beyond her old nurses' experience.

Aynia was feeling powerless. She felt that she should have been better able to protect her males. That was, after all, the idea behind the harem. A female kept exclusive mating rights to desirable males in exchange for protecting those males from other females. What kind of Queen couldn't even protect her own harem?

'I will seek vengeance!' Aynia hissed as she rose. 'I will teach the females of this Hive a lesson about violating the Queen's harem. Be they blood of my enemy or blood of my friends, I will take my vengeance, restore the honor of my males, and take dominion over what is mine.'

Aynia and Sarkany were lying on the pile of pillows in the corner of her bedchamber. Sarkany wasn't happy about being called into the Queen's chambers without his friend Moss. He stared into the fireplace.

Aynia grew tired of his sulking. She reached over and squeezed on his testicles.

Sarkany rolled away. 'Why do you do that?'

'Because I want your attention. Get your mind out of the harem.' Aynia rolled over on her stomach. 'Massage my back.'

Sarkany got up on his knees and began to work his hands over Aynia's back. As he kneaded her buttocks she spread her legs apart. Sarkany, quick to take advantage of a situation, began massaging Aynia between her legs.

'That feels good,' Aynia moaned.

'You're tense.'

'I'm angry that Thane Adders-Tongue's guards dared to touch you.'

'I wasn't hurt.'

'That's not the point,' Aynia growled. 'You're mine. When I think of them placing their hands on your body I'm outraged.'

Sarkany let his fingers lightly brush her inner thigh and pubic hair with a touch strong enough to tease but too light to please. He smiled with satisfaction as Aynia's legs spread further apart and her buttocks rose higher. 'It might not have happened if the harem was properly armed and trained as your guard.'

'Prince Moss had a sword. So did you.'

'The two of us weren't enough,' Sarkany whispered into her ear in his most seductive voice. He gently stroked her between her legs. As he began to withdraw his fingers Aynia pushed back against his hand.

'Do you like that?' he asked.

'Yes,' she admitted hesitantly. But she put her legs back together and buried her face into a pillow. 'I could almost surrender to your touch, but I can't seem take my mind off of this horrible day.'

Sarkany playfully bit Aynia's ass. She laughed and wriggled away from him.

'Ouch! Not that! Naughty boy. I should spank you.'

Sarkany lay down next to her on the pillows, stomach down. 'Go ahead. I've been punished by the best.'

Aynia got on her knees and examined the light scars on his back. 'Poor Sarkany, who beat you so?'

'In my Hive males are punished harshly from the time we're small. My Mother was very strict, and I was a mischief. One night I went too far with several ladies of the Royal Court. If it hadn't been for the timely entrance of my Mother I might have been made drone that night. Mother was very angry.'

'Your Mother did this to you?' Aynia asked, horrified.

'No. She handed me over to the Mistress of her Harem. The Mistress believed that no punishment was complete until there was blood. And apparently she wanted me for herself. The Mistress of the Harem was very jealous when she heard about my adventure. The next morning my Mother had the Mistress of the Harem executed. Much later, when I was well enough to travel, she sent me away to Ireland.'

Aynia gently rubbed Sarkany's back. 'You were exiled? I'm sorry.'

'I love it when you touch me,' Sarkany changed the subject. He was not about to start talking about his past. There was too much there that needed to remain secret.

Sarkany closed his eyes and enjoyed Aynia's touch. She was so tantalizingly close. He had to fight the impulse to turn over and wrestle her to the ground. Usually he had no problems getting a female to offer herself to him. Quite the opposite, his troubles usually stemmed from females who wouldn't take no for an answer. This Queen was a real challenge though. Every time he thought that he had her under his spell she managed to pull away from him.

Aynia leaned over and kissed Sarkany's ear.

'I like the way that your nipples rub against my back.' He told her.

'Do you ever dream of making love to me?' Aynia asked.

'Every night my lady.'

'Don't answer like that. I need the real answer.'

'That is the real answer. Sometimes I dream of making love to you and I wake up so hard that I have to go take a cold bath.'

'Turn over,' Aynia ordered him.

Sarkany did as he was told. Aynia looked for a time at his penis. There was no question that he wished to mate. He was beginning to grow hard. To help him along Aynia straddled him and rubbed her clitoris against his shaft.

Sarkany's strong willpower was all that stopped him from wrapping his arms around the Queen and thrusting into her. If he did he could lose her forever. It was a physical torture to him, but he would take things slow.

'So when you dream of making love to me, what do you dream about?' Aynia asked. She knew what she fantasized about but the minds of males were a mystery to her.

She dreamed of making love to Thorn, but she couldn't deny the attraction Sarkany held. Nor could she deny the pleasure she felt when he suckled at her breasts.

'Do you want me to show you?' Sarkany's voice dropped into a low resonating bass that enhanced his accent.

'Yes,' Aynia breathed. She stopped rubbing herself against him. Aynia was amazed at how tempting the idea was of impaling herself on Sarkany's thick, hard penis.

Sarkany neatly turned Aynia over onto her back on the pillows. He kissed her throat, her ears, and her lips gently. 'First I like to start with this.'

'Your mustache tickles.'

Sarkany stroked his thick black mustache. 'Do you want me to shave it off?'

Aynia looked at his high cheekbones, deep brown eyes, and curly black hair. 'No, it looks perfect on you,' she admitted.

'Shall I tickle you some more?' Sarkany moved his kisses to Aynia's stomach.

'Why are you and Moss so close?' Aynia asked. She wished that some small talk would take her mind off of the overwhelming desire to couple with the handsome Romanian Prince.

'I need him. It's in my blood to sire only males. If I want to be the Queen's lover I must have another male to sire her Princesses.'

'That sounds very calculating. I thought that you two were great friends.'

Sarkany shrugged. 'We are. I wouldn't have chosen him if we weren't so compatible. Moss understands my needs,' he said between kisses. 'Besides, he can't resist my charms.'

'Have you known him long?'

'We met while serving in the same military unit when I was sent to live at Swinford Hive where Mosses' Mother rules. We both love sport and adventure.'

'What adventures can a drone have?'

'It depends on how long of a leash his lady gives him. Some males need to be bound tightly to tradition. Others of us hope for a female strong enough to give us freedom. One day I will convince you to allow Moss and I to serve in the Royal Guard.'

'Enough,' Aynia warned Sarkany. 'For now consider yourself on a very short leash.'

Sarkany smiled. 'I have no objections as long as that short leash keeps me at my lady's side, or perhaps in her bed.'

'So you met Prince Moss at Swinford Hive?' Aynia changed the subject.

'When his Queen Mother told him that he was to be sent to Balnacra I begged to be sent with him,' Sarkany continued his story. 'The Queen had other ideas, which she made quite clear to me. She wanted me for her own harem. So when my friend left his Hive I stowed away with the procession bringing him here as tribute. By the time that they discovered me Moss and I were already on our way to be presented. I was very nervous when I met you. I was afraid that you would turn me away and I would have to go back to Moss's Hive.'

'You didn't look nervous. If anything I thought that you were overly confident. I almost turned you away because of it.'

'But you still accepted me.' Sarkany began kissing Aynia lower and lower on her stomach. 'In my dreams we don't talk this much.' He coaxed Aynia's thighs apart.

Aynia closed her eyes. Sarkany began caressing her stinger as he kissed her between her thighs. She never dreamed that her stinger could be the source of pleasure too.

'Do you know what you might like even better?'

'What?' Aynia murmured. She knew what her body was screaming out for her to do.

Sarkany got up on his knees. With his hard penis he teased her clitoris using short thrusts just against her as he continued to stroke her with his fingers.

Aynia shook her head. 'No, not yet,' she said, but her body wanted his penis inside of her. She wondered how something so large would fit inside her vagina. It was wider than the three fingers she sometimes slid into herself, and much longer. And yet, other females seemed to have no problem with it.

'I swear on my word as a Prince that I will not go further than this unless you ask me to. Do you like this?'

'Yes,' she admitted. Every short stroke of his tempted her to wrap her thighs around him and pull him inside of her. Each touch of his fingers on her sensitive clitoris made her want to scream out for more pressure, less pressure, or something that could bring her closer to the edge.

Sarkany knew the signs. Her lips were parted as she panted a little. Her cheeks and lips glowed deep pink. And despite her efforts not to, Aynia was thrusting her hips against him. Sarkany took a deep breath. Her scent was filling the air.

Aynia pushed away Sarkany's hand and began to stroke herself. He was doing a fine job, but she knew exactly what touch she needed to plunge into the orgasm that her body demanded.

'I love watching you touch yourself.' Sarkany said. It was the most amazingly erotic sight he'd ever seen, far beyond his dreams.

Aynia was past talking. She climaxed and thrust hard against Sarkany, taking him inside of her. After a quick, insignificant touch of pain a second wave of pleasure began to build. 'Oh,' Aynia moaned so quietly that Sarkany barely heard her. 'Fuck me. Fuck me hard.'

Sarkany pulled Aynia's ankles up to his neck as he took over thrusting. He slipped his fingers tightly around the base of his penis. The sight of Aynia stroking herself was nearly enough to make him come, but he wasn't going to just yet if he could stop it.

'I'm coming again,' Aynia said as another orgasm slammed through her body.

'I can feel it,' Sarkany told her. Between the contractions inside Aynia's vagina as she came and the wonderful feel of thrusting deep inside of her, Sarkany wasn't sure how long he could continue to thrust without coming. He made a valiant effort but finally couldn't hold back. He let go.

Moments later Sarkany smiled down at the Queen, but her eyes were closed. The smile was for him though. Once he'd come into the Queen and his fluids were inside of her she would never be able to resist him again.

The two lay on the pile of pillows, too drowsy and comfortable to think of moving. 'Are you glad now that you were brought to me without Moss?'

'Who's Moss?' Sarkany asked.

Aynia laughed. 'How did we measure up to your dreams?'

'Since I always have to end my dreams by taking a cold bath, this is much better.'

'That's hardly a glowing review.'

Sarkany took her hand and kissed her fingertips. 'That was the most incredible feeling in my life. I noticed that my lady took great pleasure also,' he started to slide his hand between her legs but she pushed it away.

'Too soon.'

'When you are ready for more pleasure I will happily provide it.'

'Where do you drones learn of these things?' She asked.

'Like what?'

'How to pleasure a female. How to pleasure each other. I would have never guessed at half of the places I enjoyed being stroked and licked.'

Sarkany nuzzled against Aynia's neck. 'I am sure that there are many more we could discover together.'

'But how do you know these things?'

'While a Princess studies everything she needs to know to be Queen, a Prince only studies the Queen.'

Aynia laughed. 'How do you study a Queen if you have no idea who you'll be married off to?'

'The basics of pleasure can be applied generally to most females. Individual variations must be adapted, of course.'

'Of course.' Aynia said seriously.

'But my lessons went beyond pleasuring you. I will know when you are in heat and when you are with child. I can smell every signal that your body sends out. I knew that you were intrigued with me at court. I knew just about how far I could push you. You were almost annoyed with me, but not quite.'

Aynia laughed. 'Am I so easy to read?'

Sarkany frowned. 'No, you're not. Much is given away by scent, but not enough and you give away nothing by your facial expression. It makes it much harder to read you.'

'Good, I like to keep you guessing.'

'It does make things much more challenging,' Sarkany admitted. And he liked a challenge. Seducing females was usually so easy for him that it lacked excitement.

'This way My Queen,' Heliotrope led Aynia down a hidden staircase to the prison cells of the hive.

Aynia wore a dark cloak with a hood that hid her face, but even in the dimly lit dungeon her disguise was inadequate. As the tallest member of the Hive, Aynia's head came dangerously close to bumping against the arches supporting the ceiling of the prison. Several times she was forced to bend down to pass safely from one chamber to another.

'We jailed them separately Majesty. In case the two were found innocent of charges I didn't want the drone's reputation compromised,' the head Jailer informed Aynia.

Aynia thought at first that the female was being sarcastic, but she appeared to be deadly serious. 'Do you believe that there is a chance of them being found innocent of treason?'

'Oh no Majesty, but only the most ingenuous Fairie would believe that a verdict equals the truth.'

'You say that my courts are flawed.'

The Jailer swallowed hard. Only an idiot would argue with the Queen. 'If I believed that only the guilty were ever charged with crimes, I would also have to believe that there's no reason for the courts to exist. Without the courts there is no chance for justice.'

'You have a very interesting view of your job Jailer. I wonder how you avoid becoming cynical.' Aynia asked.

'It's a constant struggle Majesty. Ah, here's where I keep the female, Lady Deidre.' The Jailer stopped in front of a thick wooden door and unlocked it. 'Please, mind your head. The ceilings inside are even lower than they are out here.'

Aynia nodded and entered the cell. Heliotrope followed her in.

Deidre's cell was a large room with a good-sized fireplace and enough candles to light it well. A desk, a table, and a comfortable bed furnished the room. Aynia threw back her hood and looked around.

'Majesty!' Deidre fell to her knees in front of Aynia and kissed Aynia's ringed hand.

'Your cell looks well enough,' Aynia observed. 'Poor families in my Hive live their entire lives in less space.'

'It's one of the advantages of being nobility, of the Seelie Court,' another voice spoke.

Aynia turned to face the speaker. 'Ambassador, I wish that we could have met in more pleasant circumstances.'

'I agree. I'm here to offer the support of Her Majesty, Queen Lilac of Ardcharnich Hive, to her blood relative,' the Ambassador made sure that Aynia understood that this was a family matter in the eyes of the other Queen. It was as close to a threat as the Ambassador would dare go. 'As you can well imagine, my Queen has taken a deep interest in this case. She wishes to be assured that her cousin is treated well and given due justice.'

'You may tell Her Majesty Queen Lilac that in this case her wishes are my own.'

The Ambassador bowed. 'Given the circumstances of the matter, however, I'm not so sure that justice will be done.'

'What do you mean?'

'Lady Deidre tells me that the guards who arrested her created evidence to make it appear that she was having sexual relations with your drone. While she does admit to improperly meeting him inside her chambers, she absolutely denies the charge of adultery.' The Ambassador from Ardcharnich was a lawyer by training. It showed as she pleaded Deidre's case to Aynia.

'I never touched him my Queen,' Deidre said. Tears rolled down her cheeks. 'And I can prove it.'

'If you have evidence, produce it!'

'It's in the dress that I was wearing when they came to arrest me. They stripped the both of us. My dress is probably still lying on the floor of my cell.'

'And what evidence is this?'

'I wrote a letter to you. I was resigning my post and leaving for the Hive de Chambord. If you look in my desk you will find the letter from Chambord offering me my old position. I was just saying goodbye to the Prince. I admit that I love him, but I never touched him.'

Heliotrope snorted. 'A resignation is no proof.'

'But he will tell you the same if you question him.'

'Stories can be concocted.'

Deidre turned back to Aynia. 'Please, please believe me.'

Aynia's heart was still cold. 'How did you two arrange to meet?'

'We didn't, really. Copperhead tricked the Prince into believing that I wanted to meet with him. Copperhead seems to have made up a good many messages back and forth between the two of us.' Deidre admitted bitterly.

'But you say that you love the Prince Noisi.'

'The hour of my death draws near. Why should I bother to lie at this point? Even telling the truth seems useless.' Deidre bowed her head and began to cry again.

Aynia turned to the Ambassador. 'There's a slight chance that she could prove her innocence to me.'

'What?' Deidre was again full of hope.

'I am, of course, willing to listen to your thoughts Queen Aynia,' the Ambassador said.

'But you must understand that no matter what you prove to me, the mere fact that you were found alone in a room with one of my drones is enough to have you both sentenced to death. Thane Adders-Tongue is out for blood. If I don't put you to death she'll accuse me of being soft on crime.'

'I just want to prove my innocence to you My Queen. I need for you to believe that my word is still good. What the court believes is beyond my cares.'

'No Lady Deidre, you care a great deal what the court thinks,' the Ambassador corrected her.

'Have you ever lain with a male?' Aynia asked.

'No Majesty,' Deidre admitted, confused.

'Then you possess the proof that you need. Lie down on your cot and remove your underclothes.'

Reluctantly Deidre pulled off her garments and lie down on the cot. Ashamed of what was about the happen, she turned her head to the wall.

Aynia pulled off her glove and sat down on the cot next to Deidre. She moved Deidre's thigh off to the side and slid her index finger into Deidre's vagina. At the tip of her finger she found Deidre's proof. 'Virgo Intacta. Come Ambassador, I want witnesses. Sit here and insert your finger.'

The Ambassador nodded and took Aynia's place. When she was satisfied with the evidence she moved out of the way for Heliotrope.

Heliotrope concurred. 'She's still a virgin.'

'I apologize for the lack of lubrication,' Aynia told Deidre as Deidre pulled her undergarments back on.

'I apologize for allowing Cobra-Lily to catch me in such an obvious trap.'

'Cobra-Lily!' Aynia knelt down and stared intently at Deidre. 'I knew that Copperhead was part of this, but I didn't know about Cobra-Lily. She was the one who entered my chambers with armed guards?'

'You didn't know? I thought that you knew. She was arrested along with the rest of Adders-Tongue's guards. I've heard her voice. Sounds travel far in the dungeon.'

'That little pit viper has struck at me once too often. Ambassador, I'm convinced of Lady Deidre's innocence at the charge of adultery, but as you know, she admits guilt on charges that are still capital offenses. However, even I'm not insensitive to the matter of love,' Aynia said softly as she thought of Thorn, and then of Sarkany. 'I believe that even if the two had not met alone Cobra-Lily would have falsified evidence. Tell your Queen that I seek true justice in this case.'

The Ambassador bowed. 'I will tell her that you seek the truth Queen Aynia.'

'Come Heliotrope, we have a few other calls to make. Deidre, I will do what I can, but remember, even if you escape with your life you will be banished forever from Scotland.'

Deidre nodded. She shivered. The Queen was still very angry.

Aynia gestured to the Jailer. 'Take me to the Prince's cell.'

'If your Majesty will follow me,' the Jailer led them into the most dismal part of the prison. The Jailer opened up a cell door. The room reveled was so small that the Prince could not sit down on the floor and stretch out his legs.

'I have larger closets,' Aynia gasped. 'He's a Prince, and one of my drones. Take him out of this horrible cell at once.'

'Majesty, this is the punishment for males charge with adultery.'

'Punishment? You just told me that he could be innocent!'

'He's a male Majesty. This is their lot.'

'Move him to a better cell.' Aynia looked at the pool of foul liquid on the floor. 'You'll have use of this one soon enough. I will be sending you another male, one who is guilty of far worse than this Prince stands accused of. When he is brought to you place him in here.' Aynia placed a heavy bag of gold in the Jailer's hand.

'As your Majesty commands,' the Jailer went away to prepare a new cell for Noisi.

'Help him to his feet.' Aynia ordered Heliotrope. 'Prince Noisi, this is your Queen.'

Noisi looked up at Aynia. 'My Queen, I hear your voice. I have been in the dark for long and can not see well.'

'We have only a few questions for you. Why did you do this thing to Us? Was it not enough to be a member of my Royal Harem? Was it not enough to be my drone?'

Noisi shook his head. 'It might have been enough if I had thought for a moment that I mattered to you. But I didn't. And then I had a chance to be loved.'

'A chance? You don't have the right to do with your body as you wish. You're my property!' Aynia yelled. She hoped that making love to Sarkany would kill the surging insanity of possessiveness over her harem, but Aynia once again couldn't control her anger. As a young Princess she questioned the restrictions society placed on mating males. But now as Queen she understood the physical need to maintain and protect a harem from other females.

'I wasn't talking about sex my Queen, I was talking about love.'

Aynia hit Noisi across his face. 'Don't speak to me of love. You betrayed me.'

'I betrayed your pride, not your heart.'

Aynia took a deep breath and counted to ten once, then twice. She was letting her anger get away from her. The male spoke the truth.

Heliotrope gave a small cough.

'Do you love Lady Deidre?' Aynia asked in a deceptively calm tone.

'With all my heart Majesty.'

'You don't hesitate to admit it.'

'I will die soon. I have no secrets.'

Aynia privately thought that everyone was being a bit melodramatic, but on the other hand, they were truly in danger of losing their lives. 'Did Cobra-Lily strip off your clothes when she removed you from the Royal Chambers?'

'Yes.'

'Did you ever touch Lady Deidre? Did you have sex with her?'

'No My Queen! We refused to betray you.'

Aynia nodded. 'Well enough. Prince Noisi, I will have you moved to another cell. Do not talk to anyone, not even the Jailer. When Heliotrope comes for you obey her silently and quickly. Do you understand?'

'Yes my Queen.'

Aynia sighed. 'See that he is moved to a better cell my faithful attendant.'

'Yes Your Majesty.' Heliotrope answered.

'Do you mind that I pulled you from service in the Temple?'

'No My Queen. I will always serve you first and foremost. However, I think that it's best that you forgive your other attendants, if I may be so free as to speak of this.'

'I value your opinion,' Aynia said but her tone was guarded.

'I'm growing old my Queen, and have looked forward to a quiet life in the Temple for many years. I live to serve you but I don't think that I am best suited to serve your needs now. Of course, call on me if you need me for a special assignment such as this. I will always come to help. But for your daily needs the attendants that you have now are truly some of the best.'

'I am angry beyond words with my attendants right now. Perhaps in several days I will be able to look at this situation without emotion. I think, however, that it serves me best right now for my attendants to feel the full sting of my anger so that this doesn't happen again. Besides, I think I need for my enemies to truly believe that their plan has succeeded.'

'Think? My Lady, it did succeed. You won't be allowed to pardon the lovers.'

'I have no intention of pardoning them.'

'Your Highness?' Heliotrope was shocked.

'The executions will take place as scheduled.' Aynia told Heliotrope. She turned to go. 'I must go now and question Cobra-Lily and the guards who invaded my Royal Chamber. Please go and warn Freesia and Verbena that I have task set for them tonight. Tell them to sleep well and to meet me in my chambers when the moon rises.'

Heliotrope was baffled. For a moment there she thought that Aynia was going to work out some sort of miraculous rescue for Lady Deidre and Prince Noisi. While Heliotrope believed that the two lovers deserved punishment, she was deeply shocked to see her beloved Aynia so calmly contemplating their deaths.

'Jailer,' Aynia called out.

'Yes, my Queen.'

'Captain Sage brought you several prisoners I presume.'

'Yes your Highness. They are in a shared cell.'

'Bring a torch. And a razor.'

The Jailer rushed to comply.

'Cobra-Lily,' Aynia acknowledged her with the briefest of nods.

'Fuck off bitch.'

The Jailer smacked her hand across Cobra-Lily's face. 'You will address your Queen properly.'

Cobra-Lily tried to spit on Aynia, but only managed to dribble spittle down the front of her clothes.

'Are these the guards who invaded my Royal Chambers under your command?' Aynia asked.

The guards dropped to their knees. The twelve of them were chained together so that those who hesitated to kneel down were pulled down to the floor.

'Spare us Majesty.'

'Which one of you touched my drones?'

No one spoke.

'Who was it that stripped the clothes off of my males, tied them up, and then proceeded to fondle their genitals? Show me the female who touched Prince Sarkany!' Aynia's anger was surging through her again. Some female here was going to die for touching him.

The guards looked down at the ground but they would not speak. More than one of them had taken the opportunity to lay hands on the Queen's drones. But they had no idea which drone was the one named Sarkany.

Aynia walked to the end of the line and sniffed the air around the first prisoner. The guards were both male and female, although there were far more male than females in the cell. Then she took another step and sniffed the air again. At her fifth step she paused. She could smell a scent she knew.

Her hand cupped the chin of the female before her and forced the female to look up at her. 'He had a black moustache, black curly hair, and eyes so brown they appear to be black. That is the one you undressed?'

The female finally gave a small nod.

'You made him bend over. You cupped his balls in one hand and held a knife against him with the other. Then, while you held the knife at his balls you stroked his penis. Does this accurately describe the events as you remember them?'

The guard averted her eyes.

'I will take that as a yes.' Aynia lashed with her stinger and impaled the female's hand but did not release any of her venom. Then she stepped on the fingers with the spiked heel of her black leather boot, holding the hand down as she pulled her stinger out. 'That's just a reminder to keep your hands off of my drones.'

The female screamed and clutched her hand to her chest as it spewed blood.

Quick as a blink of the eye Aynia's stinger was leveled at the other guards. One by one she slammed her stinger into their faces with such force that most were thrown backwards against the cell wall. Those who put their hands up in an effort to defend themselves were stung either in the neck or the chest.

Then she returned to the guard who touched Sarkany and stung her repeatedly in the groin.

Cobra-Lily watched her guards writhe in agony as the Queen's poison slowly worked through their systems, but she would not be cowed.

The Jailer hit the back of Cobra-Lily's knees with a club so that she fell to her knees. 'On your knees for the Queen.'

'I serve only the true Queen,' Cobra-Lily sneered. 'Shall I start talking about your little secret Aynia?'

Aynia ignored the jibe. Jailers were always fiercely loyal to the reigning Queen. The Jailer was aware of the poison that permeated her blood, she was aware of the agonizing death it would deliver if she failed to take the antidote, and she was also aware that only the Queen could deliver the antidote on a daily basis. Betraying the Queen would mean certain and painfully slow death. 'Cobra-Lily, you are charged with attempting twice to poison the Queen. How do you plead?'

'Disastrously unlucky.'

'You are charged with theft of Royal Jewels.'

'Hey, you got it all back, just in a different form. I thought that you liked that gold collar. Why didn't you wear it?'

'Call it a premonition,' Aynia told her. 'You are also charged with the death of a metal smith and a jeweler in the Guild section of the Hive. How do you plead?'

'So you found the bodies?'

'Pieces, some parts didn't burn completely in the furnaces.'

The Jailer gulped. This was sensational news. Too bad it would mean her own neck if she ever told anyone. Silence was demanded of the Jailer as much as loyalty.

'Well,' Cobra-Lily shrugged, 'they were just common workers anyway. There's plenty more where they came from. They're replaceable.'

Aynia backhanded Cobra-Lily across the face. 'Not to their families. Now what's your plea?'

'Well, I guess I'd have to say that I'm guilty of that too.'

'What rare bravado.'

'You can't touch me. My Aunt will save me,' Cobra-Lily spat out. 'She needs me to do her dirty work.'

'Your Aunt? Thane Adders-Tongue? I'm afraid that she'll never notice that you've gone missing.'

'Yes she will. She never goes anywhere without her guards, and I manage the guards.'

'You mean those guards?' Aynia pointed to the bodies on the ground. The last few to be stung were still somewhat alive. 'And yet a hue and cry hasn't been raised. No one in your own clan seems to miss you much. Could it be that Thane Adders-Tongue is so proud and full of herself that she wouldn't recognize a new guard, or even a whole new set of guards? She only sees the livery. My personal guards are in her uniforms right now. She has no idea that you're gone.'

'So you're just going to kill me? Like them?'

'Why should I spoil your surprise?' Aynia hissed. 'Jailer, hand me the razor. And lift the torch so that I can see.'

The Jailer, expecting spurting blood, turned her head away. For a Jailer she was quite squeamish about things like blood and torture. Curiosity, however, finally got the better of her. She opened one eye and squinted. Then the Jailer took a full look with both eyes. The Queen was shaving Cobra-Lily's head. Hair fell to the floor all around the prisoner.

'Majesty?' The Jailer asked. Shaving the head was a sign of sexual shame. The Jailer wondered for a moment if she had the right Fairie in the right cells.

Aynia finished shaving Cobra-Lily's head. She walked over and handed the razor back to the Jailer. For a second the Jailer thought that the Queen was about to leave but then Aynia took the torch and turned back to face the prisoner.

'The Queen trembles,' the Jailer thought.

It wasn't the cold of the dungeon. It was pure anger.

Aynia held the torch down low so that the light reflected up onto her face. Cobra-Lily shuddered a little at the effect. The Queen, who always seemed so distant and passionless before, looked sinister and menacing now. Her full height towered over

Cobra-Lily. Behind the Queen her stinger slashed through the air with a deadly swoosh as it snaked from side to side.

'Was this plot hatched specifically to hurt Deidre?'

'She was a weak spot, we just used her.'

'So it was just a plot to take control of my attendants? Or was this a personal attack on me?'

'Personal? We don't even know who the hell you are.' Cobra-Lily admitted.

Aynia kicked Cobra-Lily in the face with her spiked-heeled black leather boot, breaking Cobra-Lily's nose in a glorious gush of red blood. 'We are Queen. That's who the hell I am.'

Cobra-Lily, whose hands were shackled behind her back, lost her balance and fell on the floor.

Aynia went to the door with the Jailer. 'Cover her face with a bag, but see that it has air holes. She must live. I will send wine, food, and clothes for this prisoner tonight. My most trusted attendants will take her into exile. You will not see anything, you will not hear anything.'

'Yes my Lady.'

'Exile? Is that the best that you can do?' Cobra-Lily tried to laugh with disdain.

The cell door closed. All light disappeared. Cobra-Lily spat out blood.

In the darkness the sound carried well, the scratching sound of tiny feet with long toenails. At first there were a cautious few. Then more came. Soon the cell was swarming with rats come to feed on the dead and the dying. Cobra-Lily closed her eyes and sent up a fervent prayer to the Goddesses as rats brushed past her thighs that the blood on her face would not attract the rats to her flesh too. .

Copperhead was in a panic. He had no idea where to hide from the certain wrath of the Queen. The Hive, which housed thousands, now seemed impossibly small. The Royal Palace, Parliament, the Estates of the Seelie Court, the nobility, all were closed to him. He could chance finding Queen Carman out in the wilds again, but night would fall soon and Copperhead needed a place to pass the night inside the Hive. In the morning he would flee Balnacra.

There was only one place where a free drone could pass a night and that was in one of the pubs with the common workers. Copperhead cursed his lack of coins. Males were rarely trusted to handle money. Short of his clothes he had nothing to sell, except, of course, the fact that he was a free drone. Considering the idea of making himself a rent boy for the night, Copperhead found that he had no real qualms against it.

Now that he had a plan to follow, Copperhead walked to the poorer section of the Hive, and went in search of a pub of ill repute.

A pub that seemed to fit the bill was at the end of a dark alley that branched off of a small winding street. Copperhead recognized the street as the one he'd followed Cobra-Lily to. As he remembered the metal smith's shop was a few steps away.

No one noticed as Copperhead entered the dark, noisy pub. He moved off into a corner near the door while he waited for his eyes to adjust. There was a roaring fire burning in a massive pit on the north side of the room where a band of wandering Fairie was standing about the hearth leading a spirited songfest.

Despite the rough appearance of many of the pub's clientele the pub seemed safe enough. They were simply workers relaxing after a long day of hard work. Copperhead walked to the barkeep to inquire about purchasing some food. He had no coins, but he had a gold earring. That would be enough to buy a meal in this modest place.

'Innkeeper? I need to buy a meal and some drink.'

The barkeep frowned as she looked Copperhead over. 'Got coin drone?'

'I have this earring.' Copperhead removed it and handed it to her.

The barkeep bit the gold to test it. 'One bowl, slice of bread, two beers.'

'How about a place to sleep?'

A customer laughed at this. 'Not many drones dare fall asleep in here. You might get abducted pretty one.'

'No unaccompanied drones!' The barkeep pointed to a large hand printed sign on the wall that was surrounded by a collection of decorative plates. 'Got enough problems with the Royal Guard. License problems.' The barkeep placed a large bowl of suspicious stew in front of Copperhead along with a massive piece of bread that was well buttered and slathered with honey. Copperhead started eating quickly so that he could finish before the innkeeper decided to throw him out. As he ate the female drew a pint of honey lager and placed it next to Copperhead's elbow.

'Do you know of a place that I could go?' He asked.

'Humph,' the barkeep grumbled and went to serve her female customers.

Across the room the traveling band of Fairie banged loudly on drums to get the attention of the pub's clientele. 'We don't come here just to sing for you!' The lead female entertainer shouted out.

'Aye, we come to drink your beer!' Another member of the troop answered her.

'Well, we certainly didn't come here for the food!'

A roar of laughter swelled up from the crowd.

Copperhead turned so that he could still eat while watching the troop perform.

'Aye, that is very true. No offense innkeeper, for we know that you serve the best food that you can. Which isn't to say much. Is there a reason why the mortuary is built next door? Coincidence? Or convenience?'

'Get on with it Irish, or I'll have you and yours outside in the gutter!' The barkeep answered back with a good-natured growl.

'You know I only mean it in the spirit of fun. And now, also in the spirit of fun, we have a few tunes for you. While we sing we will pass our hat. 'Tis an ugly hat, but we love it, for it buys us our beer. Give what you can while we sing for you. But first,' the entertainer had been walking through the crowd and was by now at the bar, 'I need a whiskey to lubricate the pipes.'

The barkeep poured a shot of whiskey.

'On the house?' The entertainer asked hopefully.

'Never,' thundered the barkeep.

The entertainer placed a coin down on the counter. 'Well, it never hurts to ask, but since I'm paying for it, how about some thing a wee bit older than yesterday's bread?'

The barkeep poured a bit of amber liquid from a different bottle. The entertainer sipped it and sighed. 'Now that's what I call a fine Scottish spirit, and speaking of spirits,' the entire troop broke into a lively song about a randy ghost. It was a well-known tune and most customers joined in with the singing.

Copperhead slowly sipped his second lager while he watched the troop of entertainer's work. They sang mostly standard songs that everyone knew. While this went on an old Fairie walked through the crowd and read palms. Copperhead wanted to have his palm read but he lacked the coin to pay her. As the evening wore away the entertainers sang a haunting, sad song about an Irish Hive that was destroyed by humans. While they sang the tune a strange smoke came from the fire. It billowed out of the hearth and drifted at eye level through the crowd. The sweet scent of the smoke filled the pub. Many a customer was wiping her eyes by the end of the song, either from the effects of the smoke, or from the sad words of the song. The next day everyone from the pub found herself singing the tune at home and at work. By the end of the week everyone in the Hive knew the lyrics.

A constable walking his beat stopped in long enough to listen to the song. He saw Copperhead standing at the bar and frowned. 'I don't suppose you're going to let your clientele slip are you?' he asked the barkeep.

'He's leaving, right now,' the barkeep said as she took away the plate and pint of beer from Copperhead.

Copperhead knew better than to protest. He didn't want to cause any scene that would bring him to the attention of the Royal Guard. He headed out of the pub.

When the constable turned the corner the barkeep hurried outside and grabbed Copperhead's arm. "I know a place where you can stay the night, or longer, as long as you earn your keep. My sister has a place two streets over. Tell her I sent you.' Then the barkeep was gone.

Copperhead stood in front of the pub trying to decide what he should do. The constable returned. 'Move along drone. This isn't that type of pub.'

Copperhead scuttled along. He thought that he had the wrong alley until a seedy looking female passed him and went into a narrow doorway. Copperhead could see a crowd of females inside and more than a few drones. Taking a deep breath he went inside.

A strong family resemblance led Copperhead to the owner. She listened to his speech, then nodded her head and took him to a back hallway. He could see many curtained alcoves off of the hallway and heard unmistakable sounds coming from behind those curtains. This was definitely one of those types of pubs.

'My sister sent you along?'

'I need a place to sleep.'

'Not much sleeping going on in here. Still, you're a pretty one, aren't you? New to the game?'

'Game?'

'What you do to get thrown out of your home?'

'Um,' Copperhead thought of a story quickly. 'I got caught outside of the harem, with her sister.'

'Heard that one a few times before.' The brothel owner smiled. 'I'm Miss Tulip. This is my place, all the rules are mine, got it? Break a rule, I break your head, got it?' Tulip didn't wait for answers, so Copperhead just nodded his head. The staccato delivery continued. 'You push drinks in between customers. Never turn a customer down. No matter what she wants you to do, you do it, right? Regular customers will be your bread and butter so always make sure that they get theirs. You take a minimum of three customers a day. If you can't get it up three times a day you're out of here. If a customer takes two of you at once it counts only as half a time. My rules. If a customer picks you for the wrestling matches it counts as two as long as you win. You lose, it don't count, got it?'

Copperhead had no idea what Tulip meant by wrestling.

'Now take your clothes off and let me see what we got.'

This Copperhead understood. He pulled off his tunic and his hose. He was proud of his body and didn't mind showing it to the female Tulip.

'You got wings. You nobility?'

Copperhead nodded.

'Might charge extra for you,' Tulip licked her lips as she walked around Copperhead and ran her hands over his body. 'Soft. You never worked a day of your life, did you? Never felt a boy with skin this soft in all my life. Wouldn't mind a little taste of that myself. Later. Got business. Go out and start working.'

'Wait a second. What do I earn?'

'Three meals a day and a bed. You keep tips.'

'What about a uniform?'

Tulip cackled in a phlegmy way. 'You're wearing it sweetie. Now get out there and hustle drinks,' Tulip slapped Copperhead across the buttocks.

Grateful that this arrangement was only for one night, Copperhead went to the main pub of the brothel.

Tulip watched him walk away. 'That's one mighty cute piece of ass.'

One of Tulip's drones, having just left a customer, looked to see what Tulip was talking about. The drone frowned. New males in the bar always took regular customers away. Some customers never returned to their usual male. This drone had a steady repeat customer base that he didn't want to loose. 'He'll be in the wrestling pit tonight,' the drone observed.

'I'm sure that he will. He's got wings. Everyone loves to see nobility humiliated.'

The drone nodded. 'Too bad I just did my third of the day. I'd like to take on a piece of that myself,' he growled threateningly.

Tulip nodded. It was good to have competition between the drones. It kept them on their toes, Tulip thought as she wandered back to her seat behind a small bar in the front room. Despite the fact that she was extremely rich by now Tulip like to keep a close eye on things. So she always worked the bar herself rather than hiring the help. Besides, she was truly fond of her brothel.

Copperhead tried to walk through the crowd but every step involved a hand sliding up his inner thigh or grasping his penis or pinching his bottom. The insertion of a rather dry index finger into his anus taught him not to lean over to take drink orders. Luckily for him the brothel only served beer, and only one size of glass. The only variation in orders was the number of pints.

After about two hours of exhausting work delivering beers and removing empty glasses Copperhead was stunned to see all of the other drones lined up on a small stage and Tulip beckoning him to join them. He worked his way through the crowd and up onto the stage.

'Thanks for joining us sweetie,' Tulip said without any apparent sarcasm. 'Now patrons, I think that you know most of my boys, but I'd like to introduce the new drone. Do a little turn for the customers, show them the goods.'

Copperhead did a turn as instructed. While the crowd had seen him working on the floor they now responded as if they were seeing him for the first time. There were hoots and whistles.

'We will be holding two wrestling matches tonight. Top four to get the vote go into the ring. Sorry you loyal customers, but Leaf did his third today already and claims that he can't get it up again. I know that he's undefeated and you'd all like to see him in the ring, but it isn't to be.'

A boo went up from the crowd as Leaf obligingly pouted.

'However! We have Jonquil, who is practically undefeated. He's only lost to Leaf, so he's the odds-on favorite to pin his opponent. Let's hear by a cheer if you want him in the ring!'

The crowd cheered loudly.

'Hey Leaf, if you ain't good for anything else, get me another drink while the others are posing on stage!' A customer shouted out.

'A good point, every drone that's done his limit today is dismissed to go serve beer.' Tulip ordered the drones.

No other drones moved.

'Well, it seems that my boys all want a piece of the new drone! Let's hear your votes for who goes into the ring.'

Copperhead never understood how Tulip managed to understand the drunken shouts of her patrons but somehow she ended up with three other drones on the stage and Copperhead. The others left the stage and went to set up a small wrestling pit in the center of the room.

'Shall we let the new drone watch the first match and see what he needs to do?' Tulip asked.

The crowd seemed divided.

'All right, we'll let him watch the first match, but just to make sure he's here for the second, Leaf, shackle him to that column.'

Leaf did as he was told. Copperhead grew nervous. What was he going to see that would make him want to run away?

The pit was prepared and the customers pulled chairs close around it. They wagered eagerly on the outcome and debated the merits of the two drones preparing to wrestle. The first two contestants rubbed oil over their bodies. Their skin gleamed in the candlelight.

Tulip stood at the side of the pit. 'You both know the rules. If you're pinned, you lose.'

The two nodded.

'Well, get into the pit.'

They stepped inside and faced each other.

'Begin!'

The wrestling match began pretty much as Copperhead had imagined but his idea of being pinned was far off the mark. He watched the two drones grapple with each other. Their oiled hands slid off easily, making a hold nearly impossible. Finally one of the drones' feet slipped on the mixture of oil and sweat on the mat. His opponent took advantage and flipped the first drone down on his knees onto the mat. Then, as the first drone tried desperately to wriggle away, the second drone mounted him. Once the drone's penis was inside his opponent's anus, Tulip announced that the second drone was the winner.

The winner took his victory, pounding his penis deeper into his opponent. Then he pulled out and came on the loser's buttocks.

The loser stood up and wiped off his backside with a towel. 'You know that I hate it when you do that Fig.'

'That's why I do it,' Fig answered back saucily.

Piles of gold coins exchanged hands.

Copperhead took a deep breath. So this was why they felt that they had to force him to stay. He knew that he was bound to lose. He was not in nearly as good of physical shape as these other drones. On the other hand, what did he have to fear? How much did this differ from a session with Camellia? Then Copperhead saw the size of his opponent's penis.

'Your turn sweetie. Try to make it look good for the customers,' Tulip whispered to Copperhead. 'Don't loose too soon.'

One of the other drones was rubbing oil into Copperhead's skin. 'You don't stand any chance if you don't get hard,' the drone told him.

'I don't think that I can.' Copperhead groaned.

The other drone made a face and took Copperhead's penis into his mouth. Copperhead's penis grew hard. 'That's better.'

'It sure is.'

'Part your cheeks and let me get some oil in there for you. You don't want to get taken without some lubrication.'

'You assume that I'll loose.'

'You're supposed to loose stupid. Do you think these females want to see some snooty noble win?' The other drone whispered.

This news didn't cheer Copperhead up one bit.

'Come on boy, get into the pit,' Tulip said. She whispered something to Jonquil that caused him to break into an evil smile.

Copperhead gauged the run for the door and realized that he couldn't possibly make it. 'It's only for tonight,' he whispered to himself.

'I think that he's praying,' a customer laughed.

'Face your opponent, and begin!' Tulip ordered.

The customers began shouting.

Tulip paused at the door for a moment, and then slipped outside.

Copperhead gave his opponent a little smile. Jonquil didn't smile back. They went around in circles. Copperhead kept his backside firmly away from Jonquil.

Jonquil feinted right. Copperhead fell for the trick. Jonquil went down on one knee and put Copperhead across his other knee. Playing to the audience, Jonquil smacked Copperhead's buttocks hard with stinging strokes. The crowd went wild with approval.

Copperhead took advantage of his oiled skin and wriggled away.

They began to circle again.

This time Jonquil went straight for Copperhead's knees. Jonquil grabbed Copperhead, lifted him off of the mat, and turned him upside down. Copperhead hoped that Jonquil's hands wouldn't slide, or else Copperhead would fall and break his neck.

'Suck my cock,' Jonquil ordered the upside down Copperhead.

Copperhead took Jonquil's massive penis into his mouth. He could hardly breathe.

The crowd cheered wildly again.

Tulip came back into the pub and made a sign to Jonquil.

Jonquil finally put Copperhead down. 'Enough games. I'm going to pin you. And I'm going to fuck your ass so deep and hard that my come will shoot out of your nose.'

Copperhead gulped. Looking at the size of Jonquil's penis this was remotely possible. They resumed their wrestling stances. In seconds Copperhead was on the mat on his knees. He felt like his anus was being ripped apart, but despite Jonquil's tough words, he was entering Copperhead slowly, a little at a time, so that the massive cock wouldn't tear him.

Copperhead found himself rocking against Jonquil so that he, not Jonquil, was the one actually determining how deep Jonquil went. Copperhead was gasping and trying very hard not to come. He thought for a moment about possibly staying at the brothel for a few more days. If only Jonquil would reach around and stroke him this would be wonderful.

The front door of the brothel opened. Soon the place was filled with Royal Guards, led by Verbena. Most of the customers suddenly disappeared through back doors.

Verbena calmly picked up an overturned chair and sat it down next to the wrestling pit. She propped her feet up on the rope edge of the wrestling ring, her long legs demurely crossed at the ankles.

Jonquil looked up at her, a questioning look on his face.

'Oh no, by all means, continue,' Verbena offered.

Jonquil shrugged. Copperhead had lost his hard on, and Jonquil wasn't holding back any longer. Copperhead thought that his ass was being ripped apart.

'Come already, damn it,' Copperhead groaned.

Jonquil picked up his pace, pounding hard and deep into Copperhead. Finally he shuddered and came. Then, for good measure, he bucked against Copperhead a few more times.

'You're not much of a fuck, but at least you were tight,' Jonquil told Copperhead as he climbed out of the ring.

Verbena stood. 'Copperhead, you're charged with treason against the Queen. You are to accompany us to the prison where you will be held until your trial.' Verbena turned to Tulip and handed her a bag of gold. 'This should compensate for any lost earnings tonight.'

Tulip weighed the bag of gold in her hand. It represented a good night's take. 'It's a little light,' she complained.

Verbena frowned. 'If this is less than you make on an average night then you've been underreporting your income for taxes.'

Tulip weighed the bag once again as if to reconsider. 'Maybe this is the right amount.'

'The Queen thanks you for your information that the traitor was taking refuge here.'

'Tell the Queen, my sister and I, we're loyal to her. Look,' Tulip pointed to the wall behind her bar. On it was a massive collection of decorative plates, each featuring some moment in Queen Aynia's brief reign. 'I've got the whole set. It'll be worth a fortune some day.'

Verbena seriously doubted that, but she nodded diplomatically. Her own Mother had the complete set of plates from the reign of the prior Queen.

Adders-Tongue was enjoying her morning meal alone when a messenger came into the room. Adders-Tongue was annoyed. Her personal guard was supposed to stop this kind of thing from happening. Lately though her personal guard seemed surly and disinclined to follow her orders.

'Thane Adders-Tongue,' the messenger said between gulps of air, 'I bring news from the court.'

'Quit panting and tell me.'

'Lady Deidre and Prince Noisi pled guilty to the charges of treason and adultery.'

Adders-Tongue slowly placed her napkin down. She didn't want to show her excitement over this news. 'Was the Queen present?'

'Yes.'

'And what did she do?'

'She set an execution date.'

'When will it be?'

'Thursday morning, three days from now.'

'Thank you messenger, you're dismissed.'

The messenger walked out of the room with a frown. He ran all the way from the court to the estate and the Thane was too cheap to tip him.

Aynia and Moss were in her bedchamber alone. Aynia was quiet, deep in thought.

Moss wondered what he should do. The Queen sent for him. She specifically ordered that he be alone. Once Moss arrived in her chambers she barely acknowledged his presence. She just lay in front of the fireplace staring into the flames.

Slowly Moss slid the sheer aqua robe off of Aynia's shoulder. Her breast was exposed so that he could nurse. When he was done with the one breast he moved to the other, further pushing the robe aside until Aynia wore nothing. Except for an absentminded pat on Mosses' head Aynia didn't react to any move that Moss made.

This didn't in any way resemble the story Sarkany told about his time alone with the Queen. And Sarkany was not the boastful type. Although the Queen had her virginity to give only once Moss would've liked at the least to have her attention. A little angry and determined to get the Queen to take notice, Moss decided to become a bit bolder in his moves.

Aynia realized that Moss was turning her on her stomach, and she felt him massaging her back, but she couldn't stop thinking about the prisoners in her jail. Noisi and Deidre had betrayed her, but in truth Aynia had no feelings at all for the handsome Prince. She felt pride at possessing such a physically beautiful male but she felt no desire to actually be with him. As for Deidre, well, she was disappointed with Deidre, and her sisters, but was the virtue of a mere male worth the life of a skilled advisor?

This inability to feel the kind of possessive rage for Noisi she did for Sarkany, and the constant rumors in the Hive about her emotional coldness began to worry Aynia. Was she really so distant? Was she frigid? Was she incapable of caring about any male? No, she had true, deep feelings for Thorn.

And where Sarkany was concerned, well, there was no doubt that she could thaw for his skilled touch. Where her dreams were once dominated by gentle seduction scenes involving Thorn, now she enjoyed wilder desires centered on Sarkany. At least he was willing and able to mate with her.

As Aynia occasionally took meals in her harem she would feel Sarkany's eyes on her. She would look up and see him staring at her like a wolf eyeing prey. Then she would feel tingles of pleasure as she thought about the last time that they made love. Sometimes she would begin to daydream about commanding him to crawl under the table to lick her pussy while she continued to visit with the rest of her harem. Other times she would blush and have to look away from him.

'I executed twelve workers today,' Aynia confessed to Moss. She didn't know why she told him, but something like guilt was gnawing at her soul. If she didn't tell somebody Aynia thought that she would go mad.

'I am sorry Majesty. That must have been difficult for you.' Moss continued to massage Aynia's back, but he let his hands slide down so that he was kneading her buttocks.

'Difficult for me?'

'I'm sure that the circumstances were unhappy for you. You don't strike me as the type that would kill without a good reason.'

Aynia was not about to discuss her reasons with a male. 'Why does Thane Adders-Tongue hate me so?' She mused.

'Because she can not control you Majesty and because you are your Mother's daughter. You thwart her bids for power. You are young and beautiful and she can never be what you are. Even if she takes the power that she wants she will never become a Queen.' Moss was working Aynia's legs apart so that he could stroke her clitoris with his forefinger.

Aynia spread her legs further apart and bent her knees so that her bottom rose a little higher. She noticed that each of her drones had a different way of touching her. But each was able to get her to respond.

Moss looked down at the Queen's bottom. If he was ever going to dare this was the time. She was still distracted. Moss bent down and flicked his tongue over Aynia's pink anus.

The sensation surprised Aynia, but it felt good, very nice. She never realized how sensitive she was in that area. Moss was working her clitoris expertly with one hand as she was growing wetter and wetter while his tongue found new ways to delight her senses. He flicked his tongue over then into her anus. Aynia wished that the moment would go on forever. But as she grew used to each sensation Moss found a new way to make the pleasure grow without becoming predictable.

Aynia pushed herself up higher on her knees then moved her hands to help pull her buttocks apart.

Moss slid his fingers into her anus. They were well lubricated with her juices. 'Should I lick your pussy a little?' He whispered.

'Don't stop licking my ass,' Aynia asked him.

'I want to taste your juices. Why don't you slip you fingers into your own pussy and get them wet, then you can slide your finger into your own ass while I eat you.'

Aynia obeyed Mosses' suggestion. She slid her fingers over her clitoris again and again, ending each stroke by dipping her fingertips into her vagina. Then Moss moved her hand away gently.

'My turn Majesty. Just let me see you slide that finger in.' Moss took a deep breath as Aynia slid a finger into her own anus as she gasped with pleasure. If he weren't careful he would come soon. He reached for a cock ring and pulled it on over his penis. There was no way that he would allow himself to miss a moment of this.

Moss moved under Aynia and buried his face into her. His talented tongue worked its magic. He now had the Queen's undivided attention.

Aynia smiled down at Moss, and could see a smile in his eyes.

Moss moved back on his knees behind Aynia. 'Do you want to come? Are you ready to come?'

Aynia nodded.

Moss began working her clitoris with slightly more pressure. 'Is that good?' He asked her.

'Mmm,' Aynia answered.

'Spread your knees a little wider. You'll enjoy this more if your hips are closer to the ground.' Taking a huge chance, Moss slowly pushed just the head of his cock into Aynia's anus. Aynia wasn't sure if she was feeling pleasure or pain, but she felt herself crashing into an incredible orgasm. Moss flung off the cock ring and pushed another couple inches into Aynia.

Aynia grunted. 'No more! You're too big,' she pleaded.

Moss dared one last plunge, then held on to Aynia's hips are he came inside her.

He lay down on the ground, exhausted. Now this would be something to tell Sarkany about, and it would be Sarkany's turn to listen jealously to the details. Moss pulled Aynia to him and kissed her deeply. 'You are my fantasies come true.'

Thorn traveled north of the Island of Skye. There, in one of the sounds, he found an island that fit the needs of the Hive. Now his quest was almost complete. He wanted to leave for home but he would not give up his search until he found an alternate site for the new Hive. Another week of searching turned up no spots as suitable as the first. The Vernal Equinox was just over a week away. Finally, with just the one island to offer to his Queen, Thorn allowed himself to turn home.   .

Thoughts of Aynia, long denied, filled his head. He had put off his decision about becoming a drone. Now he knew his answer. As sweet as that one evening was with Aynia, and as much as he wanted to taste her juices again, there was no question in his mind that the life of a drone would never please him. Thorn was a soldier. It was as simple as that. His place was by the Queen, protecting her and the Hive, not in her arms. Happy with his resolve, he rode in a full gallop into the valley that was home to the Hive of Balnacra.

With his mind so occupied in thoughts of his Queen Thorn never saw the net. Once he rode into the web it was too late. His sword would not cut it; his horse could not run through it. As Thorn struggled he only became more firmly entangled in the snare.

'Let's see who we've caught here,' Snakegrass said. 'Why look, what a catch! Her most gracious Majesty, Queen Carman will be pleased. Look, my friends, we've captured the great Captain Thorn!'

CHAPTER 13

Thorn was ashamed. He was ashamed that he allowed himself to be caught. Some military leader he made. He managed to successfully complete every aspect of his mission except to arrive back at the Hive with the information he was sent out to collect. Within a couple miles of the Hive he grew careless. His mind was already on seeing his Queen again. He imagined her pleasure at seeing him back at the Hive.

Aynia asked him to return home to her. Those words carried special significance. He had been thinking about stealing a few seconds alone with Aynia again, smelling her scent, looking at her porcelain skin, perhaps kissing her wrist once again where her pulse throbbed so that he knew the beating of her heart.

But careless thoughts had betrayed him. Now he was tied to a post as Carman's prisoner. He'd searched for Carman for months and failed. All this time she had been less than a mile from the Hive. If only he could take back the last hour of his life!

Carman stood up from her makeshift Throne and dragged herself across her outdoor Throne Room to stand in front of him. He noticed that her left side was still partially paralyzed. Her left arm was not functioning and was atrophying against her body. When she walked her left foot dragged, and her left breast was much smaller than the one on the right side, as if it produced no milk. Even the left side of Carman's face seemed somehow to have slid a little below the other side of her face. There was not much of a difference, but it was enough to notice.

Carman stopped when she stood less than a foot away from Thorn. 'A spy? We have a spy Snakegrass.'

'Kill him Majesty.' Snakegrass urged.

'So it will be torture,' Thorn said without apparent concern.

'Oh no, not pain,' Carman smiled at him, but the left side of her lips did not lift up with the rest of the smile. 'I think instead that it will be pleasure.'

'Your Highness! What can you mean?'

Thorn was as curious as Snakegrass so he waited silently for Carman to explain.

'Do you know what day approaches Captain Thorn?' Carman asked. He didn't answer so she continued. 'In a week we have the Vernal Equinox. This is one of two days in a year that a Fairie Queen is fertile. I can tell that the Equinox is upon us because I am beginning to feel, well, urges. Strong urges to procreate. However, since my sister stole my Throne and my drones along with it I had no one to mate with. Until you made your timely entrance, that is.'

'I am no drone,' Thorn said, grateful once again for that fact.

'I've always fancied you Thorn, even when I was a Princess. I like your body.' Carman tore Thorn's shirt off, revealing a washboard stomach and muscular arms. 'Look at him,' Carman commanded her attendants. 'Look at those arms! What female could resist the idea of resting in those arms after making love? They're so strong.' Carman ran her fingertips longingly down Thorn's arms, then across his chest, letting her fingernails scrape his skin teasingly.

Carman smiled wickedly at Thorn again and grabbed his hose. These she also pulled away with such ease that he suspected someone cut the fabric for her.

Something fell to the ground. With difficulty Carman picked up the piece of fabric. 'What is this?' She sniffed it. 'That stink.' She sniffed it again. 'It has Aynia's stink on it. What an interesting little memento Thorn.' She tossed the pair of panties away. With another triumphant gesture she pulled away his loincloth. Now he wore only the silk ropes that tied his ankles and wrists.

Now Carman frowned. 'Unfortunately, despite such impressive,' she let her eyes linger below his waist, 'equipment, you are currently quite useless to me.'

'Thank the Goddesses,' Thorn said.

Carman slapped him hard across his face, nearly breaking his nose. 'Who let you stay in this state? Wouldn't my dear

357

sister let you suckle at her breast? No. You waste your love on her when she obviously cares nothing for you. I love you. I always have, even when you had eyes only for Aynia. Now I will give you what you seemingly could not beg from her. I will make you my drone. We will mate.'

'No!' Thorn cried out. 'Don't do this to me,' he pleaded.

'Why not?' Carman asked in real confusion.

'I don't want to be a drone. I am a soldier. That's all I am.'

'I will make you so much more. You think that you don't want to be a drone, but wait until you feel the virility stir your loins. Wait until you know the power of sex. Then you will fall on your knees and thank your new Queen for her gift.'

'No!'

Carman turned away and dragged herself back to her Throne. 'Let him stay in the sun, unclothed. When he begs for water, bring him to me. He gets no food or water until he suckles Queen's milk from my breast.'

Thorn lasted four torturous days. The sun burned his skin. His lips were dry and cracked. Finally he begged for water. Once the words passed his lips he was removed from the post and carried to Carman's private chamber in the badger burrow.

Carman lay down on her bed. Thorn was brought to the edge of the bed where her attendants forced him to his knees. He was too weak to stop them as they dropped him down to the floor. 'Leave his hands and feet tied,' Carman ordered. 'Then leave us.'

Carman unhooked the cup of her corset on her right side. She sat up on the bed with her legs over the side so that Thorn knelt between her legs. She took out a small vial and unscrewed the top. She dipped her finger into it and then rubbed the substance onto Thorn's cracked lips. 'This will smooth your lips. After all, you suckle at the breast of a Queen.'

Thorn tried to turn his head away. Could he last longer without liquid?

'Thorn, Thorn,' Carman chided him. 'I am offering a great gift. I can not begin to describe to you the power I felt after hatching as Queen. The feeling of sexuality is so powerful, so enjoyable. But mere words fail to describe it. It's like trying to describe the color green to the blind. Now, I have had to express my own milk every day since the third day of my adult life as I have no drones to nurse from my breast. Life is not easy outside the Hive. It takes a strong Fairie, an exceptional Fairie, to survive out here. I see now that Hive life makes a Queen soft.'

'Queen Aynia is not soft or weak,' Thorn protested his voice scratchy. Aynia was not weak, but her skin was deliciously soft. He closed his eyes, remembering the taste of her.

'Thorn, dear, let us not talk of the bitch who stole my Throne. Let's talk about you, and me. We can do this one of two ways. I can have someone force your mouth open and I can express my milk into your mouth. However, I think that I will enjoy this so much more if you suckle. So we will sit here and we will wait until you beg me to let you nurse.'

Carman and Thorn stared at each other for twelve more minutes. Finally Thorn opened his cracked mouth and whispered 'water.'

'I think that the way to ask is 'Please, Your Highness, Queen Carman, may I suckle at your breast and partake of Queen's milk?''

Thorn stared at Carman in stony silence.

Carman could wait no longer. 'Well, open you mouth.'

Thorn opened his mouth slowly and just barely.

'You have to open more than that, and not just the nipple, the whole areola!' Carman pushed her breast into Thorn's mouth.

Thoroughly ashamed of himself for doing this to save his life, Thorn found an excuse for compromising. He needed to complete his mission. He needed to tell his Queen, his real Queen, about the island he found. Greedily, he sucked Queen's milk from Carman's breast. It was not a great quantity of liquid, but there was something about the flavor that compelled him to taste more.

When the supply of milk dwindled he looked up at Carman's face. Her eyes were half closed and she was nearly panting. 'That's wonderful,' she purred. 'Continue.'

Disgust for his weakness and for her evil filled Thorn. 'You're out of milk, and my thirst is not slaked.'

'I'm so near to complete pleasure. Do you care to suckle lower?' She spread her legs a little further apart.

Thorn's face showed his thoughts on the idea. Carman laughed. 'Very well, I will give you a couple more days. Soon you will be able to think of nothing else.'

'I want water, just water.'

'No. We will wait. In another two hours or so I will be able to let you have more Queens' milk. Until then you can thirst.'

'Do I at least get to stand, to sit? My knees ache.'

Carman thought about it. 'I will have them lay you upon my bed. Next time we can lie together on the bed as you suckle. It will be much more comfortable for both of us.'

'Will you have them cover me?'

Carman laughed again. 'Oh no, I want to be the first to see when the Queen's milk works its magic on you. I believe the first sign is when your wings sprout. I hear that it can be quite painful.'

Thorn's wings began to sprout within hours of taking Carman's milk. At first his back ached. Then his skin seemed too tight between his shoulders. Over the space of about twenty hours the new wings pushed through his skin. Once they burst through most of the pain was gone, but his skin remained inflamed. Partially, he thought, due to the fact that Carman had him placed out in the sun again with no clothes to protect him.

The next day he was brought before Carman again in her chamber. 'You refused to come to me again yesterday to take milk.'

'I am not thirsty.'

'Yes you are. What is this?' Carman ran her hand across his cheek. 'A beard? You're becoming virile, but you need more milk.'

'I will not nurse.'

'You have no choice.' Carman hissed. 'I expressed milk all day yesterday. Do you know what happens when you drain your breast of milk more and more frequently? You produce more milk. I am heavy with it and you will take it.' Carman reached down and grabbed Thorn's scrotum. He felt sudden fear. She began to squeeze lightly. 'Now, you are going to suckle. If I don't think that you are doing your best I will squeeze a little tighter.' She demonstrated, and then let the pressure go. 'If I think that you're being a good drone, I will do this.' Carman gently massaged with her hand.

Thorn gasped. He hated himself, but he didn't want the sensation to end.

'I think that you understand your choices.' She tightened her handgrip on him. 'Now, before we begin we will have a little talk about why you were outside of your Hive.' Carman began applying pressure in just the right spot. 'You are going to talk. Tell me everything.'

Thorn fought the pain but finally complied.

The executions of Lady Deidre and Prince Noisi were to be held in public. The Queen fought against it as the two had confessed willingly in order to save the Queen the embarrassment of a trial. Adders-Tongue would not allow it. She wanted the Queen to have to face the Hive with this humiliation fresh in their minds. And Adders-Tongue was an expert on being publicly humiliated by an unfaithful drone.

That day, so long past, still seemed fresh in Adders-Tongue's mind. She acquired from a poor family a young male of great physical potential. She allowed him to take milk from her and become a drone. Then his full potential was realized. Twice as long and easily one and a half times the circumference of the penis of most drones, this drone's impressive member was worth showing off to friends. Adders-Tongue realized that was her second mistake. The first was to believe that the late Queen was actually a friend. The second was to display her drone before the late Queen and other noble ladies.

Adders-Tongue never actually lay with the drone. She wanted him to be a virgin for the next mating flight. Maybe not utilizing him was a mistake too, because he obviously leaped at the idea of bedding the Queen. Even this betrayal was not so bad, because no one knew about it. But on the day of the mating flight as Adders-Tongue took off into the sky so did the Queen and Adders-Tongue's prized male specimen flew straight past Adders-Tongue and began to couple with the Queen in plain sight of the entire Hive.

Adders-Tongue could still hear that scornful laughter in her dreams. Now she wanted Aynia to know the same humiliation.

The gallows was constructed in the Hive center. The prisoners were brought out with their mouths gagged, their hands tightly bound, and their heads covered with black sacks. Despite Adders-Tongue's calls for the prisoners to be displayed for the crowd, the Queen would not allow it. Adders-Tongue wanted Deidre's sisters to have to view Deidre with a shaved head.

Adders-Tongue was heartily disappointed with the turn out at the executions. In the center of the Hive, usually a place crowded with workers, the only Fairie present were those compelled to be there by law. Not even Adders-Tongue's kinsmen Cobra-Lily and Copperhead bothered to come, despite their important roles in concocting this embarrassment for the Queen. Adders-Tongue was also disappointed to see that the prisoners appeared to be heavily drugged. No one else seemed to care.

To Adders-Tongue's surprise the Queen retained her usually calm exterior. Through the prayers by the Priestesses and the reading of the death sentence the Queen managed to look bored by the proceedings.

'Does anyone ask for mercy for these prisoners?' Aynia asked as she stood over the doomed figures. 'Thane Adders-Tongue? Will you speak for them?'

Adders-Tongue was shocked. After all it was her plot that caught them. It was her nephew Copperhead who spied on the Queen's harem for her. Copperhead, he should have been here to see this triumph. Then again the little coward probably feared the Queen's anger.

'No. I will not beg them mercy. They are condemned. They will die.' Adders-Tongue insisted. 'I uphold our laws and traditions.'

Aynia turned to a Priestess who was recording the event on a scroll. 'Please note that Thane Adders-Tongue declined an opportunity to beg mercy for my prisoners.'

Adders-Tongue wondered what game the Queen was up to but it didn't matter. The infidelity of the Queen's drone was a wonderful public humiliation. The uppity Deidre, who had taken over Cobra-Lily's rightful position in service to the Queen, was paying the ultimate price for crossing Adders-Tongue's family. In all it was a good day.

Aynia addressed the sparse crowd before her. Deidre's sisters could not meet their Queen's gaze. Only the Ambassador from Ardcharnich Hive seemed interested in what Aynia had to say. 'Justice is a rare commodity. We believe in it, we hope for it, but too many times in our lives justice is denied. Vengeance is a terrible thing but sometimes justice and vengeance serve each other. Today I am the sword of justice, and I am the servant of vengeance. Let justice be done, and may the Goddesses have mercy on their souls.'

Aynia went to the two condemned prisoners. 'Lady Deidre, are you prepared to die?'

The figure shook its head.

Aynia plunged her scorpion's stinger into Deidre's heart. The deathblow was instantly fatal. Deidre's body fell over.

'Prince Noisi, are you prepared to die?'

He tried to speak past the gag but nothing could be made of his protests. Aynia slammed her stinger into his neck, nearly decapitating the body.

'Well, shall we go dispose of the bodies?' Aynia asked grimly.

The serious group of witnesses mutely walked outside of the Hive. Camellia and Heather supported Rose. All three sisters cried in her own way, Camellia silently, Heather stoically, and Rose loudly.

A great pyre was already lit in the valley by the Hive entrance. Aynia paused at the entrance of the Hive, hovering high at the arched doorway, where she could witness the events outside. She would not cross the threshold, as it would cause the entire Hive to follow her out. 'Place the bodies on the fire,' she commanded.

The Royal Guards threw the bodies on the fire.

The witnesses watched until the bodies became ashes.

The sun began to set, casting the valley in early shadows. The last flames flickered on the stinking pyre.

'Take their ashes and scatter them to the winds. Let them have no grave, let their spirits have no rest,' Aynia intoned.

Priestesses and other reluctant witnesses to the execution exchanged glances. This was harsh punishment indeed, even for those who committed treason. To have no grave was to be condemned to an eternity of wandering in the mists of death. With no grave for the body there would never be rest for the soul.

Even Adders-Tongue found herself surprised at the depth of Aynia's vengeance. She couldn't figure out her enemy. Did the Queen have no heart? Was she sculpted from ice? But the Queen's public demeanor would not scare Adders-Tongue from her next move. The following day, in Parliament, Adders-Tongue would make her move against the Ruling Party, using the behavior of the Queen's personal attendants, the human problem, and the matter of the enlargement of the Temple as weapons to attack the Queen and her representatives in government. It didn't matter that all of it was a tempest in a teapot. Adders-Tongue was failing miserably as the Minister of Food Harvest. If she didn't act against the Queen now she wouldn't have the power to win.

Aynia sat at her parlor table with Rose, Camellia, and Heather. The three sisters were in deep mourning for their foolish sister. Each wore the black veil of mourning, which hid nearly every part of the face, but the expression in their eyes was enough to show their anguish.

The sisters expected to be dismissed permanently from the Queen's service any second now. They did not see Verbena, Freesia, or Heliotrope, their supposed replacements in the Royal Chambers. They assumed that the reason for their absence was a small kindness of the Queen, who was probably planning to fire them in private. The one fault in this scenario was the presence of the Ambassador from Ardcharnich Hive in the Queen's private parlor. Despite what must be an awkward political situation Aynia and the Ambassador seemed to have no quarrel with each other.

Aynia appeared to be waiting for something.

They all waited together in awkward silence.

Finally there was a knock on the door. Aynia rose herself to answer it. Heliotrope looked into the room and handed Aynia a small package. Aynia took it, exchanging a smile with Heliotrope, then returned to her seat.

Aynia placed the package on the table in front of her and opened it. Inside was a basket of ripe raspberries. 'Aha, success! Do you care for a raspberry Heather? Rose? No? How about you Camellia? I guarantee that these are the sweetest berries that you will ever taste.'

'No thank you Majesty,' Heather mumbled.

'Then perhaps you would care to read the accompanying note?'

The three sisters were beginning to think that their Queen had gone mad. Not two hours ago she had put their sister to death, and now she was cheerfully handing around a basket of raspberries.

'I have no appetite Majesty,' Rose said bitterly.

'Then I shall read for you. This note reads 'Reached Chambord early this morning. Swedish emissaries refused to meet with Prince Noisi and myself, but the Hive de Chambord has graciously allowed us sanctuary as a personal favor to our Queen. Please tell my sisters that I agree that I am an idiot, and do not deserve their sisterly affections, but I hope they may find time to visit me in my exile in the next hundred years or so, after the scandal has died down a bit.' Well, the rest is more personal and meant only for me, but I think that you get the idea.'

Rose jumped up and threw her arms around Aynia's neck. 'Oh my gracious Queen!'

'Please try to remember that you're in mourning. A little decorum is called for here,' Aynia said in good humor as she released herself from Rose's suffocating embrace.

'You sent her away?' Camellia asked her astonishment showing.

'I commanded Verbena and Freesia to accompany them. I felt that it was unsafe for the two to make the journey alone, especially since they had to cross in the path of the English army. Thank the Goddess that they arrived safely.'

'But Majesty,' Heather asked with some concern, 'just who is it that you executed?'

'Heliotrope can correct me if I am wrong, but I believe that the female was Cobra-Lily and the male was Copperhead.'

'No? Yes!' Heather couldn't contain herself. She kissed Aynia and laughed out loud. 'You are truly the greatest Queen I have ever served.'

'Remember that I gave Thane Adders-Tongue a chance to beg for mercy for the condemned prisoners. If Adders-Tongue has developed a taste for blood let it flow from her own family,' Aynia said.

'But you executed those two without a trial,' Rose said.

'Don't be ungrateful,' Heather snapped. 'The Queen has shown our family great mercy.'

Aynia handed a second note to the Ambassador. 'Lady Deidre includes a note for your Queen at Ardcharnich. I hope that this concludes this painful episode for us.'

'You managed this affair quite well for such a young Queen.' The Ambassador took the note and gave her deepest bow.

'High praise indeed Ambassador.'

'I will leave now to deliver this message to my Queen.' The Ambassador said. She personally felt that Queen Aynia was much too lenient on Deidre and the drone, but on the other hand, it was the Ambassador's job to see that the best result came of the situation. Her own Queen would be pleased. Besides, she had many other intriguing rumors to discuss with her Queen. If Balnacra was having problems with human invaders in the Hive's territory, Ardcharnich would soon have the same problems. How this Queen managed the situation would teach the Ardcharnich Hive how to react. One thing was sure, the old ways were inadequate, and only the Hives that acknowledged it would survive.

'Majesty, I too am grateful for the life of my sister, but I can not help but be worried about the lack of a proper death warrant for the two that you executed.' Rose spoke her conscience.

Aynia considered for a moment before she spoke. 'I found them guilty of treason.'

'But Majesty!'

'I will not apologize for killing my enemies! Enough Rose, The matter is closed.' From Aynia's tone all around the table knew that the matter was indeed closed. No one would dare bring it up again.

Heather nodded. She saw a glimmer of the late Queen just now. If the late Queen was given to abusing her power from time to time at least she knew how to wield the power that she had. Aynia had yet to test the power at her disposal.

'Let this be a lesson to you all. Keep nothing hidden from me. If a worker's child hungers I want to know about it. If a leaf falls in the forest I want to be the first to hear the news. If I have weakness, expose it to my attention first. And if you three ever fail me again I will show you my less forgiving nature.'

The High Priestess intoned the prayers to the Goddesses. At any moment the full moon would move into position and shine down into the Temple, lending cold moonlight to the dimly lit interior.

As she lit a candle she wrestled with a decision. There were two possible 'visions' she could have this night. One supported the Queen. The other undermined the Queen's power. The High Priestess was torn. She had support from the Queen and from the Queen's enemies. The real question was who was more likely to win in the struggle?

The High Priestess was determined that the winner be the Temple.

A quick glance to the sky told her that the moon was almost in place. It was time to begin the show. The High Priestess began mumbling and quaking, her usual sign that the Goddesses were speaking to her and sending her a vision.

Then as the first moonbeams broke the horizon an icy finger of wind and mist wrapped tendrils around the High Priestess. She opened her mouth. Words would not come.

Cerridwen looked to the other priestesses. They all looked on with the usual bored expression, but Cerridwen felt that something was wrong. She exhaled. Her breath turned to ice in the air.

Foam formed at the corners of the High Priestesses' mouth. Her eyes rolled up into her head. The mist entered her open mouth.

'Beware the solstice. When the moon turns her face a red river will flow at Balnacra,' it was not the High Priestess's voice, but the voice of a multitude.

The mist withdrew back into the sky.

Cerridwen knew something was really wrong. The visions from the High Priestess always contained obvious messages. What the hell was the red river?

The High Priestess collapsed.

Cerridwen ran to her side.

Thane Adders-Tongue took her usual seat in Parliament on the first row of the six tiers of seats on the right side of the aisle, on the side of the Opposition. Adders-Tongue thought herself to be a highly cultured Fairie. She thought that she exuded charm and that many workers and nobles admired her. In reality Thane Adders-Tongue struck others as condescending. Despite her powerful position in the Opposition Party very few members of the Opposition Party liked her. Today, however, Adders-Tongue was not attempting to charm. Today she had power, she had supporters, she had position, and today she would have the floor of Parliament.

Adders-Tongue allowed her upper lip to curl a little as the weak, ineffectual Prime Minister, head of the Ruling Party, entered Parliament surrounded by friends and those who always fawn after the powerful. Soon those weaklings would be at Adders-Tongue's side. They would vie for her attention. They would plead for her to favor them. The very thought caused Adders-Tongue to make a cynical smile.

'Good Goddesses, Thane Adders-Tongue is smiling.'

'That can't be good.'

Verbena and Freesia were sitting in the section of the gallery reserved for drones. Sequestered from the female population, the drone section featured an ornately carved wooden partition that allowed the drones to look down on the proceedings below but effectively blocked those on the floor of Parliament from viewing those in the gallery. The drone's section had not seen regular use since the death of Queen Aynia's father. Because of this Verbena and Freesia found it a convenient vantage from which to spy on the proceedings in Parliament.

'What did Thane Monarda say when you left her service for our little jaunt across the channel?' Freesia asked Verbena.

'She told me that I had better not abandon her just before her daughter's wedding. So we worked out a deal. I went to France with that idiot, you-know-who, and the Queen is sending Thane Monarda's daughter a very, very, very nice wedding present.'

Freesia snorted. 'Lady Deidre, a Queen's attendant, not a lowly Princesses' attendant like us, what a fool she was. None of us would have ever betrayed the Queen like that.'

'Don't say her name, not even in here. She's dead, remember?' Verbena yawned grandly.

Freesia rubbed her back a little. 'My arms hurt from being carried across the channel. Anyway, such foolishness over a male.'

'Well,' Verbena said slowly, not completely agreeing with her friend. 'I caught a glimpse of him beneath his veil. He was, shall we say, easily the most perfect looking male in all Tuatha de Danaan? And besides, the Queen explained to us that they committed no treason. She said that all of the charges were trumped up by Adders-Tongue.'

'So, are you here spying for the Queen or Thane Monarda?' Freesia asked, wisely changing the subject. She and Verbena were friends from many years back, even before they went into service in the Royal Palace. There was no reason to jeopardize that bond over a silly drone and an adulteress attendant.

'Either one really, not that anyone specifically asked me to come today. It's become a bit of a habit. I'm amazed at how few other common workers have ever been here. They have no idea what goes on in Parliament.' Verbena told her friend.

'It's probably just as well. Most of these nobles are complete and utter fools.'

'Oh no, not all of them,' Verbena said. 'It would be wrong to accuse them all of being fools.'

'What?' Freesia asked in shock.

'The rest of them are complete and utter gits, not to be confused with being a fool. Being called a fool would be a complement.'

Freesia realized with a laugh that she was being teased. 'Oh, there's the Ambassador Cowslip from Norfolk. I can't stand that female.'

'I don't trust her. She spends way too much time at Thane Monarda's house, and she's always hinting around that our Queen is somehow inferior to English Queens.'

Freesia frowned. 'I don't know how you can stand to be in service anymore.' She turned to see late Members of Parliament literally fly down the aisle to their seats. She sighed. 'Wish I could fly.'

'What common worker wouldn't want wings? It certainly would have been helpful on our little jaunt to France to be able to fly for ourselves.'

'It's not as if the nobles need wings. We're the ones doing all the work. We need to be able to fly.'

'Good luck earning those wings,' Verbena said a little bitterly.

'All that it would take was a little Queen's Milk. One sip and hours later we're doing somersaults in the air.'

'Where would we get Queen's milk?'

Freesia thought about this for awhile. 'The Priestesses have some. Maybe one of our old comrades in arms could get some for us?'

'I doubt it. It's a pretty precious commodity. They probably keep a close eye on the entire supply.'

'What about the offering bowls on the Goddesses' altar?'

Verbena gave her friend a long cold stare that reminded Freesia of Verbena's brother, Thorn.

'I was just saying.......' Of the two Freesia was the most enthusiastic, but had much less sense than her good friend.

'Sh, the session is starting,' Verbena turned her attention to the floor below them.

On the floor of Parliament a Member in an ornate robe pounded the floor three times in slow succession with a long wooden staff to bring the session to order.

Verbena and Freesia leaned forward in their seats. Lacking amplification, it was sometimes hard to catch every word spoken on the floor. Coughing spectators, the constant shuffling of paper by aides and the harrumphing from Members on both sides of the aisle made some speeches nearly impossible to hear.

Thane Adders-Tongue was the first to speak. This was no surprise to her. She badgered other Members of Parliament all week to insure today would be the day she finally delivered her most potent political sting ever against the Queen.

'Members of Parliament, friends, today I come to speak to you of a persistent threat to the Hive. We are in danger!'

The audience in the gallery gasped theatrically.

Verbena leaned over to look at the gallery. 'Did you notice the heavy representation by members of Thane Adders-Tongue's family in the gallery? I wonder if they were coached to react by the head of their clan.'

'They're probably holding copies of her speech with written instructions in their hands. That whole clan is pure poison. Always have been, always will be.'

Adders-Tongue continued. 'Our Queen does nothing about the persistent danger by humans! Every day more of those giant barbarians make permanent dwellings near Balnacra. It is only a matter of days, maybe hours, before the humans discover the Hive and destroy it.'

Again the gallery responded.

'But does our Queen send out guards to destroy the humans? Does she work to protect the Hive? No, she does not. It might be just as well, because in this time of peril she chose to send our brave, valiant Captain Thorn away! Where is Captain Thorn Queen Aynia? Did you take him into your harem and leave us unprotected?'

This time it was not members of Adders-Tongue's family that gasped. Adders-Tongue realized that her little ad lib about the Queen and Thorn was as bad idea. Harems were not to be discussed in public.

'We are stuck with the ineffective Captain Sage, a male not worthy of his post, as events this week showed us so plainly. My guards, in an attempt to make the Queen aware of how poorly she was protected, made an example raid on the Queen's private chambers. Were they guarded? No, they were not. If my guards had been assassins the Queen would be dead right now! And if the Queen was to die tomorrow, by human hands, or by assassination as her late, great Mother was, whom would we turn to in the Hive for leadership? No one, we have no one, and do you know why? The Queen refuses to breed! She is made of ice! Clearly, if she was a normal female, she would have been able to keep her drone pleased, and he would not have been forced to go outside of her bedchamber for comfort in the arms of another female! Yes, that's what my guards found on their raid! They caught the Queen's personal attendant and one of her drones making love, in the Queen's bed! But what does the Queen do, this female of ice? Does she cry for the loss of her friend? Does she plead for the life of her drone? No, she asks me if I will plead for them. But I am a female who believes that the law must be obeyed. When I refused on principal to beg for the life of the two adulterers, did the Queen step in to forgive her friend and drone? No, she calmly executed them. Why? Because she has no passion for males! She will fail to provide the Hive with a Princess! She allowed herself to be corrupted by Lady Heather, and we all know what Lady Heather did to the Russian Queen Yelena!'

The Ruling Party of Parliament was going wild through this speech. Members were flying into Thane Adders-Tongue's face, shaking their fists. The noise on the floor of Parliament was unbelievable. Yet Thane Adders-Tongue's voice carried above the din and went on making one accusation after another against the Queen.

Verbena was on her feet, her fists balled up as if to strike. 'How dare she speak about the Queen like that? Adders-Tongue is twisting the truth every way that she can. It's not true, it's not true!'

'I think that we'd better go have a word with the Queen,' Freesia said. She was visibly worried. 'Verbena, just where did your brother go?'

'I don't know. Like Adders-Tongue I kind of thought that the Queen made Thorn a drone. We always assumed when he dropped out of sight that he had been taken into the harem. But we haven't received a bride price from the Queen. I didn't know that he was gone from the Hive. Mother will just die. She always worries about him so much.'

On the floor of Parliament Thane Adders-Tongue was still making her voice heard. 'I call for a vote of no confidence against the Ruling Party! We must send a clear message to the Queen that we demand that she mate!'

Every Member of Parliament jumped to their feet. Everyone was shouting. Freesia joined them. 'Treason! Adders-Tongue speaks treason against the Queen!'

Verbena threw her hand over Freesia's mouth and pulled her down to the floor. 'Sh! Adders-Tongue will have your head for that.'

'But she lies! Everything she says is a twisted shadow of the truth!'

'Come with me now, we must warn the Queen.' Verbena forcibly pulled her friend out of the gallery and down the stairs.

Aynia stood at the balcony near her Royal Chambers that allowed her to look down into the Hive center. She was hiding in the thick red velvet curtains, not wanting to be seen. 'Where are you Thorn? Why haven't you come back to me?' She pleaded in a whisper. She knew that the Vernal Equinox was coming. The ice that she seemed made of was beginning to melt. Every thought that she had was of males. Every dream was of mating. She was going into heat. Her twice-yearly cycle of fertility was beginning and the ancient desire to continue the Fairie line grew stronger as the moon grew fuller.

'What's the matter is our Queen getting broody?' Heather asked.

'Quite the opposite, she's thirsting in a downpour. There are males as far as the eye can see in her chambers, but I could swear that she's still a virgin. We've got to get her in the mood so to speak,' Camellia said. 'You know, break the ice, or her hymen, whatever.'

'She's pining for Thorn, it's obvious.' Rose sighed.

'Maybe she didn't expect him to be gone so long.' Heather observed cautiously. She wondered if her sisters remembered that she once vowed to get Thorn out of the way so that Aynia would concentrate on her duty to procreate.

'Maybe she sent him away on purpose, knowing that she couldn't have him.'

'You are such the romantic Rose. That doesn't make sense. If she wants him so badly why doesn't she just make him one of her drones?' Camellia asked. 'And don't say it would cause a scandal. Every Queen stoops beneath her station at one point in her reign, or two.'

'What if he refuses to become a drone?' Heather said.

'That would explain a lot. After all, to a male like Thorn the idea of being a drone might be humiliating.'

'Who cares why she hasn't been making love to any of the harem? At least she's let a number of them take her milk. Two of them are quite frequently in her company. Maybe she just hasn't felt like making love.'

'And we assume that she is a virgin. She could be fully enjoying the use of her drones every day. Just because we haven't caught her at it doesn't mean that it's not happening.'

'Adders-Tongue is making noise in Parliament again. She says that the Queen is too frigid to mate and will not give the Hive a Princess. We have to stop these rumors.'

'How?'

'Tomorrow is the Vernal Equinox. Even if our Queen is downright disinterested in mating by this time tomorrow she'll be hot for a piece of action, so to speak. As she goes into heat she won't be able to stop herself. I think that if we get a little fermented nectar into her system it would do a world of good.'

'Are you talking about thawing the Ice Princess?'

'Is that what they call Queen Aynia in Parliament?'

'Among other things.'

'I believe that should be Ice Queen,' a new voice was added to the conversation.

Rose, Camellia, and Heather turned around in guilty unison. They bowed. 'Your Majesty,' they murmured.

'I have news that may distract you from my bed. Today Adders-Tongue forced a vote of no confidence in the present government in Parliament. We all understand that a vote of no confidence in the Ruling Party is a vote of no confidence in the Queen. This business with Deidre, the human problem, the surfacing rumors of Carman's survival, all of these things have worked against me.'

'We know the source of all of these problems.'

'I can not destroy the source openly. I must find support where I can. I have lost Parliament. Without Thorn here I no longer have ears in the military, so I have no idea if I have their support.'

Heather cleared her throat. 'You have the support of the Priestesses. Your financial support of the Temple and continued reverence for the Goddesses has gone far with them.'

'The Priestesses are a small group, not even one- percent of the population. Without heavy support from the military or the workers I am in deep trouble.' Aynia sighed. Some days she hated being Queen.

'You can gain the support of the workers.' Rose said.

'How?'

'Take your mating flight tomorrow. It's hard for workers to turn on their Queen when she is carrying a Princess. It reminds them that you are the future of the Hive. I believe that Carman and Peony were both conceived in times of political crises. The workers rallied behind your mother.'

Aynia sighed. 'It has already been decided.'

'You mean that you've already made a decision about tomorrow?'

'I want you all to know that no words you say can change my mind.'

Rose put her hand over her mouth, fearing the worst. 'What is your decision Majesty?'

'Prepare a Fairie ring in the ceremonial spot in the forest. Prepare fermented Queen's milk. See that the drones sleep well in the harem tonight.'

'Then you will fly tomorrow?' Rose couldn't believe her ears.

'Tomorrow I will fly.' Aynia turned back to her bedchamber. It was time to stop dreaming foolishly of Thorn. He was obviously dead.

CHAPTER 14

The morning of the Equinox Thorn woke to find that he was tied up again. Of course he understood why Carman didn't trust him. He would sting her in an instant if he had the chance. But at least now he was minimally clothed, and he had wings. Maybe he could find a way to escape from Carman and return home to the Hive.

Carman walked across her Throne Room followed by her attendants. They held a chalice.

'Do you know what today is, Captain Thorn?' Carman asked in a flirtatious tone.

'Another hellish day in your company,' he replied.

'I missed our session in my chambers last night, but I needed my milk for something else.'

'You're nursing a nest of orphaned vipers? Careful, don't kill them with your poison.'

Carman slapped Thorn. 'I would squeeze your scrotum until your balls explode, but I have particular need of that part of your body today. And I will so enjoy making you use it.' Carman hissed into Thorn's ear. She touched her lips to the lobe of his ear, and then bit down.

Thorn opened his mouth to protest as he felt blood drip on his shoulder.

Carman quickly pinched Thorn's nose closed while Snakegrass poured the liquid from the chalice into his mouth. He tried to spit it out but he ended up swallowing half of the intoxicating liquor.

When Carman was sure that Thorn swallowed the last of the liquid he held in his mouth she released his nose. 'What you just drank, dear, is fermented Queen's milk. I have found you less than willing to take part in love making up until now, although I have you quite addicted to nursing. We know that all of your equipment works, and thanks to a nursing session where you were particularly well behaved we were able to get a test sample to check your virility. As I suspected you are quite fertile now.'

Thorn actually blushed. Snakegrass and the other attendants laughed at him.

'Fermented Queen's milk is an intoxicant that removes all inhibition to mating. It makes the body go into a fever where it must mate. I am in a heat now. But being a drone you can probably sense that.'

Thorn could but refused to admit it.

'We will allow the liquid to do its work. Then you and I will take to the sky. After some pursuit I will allow you to catch me. And, despite any rational thoughts about escaping me, you will not be able to leave until you have mated with me. You won't be able to stop yourself. You will smell my scent and it will control your mind. When you are frenzied with desire you will beg to mate with me.' Carman took a deep breath. 'I'm going wild just thinking about making love to you.'

Thorn tried to protest but the fermented Queen's milk was working into his system. His blood seemed to heat up. A scent reached his nose and he took deeper breaths in order to get a stronger whiff. The scent drove him crazy. He fought against the ropes that bound him.

'What you smell is my scent. Isn't it lovely? Don't you want to hold me close and breathe it in? But you can't, not yet. The chase is part of the foreplay. I will take off into the sky in a moment. Then they will release you. Follow my scent Thorn.' Carman turned and snapped her wings out. With a bound she was in the air. 'Come to me Thorn,' she called.

The scent was growing fainter. Thorn struggled against the ropes. He had to have that scent. Suddenly he was free. Snakegrass cut his ropes. He turned and looked at Snakegrass for a second, his mind too clouded to know what to do. All that he could think of was the scent.

'Well, fly after her.' Snakegrass told him impatiently.

Thorn nodded and unfurled his wings. With grace unthinkable for a first time flyer he took off into the air. And he loved it. He remembered what Aynia said her first day as Queen. Now he understood her exhilaration. How could she not love it? Flying was beyond words.

Thorn needed to follow the scent. He raised high in the air. The wind shifted for a moment. He started to turn towards Carman, but an intoxicating spicy scent carried on the shifted breeze. He smelled another Queen! He flew towards the source of the new scent. Aynia! It was Aynia. Of course she was taking her first mating flight today too. He breathed in the air as deeply as he could. He was honing in on her scent. He forgot Carman. He wanted to mate, and he knew where the Queen he wanted was.

While the Vernal Equinox and the Autumnal Equinoxes both marked days when the Fairie Queen was fertile, she was not the only Fairie to come into heat during that time. All females in the Hive were under the same influence of earth and sun. As a result there was little done in a Hive on those days other than mating.

Late at night while the moon shone down with cold light the Priestesses brought their servants out to the sacred grove in the forest not far from the Hive to bless it. An ancient ring of stones piled several feet high in a nearly complete circle formed an altar for the offering. Their blessing was a wild dance of exhilaration and pagan Goddess worship. The Priestesses danced nude, drank great quantities of fermented nectar, mated with their own drones as the sun rose, and then returned to the Temple to offer sacrifices up to the fertility Goddess. The only mark of their Bacchanalia left behind was a ring of toadstools marking the sacred ground.

While the dew was still heavy the ordinary workers came out of the Hive with their harems and danced through the woods, looking for private spots in which to mate. The lack of wings left the joy of flight out of their experience, but in the rosy afterglow of the day few felt a need to complain. By the time that the nobility rose from their beds and made their way outside of the

Hive most of the workers were already enjoying leisurely picnics in the woods.

Camellia once warned Aynia that when the Queen stepped outside of the Hive every remaining living being in the Hive followed her out. It was with some trepidation that Aynia realized that for her mating flight there was assembled through the woods an audience numbering in the thousands. This was to be no private affair.

Aynia made her way through the cheering and bowing throng to her temporary Throne in the Fairie circle. She gritted her teeth and smiled while waving her hand in a fittingly regal manner. Overhead, couples took mating flights, wheeling over the heads of the crowd with seeming indifference to the huge audience. Young or old, all of the nobility took part in each Equinox celebration.

Behind Aynia was an entourage of her drones. It consisted of every male in her harem with wings, a mere nine in number. Most were recently made drone in the past four days.

As she seated herself at her Throne Aynia looked critically over at the nobles of the court. This was the only time that mating males were allowed in public. Aynia noticed quite a few females looking the Royal Drones over with far too much interest. A spark of jealousy burned in her heart. Those females had their own harems. Why did they dare look at the Queen's males, and with such open leers?

Aynia understood now how before the creation of harems the Equinoxes were often marked by duels to the death for mating males by female Fairie in heat. She was feeling some murderous thoughts herself as a noble 'accidentally' brushed her hand across Wheat's loincloth.

Rose handed Aynia a large cup of fermented nectar. Aynia simply held the cup while she glowered at the Thane who appeared enraptured with Wheat, so Camellia stood up and made a toast. That started the drunken nobles around the Fairie ring on a loud boisterous round of toasts to the Queen. Aynia politely sipped with each toast, but she never let her eyes leave the group of females.

'They stare at my drones,' Aynia hissed to Camellia, her eyes narrow in jealousy.

'Then go fly with your males and get them out of public view.'

Aynia immediately blushed. 'I can't.'

'You promised to fly today.'

'I just can't,' Aynia mumbled. She was miserable. On one hand she wanted to kill the noble ladies who openly leered at her drones. On the other hand her body was crying out for some sort of release. The tension between her legs was almost unbearable. But there were strangers around, and all of them seemed to be watching her.

'This is working well,' Camellia hissed to her sisters. 'By the time our Queen takes to the sky she'll be too drunk to fly.'

'I don't think that she's actually drinking anything. I'm more worried about her murdering Thane Wisteria for making eyes at Prince Moss. Look at the Queen, she's livid. How many mating days have you seen end in fights?' Heather asked.

'It's not a real Equinox unless there's a fight,' Rose observed. 'That's why they call the Equinox blood moons.'

'She's drunk,' Camellia insisted.

'Then the drones will have no trouble catching her,' Rose replied merrily.

'You're fey.' Heather accused Rose.

'I am not.'

'Yes you are. Snap out of it. It's bad luck to be so happy. Disaster will follow, mark my words.' Heather warned Rose.

'You gloomy Scot. Why don't you snap out of it?' Rose countered.

'You breeding ninny. It's obvious that you've mated today with one of your drones. How could you when we're in service to the Queen?'

'How could I? How could I not? You should try it sometime Heather. An orgasm would do wonders for your personality.'

Heather's mouth dropped open. 'You're drunk,' she accused.

'No, just incredibly relaxed,' Rose smiled lazily. She was very pleased with herself, and her drones, and did not care who knew it.

'Sisters!' Camellia hissed. 'See how Adders-Tongue does not drink to the Queen's health.'

'Yes, we all noticed. And listen, some of the workers are booing Adders-Tongue for failing to toast to Queen.'

'So they are. But more importantly, the Queen just started unbuttoning her corset. She's beginning to unthaw. Quick, give her drones the fermented Queen's milk. It's time to get our Lady up into the sky.'

Aynia was beginning to feel quite good. At first she thought that it was the small quantity of fermented nectar that she drank, but a rush of warmth from far below her stomach warned her that the nectar was not the source. She looked over again at her drones. Funny how very attractive she found them all to be. Especially Sarkany. There was something about his black curly hair and strong body that made her ache between her legs.

'What's wrong with me?' Aynia asked herself. She could barely remain in her seat. And she was too warm, much too warm to be wearing clothes. She wanted to just leap into the air and fly.

'She's going to go at any second. Look at her,' Rose nudged Camellia. 'She keeps looking at the sky.'

'Go on, go on,' Camellia urged Aynia under her breath.

Aynia shifted in her Throne.

Camellia looked hopefully at her. 'Come on.' She whispered again.

Rose kept pushing herself up on her toes. 'Up, up.'

Camellia shook her head. 'I don't know, she hasn't moved. Look at her drones! If we don't restrain them they'll jump her where she sits.'

'As long as she gets mated,' Rose whispered.

'And she's off!' Heather said out loud as Aynia jumped to her feet and opened her wings with a crisp snap.

Aynia could fight the urge no longer. She leapt into the sky and took flight.

Heather, who worked so hard to see this day come together, felt her heart sink a little. If only she too could take flight on this day.

The workers of the Hive gave out a loud cheer. Toasts were drunk to the Queen's success.

Behind Aynia drones struggled to get free from the restraining hands of the attendants. 'Give her a good head start.'

The drones were beyond hearing caution. They smelled their Queen's scent and they were wild to reach to source. One by one they broke free and took flight after her.

Ambassador Cowslip from Norfolk Hive shook her head. 'Well, let's hope that your Queen actually allows her drones to mate with her. I heard that she's frigid.'

Adders-Tongue gave the Ambassador a sour look. 'You may have heard wrong.'

The Ambassador laughed her annoying chuckle. 'Are you or are you not the one who christened her the Ice Queen?'

'What do you want Ambassador?' Adders-Tongue asked bluntly.

The Ambassador dropped her voice. 'If she fails to mate we have several Princesses who could be freed from service to Norfolk Hive.'

Adders-Tongue gave the Ambassador a long cold stare. 'If you think that I would help put filthy English blood on a Scottish Throne you are deeply mistaken. Good day Ambassador,' she swept away with a grand gesture.

Ambassador Cowslip heard a slight snicker behind her. She turned to see the High Priestess. The High Priestess looked very amused.

'You certainly judged that one wrong,' the High Priestess said.

'I don't know what you mean,' Ambassador Cowslip sniffed.

'Oh, I think that you do,' the High Priestess's voice was silky with insinuation.

Ambassador Cowslip tried to look highly offended, but she knew that she was caught.

The High Priestess gave a small smile. 'You haven't been to the Temple to pay your respects to the Goddesses lately. I've seen you only once since you arrived at Balnacra.'

'I suppose that I have been negligent.'

'It is never wise to neglect the Temple. Someone like you might find it a source of comfort and spiritual support in these difficult times.'

Aynia flew high and fast. She knew that her drones were in pursuit but she didn't want to be caught, not yet. How she loved to fly! She put on speed and zipped dangerously through branches, leaves, and grasses. Finding a stream she zigzagged over the surface of the water, letting her feet just barely touch the water. Any human watching would have seen only an electric blue streak moving just inches from the water, then disappearing into the dense undergrowth of the forest.

'Free! I'm free!' She felt so gloriously close to shedding all the responsibilities of the Hive. Up again she soared to the sky, then low again to be near the forest floor. As she came down once again near a hollow tree, arms suddenly wrapped around her and dragged her into the hidden center of the rotted log.

She fought wildly to get away. 'No, it's too soon, it's too soon, I want to fly!' She cried out.

'Aynia.'

Aynia knew the voice. 'Thorn! My sweet Thorn, you came back to me!' Aynia stopped fighting and covered his face with kisses. 'I thought that you were dead!'

Thorn buried his face into Aynia's auburn hair. He breathed in deep to take in her scent. 'This is heaven. This is what I've been looking for.'

Aynia untangled herself from his strong arms to look at Thorn. Within seconds her smile faded. 'You are not my Thorn.'

'I am a drone,' he admitted.

'Why? How?' Aynia asked as hot tears began to fall down her cheeks. Part of it was the emotion of the mating season, but part of her tears came from deep anger.

'Carman caught me as I was coming home to you with news from my scouting mission,' Thorn reported succinctly.

'You became her drone?' Aynia fought again to get away from Thorn. 'Hers? She tried to kill me. She had my mother killed. You gave yourself to Carman? Get away from me before I forget myself and sting you.' Aynia was trembling with anger.

'You betrayed me,' she hissed.

'I didn't give myself to her.'

'Males do not become drones without taking milk.' Aynia wrested herself from Thorn's grasp. 'I thought that you were dead. I cried for the loss of you.'

'Then can't you be happy that I'm still alive?'

'Not when you belong to another female. You stink of her scent.'

Thorn took one of Aynia's tears on his finger as it trailed down her cheek. 'Then let me wash her off of me and then cover myself with your scent.'

Aynia pushed his hand away. 'I deluded myself into believing that you were tempted to give yourself to me. You pretended to want me and I believed.'

'I never pretended anything. I am who I am, Your Highness.' Thorn grabbed Aynia hard by the shoulders and forced her to look at him. 'If you can not see that it's because you don't want to.'

'You asked Carman for Queen's milk. That's what I can plainly see.' Aynia sobbed. 'It's a mystery to me how love begins, but I know now how it dies.'

'I did not betray you. Carman captured me. She forced me to drink her milk. She tortured me for days until I had to drink. I

386

would have killed myself rather than suckle at the teat of that bitch but I had to live so that I could bring you my news.'

'How noble of you. Did you think of the Hive while you lay in her arms?' Aynia asked viscously.

'I thought of you. I thought of my promise to find the Hive a safe haven. I thought of how much danger the Hive is in from the growing tide of humans moving north. I thought of the destruction of the Lanark Hive, but it all paled in comparison to the promise that I made to my Queen that I would return, not to the Hive, but to her.'

'The Lanark Hive is destroyed?' Aynia asked, taken by surprise.

'I took refuge with a wandering troop of Irish Fairie, who heard the information from another group of wanderers. They were Bean Sidhe, the Banshee,' Thorn confirmed the news. 'It was in the path of the English Army. There were no survivors. The Queen waited too long to make her decision to move the Hive. Your Highness, you must move the Hive.'

'My father was a Prince from Lanark. My Aunt was Queen. Lanark was the largest and strongest Hive in all the Tuatha de Danaan Hives. If they could not survive, how can we? What else did these Irish Fairie folk tell you?'

'Balnacra Hive can survive if you move it. That's why you sent me on my quest. I had to do anything that I could to make it back alive to tell you. I found a new sight for the Hive about twenty-four miles southwest from Balnacra. It's a small island in the Sound of Raasay. The island is hard to reach, with treacherous currents and rocks in the water all around it. There is no beach for a boat to land on even if one would survive the trip. The island is far too small to support human life, but it will support a Hive three times our size. Don't make the same mistake your Aunt made. Don't wait too long to make a decision, or the humans will make it for you.'

Aynia was angry and confused, but the truth of Thorn's words sank into her mind. She fought the crazed emotions of mating season and looked for reason. 'It is an island? Are there more than one? Is it easily found?'

'Yes. There are several islands but I marked the one I found to be best. Go south, following our stream as it flows into the loch. Then keep to the shore, for about twelve miles. Then it's another mile or so across the water. It lies between Skye and Loch Kishorn. You will smell my mark on the rocks of the shore.'

'We'll have to move the entire Hive over water. It's an enormous undertaking.'

Thorn placed his hands on Aynia's arms. 'I'm confident that it can be done, and it must be done. I saw for myself the numbers of humans moving north. It's only a matter of time before they infect this valley.'

Aynia could not hold back the emotion of her state any longer. 'You came back to me. I thought that you were dead.' She burst out again in tears.

'I gave my word that I would come back to you.'

'I hated myself for letting you go from my side, but I didn't want to stop you from doing the job that you love. I thought that it would make you stop loving me, if indeed you ever did, if I forced you to stay beside me.'

'Did I ever I love you? When did I not? I loved you when you were Princess, I worship you as Queen.'

'If you stayed in my Hive would you have become my drone?'

Thorn sighed. 'I hate this. I hate Carman for making me this way, and eventually, despite how much I love you, I would probably grow to hate you. I am not a drone by nature. I am, or was, a soldier. That's all I ever wanted to be Highness.'

Aynia nodded. 'I guess I know that to be true.'

'That's not saying that I would not have been sorely tempted,' Thorn said quickly.

'I tried everything I knew to entice you to ask,' Aynia admitted. 'I flaunted my body at you. I touched you. I made sure we had moments alone. It never seemed to make an impact on you.'

'Never Highness? I remember every detail of a brief moment before a fireplace when I tasted you.'

'I too hold that moment as a treasured memory. I was afraid that you took disgust of me. You never showed desire for me.'

'It was in my heart. My Queen, if only we could have stayed as we were.'

'I often wish I was still a Princess,' Aynia admitted.

Thorn had been fighting back his own raging desire to mate so that he could give his report. Now he allowed himself to breathe in her scent again. He held her crushingly close and kissed her.

Aynia tasted Thorn's lips. Her hands slid down his bare chest.

The hollow in the old tree rose far over their heads, ascending into darkness. Aynia snapped her wings and started levitating the two of them.

Thorn realized that they were in flight. 'Majesty, I can't resist your scent any longer.'

'Then stop resisting.'

Thorn immediately pulled her back into his embrace. They kissed for an eternity. Thorn would not be satisfied with a mere kiss though. He pushed Aynia's clothes away and suckled on her breasts with the thirst of a male denied water for over a week. Where Carman had little milk Aynia's breasts were heavy with the life giving liquid.

'Not so hard,' Aynia told him, but Thorn continued to roughly take the drink he needed from her.

When Thorn's thirst was slaked he kissed Aynia again. 'Your scent drives me mad.' He slid his hand between her legs and pushed her thighs apart. His fingers brushed lightly against her labia. 'You're so hot and wet. I want to taste you.'

Aynia spread her legs further apart. Thorn buried his face between her thighs.

Thorn licked her already sensitive clitoris onto the edge of an orgasm. 'You're fertile,' he told her. He kissed his way up her stomach, between her breasts, to her neck. 'Do you want me inside of you?'

Aynia wrapped her legs around his waist. She guided him to her. She was so close to coming, she just needed him to take her. 'Oh yes.'

Aynia moaned. This was wonderful. Everything that she wanted was here and now. Thorn was inside of her, filling her. As he stroked he worked his deft fingers over her clitoris. The sensation was too much and not enough at the same time. Aynia began to work her pelvis in rhythm with Thorn so that he would go deeper, deeper, until every muscle in her body was ready to explode.

'You're so hot and wet,' Thorn whispered into her ear. 'If I knew how this felt I wouldn't have fought being a drone.'

'See what you do to me,' Aynia put his hand back down between her legs.

Thorn felt the waves of orgasm pulse through Aynia's vagina. That sensation was all it took for him to loose control. With one last deep thrust Thorn came into Aynia.

The two slowly sank toward the ground.

'I forgot, Carman!' Thorn said with mock horror as he and Aynia lazed in the tree hollow after mating.

Aynia laughed. 'Is she still flying around expecting you to mate with her? I expect by now she's quite frustrated.'

'I can't summon the strength to fly right now much less mate again,' Thorn admitted. 'And if I could I would take you again,' he told Aynia as he buried his face once again in her hair and took deep breaths of her spiced scent. 'Unfortunately, however, she will come looking for me and I will have to go with her to keep her from going after you.'

'I am not afraid to face her,' Aynia said. 'I almost killed her once. I can destroy her this time.'

'I can't allow it Majesty.'

Aynia laughed. 'Who are you to order me about drone?' She mocked Thorn lightly.

Thorn pinned Aynia's arms to her side and met her questioning gaze with a serious frown. 'I will not allow you to put yourself in harm's way. We have mated. It's possible that you carry my child. As Captain of the Guard, and as the de facto Prince Consort, I alone have the power to control the Queen when she puts the future of the Hive at stake. Your father used this power, and I will use it too. In this you will obey me.'

Aynia's smile faded. 'I am not in the habit of being ruled by my drones.'

Thorn's infinite patience snapped. 'Don't make me bind you and imprison you in your chambers.'

The idea of Thorn tying her up and carrying her off to her bed did not have the sobering affect on Aynia that Thorn wanted it to. The vision it called to her mind was anything but unpleasant. Unable to stop it, a bubble of laughter burst out of her mouth.

'What's so funny?' Thorn asked crossly.

'The thought of you taking me to my bed and throwing me down on it. You did that once before. That time I nearly pulled you into the bed with me. Next time I won't let you get away.' She pulled him close to her and placed a hard kiss on his lips.

Thorn cursed loudly. 'Damn it Aynia, I can and will force you.'

'You called me Aynia.'

Thorn's eyes went wide. 'Forgive me Highness. Forgive the familiarity.'

'I'll forgive you if you come back with me.'

'This isn't a game. You're the Royal Mother of the Hive. You serve the Hive, I serve the Hive, and we can not change who we are. You will obey me.'

Aynia wished that there were some way that she could change this truth. As Queen she had to be practical. If Thorn stayed with Carman he might find a chance to assassinate her, and he could inform Aynia of Carman's plans.

'Where is Carman? When I return to the Hive I can send Sage to kill her.'

'Her lair is hard to find. It would be better if I led the guards to the place.'

'Tell me anyway.'

Thorn let go of Aynia's arms. He was glad to see that she finally accepted his authority over her. 'About a mile from here, where the thicket has a lot of dead undergrowth, there is a little hidden dell. The bushes growing on the hillsides above it nearly hide it. Look for a lightening struck oak to your right and a copse of pines ahead. The third landmark is a boulder shaped like a sleeping giant. Keep those over your left shoulder.'

Oak, pines, giant boulder, got it. How many attendants does she have left?'

'Five.'

'How heavily armed?'

'They have little.'

'Take my knife,' Aynia handed Thorn a small dagger that she wore in a garter. 'It isn't much, but it can do some damage.'

Thorn smiled at Aynia, but another thought came to his mind. 'How are you going to explain a Princess to your workers? Every drone of yours is going to know that he didn't mate with you, but suddenly you will be with child. Workers will ask questions.'

Aynia sighed. 'Ever practical Captain Thorn.'

'Ever realistic Queen Aynia. You must go out and mate with one of your drones.'

'You would not feel betrayed when I am with another male?'

Thorn laughed. 'Females have many males, it is the Fairie way. There are many bees; there is only one flower. Does one bee get jealous because another bee comes to taste the nectar?'

'Then it does not bother you?'

Thorn stood up. 'I must go find my other Queen and get her away from here so that she doesn't find you. My lady, I am forever in your service.' He didn't answer Aynia's question.

'Why go back to her? Why not return to the Hive with me?' Aynia had to try one last time to lure Thorn into her harem.

'I can get close to her. She does not trust me, of course, but eventually she will drop her guard and I will be there to take advantage.'

'We could be together. You could spend every night in my bed.'

'My Queen, my Aynia, I would come back if there was a future for me, but I can not serve as a soldier in my present state if I return to the Hive. I will be forced into the harem and a life of idle uselessness. You know how much I would hate that. If I stay out here I can still be a soldier. I can still take action. Please don't tempt me to stay with you.'

'A least I know that you are tempted to stay with me,' Aynia told Thorn. She sighed deeply. 'It has been heaven.' Kissing him lightly as a farewell, she turned to fly away. 'Perhaps one day when we meet again we will have the luxury of discussing our needs instead of those of the Hive.'

'You are Queen,' Thorn reminded her. 'You and the Hive are one.'

Aynia sprung into the air, not wanting to hear what Thorn was telling her. The Hive be damned, she thought bitterly. If I'm Queen why can't I once have things my way?

She buzzed back to the territory near her Hive. She had been gone about twenty minutes, not long, but her drones would be nearly crazy by now looking for her. She found it hard to summon the desire to mate again but realized that she had no choice. She had to do it and she had to make it seem like the first time.

Suddenly from two different directions behind her Sarkany and Moss appeared in the sky. Both were flying at top speed towards her. She thanked her Goddess that at least it was her two favorite drones that approached her. Thinking hastily as they made a beeline to intercept her, Aynia made a last minute zigzag that put her directly into Sarkany's path. There was no reason to deny Moss. It was just that Sarkany's coloring more closely matched Thorn's. No one would believe the blonde blue-eyed Moss as the father of an olive skinned, black haired Princess.

Sarkany couldn't believe his luck. It seemed almost as if the Queen decided to put herself into his arms at the last second. But, he told himself, she had probably just mistimed an evasive maneuver. It hardly mattered now. He had his arms wrapped around his Queen and he would not let go until he mated with her. The combined strength of their wings took the pair higher into the sky. Moss followed them.

Wheat, seeing the Queen and Sarkany together, and with Prince Moss in close pursuit, tried to catch up but could not. After a time he returned to the Fairie ring where all the other failed drones were gathering for a drink of refreshing nectar to help them to overcome the mating madness.

'Sarkany caught her,' Wheat informed the gathering between gasps. 'They both came upon her at a clearing in the forest. They were both the same distance from her, but when she went to evade Moss it put her right into Sarkany's path.' He sat down heavily and accepted a drink. He took defeat in stride. There would be many more mating flights. He had hundreds of years to work his way up through the ranks of the harem.

'Such a long time for her to evade her drones,' Adders-Tongue observed caustically. 'Perhaps our Queen does not desire to mate.'

'There have been many other long flights. New Queens often put their drones through their paces before consenting to mate, and consent she did.' Camellia reminded Adders-Tongue.

'But what good is a long flight? How does it profit the Hive? Is she thinking only of her own pleasure?'

Wheat fell back against the pillows placed around the Queen's Throne. As he did a puff of perfumed powder billowed into the air in a cloud around him, causing Adders-Tongue to go into a coughing spell. Wheat seemed not to notice. 'I'm beat, and all of these other lazy drones are worn out too.' He motioned over towards the other drones sitting around the Fairie ring. Most of them did look tired and weak. 'I bet that they all came back fifteen minutes after we took wing. Very few of us had the physical strength to stay in flight as long as the Queen did. At least we know that she mated with the fittest of her drones. And strong drones beget strong Princesses. I think that I'll start a fitness regimen tomorrow. I don't plan to be out flown next time,' Wheat said with determination as he patted his flat, muscular abdomen. He was enjoying himself immensely. For someone of his low birth to speak on equal terms with a member of the nobility was nothing short of a miracle.

'How dare you speak to me! If you were my drone I'd have you over my knee and give you a taste of leather on your ass!'

'If I was your drone I'd be fucking the Queen,' Wheat quipped back.

The noble ladies gasped, but then some dared to laugh behind their hands. Wheat was a naughty boy, but his comment was well barbed.

Adders-Tongue looked at Wheat with a condescending stare, and then turned back to Camellia. 'As Mistress of the Queen's harem you should teach these drones better to mind their manners. I did not give that drone permission to speak to me.'

Camellia pursed her lips in an effort not to join in the laughter. 'If I were you I'd be careful about speaking to him. Remember what the Queen did to the last female who was caught merely conversing with one of her drones?' Camellia put it on her mental list to have a long talk, and punishment session, with the uppity little drone.

'The Queen endangers herself by being outside this long,' Adders-Tongue changed the subject. She could not meet Camellia's laughing eyes. 'Have you noticed how very spooky the forest is today? It is almost silent.' Adders-Tongue realized suddenly that Lady Deidre's sisters surrounded her. It would be easy for them to take vengeance for Lady Deidre's death. The three females could act before anyone realized what they were doing. And all three were looking at Adders-Tongue with seriously grim expressions.

Camellia enjoyed for a brief moment the obvious discomfort of her enemy. It was good for Thane Adders-Tongue to realize how much the sisters hated her. Then, once the tension was at a perfect pitch, Camellia made small talk in a casual tone. 'Yes, the forest is very quiet today. If I didn't know better I might think that the nymphs are no longer here. The forest seems sterile, dead.'

Rose nodded her head. 'I wonder. When Queen Aynia turned down the nymph's request for help they told the Queen that they would seek help elsewhere. I wonder if those empty headed fools went to the Mountain King?'

'Surely not,' Adders-Tongue argued. 'They probably went to another more helpful and powerful source,' she said, thinking that they had gone to appeal to Carman.

'There is no other source of help around, unless you know of something we don't?' Camellia asked innocently. Would Adders-Tongue admit that Carman was alive?

Adders-Tongue was too canny of a politician to fall for this line of questioning. 'I simply can not believe that the nymphs would go to the Mountain King. He'll rape and kill them all,' she snapped. Adders-Tongue wondered nervously why her guards were sitting so far away. Couldn't they sense the tension in the air between her and the Queen's attendants?

'Yes, but are the nymphs smart enough to realize that?' Heather asked. No one answered. They all feared the answer.

Aynia, Sarkany, and Moss rose high in the sky then sank to the top canopy of the treetops. Both males were kissing Aynia everywhere. She would have laughed at their desire but felt somehow a growing urge to mate again too.

'Which one of you will it be?' Aynia asked. She expected one of them to let go and give up, but the both clung tightly to her so that she would not escape them.

'Both of us Majesty.'

'Both?' Aynia laughed at the audacity.

'We do everything together.'

Sarkany faced Aynia. He took advantage of this position to latch unto her exposed breasts. Aynia doubted that he would find much left to suckle after Thorn's greedy mouth drained her.

'My Queen is not producing milk for me,' Sarkany mentioned with a small frown.

Aynia could feel Moss's already hard penis pressing against her buttocks.

'Take me Sarkany,' Aynia whispered to him. 'Fill me. I burn for you.'

Sarkany looked a little surprised. While he had made love to the Queen several times, she was usually somewhat passive. Usually she lay staring at the fire as he coaxed her body into responded to him. Today she was reaching for him.

Moss reached around and stroked Aynia's clitoris.

She allowed him to part her legs.

'Just let me feel how wet you are,' Moss asked. With quick strokes he fingered Aynia's clitoris.

'Don't stop,' Aynia asked.

'Don't worry my love. Sarkany will take over.' Moss kissed Aynia's neck at the nape. A shiver slid down her spine despite the warmth of the sun.

Moss and Sarkany exchanged a kiss.

Sarkany rubbed the head of his penis around her outer lips. 'I want to taste your honey.'

Aynia flipped the three of them over in mid air. Quickly straddling Sarkany, she lowered herself onto him. Once they were coupled he would not be able to pull out. That suited the Queen well. There was no way that she could allow him to taste her juices. If she was already successfully mated Sarkany would be able tell. And she didn't want him to taste Thorn's juices inside of her.

Sarkany was for a moment speechless. Aynia was not like the female he was used to. On the other hand he liked her new aggressiveness. And he loved being inside her.

Aynia leaned her upper body back against Moss as she rode Sarkany. Moss moved his hand down to Aynia's clitoris and massaged her. Then, as she felt herself about to come, Moss slid his hand back around to her buttocks. He helped her to lean forward over Sarkany.

Sarkany suckled on Aynia's breast again as he firmly grabbed her at the hips and began pounding into her.

First Moss stroked her anus gently with his finger. He watched Sarkany sliding in and out of her vagina. He was hard and could not wait. Moss gently slid his erect penis inside of her anus.

Aynia gasped. 'Fill me, fill me up,' she moaned. She didn't know which sensation she wanted more, Sarkany's suckling on her nipple, the pleasure from his phallus, or the shocking pleasure from Moss working in and out of her anus. There was pleasure and sensation everywhere.

Aynia felt the delicious tension, felt the waves pass through her body in seismic ripples. 'It's too much,' she told them but didn't want them to stop.

Sarkany rolled to his side, taking Moss and Aynia with him. He lifted Aynia's upper leg until her ankle was at his neck. The angle gave him great traction to trust deeper and deeper into the Queen. He came into her hard and fast. Aynia arched up and met him one last time before Sarkany collapsed into her arms.

'My turn,' Moss reminded Sarkany. 'I haven't come yet.'

Sarkany nodded his head lazily. He wet his fingers in Aynia's vagina, then released her and flew around behind Moss. Sarkany slid two fingers into Mosses' anus. With his other hand he gently massaged Mosses' balls. The sensation was too much for Moss to deny. He came explosively, plunging as deep into Aynia's ass as he dared.

Slowly the three lovers floated down to a pine tree.

'You're supposed to be helping to keep us in the air,' Moss grumbled.

'Sorry,' Sarkany said. 'I'm too tired to fly.'

'Don't fight,' Aynia slapped their buttocks lightly. 'Let us lie in each other's arms and enjoy this fleeting moment of bliss.'

Sarkany and Moss, honored beyond words, lay each on one side of Aynia as they all enjoyed the afterglow. 'We can lay here together until the end of time my Queen, if you command it.'

'Moss, you didn't want a chance to sire a Princess?' Aynia asked.

Moss shrugged. 'Not as much as I wanted to fulfill my fantasy. Next year maybe. I'll catch you first and take you away from Sarkany.'

Sarkany laughed. 'Hey, I shared. That's the deal Prince.'

Aynia closed her eyes. 'So you two do everything together? Perhaps we'll have to explore the possibilities together.'

Sarkany and Moss kissed each other over Aynia then settled back to cuddle close to her.

Exhausted, the three of them drifted off into a deep sleep.

Carman flew back over and over the same territory. She was tiring. Her left side was not strong and her wings had trouble compensating for the difference in relative strength between her sides.

Where was Thorn? Why wasn't he in pursuit? She wasn't exactly playing hard to catch here. Wasn't he interested? No, that couldn't be. From the time that she'd forced him to drink her milk she'd noticed how he reacted to her scent. Now that he was drunk on fermented Queen's milk there was no way that he would be able to fight the urge to mate. She had seen the fever in his eyes. It burned as bright as her mating madness. But where was Thorn? How could he be avoiding her?

Movement on the ground below caught her eye. She turned and zoomed down. She caught a scent, a male scent. It was Thorn. He was hiding in the hollow of an old tree. Even drunk on fermented Queen's milk he could resist her, Carman thought bitterly. This was all Aynias' fault. If she had not partially paralyzed Carman's left side Thorn wouldn't be able to resist Carman. Or so Carman believed.

Carman flew into the hollow of the old tree. Thorn was there. He was standing with his arms folded over his chest. The stance was defiant. So was his sneer.

'Oh, so you finally tracked me down,' Thorn said sarcastically.

'Perhaps your stupid worker brain does not comprehend the idea, but in order to mate with me you have to fly after me and catch me.'

'I have no desire to mate with you.' Thorn said calmly.

'What? You drank the fermented Queen's milk. I saw the mating fever take you. When I took off in flight you fought the restraints to follow me. I saw that.'

'I suppose I did. Thank the Goddess that I'm in my right mind now.'

'How? How?' Carman stormed. Then she paused and sniffed the air. Coming closer to Thorn she sniffed his hair and face. 'Aynia!' She screamed. 'You found that bitch Aynia and fucked her. I can't believe it. She stole my Throne, she stole my beauty, and she stole my Hive. And now she, who has hundreds of drones, steals my one and only drone? How could you do that? How could you fuck her, of all the Fairie in the world? How could you have gone to her?'

'I didn't want to waste my seed in you.' Thorn commented. 'I would rather spill it on the ground.'

Carman continued to rant, stomping loudly as she paced the hollow of the tree. 'I have always loved you, but you never even noticed me. It was always that slut Aynia. That bitch even got between my mother and me. What is so special about Aynia?'

'She is *the* Queen,' Thorn said.

Carman ran up to Thorn, her stinger exposed. 'I will sting you.'

'Go ahead. I'd rather die than be your drone.'

'Shut up! I know, I'll force you to drink more fermented Queen's milk. The fever will come back, and I will not have you held back. In fact, I think that I'll just straddle you while I pour the stuff down your throat. I hope that you choke on it.'

'So do I. Anything rather than have sex with you.'

Carman screamed again. 'Stop talking this way to me. I will make you beg for my touch once the fever comes on you.'

Thorn sighed. 'Listen, if you plan to do this anytime soon I have to warn you, Aynia and I were pretty strenuous in our love making. I don't think that even with the mating fever I would be able to do my part for another two hours or so. It was deliciously exhausting.' Thorn, having mated, knew the urgency to mate that was taking over Carman's brain at this moment. The thought of having to wait another two hours before getting relief was enough to drive her crazy.

Carman grabbed Thorn. 'Come on. You're my property now. You're my drone. Let's get another cup of fermented Queen's milk for you.' She pulled Thorn out of the hollow tree.

The sound of a horse's neigh caught their attention. Carman and Thorn looked up to see a male astride a pitch black stallion. The male had a chiseled face, with high cheekbones, and a black beard that was groomed to a wicked point at the end of his sharp, cruel chin.

The male smiled and dismounted from his horse with languid casual grace.

Carman gasped. 'The Mountain King!' It was the King of the Goblins.

King Liderc slid silently across the woodland floor to Carman. Thorn, while despising Carman, hated the Mountain King even more. He stepped in front of Carman and leveled his stinger at the advancing figure.

King Liderc laughed when he saw this. 'A drone? A mere drone dares to draw his stinger on me? How,' King Liderc paused to find the word, 'romantic.'

'Fly away Carman,' Thorn warned her. 'The Mountain King can not fly. You have time to escape.'

Carman stomped her foot. 'It's Queen Carman, and I will not be ordered about by my drone.'

'I can not fly yet, but you can. Save yourself.'

Carman ignored Thorn. This new male fascinated her. He was in aspect like the Fairie, but as if glimpsed through a cracked glass. Something about this dark sensuousness stirred her.

King Liderc leaned casually against a nearby pine tree. Quietly, with sinuous voice, he began to speak. 'The nymphs came to me and told me an interesting story. They told me that the Hive of Balnacra had two Queens. I asked myself, how could this be? Two Queens! How can the Hive of Balnacra revel in such riches while I, King Liderc, the poor Mountain King, have no Queen?'

'No! I will not let you take her' Thorn warned him.

King Liderc began to advance very slowly on Thorn again. Like all Goblins he was slim with the palest skin, the darkest hair, and eyes of black. His face was narrow and cruel looking with his sunken cheeks and heavy eyebrows. He sniffed the air. 'I know what today is Majesty. Today is Equinox. And I know what that means to Fairie folk. You are fertile. I can smell it from here, and you are unmated. I can sense that too.'

Thorn stood ready, wondering if he should attack or wait for the Mountain King to make his move. For a second he wondered why he protected Carman, but did not allow himself to think on it. It was Thorn's job to protect the Fairie. Whether he liked the ones he protected or not had nothing to do with his job as a soldier.

'Is your drone too fat and lazy to take you?' King Liderc asked Carman with haughty sarcasm. 'I can tell that you desire to mate. The fever burns inside of you.'

Carman, in her right mind, would have taken flight immediately from King Liderc. But she was not in her right mind. Still unmated, she was in the grip of mating madness. She knew that Thorn could not mate with her for another several hours. However, here in front of her, was a virile male, a very virile male. She could sense that as much as he could sense her heat. There was something alluring about the cool aloofness of

King Liderc. Carman would never admit it but she was strongly attracted to him at this moment. She was, after all, unable to think of anything but sex.

'Or is it that he finds a damaged Queen too revolting to mate with?'

Carman literally growled.

'Ooh, I like that sound.' King Liderc, whose movements up to now had been languid and slow, suddenly leapt forward. With hands as strong as iron he grabbed Thorn around the waist and began to squeeze. Thorn felt his legs go numb. He tried to reach King Liderc with his stinger but King Liderc only laughed.

'Are you actually trying to sting me?' King Liderc continued to squeeze.

Thorn felt his ribs snapping as King Liderc applied unceasing pressure. It was as if a large iron band enveloped him from his lower ribs down to his thighs, an iron band that was crushing him slowly to death. Thorn tried, but could not keep his mouth closed. Thorn screamed. It was an animal howl of pain.

Carman could only watch the horrible sight in front of her.

As Thorn passed out King Liderc dropped his body to the ground.

'Is he dead?' Carman asked in a daze.

'Does it matter?' King Liderc walked back over to his black steed and mounted it. 'Come with me, be my Queen. I will quench the fever that burns in your loins. Is your pussy throbbing, aching with desire, the need for sex? I will give that to you. I will be your King. I will stroke you until your ripe fruits gush nectar onto my tongue. I will release your desire.'

Carman closed her eyes for a second and breathed in the scent he exuded. Yes, she wanted sex. She wanted it now. 'Take me with you,' she said.

Riding over to Carman King Liderc easily lifted her up onto the saddle in front of him. Holding her still with his iron grasp, he touched spur to horseflesh. In seconds they were headed underground, into the Hall of the Mountain King.

'I bring you a new Queen!' King Liderc told his Goblins. He slid off of his horse and pulled Carman down next to him.

Carman, still stunned, gazed into the darkness. She realized that there were hundreds of goblins there in the darkness around her. She could not see them but she could hear them. Much too late to do herself any good, Carman let out a scream.

King Liderc laughed. So did all the other goblins. 'Funny, the nymphs said the same thing when they came here.'

Now the legions of goblins began hooting loudly. The sound made Carman cringe.

'Well, you have seen my Queen. Now I will go mate her.' There was a cheer as King Liderc clamped his fist around Carman's wrist and dragged her to his chambers.

CHAPTER 15

'Why do the stones sing?' Moss asked Aynia lazily.

'Sing?' Aynia asked with immediate concern. She raised her head from where it rested on his arm. She heard the strange sound too.

Sarkany understood that something was terribly wrong. 'What is it?' He asked.

'Come, we must dress and fly.' Aynia pulled on her clothes rapidly. Watching Sarkany dress she was filled with a sudden fondness for him. She went over and kissed him on his cheek. 'I look forward to exploring your body with more leisure in the future,' she told him with a husky voice.

Sarkany took a deep, satisfied breath. 'My Queen.' He bowed to her.

'What about me?' Moss asked petulantly.

'I have other ideas for you, wicked ideas.'

Moss grinned. 'I am at your command.'

Together they took flight. In no time they alit at the Fairie ring in the clearing.

Many questioning eyes turned towards Aynia.

'Majesty,' Camellia bowed and smiled.

'Can you hear it? The stones are singing.' The tone of Aynia's voice was enough to alert her attendants. Indeed, the stones of the valley resonated with an eerie hum.

'The Mountain King!'

The Royal Guards, ashamed to be caught unawares of a dangerous situation so near the Hive, came immediately to their feet. They swarmed around their Queen.

All the Fairie folk jumped up in alarm. The Mountain King was a natural enemy to the Hive. Much more feared than humans, crueler than any troll, these distant relations to the Fairies were the only magical creatures that actively sought to destroy Fairie Hives.

'Why does he come to the surface?' Aynia asked herself. 'The nymphs told me that they would take any measures to protect this valley. Damn empty headed nymphs! The Mountain King! If they went to him they're all dead. If he thinks that we're weak he will come for us. Hurry, everyone into the Hive!' Aynia needn't have commanded her subjects. At the first mention of the Mountain King a panicked retreat into the Hive began.

'My Queen, you must come inside!' Captain Sage warned her.

Aynia stopped. 'What was that sound?'

Everyone heard it, but no one wanted to admit it.

Aynia's heart raced. She knew instinctively, despite the primal nature of the scream, that it was Thorn. Aynia tried to free herself from restraining arms but she was weary and her guards insistent. They and the drones swarmed over the Queen, lifted her up, and swept her towards the Hive like the current of a relentless river. Within moments she was virtually a prisoner in her own Palace.

There were some torches in the private chambers of the Mountain King. The light was only enough for Carman to make out the shapes of furniture. She rubbed her wrist where King Liderc held it. Backing away from him she moved across the chamber cautiously.

King Liderc stripped off his clothes with speed. Then he went to a table and poured himself a cup of wine. 'Do you care for any?' He offered Carman a cup.

She shook her head no.

'Suit yourself. I don't really care.' He put his own cup down and advanced on her, again moving with languid grace that belied the speed with which he moved. In seconds Carman was trying to defend herself as he ripped off her clothes.

Carman backed up, away from the onslaught. She crossed her hands over her chest in a feeble attempt at modesty. She stopped when she felt a piece of furniture against the back of her knee.

'So you lead me to the bed right away? That's what I like, a Queen who can read my mind.'

Carman turned and saw that it was indeed a bed that she had trapped herself against. With new determination she turned back to King Liderc and brought forward her stinger.

'Oh, I like a female who fights back. It gives the love making a sweaty, desperate feel. Promise me that you'll scream.'

Carman lunged with her stinger, going straight for King Liderc's heart. Her stinger made contact, but he only laughed at her.

'Foolish Fairie. My skin is made of stone. My heart is made of stone. I will show you what else of me is as hard as stone.' His voice fell into a low rumble.

Carman tried again and again to sting the King. It still had no effect.

'I grow tired of this,' King Liderc told her. He pushed her down on the bed and fell on top of her.

'What is that scent?' Carman asked. She could smell this slightly earthy sent that excited her senses. Already mad to mate, the scent was fogging her brain.

'When you want me, spread your legs apart. I can wait, but I doubt that you can.'

Carman tried to slide her own hand between her legs.

'No my pet, I can not allow you to please yourself. If you want relief you must allow me to provide it.'

Between the intoxicating scent and the silky voice of King Liderc, Carman could no longer summon up the strength to resist him. She parted her legs, bending her knees.

King Liderc pushed apart her thighs even more with a strong hand and he began to lick Carman roughly. His tongue was like a cat's. Carman wriggled but could not move. She was well pinned. For such a small appearing male King Liderc's body was surprisingly heavy.

Despite her revulsion Carman could not deny the sensation she was feeling as King Liderc licked her. She had felt it before when she forced Thorn to take her milk, but not these stronger waves and contractions passing through her body.

King Liderc pushed Carman's knees up to her chest. She did not protest. He smiled. 'Good, my new Queen likes rough treatment.'

'I do not,' Carman retorted.

'Your wetness belies that.' He fingered and stroked her as she felt, much against her will, the deep madness of the mating season once again overtake her mind. 'This is what I offered to you, my pet. Let's not pretend that you don't burn to be mated,'

King Liderc watched with a bemused expression on his face as Carman climaxed. Personally he didn't care if his lady took pleasure, but the chances of her conceiving were better if she did, so he took the pains tonight to bring her pleasure. Once she carried his prince she would not be so lucky.

Carman gasped, her back arching as every muscle in her body contracted wonderfully. The moment of bliss was short lived. King Liderc took this moment to enter her. Carman screamed. He was as hard as stone, and despite her wetness, dry as dust. Each thrust was like stone rasping against raw skin. She struggled to get away.

Suddenly a new and horrible sensation was inside her. Fire! Her womb felt that it was on fire. 'I die, I die!' She screamed to King Liderc.

King Liderc laughed. 'That's my seed.'

Carman calmed only a little as she realized what he said was true. In her mind's eye she could see into her womb. She could see her egg; she could see his molten lava sperm swimming towards it. Then she could see conception. Clarity overtook her mind. She was mated to King Liderc. She would give birth to a prince. She would spend the rest of her life in this underground world where there was no light. Carman would be the Queen of this Hive, a Hive that was ruled by its males; not its females. And this King would take her night after night in this horrible

408

painful way, using her for his own pleasure, caring not at all for hers.

At least that was what he believed.

Any other female would have gone mad at this thought. Not Carman. Carman began to plot a way to bring this male to his knees.

'Where are they?' Snakegrass asked for the tenth time in a many minutes as she paced the full length of Carman's outdoor throne room.

The other four attendants shrugged. They were not among Carman's original attendants. Since entering service in Carman's chambers they'd survived a day-long massacre, ran for their lives through the Hive, and were now living in a miserable dusty hole in the ground with little food. Carman was a demanding Queen to serve. By now she was universally despised. These attendants did not care where she was.

'I will search for her. You four stay here in case she returns. The Queen will be tired and hungry. Make sure that there is ample food and drink for her. Refresh her bed. When Thorn returns be sure to chain him.'

The attendants nodded but showed no signs of obeying Snakegrasses' commands.

Snakegrass flew away brooding on her own thoughts as she searched for signs of her Queen. Many years ago her Aunt, Thane Adders-Tongue, placed Snakegrass in service to Carman. An attendant served her princess with pure loyalty for several reasons. Failure to serve well always meant death. That was the downside. The upside was the possibility that the princess would become Queen. But what then? A princess's attendants were set aside for professional staff such as the sisters brought in for Queen Aynia. The old attendants were placed in the Temple to become Priestesses or were retired to a small pension. After living in the Royal Palace neither choice appealed to Snakegrass.

Realistically even those possible futures would be denied to Snakegrass. Carman had little chance of taking control of the

Hive away from Aynia. Aynia was acknowledged by the common workers to be the rightful Queen. Carman was damaged and faced charges of treason if she returned to the Hive. Snakegrass sighed. Her course was a losing one, her future bleak, but with nothing left to loose she would stay beside Carman to the bitter end.

Hours later Snakegrass spied Thorn's body in a small clearing. She landed near him. His face was pale and his breathing was labored. She could not revive him.

Snakegrass flew quickly to the hidden glen to gather supplies. The other attendants were gone. So were most of the food, blankets, and other supplies. Cursing under her breath, Snakegrass gathered what little was left and flew back to Thorn.

Captain Sage and his men found Carman's hideout from the directions provided by the Queen. They searched the area but found little. Even the ashes of the fire were growing cold. It was clear that the rogue Queen and her attendants were gone from this site. Sage's head sunk forward. It was another failure. One day his Queen would stop being so forgiving and he would face a public execution like her drone, Prince Noisi. Sage shuddered. Was it the Queen's sting that killed the Prince, or was it the near decapitation? Either way Sage did not look forward to reporting his most recent failure to the Ice Queen Aynia.

Thorn woke in a fit of painful coughs. He was bound from just under his arms to his hips in a tight swaddling. It was night. A small fire flickered and produced too much smoke. On the other side of the clearing, just visible through the smoke, was a female.

'The Mountain King,' Thorn tried to warn her.

The female moved closer.

'The Mountain King,' Thorn repeated with difficulty.

'The Mountain King has Queen Carman?' Snakegrass asked him.

Thorn tried to nod. It was hard to speak.

'I guess that's how your ribs were broken. Did you try to defend her or did you just let him take her?'

Thorn's eyes narrowed with anger.

Snakegrass nodded. 'Of course you tried to save her. But did you mate with her first? No, probably not. A mated female would have been no use to the Mountain King.'

Thorn turned his face away from the smoke of the fire.

'I have not mated today yet either,' Snakegrass said in a very different voice than she had ever used around Thorn. 'Carman may not forgive me for making use of her drone, but even we common workers have our needs.'

Thorn looked back at Snakegrass, his eyes wide. Surely this female did not mean to mate with him? Most of his ribs were broken and his whole body ached. He tried feebly to put up a hand to ward her off, but Snakegrass laughed at the gesture.

'I left the important bits unwrapped. Here,' she dropped a liquid into his mouth.

Thorn tried to spit out the fermented Queen's milk but the burning of his tongue told him that some remained in his mouth.

'Oh, that begins to work right away,' Snakegrass crooned. Not gently enough she pulled away Thorn's tights. 'There's a good soldier, standing up and saluting me.'

'No,' Thorn groaned.

Snakegrass slipped off her clothes and straddled Thorn. 'Under these circumstances I'll do all of the work. Just lie there and don't say a thing.' Snakegrass lowered herself onto Thorn's cock and began moving.

Thorn tried to push her off, but his arms were weak and it hurt to move. Suddenly he passed out again.

When Thorn woke again the sky was the pale silvery color of pre-dawn. The fire was almost out. Dew hung heavily from every surface. Even the blanket draped over him was damp. Snakegrass wandered back into camp carrying twigs and leaves for the fire. She dumped some of the kindling into the fire ring and poked at it with a stick.

When the fire began to smoke again she wandered over to Thorn and looked down at him. She used the tip of her boot to nudge him. 'You're awake,' she said in a flat voice.

Thorn looked up at her. 'Yes I am.'

'Good. I have to get you to sit up to eat.' Snakegrass bent down and tried to help Thorn into a sitting position.

The pain was incredible. Thorn gasped.

'Come on big boy; let's get you over closer to the fire.'

'That's a pretty lousy fire.'

'When you are better building the fire will be one of your duties. Until then don't anger me. Drones should speak only when spoken to. Even with your injuries I will punish you, understand?'

'Do you mean like last night?' Thorn asked.

'You failed last night,' Snakegrass growled. 'A drone that can not please his mistress is a poor excuse for a drone. Remember, with Queen Carman held prisoner by the Mountain King you are nothing but a free drone. I will keep you at my pleasure, and for my pleasure, as long as you serve me well.'

Thorn frowned. He was really beginning to hate being a drone.

'Eat, you need your strength.' Snakegrass handed Thorn a bowl of barely warm porridge. Then she took the blanket and wrapped it around his back to help keep him warm.

Carman paced the chamber where she was held for hours. Gradually she grew accustomed to the dark. She didn't bother to see if the door to the chamber was guarded. When King Liderc left her he turned a lock on the door that was badly in need of oiling. The screeching protest of the metal told her that she was locked in.

Once Carman's eyes were adjusted to the dark enough for her to see she began a methodical search of the room. The walls were solid rock. A carpet covered the granite floor from wall to wall. By moving the furniture she was able to roll the rug section by section until she was convinced that there were no trap doors. The effort exhausted her. After she moved the furniture back she fell asleep again.

When Carman awoke she saw King Liderc sitting at the long heavy wooden table in the center of the room. He was eating his dinner and watching her with a faint smile of amusement.

By now Carman was starved, so she rose and went to the table. She sat opposite King Liderc, at the far end of the table, where another plate was laid out.

'Normally, my Queen, we do not allow our workers to lie in bed all day.'

'I did not lie in bed all day.'

'I noticed. You moved all of the furniture. Are you redecorating? I must confess that I am a long time bachelor and very set in my ways. This room hasn't been changed since I moved here from Carpathia. It did not please me to see my chamber altered.'

'I was searching for an escape route, a secret room, a hidden tunnel.'

King Liderc laughed. 'Good for you. Very enterprising.'

'I amuse you?' Carman was offended.

'Yes. You do. I can not think why, but you do. Perhaps because I was expecting to find that you had hung yourself, or fallen on your own stinger.'

Carman took a sip of her wine. 'I am not the type.'

'No, perhaps you're not,' he looked her over with a thoughtful expression on his face.

'I have escaped certain death before.'

'But my dear, I do not plan to kill you. I never plan to kill my females. They just seem to take it upon themselves to die. Sometimes they take their own lives quickly. Other times they die slowly over time, starving themselves, pining away for the overworld.'

Carman took a bite of her food. 'Again, I am not the type.'

'No. You're not.'

'I would like some clothes. You tore mine off last night and the shreds of cloth left are not fit for a worker, much less a Queen.'

'What incentive do I have to give you any clothes? I like the idea of coming home to my chamber and having my female readily accessible.'

'Clothes would not make me any less accessible to you. You can tear through anything with those hands.'

'True, but I still don't think that I will give you anything to wear.'

'Why not?' Carman demanded.

'Because you have not earned clothes yet, my dear.'

'I carry your damned prince. Isn't that enough?'

'No. It's not. Any female can be impregnated.'

Carman snorted. 'But how many survive to give birth?

'Enough. The goblins are legion.'

'Then what must I do to get some clothes?'

'Come here.'

'What?'

'First I require that you should obey me, always. I say come here. If I have to say it again I will take this whip,' King Liderc raised a riding crop that lay on the table near his plate, 'and I will put you over my knee, and I will beat you into submission.'

The sinuous voice of King Liderc was quiet, but Carman had no doubt as to how sincerely he meant what he said.

'You assume that I would dislike that.'

'You assume that I would dislike that, my lord,' King Liderc corrected Carman.

'My lord,' Carman smiled grudgingly.

'Come here,' he ordered her again in his quiet voice.

Carman rose and went to the other end of the table. King Liderc took her hand. He pulled her into his lap. 'This is better. Always obey me. Here I am the Lord, and you are only my servant. If you behave I will make your life bearable.'

'My Dread Lord,' Carman said before kissing King Liderc. It was the night after the Vernal Equinox, she was already mated, but somehow since he came into the room she could only think of mating with him again.

King Liderc slid his hand between her legs. 'You're already damp,' he said with surprise.

'I was dreaming of you.' Carman turned toward King Liderc and straddled him in the chair. Being made partially of stone he was already hard and ready for her. Carman lowered herself onto him. It was still painful, but not a bad as the night before. 'Let me show you what I dreamed of my lord.'

King Liderc would have never thought it possible, but he was shocked. This strange Fairie was not just allowing him to touch her; she was impaling herself upon him with apparent delight. Not that he didn't enjoy it, quite the reverse. Something about Carman excited him. It was more than that seductive scent she gave off. There was some kind of madness in her. She was potentially dangerous. For the calm, eerie King of the Goblins that touch of danger was excitingly different.

Carman lifted herself off of King Liderc and stood up. King Liderc wondered what she was planning next. She turned around and pushed his dinner plate away on the tabletop. Then she leaned face down over the table and spread her legs apart. Looking back over her shoulder at him, she smiled. 'My Dread Lord, fill me with your fire again.'

King Liderc rose to her challenge. Standing up, he slid into her and began to pump hard against her, hoping that he was hurting her, hoping that she would beg for him stop, but she only began to moan deep in her throat. He held back, but finally could not as she bucked against him. He could feel her juices flowing.

'I burn!' Carman cried out as King Liderc came into her.

He sat down again in his chair. Carman lay across the tabletop. Slowly she rose up and turned around. 'May I have some clothes now my lord?'

King Liderc picked up his riding crop and smacked it smartly across her buttocks. 'We will see. Go and wait for me in the bed. When I am done eating I will teach you further what I like.'

Carman smiled. 'I hear and obey master.' The sarcasm in her voice was lost on him. King Liderc only heard what he wanted to.

Normally, in the course of a day, King Liderc woke, took his morning meal alone in his chamber then spent the day attending to matters of state. Later, when he was ready to sleep, he retired to his chamber, ate dinner alone, and then slept.

It did not go without remark among his goblins that since their King had taken prisoner the Fairie Carman he now visited his chamber several times during the day. Goblin minds, due in no small part to the place in which they lived, were low and uncouth. Many a comment about their King's virility filled the goblin gossip for days.

No matter what time of the day or night he entered his chambers King Liderc found that Carman greeted him enthusiastically. She would leap off the bed and run to him. Sometimes before he could lock the door she was covering him with kisses and tearing at his clothes. Several times the King had not gotten past his threshold before Carman's legs were wrapped around his waist and he was coupled with her. King Liderc was, in the space of a few short days, well pleased with his bride.

On the fifth day King Liderc returned to his chamber in the middle of the day to find Carman lounging in his bed. She merely glanced up at him and yawned.

'What is the meaning of this?' King Liderc demanded to know. Anticipating her usual greeting the Mountain King had walked back to his chamber with a spring in his step and a stiff dick in his trousers.

'The meaning of what?'

'Is this how you greet your Lord and Master?'

'If I were hungry I would eat, but as my hunger has been recently slaked I decline to dine.'

'What is this talk of eating?'

'It is a metaphor Lord.' Carman said with contempt in her voice.

'I know what it is. I want to know what you mean. Who was with you? Who dared to lie with my Queen?' King Liderc' eyes glowed red with anger.

'I do not know one goblin from another Lord. You keep me locked away from all company. In your jealousy you provided the perfect opportunity for the rape. I am confined and unclothed and unable to defend myself.'

King Liderc's dark visage infused with blood. 'Who was he?' He shouted in a voice that moved the granite boulders of the overworld. King Liderc moved with his lithe speed to the side of the bed. He grabbed Carman's wrist and pulled her up to his face. 'You tell me who he was.'

'One goblin is as like another my Lord. When I heard the grating sound of the lock turning I ran to the door in my customary manner, but I recognized that it was not my Lord come to make love to me. I ran across the room to escape him, but he locked the door and I was trapped in here with him. He took me here, in your bed.' Carman pointed to the mattress.

'I will only ask you one more time,' King Liderc said through gritted teeth. 'Who was he?'

'He did have a key. Perhaps he was one of the guards at my door,' Carman suggested.

King Liderc threw her back down on the bed and stomped across the floor. He unlocked the massive wooden door and swung it open. There was a surprised cry then Carman heard bones crush.

Another goblin cried out. 'What have we done my Lord?'

There was a sound like a goblin struggling to breathe through a crushed windpipe, than another ominous crashing of bones. King Liderc came back into his chamber. He closed the door. Glancing down at his hand he saw blood. Casually, he wiped it off on his thigh.

'You killed both of them my Lord?' Carman asked.

'I was not sure which one touched you. Besides, if someone entered my chamber, they let him through.'

Carman held out her arms to King Liderc. 'Let me thank my protector properly.'

King Liderc slid into the bed. Carman wrapped her arms around him and stroked his arm.

'I know that a Fairie Queen may kill a goblin. I just don't know how. Tell me the secret, so that in the future I can protect myself,' Carman said slyly.

King Liderc smiled. 'I would prefer to instruct an asp how to sink its fangs into my flesh.'

'You do not trust me my Dread Lord?' Carman asked with slight indignation.

King Liderc pulled Carman close and rolled the two of them over so that he was lying on top of her. He kissed her slowly. 'I will never trust you. If you had the power to you would stab me in the back.'

Carman gave a contented sigh. 'My Lord knows me so well. But tell me, how shall you protect me in the future? You can not spend the entire day in these chambers with me. Then you would be your own prisoner. Not that I would mind spending all day in my Lord's arms,' she added quickly.

'Perhaps, if you are well behaved, I will have you spend the day at my side. You are, after all, now my Queen. You should start to be present at court. That way my subjects can view how your womb bulges with my son.'

Carman laughed. 'It will be easy for them to see. I still have no clothes.'

'I like you this way,' King Liderc's voice rumbled into her ear. 'I like the feel of your naked buttocks when you sit in my lap. I like to know that you have nothing to hide. I like to be able to kiss you here,' as he demonstrated, 'and touch you here,' he showed her again.

Carman obliging wriggled against him.

Carman had little respect for males. Her opinion was common among Fairie females. Most Fairie felt that outside of mating males were of no use. Carman observed that King Liderc, who had once seemed like a very formidable foe, was now a tame drone. She tested her theory by concocting a rape story. As she suspected, King Liderc was now more than willing to kill his own just for a chance to mate with her. It was a weakness inherent to all males. They just could not manage to think beyond their own sexual cravings.

Now that she held King Liderc in the palm of her hand Carman was determined to manipulate him in order to get the things that she wanted most. She already had her freedom from his chamber and clothing to wear. Next she needed access to Snakegrass. Eventually she would talk him into helping her to overthrow the Hive. But before she let him do that for her Carman had to discover the secret to killing the goblins. She knew that as a Fairie Queen she had the power, but how? Once she knew how to kill King Liderc she could use him to take back the Throne, then dispose of him as she would any useless drone. After that she would reign supreme and there would be no one to stop her.

CHAPTER 16

Thorn was pleased to find he no longer felt as much pain when he moved. He was not pleased, however, when Snakegrass began to unwrap the tight bandages from his rib case. 'Don't remove those!'

'I have to Thorn, or you'll get pneumonia. You need to be able to take a deep breath.'

'I can,' but when he tried he was wracked with pain.

'And we need to get you walking soon.'

'I don't think that I can.'

'You will. Stop arguing with me,' Snakegrass said. She stooped in front of him and buckled a think leather strap around his ankle.

'What is that for?'

'I want to make sure you don't escape. You could be faking how badly you're injured. Now stand.'

'I can't.'

Snakegrass grabbed Thorn's pubic hair and yanked up. To his surprise, Thorn found himself standing, although he had to lean against a tree for support.

'That's much better.' Snakegrass expertly fastened a leather cock ring on Thorn with a leather strap that separated his testicles. She attached a chain from the ankle strap through a ring on the strap at his scrotum. She tugged on the chain.

Pain shot through Thorn's balls. His knees nearly buckled. 'Ouch.'

'Good. This will permit you to walk but not run. And this,' Snakegrass attached another chain to the ring and pulled it between Thorn's buttocks up to his wings, 'will stop you from flying.' Again she tugged on the chain.

Thorn sank to his knees as the pain ripped through his scrotum. 'If you keep doing that what good will I be to you?' He gasped. 'I can't give you pleasure.'

420

'You will be a lot of use to me. You will find food, you will build us shelter, and you will help me find a way to rescue Queen Carman from the Mountain King. Besides, what makes you think that I don't take pleasure in seeing you on your knees in pain pet?' Snakegrass stood in front of Thorn. She slid her fingers into her crotch then wiped the juices onto Thorn's lips. 'Lick my fingers,' she ordered. When Thorn was slow to comply she took a stick and tugged lightly on the chain to Thorn's cock ring.

Thorn grunted. Then he obliging opened his mouth and licked her fingers. 'Good boy,' Snakegrass crooned. She slid her fingers back inside her pussy. 'Do you want more? Don't speak, just nod your head yes.'

It took just one more tug of the chain to get Thorn to nod his head.

Days later Snakegrass and Thorn hiked within sight of the Hall of the Mountain King. 'I cannot get any closer,' Snakegrass hissed. 'If the goblins smell me they will come out and capture me. Go to the oak at the edge of the forest and carve this sign into it.' Snakegrass showed Thorn a drawing on a piece of paper.

Thorn held the knife in his hand. He could stab Snakegrass. Obviously Snakegrass thought of this too. She moved beyond his reach.

Thorn walked gingerly over to the oak. It took some time. Despite Snakegrasses' assertion that he could walk, any step with a normal stride would cause the cock ring to tug uncomfortably on his balls. He was forced to take small steps with a funny little walk he remembered many drones in the Hive using. Apparently under their hose many drones were hobbled the same as he was now. If he could only stand the pain in his balls he could walk across the valley and return to the Hive. Surely Aynia would remove the torturous device.

Once out of sight of Snakegrass he opened his wings experimentally. Immediately he regretted the attempt. He curled up on the ground and tried not to throw up.

'That took you far too long,' Snakegrass snapped when Thorn returned to her hiding place. 'We have many more of these to do.' She peered at his face, then took the knife from him and inspected the cock ring and chains. 'You didn't try to cut the hobble off or remove it, so you must have tried to fly.'

Thorn groaned. Why hadn't he thought to cut the leather strip around his ankle?

'Bad boy, I'm sure that you won't try to fly again any time soon.' Snakegrass chuckled. 'It seems as if the attempt brought its own punishment, doesn't it? I'm sorry to say that it does not.' Snakegrass grabbed the chain and pulled Thorn over to a tree. She pulled his hands back around the tree and slipped a pair of cuffs on his wrists. The cuffs rubbed his skin raw.

All night long Snakegrass forced Thorn to drink sips of the fermented Queen's Milk. Then she sat before him and laughed as he screamed in frustration as he tried to get to her to mate. By sunup blood flowed freely from his wrists.

The goblins that accompanied Carman to the surface were nervous. They did not like being ordered around by their new Queen and they hated being exposed out on the surface.

'Wait here,' Carman commanded. She dismounted and began to walk away from the goblin guard. Carman saw the signs carved into an oak tree. She read the signs and looked to see where the next marked tree was. She saw it off in the distance. Quickly, without warning to her escort, she took off into the woods.

The guards were unsure of what to do. No goblin ever questioned King Liderc. This female was another matter altogether. Indecision froze them. Soon Carman was too far out of sight to follow.

'Snakegrass!' Carman hissed.

Snakegrass didn't believe her ears at first. 'Queen Carman?' She jumped up with joy and ran to the source of the voice. But when she saw Carman she fell back.

'What's the matter with you?' Carman demanded. 'Is this how you treat your Queen?'

'I, um, how did you escape the Mountain King?' Snakegrass asked.

'I didn't escape. He's my new ally. Right now I'm plotting with him to take control of the Hive back from Aynia. But I need your help.'

Snakegrass shook her head and began backing away from Carman. 'You've mated with the Mountain King.'

Carman shook her head. 'No, no, I carry Thorn's child. The Mountain King is my ally.'

'I can tell. You've mated with the goblin. He's the enemy of all the Fairie folk, and you mated with him,' Snakegrass said in disgust. 'You're no longer Fairie.'

Carman's anger welled up. 'How dare you talk to your Queen like that?'

Snakegrass turned her back on Carman and began to walk away. 'You are no longer a Fairie Queen.' She could see that Carman's wings were no longer clear like a Queen's. While still iridescent, they were now jet black. And Carman had taken on the pallor of a goblin.

Carman lunged at Snakegrass. Hearing the scuffle, Thorn limped out of the glen. He saw the attack on Snakegrass but did not go to her side. He had no love for his current mistress. On the other hand, this might be his chance to kill Carman. Once he killed her he could go home to the Hive.

Thorn sized up the situation. He could not run in to the fight since he was hobbled. He would have to slowly work his way closer to Carman without being seen.

Snakegrass drew her dagger and tried to stab Carman. Carman knocked the blade away. Her stinger drawn, Carman wasted no time. Using the last of her venom she stung Snakegrass to death. Snakegrasses' eyes rolled up and foam fell from the corners of her mouth.

Carman pulled her sword and hacked off Snakegrasses' head. Placing the head on the ground near the small campfire,

Carman laughed at the stunned expression frozen on Snakegrasses' face.

Thorn watched, horrified.

Carman stripped of her blood soaked clothes. Then she picked up Snakegrasses' head by the hair and began a wild dance around the clearing.

Thorn got quietly sick.

Soon the goblin guard caught up with Carman. They dared not return to the underworld without their Queen. Not wanting to touch her, the goblins wrapped Carman in the blanket they found on the ground and bore her home.

Thorn hobbled over to the campsite and grabbed the bloody sword left behind. He used it to cut the ankle strap off. Later, when he had a more precise weapon, he would work on freeing himself from the cock ring. Silently he followed the trail the goblin's horses made through the woods. The goblins were so deeply preoccupied with their mad Queen that they didn't notice Thorn following them back to the Hall.

Sage and his guards found the body of Snakegrass the next day. Sage decided to spare Queen Aynia the details, especially about the flies and smell. He did warn her though that there were signs of goblins in the clearing.

Aynia listened to Sage give his report with little interest. She was sure that she heard Thorn scream in the woods but no one mentioned finding his body. During the mating flight she was convinced that it was best to let Thorn go. Now that she was sure he was dead or mortally wounded she hated herself for not commanding him into her harem.

It was several days since the mating flight and the entire Hive still talked in the hushed voices of hangover victims. Many Fairie tiptoed through their days with expressions of mixed embarrassment and regret. Aynia knew that feeling. Worse, she knew that every eye in the Hive as on her sheets to see if her cycle would begin or if she was with child. When she thought about the private nature of sex and the very public acts she committed with her drones she crawled into bed and pulled the blankets over her head.

Aynia wondered: How many other Fairie were nearby watching her as she allowed Moss to penetrate her from behind? Was she the laughing stock of the Hive? Would she repulse all the workers if they knew what she had done? And how much she had enjoyed it?

Buried under the covers Aynia also thought about Thorn. Their lovemaking had been wonderful, beyond her dreams, but Thorn the drone would never be the same to her as Thorn the Captain of the Guard. Somehow their relationship was altered. Besides, in recent weeks a new male began to figure prominently in her thoughts. It was Sarkany's touch she longed for. He knew where to caress her. He enjoyed serving her.

Thinking of the drones in her harem brought a familiar full felling in Aynia's breasts. She needed to call for a male to suckle. But what male could she face? Did the Princes discuss the mating flight with the rest of her harem? Aynia was too embarrassed to call for one of them.

Using her only alternative, Aynia massaged her breast and began to express her milk into a bowl by hand.

'How fares our Queen today?' Heather asked as she tried to get around Rose. Rose refused to let her sister pass into Aynia's bedchamber. 'Has she at least gotten out of bed?'

'She neither eats nor sleeps. For two days now she has been unable to rise. If she does not walk soon I fear that she will become weak.' Rose sniffled.

'She wallows in pity.'

'No, no, she is ill. Maybe she is pregnant,' Rose said hopefully.

'Pregnancy is not a state of sickness. It's a natural state for a female body. She does not rise because she chooses not to.' Heather said with open contempt.

Camellia came out into the hallway to listen in on her sister's conversation. 'You are full of anger at our Queen today. Are you angry that she didn't just turn to you and say 'take me Heather'? Or are you angry because she enjoyed her drones for once in the way she was meant to?'

Heather got toe to toe with Camellia. 'Watch your mouth. Sister or not, I'll whip you black and blue if you talk to me like that again.'

Camellia would not be intimidated. 'Who will whip whom? You're straying into my area of expertise. She doesn't want you Heather. Get over it.'

Rose stepped between her two sisters. 'The Queen, don't upset the Queen with your petty squabbles.'

Heather sneered. 'So, you take her side now too? Our Queen indulges herself in this mood. The humans are building a settlement five miles away from this Hive. Parliament is becoming more and more critical of our Queen every day. This is a crisis and the Hive needs a leader. I will give them their leader if it means dragging the Queen kicking and screaming from her bed.'

'Heather, no! You can not lay a hand on her! It would mean your life! Our sister Deidre was shown great mercy by the Queen when she broke the law, but we can not and should not expect the same indulgence. Please do not touch our Queen in anger.'

'Then I will devise some other plan to get her out of bed. Make no mistake of my intentions. By this time tomorrow I will see our Queen on her feet.' Heather turned around and swept out of the Royal Chambers, leaving behind a fearful Rose and Camellia.

'What do you think she'll do?'

Camellia shook her head. 'Heather is very stubborn about some things. I have no idea about which course of action she will choose. I think it best that we prepare ourselves for tomorrow. I fear we may have to bury a sister.'

Thorn followed the goblin guards underground. If they knew that he entered the Hall they seemed not to care. In truth there was little that he could do against the goblins. He was one Fairie with one sword and one stinger. The goblins were legion. Still, they seemed unaware of his presence, so he darted into the first hiding place he could find.

The entrance to the Hall closed behind the goblins as they carried Carman back to their King. When all the goblins were out of sight Thorn went over to inspect the entrance. He could see no seam in the boulder. The entrance was magical and he didn't have the key. He would need time to accustom his eyes to the pitch black of the underworld and he would need to learn the key to opening the boulder. There was nothing for Thorn to do but wait.

As hours passed it became apparent that the goblins rarely ventured out to the surface. Thorn began to despair that the entrance would ever open again. However, throughout the hours he began to be able to see. The underworld was not completely without light, although the light that did exist was extremely subdued.

Once the shock of the raw earthy smell passed Thorn was able to make out some scents. There was a strong male smell that bordered on stink. Harder to discern was a female scent. It vaguely resembled a Queen's scent but lacked the aphrodisiac quality of Aynia's smell. Thorn recognized it as Carman's scent. Once he had been crazed to get to that smell. Now it seemed different. Perhaps it was the lack of the fermented Queen's milk to drive him into a mating frenzy. Or perhaps it was because Carman was no longer in heat. Either way her scent lacked the pheromones it once held.

Hours later Thorn realized that there were other female scents. Goblins had no females of their own so these had to be captured females. Thorn got up out of his hiding place. His legs were beginning to cramp and it didn't seem that the goblins would be leaving their lair any time soon, so he decided to go find out what females were trapped in this gloomy world with him.

'You seem to be covered in blood,' King Liderc commented dryly as the goblin guards carried Carman into the King's bedchamber.

The guards, all too aware of the fate of those who were accused of touching the new Queen, were visibly shaking as they deposited the nude, blood soaked Carman on the bed. Slowly, so as not to arouse the notice of their King, the guards backed towards the door. Once beyond the threshold they gently closed the door. Despite their care the hinges squeaked ominously. When the door was closed they bolted away from the hallway.

Carman ignored King Liderc's comment. She scratched as her arm, but the dried blood on her skin would not flake off.

'Meeting didn't go quite as planned my dear?'

Carman merely grunted and went to the wash basin. She dunked the sponge into cold water, lathered soap onto it, and began to scrub her skin until it was raw.

King Liderc walked over and took the sponge from her hand. Carman glared at him for a moment. He rinsed off the sponge and began to cleanse her skin. 'What happened?'

Carman rinsed out her mouth and spat bloody water out. With a great sigh she braced her arms against the dark wood chest. She could not believe that she failed to escape when she had the chance. What lunacy overtook her mind that she allowed the goblins to bring her back to this prison?

'I asked you a question,' the King growled at her.

A shiver went down Carman's back. She turned suddenly and knocked King Liderc to the floor. He was much stronger than she was but the suddenness of her move surprised him. In a second Carman was straddling him and tearing at his clothes. 'Make love to me,' Carman demanded.

King Liderc laughed. 'What ever happened to you up on the surface?'

Carman silenced his laughter with an intense kiss. Her hands found what she was looking for, a way past his leather codpiece. She guided him into her as she kissed him. Then she gently bit down on his lip, gradually increasing pressure. He

428

turned away. This time Carman laughed at him. But she continued to grind her pelvis against him.

'I want to know why you're covered in blood.'

Carman placed her finger against his lips. 'Sh. You're distracting yourself my dark lord.'

King Liderc placed his hands on Carman's hips and rolled her onto her back. Bringing her ankles to his shoulders, he plunged into her with powerful strokes. After he came he remained inside of her. They lay entwined on the floor.

Carman finally looked into his eyes. Her hand went to touch a lock of hair that curled just over his temple. 'My sister, Aynia, turned my former attendant, Snakegrass, against me. As you can well imagine it took some persuasion to extract a full confession from Snakegrass. Thus the blood.' Lying came as naturally to her as breathing.

'I thought that no attendant could be turned. Isn't that one of those things that the Fairie are always so proud of? The incorruptibility of their attendants?'

'She didn't so much turn against me as you.' Carman said slowly.

'What do you mean?'

'Snakegrass confessed that Aynia is amassing a Fairie army to attack your goblin empire. She tried to turn me against you, my love. She tried to get me to fight on the side of the Fairie. After all, two Queens are better than one. But I refused.'

'Why would Aynia decide to attack me?' King Liderc asked.

Carman thought about this for a moment. All that she said was a lie but the foolish male tended to believe what she said. Now was a critical move. She had to think of a plausible reason. 'Don't you know?'

King Liderc shrugged. 'The Fairie and the goblins are not such enemies as you might think my queen. On the continent where I come from the courts are not as formal as they are here. The goblin and Fairie live side by side. After all, we are cousins. Who do you think gifted the onyx Temple to the Hive at

Balnacra? It was a dark Prince. I can't imagine why the Fairie would suddenly take it their heads that the goblins are enemies.'

'You killed Aynia's father. She loved him very much and she has sworn vengeance.' Carman reminded him.

'That was not I. It was my uncle. I am but lately come to take dominion over this land. But I know of that unfortunate accident. My uncle was informed that the late Queen wished to mate with him. What he went to the rendezvous he was in a mating frenzy. Then this foolish drone stepped in his way. He didn't mean to kill the Prince. He just wanted the rival out of his way so that he could mate with the Queen. You know the mating madness. You know how easy it is to do something that you later regret.'

Carman almost nodded in agreement as she ran her hand across her swelling abdomen. 'Aynia does not care to hear about accidents. And as far as she's concerned you are your uncle. The Fairie do not recognize the goblin as individuals. She wants you dead. She's plotting against you right now. Take care my love,' Carman hissed into his ear. She pressed King Liderc's head to the cushion of her bosom. 'You must strike at her first. You must kill Aynia before she kills you.'

Thorn moved deeper into the underworld of the goblins. As tunnels twisted he lost all sense of direction. He despaired of finding his way back to the overworld. Never once did he think of turning back though. His efforts were concentrated on finding the females hidden in the hall. Once they were free he could turn to his real mission, finding and killing Carman.

The scent of females finally led him to the nymphs. Above the smell of earth and damp a honeyed odor called to him. He knew that there were females ripe for mating nearby. At every intersection of tunnel he would pause and breathe in deeply to find the source of the scent.

In the end Thorn was surprised to find the nymphs were caged more by their despair than actual boundaries to escape. The females were in an unlocked room where they lounged

430

listlessly across sparse furnishings. After waiting for a lone goblin to saunter past the room Thorn opened the door to see twenty mournful nymphs much in need of sunlight's touch.

The nymphs at first did not respond to Thorn's entrance. A few whimpered. Then one stood. 'It's Captain Thorn!'

The other females instantly turned their attention to him.

'Thorn!' Their voices echoed with desperate need and hope.

Thorn looked at the gaunt faces and stepped back. The nymphs were all coming towards him now.

'He's a drone! Thorn is a drone!' One of the nymphs cried out.

In a second five females were on him, tearing at this clothes. 'Mate with me Thorn,' they cried out. Their high wails bounced weirdly off the stone walls of their chamber.

'Wait, wait!' Thorn shouted. 'Quiet!'

Nymph hands caressed him in the most private places. Despite his alarm his erection was growing quickly. There was great allure in having the nymphs throw themselves at him. After all, how many males did nymphs pursue?

'We must be quiet ladies, or the goblins will hear us. I have come to rescue you.'

'The goblins,' the females wailed. Some ran across the room in terror at the mention of their captors.

The water nymph crossed the room. She was still the leader among these females despite the look of death on her face. 'Captain Thorn, the goblins hold us here to mate with them. They come each day to check for those of us who are ripe for mating. You are now a drone, you can help us.'

'I can help you by letting you all escape.'

'Possibly, but first, because escape may take time, you must mate with those of us who are fertile. Save us from the embrace of the Mountain King.'

'It is a better plan to flee now.' Thorn argued.

'The Mountain King only leaves the underworld every three or four days Thorn. If we attempt to escape before then they will search for us. By then it will be too late for some of us, too late for me. I know that it is my time. If the Mountain King fills me with his seed I will become goblin and the thought of that nearly makes me mad. Please Thorn, you are drone, if you mate with me, with us, you will save us from the fate of the goblins. When it is time to escape we will go with you.'

The water nymph took Thorn's hand. 'For the love of the Goddesses Thorn, let me bear your child.' She stared at him until he had to look away.

With a small sigh Thorn simply said, 'how often do the goblin guards come by, and can you hide me safely?'

The water nymph gave a small sad smile and led Thorn to a pallet near the back wall. 'We will protect our stud. What happened to your wrists?' She looked at the mean scabs forming above his hands.

'Snakegrass tied me to a tree and force-fed fermented Queen's milk to me. I guess under its influence I didn't realize what I was doing,' he frowned.

'We have herbs. Don't worry Thorn. We will care for your wounds, and we will heal all of your pains.'

Thorn revealed the cock ring. 'Can you do something about this?' he asked.

The nymph laughed. 'Can I do something about your hard penis? Yes, I believe that I can.'

'I meant the cock ring. It pains me. It makes it difficult to mate.'

'It controls you,' the nymph said with a twinkle in her eye.

'If you don't find a way to remove it I will leave you to the mercy of the Mountain King,' he threatened.

Several of the nymphs began to wail again.

'I will remove it,' the water nymph finally agreed, 'but only after you've mated with me.'

Thorn crossed his arms over his chest in a defiant stance. 'Now or never.'

The nymph shrugged. 'I suppose now. As if I have a real choice.' With cool fingers she explored around Thorn's scrotum awhile longer than Thorn felt she needed to, but finally the hated ring was removed and the chain binding his wings came off.

Thorn sighed. He was freed.

'A deal is a deal Captain. Come, chase me.'

'Why do I need to chase you when you're standing right in front of me?' Thorn asked.

'Because it is the way,' the nymph said with a wink. She sprinted across the room.

Thorn followed.

'What shall I do about the Queen?' Heather asked the High Priestess.

'Is she with child?'

'I believe so. She is near her cycle but I've seen no blood on her sheets.'

'Guessing is not good enough. We must know for certain. You forget that your life swings in the balance here. If the Queen is not mated I will have you killed.'

'I did everything I could to get her to mate,' Heather said, shocked at the accusation. 'I got rid of Thorn, I got her to transform more of her males into drones, and she did take the mating flight.'

The High Priestess raised her hand and the sound of a small clear bell echoed in the cold room.

Another Priestess brought in a small child, a girl. Heather met the child's eyes and gasped. It was Rose's youngest child, Heather's niece.

The High Priestess ran an overly long fingernail down the side of the child's bared throat. 'They are so fragile at this age,' the High Priestess said. Small blood droplets welled along the line drawn down the child's neck. The High Priestess looked back at Heather and met her horrified gaze with eyes like cold steel. 'Mark me well Lady Heather, there is no forgiveness for failure when you serve a Queen.'

Heather was in a panic. Her long strides took her across the Hive center in minutes. Curious workers watched her progress. When most of the Seelie Court wished to get somewhere in haste they flew, but Heather's wing was still not right after the attack in Russia. Heather paid the commoners no attention as she swept past. As she entered the palace one of the workers began running for Thane Adders-Tongue's estate.

Rose jumped as Heather slammed open the doors of the Royal Chambers. She didn't like the look on Heather's face.

Camellia rose from her seat slowly but she also looked very concerned.

Heather strode right up to Captain Sage. Her fear was boiling out as anger and she had found a target for her wrath.

Picking Sage up from his chair she slammed him against a wall. 'I was able to walk into this Palace and into the Royal Chambers without once being stopped or questioned by your guard. You are so pathetically incapable of protecting the Queen that we're lucky that she isn't dead already. How many times do you have to be told to place a guard at all times outside the Palace, inside the Palace, at the entrance to the Royal Chambers, and all along the hallways? Everyone entering is to be questioned and searched, everyone! I don't care if they are a trusted advisor, you stop them and you search them, got it? Quite frankly, if I were the Queen I would have my stinger in your heart. You're a fool and an incompetent. Or are you? Maybe you only appear to be a bumbling fool. After all, one would be hard pressed to fail at their job as many times as you have without trying to. Either you're a danger to the Queen by your sheer lack of competence or you're in league with the enemies of the Queen. Either way I accuse you of treason for failing to protect our Queen. Report at once to the Jailer in the dungeon. I will begin preparing charges against you immediately.'

'Put him down Heather,' a calm voice commanded.

Heather threw Captain Sage to the floor, but her spiked heel came down on the back of his hand so that he could not move.

'Stand down Heather,' Aynia ordered. She stood at the door to her bedchamber. The diaphanous but sheer black cloak accentuated how very pale and thin the Queen was, but her voice carried a tone of authority rarely heard before, and her chin jutted out stubbornly in a good imitation of her mother, the late Queen.

'I will not.' Heather growled. 'I am doing what needs to be done, what should have been done a month ago.'

'This is not for you to do Heather.' As Aynia neared the edges of her cloak moved like tendrils of smoke across the floor.

'Isn't it?' Heather asked in mock disbelief. 'If I don't who will?'

'Don't do this sister,' Rose pleaded with tears in her voice.

'For the sake of the Goddess Heather, come to your senses,' Camellia tried to place a warning hand on Heather's arm, but Heather angrily shook it away.

'This is not for you to do,' Aynia repeated.

'And who are you to tell me what to do?' Heather got right up into Aynia's face and shook her finger inches from Aynia's nose. 'I will make the rules, I will lead the Hive, because unlike you I am a leader and I will not allow this Hive to wither and die!'

Aynia's eyes flashed with anger. 'You forget yourself Madame. How dare you talk to Us this way! We are Queen.' Aynia indeed looked every inch a Queen at the moment.

'I do not forget that Lady, but perhaps you do.' Heather sneered at Aynia.

Aynia trembled with anger. 'Lady Heather, you are dismissed from my service. Leave Our Royal Chamber at once. You are committed to the Temple. If you try to leave the sanctuary offered you there I promise that you will die.'

Heather bowed to Aynia in true genuflection. 'Yes Majesty.' Heather could not stop the tear that formed in the corner of her eye. She took one last look at the regal face then backed out of the room bowing.

A long awkward silence followed. Aynia finally took a deep breath and turned to Camellia and Rose. 'I will spare her life as long as she remains locked away in the Temple. But she is dead to Us. We will not speak her name again.'

Rose burst into tears and looked away.

Camellia uttered a harsh expletive.

Aynia turned on her heel and swept back to her chamber door. There she paused, looking down at Captain Sage. In a frighteningly calm voice Aynia said, 'Tell Prince Sarkany and Prince Moss that they now share command of my guard. And send the usual dowry to the family of Captain Sage. Come Sage,' she put her hands out to him and as he rose to take them Aynia pulled Sage into her sweeping cloak, placing his trembling lips to her bared breast.

Aynia sat with the Master Builder of the Hive. 'You do understand that if word escapes of this it will be your life.'

'Yes my Queen.'

'And that of your entire clan.' Aynia nearly hesitated to make this threat, but it had to be done.

The Master Builder gulped. She had no daughters, but she had nieces. 'The new Hive will be kept secret.'

'Good. Then choose your workers and submit a list to me. In three days the first Hive builders will leave for the new sight.'

The Master Builder decided to put the best face possible on her fate. 'It is quite a privilege to design a new Hive from scratch rather than simply spending my talents on repairing this one.'

'Quite,' Aynia agreed and took a slow sip of her tea from a delicate china cup.

'We will need to move food, supplies, everything.'

'I expect you to build food storage first. Above all we must have food to survive the coming winter. When it comes time to leave Balnacra I don't know if we'll be able to take much with us. It is imperative that the workers that go with you bring everything that they own.'

'How will we move them across the water?'

'Leave that to me.'

The High Priestess and Ambassador Cowslip from Norfolk Hive were playing chess in the Ambassador's chamber. The High Priestess was winning.

'Do you really think that the Queen will try to move this Hive?' Ambassador Cowslip deliberately provoked the High Priestess.

The High Priestess's hand hovered over a piece. 'There has been no sight of Captain Thorn. Chances are that he's dead by now. Without his information I don't see how the Queen can ever hope to move the Hive.' She let her hand fall on another piece.

Ambassador Cowslip was quick to react. She attacked the High Priestess's Queen, replacing that piece with her own Queen. 'You left your Queen exposed,' Cowslip explained.

'Well, some sacrifices must be made.' The High Priestess said philosophically as she leisurely moved her bishop across the board. 'Checkmate.'

'You sent for me, my Queen?' Sarkany asked.

'Let me see you in your uniform.' Aynia looked him up and down. She reached out and stroked the front of his hose. 'The tunic is a little short.'

Sarkany tuned around, showing her that his well-shaped buttocks were also visible. 'I do seem to be exposed,' Sarkany agreed.

'Perhaps you need different uniforms. Look into it.'

'I must be allowed to speak with the tailors.'

'I don't like the idea of you mingling with the workers.' Aynia didn't like the idea of her handsome drone being exposed to other females. Sarkany did not interpret her words the same way.

'In my Mother's Hive we did not observe such great distinctions between the classes. The relationship was much more casual.'

'That is not the way here,' Aynia reminded him. As they talked she ran her hand between his thighs. The distraction was making it difficult for Sarkany to focus on the conversation. 'We are more civilized,' she said, then immediately regretted the comment.

Sarkany didn't dare step away from her caresses, but his expression showed his anger. 'Yes, but in Romania my Mother does not have a population on the edge of rebellion.'

Aynia frowned. She could think of an angry retort, but what he said was true. The Hive was spinning out of her control. At some point she would have to deal with the tensions building in the Hive.

'I should have you punished for that, but I know that what you say is true. I have missed so many opportunities. I should have reached out to the nobility. Now I fear that it may be too late to repair the damage.' She lapsed into quiet.

'Um, Majesty,' Sarkany said quietly minutes later.

'Yes,' Aynia looked up at him. She'd been deep in her own thoughts.

'If you continue to…' he looked down meaningfully to the front of his tights. Aynia had been stroking him while she thought. Now he was very hard. 'I'd hate to stain my hose just before my watch. Lady Camellia would get the wrong idea and grab her whip.'

Aynia smiled and stood up to embrace him. 'I don't know, maybe I like the way these uniforms look.' She kissed Sarkany passionately. 'And maybe you could use a little discipline.'

'I think that the tights are too, well, tight.'

Aynia pulled Sarkany to her bed and pushed him down on it. Then, with a mischievous smile, she straddled his face.

Sarkany pulled aside the crotch of her corset and plunged his tongue inside of her.

Aynia pulled down the top of Sarkany's hose and took Sarkany's hard penis into her mouth. She varied long strokes of her tongue with nibbling kisses.

'Majesty, if you do that I will not last long,' Sarkany complained.

Aynia bared her teeth and ran them up the length of his penis, scraping just enough to let him feel the edge. Then she took her hand and began stroking him while her lips played with the head of his penis. The arousal was too much. He came into her mouth.

Aynia licked the last drops of cum off of the tip of his penis then rolled over on the bed and smiled. Her hand went to his cock and began to caress it. To her amazement he began to grow hard again.

'I didn't think that this was possible.'

'Sometimes I can with proper incentive.'

Aynia closed her eyes and breathed in his scent. She was ripe for him, so close to climaxing just from thinking about him inside of her. She got up on her knees. 'Is this proper incentive?'

Sarkany got on his knees behind her and thrust into Aynia. His hand reached around to stroke her. 'You are so hard,' she moaned.

'Like a rock.'

Aynia bucked against him, magnifying each of his thrusts.

Sarkany caressed her buttocks. A thought came to mind. He spanked her hard.

Aynia did not protest. She wriggled a little and grunted. Her entire focus was on the orgasm about to climax inside of her.

Sarkany spanked her again. 'Say that you're mine,' he ordered her.

Aynia shook her head no.

Sarkany slapped her buttocks again so that the sound rang through her chamber. 'Say that you're mine.'

'I'm yours,' Aynia finally said. She should have been angry with him for daring to command her, but she felt comfort in submitting to his strength.

'You belong to me.' Sarkany purred. 'You are my Queen, and you belong to me.' He thrust hard into her as she yelled out in pleasure and they came together.

Cerridwen looked at the drugged child chained to the High Priestess's chair and shivered. The High Priestess called her naive, but Cerridwen felt deeply that the Priestesses at the Temple, above all others, should not be behaving in this unethical manner. 'Your Grace,' Cerridwen said to get the High Priestess's attention.

'Yes?' The High Priestess was not pleased to see Cerridwen. Despite the fact that Cerridwen was her current lover, the High Priestess did not like Cerridwen much.

Ambassador Cowslip looked on with disdain at Cerridwen from her seat near the High Priestess.

'I must protest. The use of this child against the Lady Heather is unconscionable.'

'I've warned you before about questioning my actions. I am the supreme moral authority here.'

'Are you? Are you really?' Cerridwen asked. 'Nothing that I've seen suggests any ethical or moral core.'

'Really?' The High Priestess raised an eyebrow.

'On one hand you manipulate and threaten the right hand of the Queen to make sure that the Queen breeds. On the other hand, you plot with her enemies who would place another Queen on the Throne.' Cerridwen glared at Ambassador Cowslip. 'Why would you do such a thing?'

The High Priestess cracked a small sour smile. Finally Cerridwen was growing up and seeing the world for what it was. 'I am keeping my options open.'

'Your options? What about the Hive? What about the Queen?'

'The Hive and the Queen be dammed. The Temple has always been in a position of subordinate power. We rely on the Nobles for funds, the workers for mindless devotion, and the Queen for her milk. I tire of these limits to my power. I see a chance here to seize control of the Throne. And I will take that chance, from a safe distance, of course.'

'I can't let you do that,' Cerridwen challenged the High Priestess. Both her voice and her body quaked with emotion. 'I will not stand idly by while you subvert the natural balance.'

'Oh, I believe that you will stand idly by. Pin her stinger quickly!' The High Priestess commanded the other priestesses.

Cerridwen tried to fight but was quickly overpowered, gagged, and bound foot and hand. She could not struggle against the powerful females who dragged her to an alcove in the chamber. There a clamp went around her waist so that she was chained to the back wall.

'Place food and water with her,' the High Priestess commanded.

'Why?' An incredulous priestess asked.

'Let the Goddesses decide if she lives or dies. Her death won't be by my hand.'

Cerridwen tried to scream as she saw the priestess begin to build a wall less than a foot from her face. Tears ran down her cheeks.

When the wall was three feet high the High Priestess glanced at Rose's daughter. 'Throw in the female child as well. We don't want to risk someone running home to Mommy.'

Ambassador Cowslip pressed her lips together. Every thought that she ever had about the Scots being barbarians was being played out in front of her. Not that there weren't a few bodies entombed in the walls of her home Hive in Norfolk, but at least those bones weren't fresh.

'Won't someone come looking for the child?' Ambassador Cowslip asked.

'Oh, she'll be missed. That's the point.' The High Priestess sipped a taste of wine while she watched the child's face disappear behind a layer of bricks. 'As my special gift to you I'm going to lay this death at the door of Thane Adders-Tongue.'

'A gift to me?'

The High Priestesses' eyes turned to the color of cold steel. 'You were very sloppy, talking so loosely with Thane Adders-Tongue about your English Princess. She might hate the Queen, but Thane Adders-Tongue hates the English more. If pushed she could take the side of the Queen against us. So I will put this blood on her hands and either the Queen or the Queen's attendants will kill her for us.'

'But how will you stop your own priestesses from talking? If one is willing to turn against you the others might too.'

'I had a vision last night, from the Goddesses of course. It seems that the Temple is now a silent order. Only I shall speak for the Temple from now on. The punishment for speaking is harsh.' The High Priestess pulled the silver cover off of a plate next to her throne. On the plate, three tongues.

CHAPTER 17

Tulip frowned as she surveyed her brothel from behind the bar. Earlier that morning a section of the Hive walls gave way. One of those walls was part of her sister's tavern a couple streets over. The patrons moved their business over to Tulip's place, which was a good thing, but there was an ugly mood running through the crowd, and that was bad.

Tulip's sister sat next to her behind the bar and glumly drew pints for clients. Tulip's brothel was plain and crude compared to the lovely carved wood interior of her own place. And the presence of free drones made her nervous. She wondered idly if the young noble she'd sent over from her place a month ago was still here, or if he even came. A nice looking piece like that wandering the streets could have easily been abducted into a harem by some quick thinking female, never to be seen again.

'I say what's the Queen going to do about it? We're still digging out our dead and no one but us cares,' a very drunken patron spoke out loudly.

'Sh!'

'Don't shush me. I'll speak my mind.'

The crowd rumbled as attention went to the female.

'Some things need to be said. Some things I have to say,' the female went on. Tears began to fill her eyes. 'I saw a child's arm under the rubble. It twitched. It twitched for ten minutes as we dug like madwomen. Then it stopped. I didn't stop digging, but I knew the child was gone,' the female lapsed into sobs. Neighbors patted and rubbed her back in sympathy. She sobbed but began to speak again. 'It wasn't as if it was a surprise. We've known for years that the walls would eventually give out.' She pounded a rough hand against the wooden tabletop. 'The Queen should have done something!'

Tulip had heard enough. She pushed her large bulk through the tables to the small front stage. 'That's it! I've had all I'll take. Anyone wants to speak against the Queen in my place will get a knife to the ribs.'

The crowd grumbled.

'You drunken idiots have short memories. The Queen, on one of her first days on the Throne, spoke about the need to fix the Hive. But the Thane Adders-Tongue raised a fight about it. She ridiculed the Queen for days from the floor of Parliament about it. Don't you remember?'

'Who listens to what they say in Parliament? It has nothing to do with us,' a worker grumbled.

'If you actually got off your butts and went down to listen you'd hear a great deal that has to do with you. You have no one to blame but yourselves if you're ignorant about what Parliament is up to.'

'Even if we went to hear, how could we complain? They ignore you if you shout down from the gallery. And I don't even know who represents my section of the Hive.'

'Whose fault might that be? Did you even bother to vote?'

'Why vote? The noble who wins won't listen to us anyway.'

'Then run for a seat in Parliament and make your voice heard from the floor.'

The tavern went silent.

'Are we allowed to do that?' Someone finally asked.

'Yes,' Tulip said, exasperated.

'No worker has ever won a seat in Parliament before.'

'In your memory has any worker ever run?' Tulip asked the crowd.

A murmur went through the tables.

'Good Goddesses, can't you see that we need to stand up for ourselves? Maybe if we did that and we supported our Queen we could have a safe place to live,' Tulip told them.

'Tulip for Parliament!'

Tulip glared back towards the bar, recognizing her sister's voice. 'Ah now, don't start that,' she grumbled.

The crowd took up the chant.

444

Tulip walked off the stage and pushed her way back to the bar. 'I'll thank you to keep your trap shut in the future sister.'

Tulip's sister smiled for the first time since the collapse of the wall. 'It gives me a giggle to think of you being called the Honorable Tulip.'

Tulip also smiled. 'You know, I kind of like the sound of that.'

Rose handed a note to Aynia with a trembling hand.

'Rose, what is it?' Aynia asked her.

Rose pointed to the letter. She was unable to speak.

'This isn't in Heather's handwriting,' Aynia observed, but the note was on Temple stationary.

'It is signed by the High Priestess,' Camellia noted. She already read the note.

Rose began to cry. 'If this it true, I don't know what I'll do.'

The note was blunt. It accused Thane Adders-Tongue of abducting and killing Rose's daughter. As proof the High Priestess enclosed a lock of black curly hair and a small bracelet. Everyone in the room recognized the gold bangle. The bracelet was a gift from Aynia to the girl for her last birthday.

'Why does she say that the message is from Heather?' Aynia asked. 'If the High Priestess wrote the note and signed the note why does she not say that the message is from her also? This is curious.'

Rose took a deep breath. 'It doesn't matter who wrote the dammed note. My daughter is dead.'

'The High Priestess has been holding the other priestesses incommunicado. Heather would not have been allowed to write to us,' Camellia informed Aynia.

'I demand justice,' Rose said through gritted teeth. Her temper, though slow to light, was beginning to blaze. When Rose lost her temper she did so in grand fashion.

'There is no such thing as justice when a child dies,' Camellia snorted. 'This note from the High Priestess will never stand up in court. It's hearsay. We could never get a conviction.'

Aynia took Rose's hand into her own. 'I know how you feel about skirting the legal system, but if you say the word, Rose, I will give you more than justice. I will give you blood.'

Rose stood silent for a moment, swayed between her deep ethical beliefs, and her anguish over the death of her daughter. Slow to anger, once pushed over the edge Rose's rage was hard to contain. She saw red. Her sweet child was murdered. 'Blood,' she finally croaked out. 'Give me blood.'

'Drones! She places her drones in charge of the Royal Guard!' Adders-Tongue denounced Aynia from the floor of Parliament. 'She disgraces us, she disgraces her drones, and she disgraces the Hive!'

The gallery above Parliament buzzed with angry whispers. One worker could stand it no longer. 'But you felt that it was all right for my drone to work collecting food! He was exposed to everyone as he worked among other females! Only the Queen saved my drone from public eyes. Who are you to speak?'

'What are you going to do about the collapse of the chambers in the worker's quarters,' demanded another angry worker, alluding to the fatal cave in that morning in the poorest section of the Hive. Since Tulip's speech in her bar more and more workers were attending Parliament, and they didn't like what they saw.

'Since when does Parliament listen to the voices from the gallery? There are rules for being heard here, and your voice is not allowed!' Adders-Tongue yelled at the angry mob.

'This is our parliament!' The workers in the gallery yelled.

'Have them taken away,' Adders-Tongue demanded.

Parliament erupted into mayhem as the workers stormed the floor. Adder-Tongue and the other noble members of Parliament flew for the safety of their estate chambers.

Back at her estate Thane Adders-Tongue angrily slapped her gloves into the hand of a waiting maid. 'One can not even conduct Hive business in Parliament anymore. Ever since the Queen's mating flight the mood in the Hive has turned downright ugly.'

The maid held her face in a mask. She lost two family members because of the cave in. The ugly mood in the Hive was due to Parliament's uncaring attitude towards the common workers and in particular Thane Adders-Tongue's careless and widely repeated remarks about the cave in. It was not due to the Queen's suddenly visible drones. No one really cared about the males once the novelty wore off.

The maid followed Adders-Tongue into the parlor.

'Take my cloak. Wake up girl.' Adders-Tongue snapped.

As the maid reached for the cloak, Adders-Tongue deliberately let it slip from her fingers and onto the floor. Hiding an expression of pure hatred the maid reached down to pick it up.

'You're losing it girl. I should have never let you have that half-day off. Days off just make servants soft.'

The maid was thankful that Adders-Tongue could not read minds. The maid took her half day off to attend the funeral of her sister and Aunt. But in a way the maid was grateful for Adders-Tongue's remarks.

'I probably need to remind you that I am going to the theater tonight. Come upstairs and help me dress.' Adders-Tongue walked up the stairs to her bedchamber.

The maid followed.

'I will wear the black dress. Not that one, fool. The evening one.' Adders-Tongue snapped.

The maid helped to slip the dress on.

Adders-Tongue sat down at her vanity to apply makeup as the maid brushed and styled her hair.

'Jewelry Madame?' The maid dared to suggest, hoping that her voice did not betray any excitement.

'Maybe, no.'

The maid brought out an exquisite box and began to open it.

'I said no. Are you going deaf as well?' Adders-Tongue snapped.

The box opened. Revealed to the candle light of the bedchamber, the pure gold necklace sparkled.

Adders-Tongue's greedy eyes glistened. 'That is lovely. But it isn't mine.'

The maid placed on a pair of gloves.

'What are you doing?'

'I didn't want to get my fingerprints on the fine gold and dull the finish,' the maid explained.

'Humph, I guess so. Here, let me try it on.' Adders-Tongue waited for the maid to place the necklace around her neck and then admired it in the mirror. 'It is beautiful. But this is not one of my pieces. Where did it come from?'

The maid did not answer.

'Where did it come from?' Adders-Tongue demanded.

She looked into the mirror. Standing behind her was a different female. The maid bolted from the room.

'You! What are you doing in my house?'

'Where is my daughter's body?'

'I have no idea where your damn whelp is,' Adders-Tongue said.

It was the wrong answer. Rose reached out and turned the clasp so that the necklace tightened around Adders-Tongue's neck.

The maid was warned of two things. One, to never let the gold necklace touch her skin, for it meant certain death. The second, not to look on the Thane Adders-Tongue as the poison set to work. The death would not be pretty.

This last warning was real. As the maid ran from the estate she could hear the terrible tortured screams from Adders-Tongue.

The maid rushed across the Hive center to her clandestine meeting. The events of this amazing day rushed through her mind. It was an odd thing, the maid reflected, to look up from scrubbing a floor and to see the loveliest male she had ever set eyes on, a drone with high cheekbones and thick black moustache, standing at attention in the front hallway of the Thane's estate. Behind him stood another drone with eyes of deep blue and hair the color of honey. Between the males was a motherly female in a thick green cloak who demanded to search the Thane's estate. The woman expressed such sorrow over the loss of the maid's loved ones that the maid never doubted the sorrow was genuine. After that came the gentle request, could she give something to Adders-Tongue? Would she be willing to be a party to this?

The maid never hesitated. It was with great surprise that she realized there would be a reward. Wasn't the death of Adders-Tongue rewarding enough?

As the maid ran to her appointed meeting with the assassins she knew that this could be a trap. She herself could be about to die. It didn't matter. Family was avenged.

The maid slipped into the dungeon as the jailer opened the door for her.

The maid paused. She was supposed to meet with the assassin. But this was a different female. She threw herself at the foot of the Queen. 'It is done,' she said. Her forehead touched the damp floor of the dungeon.

Aynia nodded. 'I thank you.'

'I did it for my family.' The maid looked up at Aynia. The Queen's head nearly touched the roof of the dungeon. Now the maid began to shudder. The dungeon was cold and dark. The maid realized that the Queen only had to make a motion and the maid would be locked down here for life.

'Lady Rose did not inform me if you two decided on your reward.' Aynia said in a soothing voice.

'I need nothing Majesty, I swear it.' The maid gulped. She saw beyond the Queen and gave a small gasp. Her entire clan was here in the dungeon. Was her whole family to pay to keep the Queen's secret?

'I insist,' Aynia's cool voice snaked down the maid's back, causing her to shiver. Aynia chose not to notice how the maid feared her. 'There was danger that the Thane would recognize the necklace Cobra-Lily sent to me. There was also danger that despite the gloves the poison would reach your skin.'

'I need nothing, Majesty,' the maid whispered now and trembled.

'If you could name anything, what would you have? Speak your heart to me.'

The maid suddenly grew bold. If she were meant to die today she would at least speak her mind before the Queen. She sat back on her heels and looked into the Queen's regally serene face. 'I want wings. I want my whole family to have wings,' the maid made a sweeping gesture towards her cowering kin. 'And I want a decent place for us to live, where the walls won't crumble in and kill us as we sleep, where the entire family doesn't have to live in a one room chamber.'

A fleeting smile played across Aynia's face. 'That is more than one thing.'

The maid was greatly relieved that the Queen's tone betrayed no anger. However, the Queen was notorious for her icy demeanor. Who knew what thoughts crossed the Queen's mind as a mere worker confronted her about the miserable living conditions in the Hive?

'Perhaps if you have one you can have another,' Aynia mused more to herself than to the maid. Aynia paced the dungeon floor, bowing her head slightly to avoid the low beams of the roof. Making up her mind, Aynia turned to the assembled workers. 'I will give you all Queens' milk if you in turn swear your dying loyalty to me. Swear that what I say to you will never be spoken to another worker.'

The family took little time in dropping to their knees and loudly swearing their loyalty. Like the maid they were convinced that the Queen meant to kill or jail them.

'If I give you your wings you must all go at once on a dangerous trip with the master builder. I am moving the Hive.'

The family gasped. So did the jailer. 'If the other workers in this Hive only knew what secrets a Queen hides in her dungeon they would be amazed,' the jailer mused to herself. But it was not worth her life to tell the gossip that she knew.

'We must move from Balnacra or the Hive will die,' Aynia explained. 'You, the workers, know this better than any others in the Hive. You know how unsound the structure has become. You know the danger that you and your children live in.' Aynia walked over and touched the cheek of a small girl who then tried to hide in her mother's skirts. 'I tell this to the nobles, I speak of it to Members of Parliament, I have dialogs with the High Priestesses, but none will listen to me. They feel safe within the walls of their own chambers. They do not understand the danger to the common workers as I do.'

The maid and her family nodded. It never occurred to them that their Queen knew of their suffering.

'But the structure to the Hive is not the only danger we face. We are powerless to stop the flow of humans into our valley. It is only a matter of time before Balnacra is destroyed under an anti-Fairie spell. Tell me, if I give you your wings will you go and help to start to build our new home? I give my solemn word that in the new Hive no worker will be forced to live in squalid chambers.'

'But where will we go?'

'To the coast,' Aynia told her.

'That is almost a week from here,' wailed the maid's mother.

'On foot yes,' Aynia explained, 'but on wing you could make it in less than two days.'

The family huddled into a corner of the dungeon to discuss the Queen's proposition. In the end it was the maid who made the final argument. 'If we say no, will we ever be able to leave this dungeon alive?'

A unanimous decision was quickly made.

King Liderc looked suspiciously about the room full of nymphs. Something was not right here. Something did not smell right. His eyes narrowed. 'I thought one or two of you were nearing your fertile period.'

'We do not cycle in the underworld,' a foolishly bold nymph told him.

King Liderc laughed. 'Practice whatever magic you wish to stop nature, but in time you will become fertile, and I will be here to fill you with my seed. It is good to see you in high spirits though,' King Liderc lifted the chin of the defiant nymph with his finger. 'Because I prefer my females with a little fight left in them.' He turned and left the room.

Once the door was closed the nymphs sighed and rose from their places. 'You see Thorn, we can hide you,' the water nymph told Thorn.

Thorn nodded in agreement.

Two nymphs lay down beside Thorn and began to run their hands teasingly under his clothes. 'Chase me Thorn.'

'Yes, chase us.'

Thorn groaned. The nymphs lived for the chase. And four times a day they insisted on being caught.

The water nymph kneeled down beside Thorn. 'The Mountain King did not mate with me. He did not sense my fertility.' She took Thorn's hand and rested it lightly on her flat stomach. 'It must mean that I carry your child. I am safe now Thorn, mighty Thorn, our protector.'

'Yes, Thorn, our protector. Give me your child too,' a nymph pouted fetchingly as she tried to pull Thorn onto his feet.

Thorn groaned. 'I'm too tired to chase nymphs right now.' But he knew his protest was weak. There was something about the sight of a fleeing nymph that brought him to his feet and made his penis hard with desire. Now he knew why the Fairie females warned Fairie males away from nymphs. The nymphs would run a male to death before they were sated.

'Sometimes I wonder if it was a good idea to make you Captain of the Guard. You have been very busy.' Aynia held out her hand to Sarkany.

Sarkany smiled at her as he crossed the room to her. Taking her hand, he turned it over and pressed his lips to her palm. 'You only need call for me and I will be at your side. After all, I live to serve.'

'Does it make you happy?' Aynia asked although the answer was already in his eyes.

Sarkany weighed his words carefully. 'For a male like me it is the only thing that makes life in the harem palatable.'

'Hardly a glowing review. How are security matters?'

'Sage was a dammed idiot.' Sarkany did not mince words. 'You were wide open to attack. Why did you take him into the harem? Now he's making noise about rejoining the guard.'

'His mother is in service to the biggest gossip in the Hive. I had to dismiss him from the guard for my own sake but I couldn't chance him going to live with his mother and giving her information about life in the Palace. Imagine what stories he could tell. And they would spread like wildfire through the Hive. I had no choice Sarkany. I had to silence him one way or another. My harem seemed like the kinder prison.'

'Well, if Sage thinks that just because he was in charge once that Prince Moss and I are going to let him have any authority, he's dead wrong. I can barely tolerate the fool.'

Aynia slowly ran a finger up the front of Sarkany's crotch. 'When you get angry,' she told him, 'your accent gets much heavier.'

'Mmm, yes,' Sarkany answered. He stared down as Aynia's finger leisurely traced the outline of his hardening cock. Then she took her fingernails and lightly rasped them against the head of his penis. The sensation was maddeningly pleasurable.

'So you like serving as my Captain of the Guard?' Aynia asked in normal conversational tones.

Sarkany knew that if he did not play the game and act as if nothing unusual was happening, she would keep him in this torment for hours. Since mating the Queen was becoming sexually aggressive with her drones. So Sarkany stood at attention and focused on a spot far away and tried very hard not to try to lean against her hand or to lose the thread of the conversation. 'At least as Captain of the Guard I feel useful. All of the drones now serving in the guard are much happier.'

Aynia nodded. Lady Camellia reported the drastic drop in the number of fights in the harem since the drones began serving in the Palace guard. Certainly the amount of furniture destroyed in shinty matches led by Moss and Sarkany had dropped dramatically. In fact all incidence of punishable transgression had dropped off. Aynia might have imagined it, but she felt that Lady Camellia was not entirely pleased about this development.

'Why is it that I can not stay away from you?' Aynia asked Sarkany. 'From the moment you first kissed my hand, it is as if...' she frowned and looked down at her palm. It was as if she could still feel his kiss. She touched her fingers to her palm and lightly ran her fingers over the skin. 'Like an echo,' she muttered.

'As if what?' Sarkany asked. If Aynia had looked up at him she might have noticed the wary look in his eyes.

'It's as if you're in my blood and it makes me long for your touch.'

Sarkany laughed. 'That's because I am such a skilled lover.' He kissed her bare shoulder.

'It's not that,' Aynia said, still absorbed with her palm.

'You wound me,' Sarkany said in a hurt voice.

Aynia looked up and smiled. 'I didn't mean it that way.' She took a deep breath. 'Even your scent is different. It enters my brain and makes me crazy for you.'

'Good.' Sarkany removed the last of her clothes.

'Undress for me,' Aynia commanded Sarkany.

He pulled off his tunic and tossed it onto the floor. Then he slowly teased off his hose, finally freeing his hard cock.

Aynia slid her hand down the length of the shaft. Moving onto her knees she took first one his balls and then the other into her mouth, slowly sucking on each one. 'I love the smell of you,' she told him.

Sarkany could only nod.

Aynia ran her tongue roughly up the underside of his penis, and then gently flicked her tongue across the head.

Sarkany tried to plunge his penis deeper into her mouth, but Aynia shook her head.

She held her lips tight against his penis as she worked her way up and down his shaft, going deeper each time. Then Aynia pulled back and worked only around the head of his penis with light brushes from her tongue. While she did this one of her hands gently massaged his balls.

'I want to fuck you,' Sarkany finally groaned.

'And you shall.' Aynia gave one last lingering lick then she lay down on the fur rug in front of the fireplace. Her hand went protectively to her abdomen. 'I am mated. Why is it that I think of nothing now but making love?'

Sarkany solemnly kissed Aynia at her navel and then brought his kisses lower. With much more patience than he felt he gently moved her legs apart. 'It is common for females. Once the pressure of mating goes away you are free to more fully enjoy your needs.'

'And you know this because?'

'I told you, when you are a Prince all that you study is the Queen. I know, for instance, that you go wild when I lick you like this,' Sarkany lapped at her clitoris with rough stokes. 'But you really hate it when I do this,' he said as he slid a dry finger inside of her.

'Stop that,' Aynia grumbled.

'My point exactly.'

'Sometimes I think that I feel her move,' Aynia confessed.

'Who?'

'Our Princess.'

Sarkany stopped licking for a moment. 'Princess? How do you know?'

Aynia smiled. 'Ha! So there are some things that a Queen knows that her drone does not.'

'You know for sure that it is a Princess, or do you guess?'

'I can't explain it, but I know the child is female.'

455

'Then she is not mine.' Sarkany said in a distant, cold voice.

'What do you mean?'

'I told you once that I couldn't sire females. It is my fate. If you carry a Princess then you carry another drone's child.'

'How do you know that you can only sire male children?' Both Sarkany and Aynia now eyed each other suspiciously.

'Who did you mate with beside me?' Sarkany's voice rumbled with barely controlled anger.

Aynia pulled herself up into a sitting position. 'You may remember your best friend, Prince Moss?'

'He only took you through the anus. I don't see how he could have possibly sired your Princess.' Sarkany, not thinking clearly about whom he was with, grabbed Aynia's arm. 'Who was he?' Sarkany growled.

'How could you possibly know that you sire only males?' Aynia was not about to allow Sarkany to avoid her question. Somewhere in her mind an alarm was sounding, but she couldn't remember why.

'It is my fate,' Sarkany said, releasing her arm. 'It was my father's fate too. My mother would only mate with him, and she bore male child after male child until she finally put him to death rather than mate with him again. All of my brothers and I share the curse. It is in our blood. That is why I need Moss. He was to mate with you to bring the female child, but this first time he gave you to me. One Prince, after all, is not a tragedy. But Moss didn't mate with you at the Equinox. So tell me, who is the lucky drone?'

Aynia looked back at her hand. 'Thorn.'

'Thorn? The missing and presumed dead Captain Thorn?'

Aynia realized that it was time to confess. 'He was on a mission for me. When he was returning Carman caught him and turned him into a drone. He was on the mating flight with her when our paths crossed. He mated with me instead.'

'So you finally got to fuck your great love, Captain Thorn. Why didn't you just bring him back here and put him into the harem?' Sarkany asked bitterly.

'Because we agreed that he needed to be free to pursue Carman for me.' Aynia felt a blast of anger flare up in her blood. She realized that it was Sarkany's emotions that flowed under her skin.

'Oh, so he gets to be free from the dammed harem, but I don't? I'm such a fool. I thought that you were glad that I caught you on the mating flight. You looked so relieved when I found you. It made me think that you cared for me. Now I know that you were just glad that we mated so that you could claim that your bastard Princess was legitimate. Was I the lucky one because Thorn and I share similar coloring so no one would question that I was the father of the child?' Sarkany stood up, his eyes blazing with fury.

'Sarkany, no it wasn't like that,' Aynia protested, even though Sarkany had cut straight to the heart of the matter. She had indeed chosen to mate with Sarkany because a child of Thorn's could be passed off as his. 'Let me try to explain.'

'Explain nothing my Queen. After all, you are free to do with your body as you please.' Sarkany stomped out of the room, dramatically slamming the doors of the bedchamber closed.

The nobles gathered at Thane Monarda's chambers. This morning the talk was not idle gossip.

Verbena watched the noble ladies through a curtain and thought 'they are terrified.' She wanted to stay to listen, but Monarda sent her to the kitchens for a tray.

Thane Monarda putted her daughter's hand and gave a brave little smile. 'Given the atmosphere in the Hive I'm not sure that a big wedding is a good idea right now. After all, when a new family is formed it means a new chamber. At least it does for us. The poor just stay in the chamber they share with their parents and siblings.'

'Can you imagine?' A noble lady snickered.

'How can they stand to live like that?' Another lady asked as if the workers had a choice in the matter.

Ambassador Cowslip from Norfolk cleared her throat. 'I must agree with our distinguished hostess. In the interest of peace it is best to downplay things right now. The Queen obviously has no control over the workers anymore.'

'We can't let the poor scare us,' another female complained. 'Are we supposed to stop living just because a few of them died?'

'I don't mean to stop the wedding entirely, I just think that we should make it all less public. Better safe than sorry,' Thane Monarda said with false cheerfulness. Her daughter made a face and pulled her hand away from her mother's.

A wedding was very important to a female Fairie. It was a sign that she had arrived. If other females trusted her with their sons it meant that she was ready to take her place as a full adult in society. More importantly, it meant that she could have a male pleasure her every night. And the next Equinox that came she would be allowed to exit the Hive with all of the other married females and take part in the mating rituals.

'Nonsense. The poor are poor because they lack the moral strength to escape their situation. If they really wanted to better themselves they could. Adders-Tongue was right.'

Everyone in the room shivered. The mention of the late Thane Adders-Tongue was sobering.

'Did you hear that they burned her body at night to stop riots?'

'Does anyone know what killed her?'

'And has anyone noticed how hard it is to find any help now days? The stores have no clerks, and I have been looking for a cook for a week.'

Thane Monarda frowned. 'Did anyone hear any rumors about what killed Thane Adders-Tongue?'

'She had a mysterious rash around her neck.'

'How do you know?'

'My under parlor maid's sister is a mortician. I wanted to get more information but the silly girl simply vanished.'

Ambassador Cowslip smiled over her teacup. Months of silent waiting were finally producing a useful opening. 'Things like this simply do not happen in English Hives,' she sniffed.

'Oh my Goddesses,' Thane Monarda said as an idea popped into her head. 'Servants vanishing without a trace, a body so gruesome it gets burned without a decent burial. Are you blind? Can you not see it? It all adds up to just one conclusion. It's the plague!'

'Bring Prince Sarkany to me,' Aynia commanded Camellia.

'The Prince is ill Your Highness.'

Aynia stopped pacing and stared at Camellia until Camellia flinched. 'I did not ask if he was ill. Bring him to me.'

'Yes Your Majesty.'

Camellia went to the harem. She had no idea what was going on between the Queen and her drone but if the Queen wanted this reluctant Prince she would have him.

'Prince Sarkany, come with me.' Camellia ordered.

'No.' Sarkany said. He leisurely met Camellia's gaze with insolence then deliberately, slowly, looked away.

'You play a dangerous game drone.' Camellia snapped a bullwhip so that it sliced the pillow cover near his ear.

'Go ahead, draw blood. She can not have me if I am too damaged to be presented. So do your worst.' Sarkany pulled off his shirt and exposed his scarred back.

Camellia was not having any of it. She was in charge of the harem. Grabbing Sarkany by his hair she started to pull him off of his bed. When he fought back she slipped a hand down to his balls and grabbed his pubic hairs. 'The Queen won't mind if I deliver you hairless,' she threatened.

Sarkany wanted to protest but he was in no position to complain. To his dismay Camellia dragged him to Aynia's bedchamber by his short hairs the entire way. With Camellia you either obeyed immediately or you paid. There was no such thing as half measures.

'Majesty, the drone you requested.' Camellia expertly slapped cuffs on Sarkany's wrists. 'If I were you,' she whispered into Sarkany's ear, 'I'd worry less about who sired her current child and worry more about who sleeps with her every night.' Camellia then left the room. She wanted no part of a lover's spat.

Aynia smiled a little. 'I wonder what I should do with you. Should I take a whip and punish you for avoiding me?' She asked. As she walked behind Sarkany she slapped one buttock with her hand. 'When your Queen commands your presence you come.'

'Do what you want to me,' Sarkany said. 'Do you think that you are the first female to demand that I come running to her side? Do you think that you are the first female I've disobeyed?'

'You've made it quite clear that you have a history,' Aynia admitted.

'Apparently I am not the only one.'

'I am Queen, Sarkany. I have many drones, and I can mate with any one of them I so desire.'

'Then go mate with another one of your many drones and leave me alone.'

'I can't do that.' Aynia released the cuffs on Sarkany's wrists. 'I can't explain it, but you probably have the answer. Why is it that I think of nothing but you? Why is it that I can barely stand to have another male suckle from my breasts? Why is it that my blood begs to have you near? Why is it that the mere sight of you starts my juices to flow? I think that you have answers.'

Sarkany rubbed his wrists and waited for Aynia to speak again.

Aynia felt in her blood that her bond with Sarkany was slipping away. He would never forgive her deception. 'Please forgive me,' she whispered in his ear as she stood behind him, her breasts so lightly pressed to his bare back. 'Please.'

The second please was almost a whisper. The warmth of her breath and the feel of her body so close and so desperately wanting him made Sarkany close his eyes and bite down on his lip. He would not let himself forgive the Queen. No matter what the rules of society were, this female was his, and he would not share her.

Aynia sighed. This was not the meeting she envisioned. Everything was wrong. 'You may go,' she said in defeat.

'As you wish my Queen,' Sarkany said politely, but the words had an edge to them. He turned to leave the room.

Sure that she was alone, Aynia sunk down to her knees and covered her face with her hands. She could hold it back no more. A sob shook her. 'Everyone I love leaves me,' she wailed as her hands trembled.

Sarkany, hidden in the shadow of the door, faltered for a moment. The Queen looked so vulnerable. In the dim light of the candles darkness seemed to creep to her side and threatened to overtake her. Torn between her need and his pride, he finally turned away.

Rose passed Sarkany in the hallway of the Royal Chamber as he returned to the harem. She searched his face, recognizing anger. 'Prince Sarkany,' she greeted him, nodding her head.

'The Queen needs you,' Sarkany said stiffly.

'Does she need me, or does she need you?' Rose asked.

Sarkany opened the door of the harem. 'My watch on the Guard starts in a minute.'

'There is more to protect of the Queen than her Palace.' Rose told him.

Sarkany answered Rose by slamming the door of the harem closed in her face.

Rose took a deep breath. There was a time to enforce protocol and there was a time to turn a blind eye. Besides, if the Queen were half as distressed as her drone she would need someone to talk to right now.

Rose slipped into the room and steered Aynia to the bath. As they waded into the water Rose began to scrub Aynia's back. "Your Highness, you must begin to think of finding replacement attendants. We could have survived without Deidre or,' Rose paused and swallowed hard, 'Heather. But with both gone, well, matters are beginning to get very complicated.'

'I do not want to think about that now,' Aynia warned Rose.

"Majesty, you need the council of trained attendants. Since the death of my daughter I am not serving you to my best potential. And Camellia has her hands full with your harem.'

'I will keep my own council,' Aynia said in a cool tone that warned Rose away from the subject.

Rose took another deep breath and decided to change to a different, but equally dangerous, subject. 'I heard a story once about a Queen who was so wild with fermented nectar at an equinox that she flew straight to her drones and tried to mate with them right there in the Fairie ring.'

'I'm in no mood for stories Rose.' Aynia growled.

'Not one single drone could get hard enough to mate her. Males pursue, females are chased.'

'I'm not a damn nymph' Aynia argued.

'No. But there is a reason why you take off in the sky first and the drones chase you. It is in our blood. The chase is the foreplay.'

'I tire of this Rose, what is your point?'

'You said it yourself. You can command him to come to you, but you can't make him want to be with you. Give him time.'

'He acts as if I betrayed him.'

'If it was any other male but Thorn he would not have cared. Thorn is his only real rival and Sarkany knows it. He's afraid that you'll bring Thorn into the harem.'

'That won't happen. There is no reason for him to be jealous of Thorn.'

'Thorn knows it, you know it, but Sarkany does not.' Rose counseled in her motherly way. 'Let him be for awhile. After all, males desire the touch of a female more often that a female needs a male.'

'Then what happens?'

'The chase begins again.'

Thane Monarda shrank back a little from Verbena as Verbena came in to brush her hair.

'My lady?' Verbena asked. There was fear in Monarda's eyes.

'Where did you go on your day off?' Thane Monarda demanded to know.

Verbena frowned. 'My day off is my day Lady. I do not discuss it with you.'

'Tell me,' Monarda's voice rose hysterically.

'A lady does not talk about such things with one of her betters.'

Monarda's stinger whipped through the air. She was too far from Verbena to strike, but the threat hung in the air between them.

Verbena moved away very slowly. 'I was at Tulip's.'

'What is that?'

'It is a public house that provides private entertainment.'

'A brothel.'

'If you prefer,' Verbena acknowledged the truth.

'Was it at the section of the Hive near the cave in?'

'Tulip's sister's pub lost two walls. It is very near by.'

'Then you might be infected. Get away from me.'

'Infected?' Verbena asked, confused.

'I know. They might deny it, but I know, I figured it out! Plague! Plague stalks the Hive.'

Verbena controlled her urge to laugh. 'What signs have you seen?'

'Everyone whispers about Thane Adders-Tongue. She died so mysteriously. And they say that her body was,' Thane Monarda paused dramatically, 'horribly disfigured. A rash all over her throat, deep scratch marks made by her own hands as if she was trying to rip her very flesh away, and the expression on her face was supposed to be gruesome.'

'I heard the same tales, but I heard that Cobra-Lily, her niece, sent a poisoned necklace to Thane Adders-Tongue. It seems that Cobra-Lily grew tired of waiting for her inheritance. And no one has seen Cobra-Lily since Adders-Tongue's death. She can not be found.' Verbena didn't bother to mention that this was because Cobra-Lily's ashes were scattered all across the valley of Balnacra.

'What poison could do that?' Monarda asked. She lowered her stinger.

'Come now Lady; let us not pretend not to know how to kill. Poisons were much more fashionable when you were young than they are now, but we all know our wood-lore. There are some lethal brews that can enter the blood through a scratch. Desperate to remove the venom, the victim could inflict terrible damage on herself.'

Monarda nodded her head slowly. 'Perhaps, but that does not explain all the missing workers.'

Verbena's eyes grew wide. 'What missing workers?'

'Haven't you noticed?' Monarda's voice dropped into a whisper again as if she was in a public place and not her own boudoir. 'The Hive is not as crowded as it was before. All the nobility are here but our servants have gone missing. I think that they are all dying from the plague and the Queen is keeping it quiet by destroying the bodies. At first my friends laughed at me, but they are beginning to listen.'

'You told all of your friends this tale?' Verbena asked quietly.

'Oh yes.'

'Did you ask the Queen for an explanation?'

'The Queen?' Monarda sniffed. 'I don't trust her anymore. After all, as Ambassador Cowslip said, a Queen must be available to her nobles. We are the Royal Court after all. She ignores us. She has no friends in the nobility and she makes no effort to seek our advice.'

'Oh,' was all that Verbena could say. This lady was once the most ardent royalist in the Hive.

Verbena slipped into the Palace with the rest of the throngs attending court that day. Once past the first set of guards though she ducked around a hallway and into an alcove. Moments later five guards confronted her.

'You should not be here worker,' one of the guards told her.

'I'm not a worker,' Verbena told him tartly. 'I'm Lady Verbena.'

'You have no wings.'

'I served the Queen when she was Princess. I was awarded the title.'

The guard frowned. 'Be that as it may, you should not be here. We will escort you to the Captain of the Guard for further questioning.'

Verbena did not tell the Guard that she was seeking the Captain. She meekly followed the males to Thorn's old office.

Sarkany looked up from his desk and raised an eyebrow.

Verbena took a deep breath to steady her nerves. This male was a drone. His very scent filled the air with hints of his power. 'Captain,' she began, but he cut her off.

'There has been a change in the Guard at the Palace,' Sarkany informed her. 'It is no longer a simple thing to sneak in to the Royal Chamber.'

'He is so angry,' Verbena thought. 'I,' she started to speak again, but once again was stopped.

'If you wanted to see the Queen you should have gone into the Royal Court with everyone else.' Sarkany leaned back in his chair. 'So tell me, why did you sneak into this hallway?'

Given the chance at last to speak, Verbena hesitated. 'I came to see the Captain of the Guard.'

'You found me.'

Now Verbena felt embarrassed. When she spoke to Thane Monarda she felt deeply worried. Quickly reviewing the conversation in her mind it all seemed so silly.

'You wanted to tell me something?'

'Suddenly it doesn't seem important. I, just, well.' Where could she start?

His voice was unexpectedly soft. 'You are Captain Thorn's sister.'

It wasn't a question, but she nodded her head.

'Something you have seen or heard worried you enough to try to come warn the Queen. You served her once.'

Verbena sat up straight. 'I serve her still.'

'Leave us,' Sarkany ordered the guard. When they were gone he turned back to Verbena. 'Tell me.'

Verbena looked into the Captain's eyes and began to tell her story. She talked of Thane Monarda. She told about the rumors about the plague. She mentioned the fact that many workers were mysteriously missing from the Hive and how the Nobles were noticing it. She also talked about Ambassador Cowslip from Norfolk Hive and her deep suspicions of the motives of the English Fairie. When she finished she looked again into Sarkany's strong masculine face hoping to see some sort of answer. 'I've been sending warning notes to the Queen but she does not answer them. The Hive is uneasy Captain. The workers are still very angry about the cave in and the nobles are turning against the Queen. Something bad is going to happen.'

'Well,' Sarkany said, 'thank you for coming here and telling me this.' He stood up. The interview was over.

Verbena gasped. He was simply dismissing her and her fears. 'Captain,' she said, 'please, you must listen to my warning.'

Sarkany's eyes narrowed. 'Why? Because you're Thorn's sister?'

'No, you should believe me because we both serve the Queen. I'm telling you about a rumor that could tear this Hive apart.'

Sarkany firmly led Verbena to the door. 'Thank you for coming. Don't try this stunt again Lady Verbena. If I catch you in the private corridors of the Palace I will have you thrown into the dungeon.' With a gentle push he placed her outside the door and shut it in her face.

When Lady Verbena was gone Sarkany went to the desk and pulled out a number of notes, all addressed to Aynia. It took him some time but he was finally able to crack the code that hid the real messages. The reading was enlightening if one wanted to realize how very close the Hive was to the brink of revolution.

Sarkany frowned. It would never do for the Queen to know that he was reading the messages meant for her eyes only. After all, he smiled grimly to himself; he didn't want her getting upset in her delicate condition. Besides, he certainly did not want her to know that he stopped passing the messages along weeks ago. Sarkany fed the notes to the fire until the paper was nothing but ash. Then he stirred the ashes so that no one would ever guess he burned anything other than logs in the fireplace.

Carman bit down on King Liderc's earlobe none too gently.

'I'm awake,' he told her in a grumpy voice. 'What is it that you want?'

'What will you do about the Hive?'

'I grow tired of this conversation.'

'I grow tired of warning you about the threat that she poses.'

King Liderc snorted. 'She does not threaten me.'

Carman slammed a pillow down in frustration. 'If you were a real male you would not sit here and take this from her.'

King Liderc sat up and turned to stare at Carman with an expression that made braver goblins soil their pants. 'What did you say?' His voice rumbled with anger.

'I said that if you were a real male you would go and kill that bitch.'

King Liderc grabbed Carman's wrist and bent it back until she whimpered. Then he began to fill the room with his seductive scent. Despite her pain Carman could not help the desire she felt.

'Do you want me?' he asked her.

Carman gritted her teeth rather than answer.

He let go of her wrist and got out of the bed. He crossed the room with his lightening speed. On the table was a small whip. He picked it up and smacked it against his palm.

Carman closed her eyes. There was no escaping it though. His scent was drawn in with every breath until she could no longer deny the ache she felt to have him inside of her.

'Crawl to me.' He commanded.

Carman hated herself, but she crawled off of the bed and crossed the floor. Still on her hands and knees, she stopped at his feet.

'Do you want me?'

'Yes My Lord,' Carman admitted.

He walked around behind her. 'Touch yourself.'

Carman protested, but he lightly touched the edge of the whip to her clitoris. 'You will touch yourself.'

Carman slid her one hand between her legs. She was already wet with desire. Her own touch gave her pleasure but she wanted him.

'Arch your back more. And spread your knees.' King Liderc sat casually on the edge of a table, enjoying the show at Carman's fingers desperately rubbed against her clitoris.

Carman's breath came in ragged gasps. The pleasure was building.

'Stop.'

Carman groaned. 'I was so close.' A light lash against her backside stopped her from protesting out loud.

'I know that.'

They sat in silence for a moment, and then he told her 'begin again.'

Carman's hand gratefully slid between her legs again. Using at first two, then three fingers, she finger fucked herself. It was far short of what she needed inside of her but it did help relieve some of the desire.

'Stop.'

Time and again King Liderc took her to the brink but would not allow her to climax. And not enough time was allowed to pass for her passion to cool. He kept her always walking the fine line between the two.

'Do you want me?' He asked her again.

'Yes.' Carman whispered. She was near to exhaustion. Tears of frustration dropped down her cheeks and her own juices flowed down her inner thigh.

'Yes what?'

'Yes My Lord.' Carman trembled. 'Please,' she whispered.

'Please what?'

'Please end my agony My Lord. Allow me to come.'

King Liderc got on his knees behind her. 'Bring yourself to climax.'

Carman sobbed as she put her hand to her clitoris again. Was he playing with her again?

Just as she felt the wave beginning to build he entered her, slamming into her as he held onto her hips. She pounded back against her lord until, relieved and satisfied; her body broke into an orgasm of ferocious strength. Carman closed her eyes for a moment as her entire body shook. When she opened her eyes again the expression on her face was so cold and angry that it would have terrified King Liderc to see it.

Ambassador Cowslip made a small face as Prince Moss and the rest of the Royal Guard passed by in the hallway outside the room where a state dinner was being held. 'None of my business, of course, but in England we respect the old ways. None of our Queens would allow this, much less condone it.'

Her audience followed her gaze. The uniforms of the Royal Guards were not designed to be worn by drones. Very masculine shapes strained against tights in places not hidden well enough by tunics. Appreciative female eyes caressed male buttocks as they passed by.

'I don't know,' a Lady admitted, 'I don't mind the view.'

'Of course not, but he isn't one of your brothers is he?'

The Lady shook her head. 'She wouldn't put Noble members of her harem out on display like that, would she?'

The Ambassador nodded towards Moss. 'He's a Prince.'

Sarkany knocked on Camellia's chamber door.

'Enter.' Camellia was genuinely surprised to see Sarkany when she looked up. 'Prince Sarkany, what brings you here?' Many males in the harem initially feared the Mistress Camellia. After time, once they grew accustomed to her strict rules, the drones found her to be a good source of guidance. Nearly every male found his way into Camellia's office at some point. Sarkany was not one of them.

Sarkany paused at the door as if to reconsider, then he closed the door and came into the office. 'We must speak.'

'Have a seat Prince. Although I tell you right now that I will not get involved in this little spat between you and the Queen. Some things males and females must work out on their own.'

Sarkany shook his head. 'This has nothing to do with that. This is much more important.'

'What is more important than your relationship with the Queen?'

'I must leave the harem. I am asking your permission to go.'

Camellia laughed. 'If you weren't so serious I'd toss you over my knee right now for the impertinence. Why do you think that you need to leave the harem?'

Sarkany explained to Camellia his reasons in detail.

Camellia listened with a grave expression on her face. 'Compelling reasons, I agree.'

'I must go.'

'I understand why you think that you must.'

'Then you will let me go?' Sarkany asked.

'You could have slipped out without telling me, and you could have ordered your Guard to cover for you. With so many drones in and out of the harem for duty in the Guard I don't know where half of them are at the time. It makes running a harem properly hell,' Camellia grumbled.

'I didn't want to put you in an awkward position. At some point the Queen might demand my presence. What would you do if you couldn't find me then? No, it is better that I am honest with you.'

Camellia nodded. 'I'm surprised that you would consider my position. We have been at odds many times.'

'But we are not enemies.'

'No.'

Camellia leaned back in her chair and thought for a moment. Of course she would let him go. That was already decided. But she needed to regain her power over him. 'I will let you go,' she told Sarkany, 'if you revel to me the magic that you have over the Queen.'

'I have no magic over the Queen.'

'Yes you do.' Camellia got up from behind her desk and walked around to Sarkany's chair. She stood behind him but he did not try to look around to see her. She leaned down to whisper into his ear. 'I could torture it out of you. I could take the most delicate parts of your flesh and hurt them so that your screams wake the dead.'

Camellia stood up and went on in a normal voice. 'I could go on with threats, but you above all know what the Mistress of the Harem is capable of. Your back shows proof enough of that.'

Sarkany clenched his jaw. The scars still ached on cold days. He doubted that he could survive another night like that one. Then again, he'd been only a boy before. Now he was a physically powerful drone. The idea gave him pause. Throughout any male Fairie's life the idea of the superiority of the female was strongly enforced. Most males simply assumed that they did not have the physical power to dominate a female. As most drones were kept physically inactive in a harem from the onset of their full maturity it was probably true that most males were physically inferior to the females. But Sarkany kept himself in top physical condition. He could probably overpower Camellia.

Camellia sat back down at her chair. 'Come on, just tell me,' she said in a comradely tone.

Sarkany had to smile. 'I can't tell you. I could show you, but it would cause a small problem.'

'Aha! You admit that you have some hold over the Queen!'

'Yes. I admit it.'

'So, what is the deep dark secret?'

'Ask your sister Heather. She knows, or at least she's witnessed it.'

Camellia frowned. 'The High Priestess is holding all of the priestesses at the Temple incommunicado. She says that the Goddesses told her that every priestess except her must take a vow of silence. If they talk she's threatened to cut out their tongues. If they write she'll cut off their hands. I don't like this development.'

'I wondered why the Queen stopped getting messages from her old attendants. You see why it is imperative that I go.'

'Show me your magic.'

'You would stop me from my mission just to know this one thing? You fool!'

Camellia's eyes narrowed. 'I will make you pay for that Prince.'

'Lady Heather could barely stand to look at herself in a mirror after I was done showing her. Do you want to risk the same humiliation?'

'Bring it on drone. I can take any magical power you've got.'

Camellia and Sarkany glared across the desk.

'You brought this on yourself,' Sarkany warned her.

'No,' Sarkany smiled cruelly at Camellia.

She whimpered. 'Sarkany…'

'No.' He rolled out of her bed and pulled his soft gray tunic over his head.

'Just once more.'

Sarkany leaned over Camellia and kissed her gently on her forehead. 'Your mind should start to clear now.'

Camellia's eyes began to focus. She looked around and went bright red. She was naked in her bed. Sarkany was casually dressing across the room. 'No, no, no, this can not have happened!'

Sarkany didn't say a word but he looked at her with a frank expression that made her wince.

'What in the?' Camellia did not finish the thought. She looked down at her sheets and rubbed two fingers against the silk. Her finger came up bloodied.

Finally Sarkany looked a little disconcerted. 'It never occurred to me that you were still virgin.'

Camellia flew across the room at Sarkany. She pounded him with her fists. 'Damn you. How could you?'

'You insisted. In fact, you insisted several times. I warned you not to make me show you my powers. It was quite a surprise to me, well, your reputation, one would not have guessed you were still a virgin.'

'There is much one can do without intercourse. I suppose, though, that I cannot blame you. I did, literally, ask for it.' Camellia was not happy, but she felt that she was to blame for the situation. 'So this is how you affect the Queen?'

He shook his head. 'This is what I try to do to the Queen. She seems somewhat immune to it though. Not like you or your sister. Both you and Lady Heather are very easy.'

'You're a real bastard. You know that, don't you?' Camellia asked.

'You have no idea.'

'But I am beginning to get the picture.' She moved back to her desk and sat down with exaggerated care. 'Oh Goddesses, did you have to spank me too?'

'Let's just call that payback. I don't like being publicly flogged.'

'How about privately?' Camellia asked in a husky voice, and then she laughed.

'Not even in private.' Sarkany tossed a dildo on the desk in front of Camellia and then sat down across from her. 'You had a few cute pet names for that. But since most were variations on my name I'll spare you the list.'

'So you didn't do the deed yourself?' Camellia asked in surprise. She was realizing just how very sore she was front and back. For the next few days sitting and walking would be a painful experience.

'I know what happened to the last drone who betrayed the Queen.'

Camellia didn't try to hide her smile. 'I've made my decision, a painful one to be sure. I'll let you go from the Hive. I'll even find a way to smuggle you out and get you some supplies. But I ask one thing in return.'

'What?'

'Don't ever come visit me in my office again.'

The English army gathered near the water of the loch and made camp. They were cold and miserable. Two days ago they met an army of Scots from a lowland clan at a small bridge. The fighting was intense. Then, in a sudden downpour, the Scots disappeared as if by magic. The next day the English took up the trail, smelling victory. Ravens were beginning to follow the army by the hundreds, knowing that were the English Knights camped there would be carrion.

Camellia sat with her feet up on the table. Rose walked by and swatted at Camellia's feet with a towel, but Camellia ignored her.

Aynia was pacing by her fireplace. Her resemblance to a caged predator was enhanced by her snarling commentary aimed at Camellia.

'Seventy percent of the workers are ready to move on to the new Hive. Unfortunately with all this whispering about plague I don't dare let them make the trip.'

'They can't be seen in the Hive anyway Majesty. If the nobility see the workers with wings it's going to open you up to all kinds of questions that you don't want to answer,' Camellia reminded Aynia.

'Eventually you will have to tell the nobility about the new hive,' Rose added.

Aynia sat down but she squirmed uncomfortably in her chair.

'If you need to have a male suckle Majesty, I can send Camellia to the harem,' Rose offered.

Camellia chuckled. 'I don't think that's the source of the Queen's discomfort.'

Aynia glared at Camellia then jumped up and began pacing again. The tension in the air was making Rose uncomfortable, but Camellia had an amused smile on her lips.

'Then what is it Majesty?' Rose asked. 'Can I help you with something?'

'It has been four days,' Aynia complained. 'You promised me that he would come back to me Rose, but he hasn't.'

'Oh! Rose's eyes went wide. 'Your Majesty does have a number of other drones.'

'I don't want another drone.' Aynia snarled. Reaching a decision, Aynia stopped pacing and went to her bedchamber door. 'Don't disturb me,' she said as she slammed the doors closed.

'Camellia, what is the Queen going to do?'

'I think that she's going to take matters into her own hands, so to speak,' Camellia told Rose with a broad wink.

Rose wrung her hands. 'This is not good. We can't have her distracted like this. Can't you talk to the Prince about this and make him see reason?'

'No, I can't talk to him,' Camellia said firmly.

'Why not?'

'Because Prince Sarkany is not here.'

Rose gasped. 'Where is he Camellia?'

'He is gone from the harem. For his sake, and hers, you must promise to keep this quiet.'

'What are you going to do about this?' Rose was worried. Drones did not go missing from harems. Of course, by serving in the Royal Guard the Queen's drones were much freer than most drones. Aynia's drones were no longer confined to the insulated environs of the harem.

'I'm not going to do anything. And either are you.'

'Not even search for him?'

Camellia gave her older sister a weary look. 'I know where he is, but he is not in the harem. Please, don't ask any more questions.'

Thorn wanted to sleep. He needed desperately to sleep. If only the damn nymphs would stop running from him. As soon as they started the chase his body demanded he join in. By his own count he had impregnated five of the nymphs. Blessedly those nymphs were no longer interested in being chased. That still left seventeen nubile and scantily clad females to go. The thought of them made him exhausted.

'Thorn!'

'Come chase us Thorn,' the nymphs urged him.

Thorn buried his head deeper into the pillow, trying not to hear their taunting voices. 'Go away,' he yelled. He understood how a troop of nymphs could kill a human male in one night. Humans called them the willies. The humans claimed that the female spirits danced them to death. Thorn knew better. The nymphs mated males to death. Not for the first time Thorn wished that he was never made a drone.

A nymph took Thorn's rigid penis into her mouth and took the entire shaft down her throat. Another nymph brushed her breasts against his bare back. If only he could grab the nymph in front of him and pin her down he wouldn't have to chase them for several hours. Thorn lunged out to grab the female, but she laughed at him and danced away.

'Come on Thorn! Chase after me,' the nymph urged.

'Yes, chase me,' the chorus went.

Thorn groaned and stared to rise, but the sound of the door opening terrified the nymphs. Thorn was quickly and masterfully hidden.

King Liderc entered the room, followed by Carman.

From his hiding place Thorn allowed himself a quick peek at the room. His enemy was so close.

King Liderc strode around the room, sniffing the air. 'None yet. I don't know what magic you use nymphs, but sooner or later nature will run her course with you.' He went from female to female, sniffing each one. Some he stood by longer than he did others. 'Soon,' he would mutter as the nymphs quaked.

'Tomorrow, same time ladies?' King Liderc asked before he left the room.

Carman, however, remained.

She walked from nymph to nymph, glaring at them. Finally she stopped by the water nymph. 'You are with child. Don't deny it. I can tell these things.'

The nymph stood up. 'Then I won't deny it.'

'King Liderc tells me that none of you have been mated, so how is this?' Carman asked.

'Well,' the water nymph said slyly. 'I doubt that he'd want to tell you that he spends his days chasing us. You didn't expect him to admit it in front of you, did you?'

Carman almost shook in her anger. 'What do you mean?'

The other nymphs liked this game, so they joined in. 'He comes down here and chases us all day. He likes the variety, or so he said.'

Carman pulled the water nymph by her hair across the floor. 'If you bear his child so help me I will cut the babe from your womb.'

'That will start my cycle again,' the water nymph said bravely, meeting Carman's fierce gaze. 'Then your King will come down again to mount me every day until he puts another Prince into my womb.'

'You assume that I meant to leave you alive,' Carman growled.

Carman followed King Liderc back to their chamber. She was fuming, but slowly her angry expression turned thoughtful. By the time she entered the room she was deceptively calm.

As they sat down to their dinner Carman sighed loudly.

King Liderc ignored her.

She sighed again.

He continued to eat.

Carman pushed her plate away loudly and again sighed with so much force that King Liderc finally looked up.

'What is wrong?'

'Oh, nothing,' Carman said.

King Liderc shrugged at went back to his meal.

Carman's eyes narrowed to angry slits, but kept her temper in tight reign. 'I suppose now that I carry your Prince you have no interest in me,' she said with a slight tremor to her voice.

King Liderc laughed. 'If you need servicing go lie on the bed and spread your legs. I'll be over presently, as soon as I finish this meal.'

She could have killed him, if she only knew how. 'Snakegrass told me that my sister Aynia is so much more beautiful than I am. It's probably just because she isn't mated yet.'

'The Fairie Queen is unmated?'

Carman knew that she had King Liderc's full attention when he set his fork down quietly. 'No, apparently she refused to take her mating flight.'

'And she is beautiful?'

Carman frowned. 'Oh, if you like that kind of thing, red hair, creamy white skin, ample bosom, wide hips,' she traced an exaggerated female form in the air with her hands.

'A redhead?'

'Yes,' Carman said impatiently.

'Hmmm,' King Liderc mused. 'Perhaps I should go see this Queen for myself. 'She is truly unmated?'

Carman shrugged. 'Snakegrass might have been wrong.'

Sarkany hovered over the workers assembled on the rocky shore of the small island. A thrill ran down his back. There were so many more here than he had dared to hope for. Sixty was not a big army, but it was big enough for what he had planned. After all, he knew the size of the forces he would be up against, and they were limited in number.

To his right came a displeased voice. 'You simply cannot take this many of my workers.'

'I'm not taking them, they are following me,' Sarkany informed the master builder.

'Don't play word games with me drone. It comes down to this; you are leaving me with no workforce for the new Hive. My completion date is getting pushed too far back. The Queen will be most displeased.'

Sarkany flew up to the master builder so that he was right in her face. His voice almost purred, but the growl was audible just underneath. 'The Queen is the least of your worries. Let me take care of her.' It was clear that the Master Builder was not pleased at having to deal with a male, especially a drone. Ever since his arrival at the building site on the island Sarkany had endured outright hostility and many a suggestion that he retire to the harem where he belonged. The criticism stung. However, society in the Hive was changing right before their eyes and if the Master Builder could not accept and change Sarkany would be glad to bury her along with anyone else that opposed him.

'Fine, do what you plan to do drone. But when it's all over if you're dead and buried how will I explain this?'

'If I am dead and buried, those who come looking for you will not be after explanations. They will be out for blood. Besides, you have at least two thousand other workers here. What difference will the loss of sixty make?'

The Master Builder finally dropped her gaze from Sarkany's. 'You're lucky that you convinced this many females to follow a mere drone,' she grumbled. 'I guess that means you have the crazy ones. Good riddance.'

Sarkany did not allow himself to smile. His power here was tenuous at best, based partially on exaggerations and lies. It would do no good to further antagonize the Master Builder.

He turned to address his troops. 'It will take us a full day to fly to Balnacra. Be sure to carry enough provisions. And be very careful. There are many humans in the Highlands now.'

'We're not afraid of them,' a worker shouted out.

'No, but we don't have time to deal with them. We must be on the move.' Sarkany surveyed his army. They might not be trained, but they were eager. 'To Balnacra!'

'To Balnacra!' the rabble shouted.

'Vive Scotia!'

The workers roared approval and en mass took to wing for the Hive.

Thorn was backing away from the nymphs. 'No, not today. I need my strength.'

'Chase me Thorn,' several called out as they started to run from him.

'No, not today,' Thorn repeated firmly.

'Your lips say no, but your penis says yes,' a nymph laughed as she reached down and gave him a playful squeeze.

'Don't do that,' Thorn slapped her hand away. 'Listen, you need to concentrate. I heard the goblins say that they were going to leave the Hall today. This is our chance to escape. But I need my strength.' He moved another wandering hand from his body. 'Don't you all want to go to the surface again? Don't you want to see the sun?'

'The sun?' The nymphs said as if in a daze.

'The sun, the big ball of fire in the sky, you know.' Thorn said with the little bit of patience he had left.

'Oh yes, we want to go to the surface again!'

'Good.'

'When'

'Later.'

The nymphs pouted prettily. 'We want to go now.'

'We have to wait for the goblins to leave,' Thorn explained.

'What will we do while we wait?'

'I don't know,' Thorn sighed.

'I do, chase me Thorn!'

'Yes, chase me!'

Thorn sighed. It was going to be a very long day.

'What about Parliament?' Ambassador Cowslip asked Thane Monarda.

'The Queen already suffered a vote of no confidence.'

'That was before Thane Adders-Tongue died. Since then the Queen has wooed back support.' Ambassador Cowslip failed to mention that she was partially responsible for Adders-Tongue's death.

'But the majority will still side with us. It is time the truth comes out about the plague,' Thane Monarda argued.

Ambassador Cowslip shuddered. She didn't believe that plague stalked the Hive. If it did it was a very selective plague that only affected the workers. As much as the Ambassador believed in the superiority of the nobles she did not believe that plague gave a damn about class. However, if it took rumors of plague to bring this, the last great Hive in Scotland, under English power, then by the Goddesses the Ambassador would fan the flames of fear.

'Where else can the Queen look to for support?'

Thane Monarda laughed bitterly. 'The Queen will foolishly look to the Temple, but I doubt that she will find any support there. The High Priestess is like all clergy. She will stand aside until a clear winner comes forward. Then the Temple will throw its support behind the powerful. The priestesses are interested in preserving their own skins. They don't care who the Queen is as long as they can have her milk.'

Cowslip had to agree with this. The High Priestess had said as much in her final conversation with the unfortunate Cerridwen.

'And the Royal Guard?'

'They are trained from birth to be drones, playthings for the Queen. They will obey the first strong female that commands them.'

Ambassador Cowslip licked her lips. 'What about the workers?'

'Once they hear about the plague they will be too panicked to do anything. Again, all it takes is a strong female telling them what to do.'

Ambassador Cowslip shrugged. 'If you are sure of gaining support for this uprising, well then, do as you will. Of course, I am just a disinterested observer.'

Prince Moss barged into the Queen's parlor. 'Your Highness!'

Aynia looked up from the pile of papers she was reading as she ate her breakfast. 'Prince,' she acknowledged him briefly. If she was annoyed at Moss she barely showed it.

'There is an army forming in the Hive center.'

Aynia looked over at Rose. 'Get Camellia, Gather the drones. Bring my body armor.'

Rose nodded and ran to the harem. She threw open the door and ran inside. Camellia stormed out of her room. 'What in the name of the great Goddesses possessed you to break into the Queen's harem?'

'There's an army in the Hive center. The Queen calls for her drones.'

Camellia's eyes grew wide for only a second. Then she whirled away, well in command of her domain. 'Battle stations! All drones to arms. It is time to protect the Queen!'

Rose breathed a sigh of relief. Camellia's calm manner did much to improve her nerves. She returned to Aynia's side.

Aynia was equally calm and in command. 'What army is it in the Hive center?' She asked Prince Moss.

'Nobles. It looks like Thane Monarda is leading them.'

'Thane Monarda? Isn't Verbena in her service? Why didn't she warn me?' Since Thane Adders-Tongue's death the frequency of messages to Aynia from her old attendants had dropped off sharply. Aynia mentioned the loss of the messages to Sarkany but he assured her it was because there was no news to pass on.

Moss frowned. 'Well, Lady Verbena did come to talk to Prince Sarkany several days ago.'

'About?'

'Sarkany made us leave the room.'

Aynia stomped her foot impatiently. 'Then go get Sarkany. Drag him in here if you must, but bring him to me.'

Moss paled. 'Highness, I don't know where he is. He disappeared five days ago.'

'Quiet!' Thorn ordered. 'Make any noise and we're all dead,' he warned the nymphs.

There were no guards in the tunnels. The goblins knew that once their kingdom was sealed at the magic gate no enemy could enter or escape. This explained the lack of locking doors on the chambers they used as prisons and the lack of patrols in their tunnels. Still Thorn was wary. They had to time their escape carefully.

The main problem was the twisting path of the tunnels. Thorn had traced the scent of the nymphs to find their cell. Now he had to find a way back to the hall. A flickering candle gave the clue to find the way. They followed the current of air upstream.

Once in the main hall the nymphs and Thorn had to weave their way past the goblins there. Many times the goblins came too close, almost detecting their presence, but finally Thorn and the nymphs were secreted about the door to the hall. Now they only had to wait for the door to be opened.

'I don't know why I indulge you so,' King Liderc grumbled at Carman. 'There is no good reason for us to ride through the overworld. I should be at the front of my forces as they tunnel to the Hive. We're going to have to join them in the tunnel at the last minute anyway.'

'Only animals burrow,' Carman hissed.

'Are you calling me an animal?' King Liderc stepped towards her, his hand raised menacingly.

'Yes,' Carman admitted. 'You're an animal in bed,' she said as if teasing him.

King Liderc pulled Carman to him and gave her a rough kiss. 'You saved that one nicely.'

'Yes My Lord,' Carman admitted. She slipped her hand down the front of his hose. 'Save this thought for later. We may need a battering ram to break down the gates of the Hive.'

Thorn gasped. King Liderc was going to assault the Hive? But why, he wondered. A glimpse of Carman answered that question.

King Liderc laughed and moved away to give his goblin troops last minute commands.

Carman watched him walk away. 'Always thinking with your penis My Lord,' she said quietly. 'Once you figure out where males keep their brains you can lead them around by their balls and make them do anything.'

Thorn frowned. His hand shot out and grabbed the wandering hand of a nymph who was stroking his crotch. 'Stop it,' he whispered.

'Queen Carman is right,' the nymph giggled. 'Males are so easily led about.'

'Get your hands off of me. And move away. Further away. I don't want a single nymph close enough to touch me,' he warned them. 'For the love of the Goddesses, keep your minds focused on escape. Can you all do that?'

Carman and King Liderc mounted matching black horses. 'Meet us at the Hive!' King Liderc ordered his goblin army as they rode to the entrance of the Hall. But just as he was about to give the magic command to open the gate King Liderc stopped. Then he sniffed the air.

Carman, growing greatly impatient to take the Throne back from Aynia, grumbled. 'What is it now?'

'I smell something. I smell females, and I smell a male.'

'You smell you, and you smell me. Come on, let's ride.'

'I do not smell my own scent,' the King growled.

'You are anticipating the scent of Aynia. You can't wait to mate with her, can you?' Carman snapped.

King Liderc leaned over to Carman. 'Shall I have both of you in my bed at the same time?' He brushed his finger across her lips.

Carman barred he teeth and tried to bite him, but he laughed and pulled away in time.

'Jealous my pet? Don't worry; you'll always be my first Queen.'

Carman's answer to this was obscured by the rumbling of the gate at the entrance to the Hall of the Mountain King as the boulder opened to let the King and Queen of the goblins ride out.

Thorn was not about to take a chance at missing the narrow window of opportunity to escape. As soon as the horses were clear of the gate he and the nymphs ran for the crack in the boulder. 'Run, run,' he yelled to the nymphs. 'Run for your lives!'

Thorn didn't care if the goblins heard him and the nymphs making their escape. He would rather take his chances being seen in the overworld than being stuck forever in the underworld.

Carman and the King, however, never looked back, and never saw Thorn or the nymphs as they emerged from the darkness for the first time in days.

'I must go warn the Queen,' Thorn told the nymphs.

'Don't leave us Thorn,' the nymphs pleaded.

'Then come with me,' he told them.

The nymphs stopped. 'We asked the Queen for help once. She refused. That's how we came to be prisoners of the Mountain King. If she is in need of help now we will not assist her.'

'I must serve my Queen.'

'Be our King Thorn. We will care for you. We will be your harem. Stay with us Thorn.'

'Yes, stay with us,' the nymphs urged him. Hands began to stroke him in intimate places. Caresses touched his inner thigh, his buttocks, and his balls.

Thorn pushed the hands away firmly. 'No. Ladies, it has been anything but a pleasure. If I stayed with you it would be the death of me.'

The water nymph smiled. 'But what a way to go.'

'I never thought that I'd see the day when a drone chose death over sex, but now I have. I would rather die fighting for my Queen than make love to another one of you. Goodbye.' Thorn took off into the air flew in a beeline for the Hive.

'We strike now!' Monarda told her friends.

The Hive center was crowded for the first time in a month as the nobles who backed Thane Monarda followed her to the steps of the Royal Palace. Other nobles who were too cowardly to commit to revolution still hovered nearby; ready to jump in with any winning side that emerged from the fray.

Curious workers also lingered longer than usual in the Hive center. They recognized most of the Nobility. The mere fact that so many of the Nobility were gathered together made more than one worker curious. The fact that they were armed was even more interesting.

Thane Monarda boldly banged on the front door of the Palace. A moment passed, and then she banged again.

Nervous laughter erupted from several places in the crowd until finally Prince Moss and the rest of the Royal Guard appeared on the top step of the Palace terrace from a door far to the left of where Monarda and her fellow rebels were standing.

The mob looked on at the drones in their uniforms. There was no denying that the Queen's drones filled out their tights well.

Moss looked at the crowd with only the hint of curiosity. 'May I help you, Thane Monarda?' He asked ever so politely.

'We, we've come to confront the Queen!' Monarda said in a voice that started off strongly then dropped off into a pleading tone.

'The Queen is not holding court until after lunch today. If you would be so good as to return then she will be listening to petitioners.'

Monarda frowned. She felt ridiculous. Did this drone not understand that this was a serious matter? 'I demand to see the Queen. We all demand to see the Queen immediately!'

Moss was about to speak but was interrupted by Aynia. 'We are listening,' Aynia said as she gently floated down from the balcony above the Hive Center. The gauzy white dress she wore was thick enough to hide her body armor, but clingy enough in the right places to show the unmistakable swell of her abdomen. It was an old style dress, no longer fashionable, but the new fashions hid pregnancy too well.

'Everyone pities the pregnant lady,' Camellia quipped about the dress as Aynia put on her Hive Tartan sash.

Aynia's reply was vulgar enough to make even Camellia blush.

'You wished to speak with me Thane Monarda? All of you?' Aynia met the eyes of each noble with her calm gaze. One by one they dropped their eyes to the ground, too ashamed to meet the Queen's serene visage.

Someone pushed Thane Monarda ahead of the group. She looked back and immediately suspected Ambassador Cowslip from Norfolk. Her eyes narrowed to angry slits, but she turned back to the Queen. 'We know that there is plague loose in the Hive, and we demand that you do something about it.'

'Plague? There is no plague,' Aynia said as if she was talking to a small child.

'Yes there is! We know it! How else do you explain the death of Thane Adders-Tongue?'

'Cobra-Lily, her niece, sent her a poisoned necklace.'

'Then why are all of the workers disappearing? What are you doing with the bodies?'

Aynia opened her mouth to speak but a strange low rumbling came up from the ground.

'The Queen!' Moss and his guards grabbed Aynia gently and flew with her back up to the balcony.

From the poorer section of the Hive a wave of workers ran into the Hive Center. Behind them the Hive was crumbling, imploding. No one else moved. They were in shock.

Suddenly the floor ripped apart right in front of the stairs to the Palace.

Nobles who panicked and forgot to take to wing fell into the fissure. Those who remembered to fly banged into each other in their panic.

Ambassador Cowslip ran for the Temple doors.

The workers who were running from their section of the Hive stopped at the edge of the fissure. They had no wings to rise above it. Panicked workers behind them pushed the front ones to the edge, and finally into, the tremendous hole in the floor.

Aynia looked to Moss. 'Do something! Get your guards out there and turn the crowd before they stampede into the hole!'

'Your Majesty will be unprotected!'

'Get down there and save my subjects!' Aynia commanded them. When they wavered she took Moss by the arm and shoved him to the edge of the balcony. 'Just go!'

Moss and the rest of the guards flew down to the crowd, trying in vain to be heard above the panicked masses.

Suddenly as it began the rumbling noise stopped. Then there was another sound, a hissing discordance, rising from the fissure. A black horse galloped out of the ground; on its back, King Liderc. Behind him hundreds of goblins climbed out of the black earth and spilled into the Hive.

Now the workers ran in the opposite direction. Children fell under hundreds of feet, crying out once then no more. Nobles turned the weapons they meant to use against the Queen to a pitched battle with the goblin army.

The Royal Guard flew in to protect the workers and to direct them to safety. Prince Moss swooped down and pulled a juvenile female from harm's way as she was knocked to the ground under a surge of panicked workers. The female clung for dear life to Moss's neck when he tried to put her down in a safe place.

Wheat directed traffic towards the noble's estates, commanding the drones near him to stop the workers from running back into the weakest section of the Hive.

The goblins continued to pour into the Hive from the fissure. Fairie forces were split. Thane Monarda and her nobles were pinned against the fortified façade of the Palace. They fought but the struggle did not last long. It took moments for sixty or more to lose their lives. The others who could still fly took to wing.

The goblins turned their efforts to invading the Palace. When they could not breach the front doors the goblins scurried back to the fissure and went underground, hoping to tunnel into the palace halls.

Then there was quiet. The only sounds were ominous creaking noises from the remaining walls of the Hive.

King Liderc slid off of his horse and walked in his languid manner to the steps of the Royal Palace. Seemingly oblivious to the bodies and blood around him, he looked only to Aynia. He slid off his gloves and gave a deep bow. 'Queen Aynia?'

'Mountain King.' Aynia acknowledged his presence with a small nod of her head as she looked down at him from her balcony.

'You are indeed lovely Queen Aynia. I heard rumors, but none do you justice.'

Aynia closed her eyes for a second. The Mountain King was releasing his scent into the air. 'You woo strangely Goblin,' Aynia told him.

King Liderc paused and smiled his most dangerous smile. 'In truth, my dear, I came not to woo.'

'Then why are you here?' Aynia showed no fear. She was as icy and calm as the Mountain King was. 'Ah, she sent you. She has you well trained drone. You heel to her command,' she mocked.

'I answer to no female!' King Liderc shouted, his face betraying his anger. Then he took a deep, calming breath. Again he matched Aynia's detached calm, but inside he seethed.

'I heard a rumor that you meant to go to war against me. I came to ask if this is true,' he looked up to her on the balcony.

'We are not at war with you, Your Majesty. Go home.'

'But I can not. After seeing your beauty I simply must have you. Come to me,' he commanded in a voice that almost made Aynia's feet move of their own accord. Many of the other females in the Hive also found themselves moving towards King Liderc as if hypnotized.

After feeling the sting of the Queen's mocking he would stop at nothing to possess, subdue, and humiliate her for daring to call him a drone.

Aynia shook her head as if to break the spell. She gasped and turned back into her Palace. The red velvet curtain dropped down and hid her from his sight. Aynia took a deep breath of the untainted air in the palace to clear her mind, and then she ran.

Thorn zoomed across the valley; weaving a lunatic trail above and around obstacles no sane Fairie would pass at half the speed. In his haste he never saw the danger until he suddenly went cartwheeling through the air. He stopped when he slammed into the rough bark of a pine tree.

He hurt all over but nothing was broken so he took off from the branch and flew in the direction of the Hive, this time with more caution. Then he spied his assailant. Innocent eyes looked past him as if he was invisible. The dreaded tail swished back and forth as the horse, oblivious to the damage she'd caused, nibbled on grass.

Thorn made a face at the horse and continued on his way, only to be stopped by the sight of humans in the valley. He longed to kill them but there was no time. He had to go help Aynia fight the goblins. However, he wasn't about to risk flying straight through the human's war camp. A sense of dread and emergency filled his heart as he skirted the edge of the woods.

As Thorn reached the north border of the camp where the berry thickets grew dense and impenetrable to humans Thorn ran into another obstacle. Suddenly he found himself surrounded by an army of workers.

'We must get to the Hive!' Thorn called out.

'It's Thorn!' Some of the workers recognized him.

'But he's a drone!'

Sarkany rose in front of Thorn. 'Captain Thorn.'

'Prince Sarkany,' Thorn nodded and tried to take off. 'I must get to the Queen.'

Sarkany placed a hand on Thorn's arm, holding him back more with words than by force. 'Oh yes, the great Captain Thorn. It's time to make your grand entrance. I'm sure that the Queen will be thrilled. She'll probably lie down and spread her legs when she sees you.'

Thorn threw a punch into Sarkany's jaw.

Sarkany rose and flew at Thorn. They wrestled across the sky.

'The goblins are attacking the Hive! The Queen is in danger. We must go save her,' Thorn grunted. Sarkany was smaller than Thorn but he had the ability to move with lightening speed and to land solid punches that hurt.

Sarkany stopped swinging at Thorn and frowned. 'The Mountain King is after the Queen?'

'Yes! The goblin army is marching to attack the Hive. They could be there right now.'

'Then I suppose that this would be a good moment to bring my army to the Hive,' Sarkany mused.

'What are you talking about?' Thorn asked.

'Opportunity Captain, let's go to the Queen.'

Thorn stared at the Prince for a moment then shrugged. Whatever Sarkany was planning was of no concern. The only thing on Thorn's mind was the safety of the Queen.

Thorn and Sarkany rose in the air and resumed their flight through the woods, followed closely by sixty armed workers.

Aynia ran through the halls of the palace. At every junction she peered around the corner to see if goblins were inside the palace yet. Before long the hallways were infested with them. They were tearing the palace to shreds searching for her.

'The Queen!' a goblin gave out the alarm.

Aynia took to wing. She had one defense if she could reach it. But time was running out. The hallways were filling with more goblins as each second passed.

Some of the passageways had ceilings so low that her legs passed perilously close to the heads of the goblins. Some goblins lobbed spears at her. Once glanced off of her back and brought her down. As goblins began to surround her Aynia forced herself to leap into the air, launching herself into a twist that landed her far down the hallway beyond the goblins.

Aynia somersaulted into the next hallway. Her back was burning with pain. The blow from the spear and the fall to the ground severely damaged one of her wings. Looking down at the wet sensation on her leg, Aynia was shocked to see blood drawn. One of the spears had found its mark.

Aynia didn't think about stopping. She was close to her goal, the Royal vaults. She stepped into the hallway were the Princesses chambers were. She could see the vault of Royal Jelly at the end of the hallway. Aynia broke into a run.

Suddenly the tiles on the ground erupted as forty goblins clawed up through the floor. Aynia fell and rolled.

She came to her feet and yanked open the door in front of her, finding herself in her old chamber.

The room was empty and dusty. The grid lies were still tapped off from the battle between Carman and her. Dark brown stains, probably dried blood, marked the floor in more than one spot. Memories of that day glued Aynia to a spot just inside the door.

The sound of goblins throwing themselves against the door to the chamber brought Aynia to her senses. Rushing across the room to the small back chamber where she lived and slept for nearly one hundred seventy years as a Princess, Aynia found the secret knob and pulled it.

A hidden door popped open. Aynia shoved it open just wide enough to slip past. The passageway was built for a princess, not a Queen. It was a very tight fit but Aynia shut the door behind her and began crawling to safety.

CHAPTER 18

Thorn and Sarkany reached the entrance to the Hive at the same time. Both paused as they saw the great destruction.

'Do you hear that?' Thorn whispered.

'Is that the walls?' Sarkany asked.

'I think so. I wonder if the goblins are here yet.'

'It could cave at any moment.'

'Sh,' Thorn hushed Sarkany. They ducked down just in time to avoid being sighted by several goblins. 'I guess that the goblins are here. We need a plan.'

'Well, I have a small army. We could use them,' Sarkany suggested sarcastically.

'Yes, and just why did you raise an army?' Thorn asked suspiciously.

'It's a long story. Right now we have to figure out a plan.'

'I think that I already said that. If the Hive is about to fall down we need to evacuate it.'

'Then there is the small matter of the goblins.'

'I'm not forgetting that Prince,' Thorn snapped. They were united in their desire to save Aynia but distrust still came between them.

Sarkany peered back into the Hive center. 'Tell you what; we'll split the forces…'

'I think that I'm much more qualified than a dilettante like you to plan our strategy.'

'I've have more than enough experience Thorn.'

Thorn made a disparaging noise.

'I've been Captain of the Queen's guard for quite some time now and I had several years of military experience in another Hive. Don't make the mistake of thinking that I'm a typical drone.'

Thorn was sputtering. 'You? Captain of her Guard? She let a drone lead the Guard?'

'Jealous?' Sarkany taunted him.

494

'Angry.'

'Good.'

'I could have continued to serve in the Guard,' Thorn swore softly but thoroughly.

So did Sarkany. 'We don't have time to do this now. The Queen is in danger. Listen, why don't you go rescue workers? I'll go find the Queen. We won't worry about taking on the goblins and we won't try to save the Hive. We just save whom we can and get the hell out of there, agreed?'

Thorn nodded. 'Agreed. How long do you need?'

'I don't have a clue,' Sarkany admitted. 'But I won't leave until I find the Queen.'

'Some great plan Prince. Let's give it an hour. After that we meet here and make further plans, right?'

'Right,' Sarkany began to turn away but turned back to face Thorn. 'The Queen is mated. I thought that you should know.' Sarkany offered his hand to Thorn.

Thorn regarded it for only a moment before taking it.

The two drones returned to their makeshift army and began the task of selecting the troops they needed for their plans.

Aynia had several close moments as she squeezed through the narrow passageway. Her growing abdomen scraped the walls at a few spots. Finally the end of the tunnel was before her. She pushed the release mechanism and crawled out into the Temple. As she emerged strong hands grabbed her and pulled her out of the sanctuary and into the private chamber of the High Priestess.

Once in the room Aynia shook off the offending hands. Then she removed cobwebs from her hair. 'What is the meaning of this?' Aynia demanded angrily.

The High Priestess looked at Aynia with a smirk on her face. 'Did I not mention that many Fairie find the Temple a source of comfort during times of crises Ambassador?' she asked in a mocking tone.

Ambassador Cowslip came from behind the High Priestess's throne.

Robed priestesses lined the room, their faces hidden by hoods.

'What is this about?' Aynia asked.

'I got a better deal,' the High Priestess explained.

'I don't know what you think that you have, but goblins are invading the Hive and I need Royal Jelly.'

'No.'

'No? I don't know who you think you are or what you think you're doing, but any second the goblins could invade this Temple, and it isn't exactly a social call.'

'Goblins Highness? Don't you mean that the nobles are revolting against your reign? Face it, your time is over. It's time for a new order here in the Hive. When you are executed we will send to England for a new Princess and we will start over with a Queen who knows her place, a Queen who understands that she is subject to the Goddesses.'

'You would put English blood on my Throne?' Aynia was aghast at the thought.

'It is my turn to rule Highness. I have worked for years to get to this place of power. Do you think that I would let you tear it all apart with your new Hive? No. We will stay here.'

Aynia shook her head. 'This is hardly the time to discuss all of this. There are, in truth, goblins in the Hive. I need Royal Jelly to kill them.'

'And I told you no. From now on I don't take orders from you.'

Ambassador Cowslip smirked. 'Good heavens, she looks frightful. No proper Queen would gad about looking like that.'

Aynia drew in a deep breath. The Ambassador and the High Priestess shared a triumphant glance.

They should not have taken their eyes off of Aynia. In a second her stinger was out.

'I claim diplomatic immunity,' Ambassador Cowslip cried out. Her hands were out in front of her face as if to ward off the Queen's wrath.

'Denied,' Aynia growled. She plunged her stinger straight into the Ambassador's heart. Ambassador Cowslip tried to fly away but was impaled on the end of the Queen's stinger.

Fear suddenly showed in the High Priestesses eyes.

'Give me Royal Jelly,' Aynia hissed.

'No!' The High Priestess tried to run from her throne, but Aynia's stinger lashed out and stabbed her through the back.

'Now, someone is going to tell me how to get some Royal Jelly!' Aynia yelled out so that the assembled Priestesses quaked.

One hooded figure stepped forward. 'I know the secret Highness, if you will trust me.' The female pushed back her hood.

'Lady Heather!'

'Do you trust me my Queen?'

'With my life.' The two females clasped arms. Aynia took Heather's hand and allowed her to lead her into another room.

The leader of the English army looked across the valley. He didn't like it one bit. The moon was new. Her face was turned, providing no light. It was the summer solstice but a winter chill permeated this Highland valley. Mist clung to the ground. Men standing twenty feet away were wrapped in the cool fog up to their waists. Beyond them, where the grasses gave way to forest, the mist obscured towering trees.

The valley was deadly quiet.

The horses sensed the nervousness of the men. They snorted and pawed the ground.

Even the ravens were still.

Suddenly, everywhere, Scots rose up from the ground. The battle was joined.

Sarkany was not prepared for the destruction he saw as his army slipped into the Hive. Obviously a battle had been fought in the Hive center. He saw the bodies of nobles that he knew and wondered if they were killed in a fight with the Queen's troops or in a fight with the goblins.

Over the smell of blood and death he could sense a faint whiff of the Queen's scent. Silently motioning to his troops, Sarkany headed for the Temple.

Thorn and his contingent were horrified at the scenes they saw. Workers, young and old, lay on the ground, trampled to death. As they moved into the poorer sections of the Hive they saw more Fairie who were killed by falling walls. In some places only a foot or a hand marked where bodies lie under tons of rubble. The population was in a panic, with good reason, but a panicked mob was a dangerous mob, so Thorn moved ahead with great caution.

They turned a corner and were suddenly beset by a hundred goblins.

'I must take your milk,' Heather informed Aynia.

'I hope that you know what you're doing.' Aynia sat down and unlatched the cup of her corset.

'Majesty, I would not presume…'

'Heather, my people are under attack, the Hive is falling down around us, and the Mountain King is trying to abduct me. At this point I will do anything I have to.'

'Wait until I tell you before you make that decision.' Heather eyed the Queen's breast. She stood between Aynia's thighs. Then, with a deep breath, she latched on and began to suckle.

Aynia closed her eyes. 'Your lips are very soft Heather. This feels so different from when my drones take milk.'

Heather looked up at the Queen but did not stop nursing. Slowly she began pushing Aynia's skirt up above her thighs. Aynia felt Heather's fingers lightly brush across her skin. She parted her legs a little more.

Heather kissed Aynia on the mouth as she used her hand to express more milk from Aynia's breast. Aynia opened her mouth and allowed Heather's tongue to dart inside.

Aynia felt Heather's hand in her hair. She turned her face into the hand so that Heather caressed her cheek.

Heather kissed the hollow of Aynia's neck, and licked the warm skin with her tongue. She trailed her kisses down between Aynia's breasts and across her abdomen.

'My Queen, I will show you what I need for you to do for me.' Heather bent down and began to suckle on Aynia's clitoris. Aynia spread her legs as Heather expertly darted her tongue in and out of Aynia's vagina.

'Do you like that my Queen?' Heather asked breathlessly.

Aynia moaned. 'I love it.'

'Your juices are growing sweet. Can you come in my mouth?'

'Yes,' Aynia's back arched as she came.

Heather quickly took off her own skirt. 'I will take a little more milk from your other breast. Then I need for you to make me come while I say the prayers. My juices will be the Royal Jelly, so save them somehow.'

Aynia nodded.

As soon as Heather took the milk she needed from Aynia's other breast the two switched places. Aynia did not immediately go down on Heather. She slowly unlatched the cup of Heather's corset. 'I've always wondered what it tastes like,' Aynia admitted.

She flicked her tongue experimentally over Heather's nipple. Heather's nipple went hard. Then Aynia put the entire areola into her mouth and began to suckle. With her hand she roughly massaged Heather's breast.

'How is it Majesty?' Heather asked.

'Interesting, did you like that?'

'Oh yes,' Heather moaned.

Aynia slid her fingers slowly inside of Heather. 'And do you want this?' She asked.

'Yes.'

Aynia finger fucked Heather to get her fingers wet. Then she raised them to her mouth and flicked her tongue over the fingers to taste the juices. 'These aren't Royal Jelly yet. You better start your spell.'

'Prayers,' Heather corrected her. 'They're prayers, not spells.'

Aynia bent down on her knees and tentatively tasted Heather. She licked outside the labia while working her fingers back inside of Heather. When her fingers were well wetted again Aynia slid the fingers into Heather's anus and put her thumb into Heather's vagina. Aynia then sucked and teased Heather's clitoris.

Heather was saying the prayers out loud, but then lapsed into silent intonation as her wildest fantasy came true. She opened her eyes and saw the Queen's red head between her thighs. She tried to spread her legs further apart. This was heaven. The Queen was on her knees and going down on her.

Aynia suddenly noted the change in flavor of Heather's juices. They were also beginning to take on the distinctive slick texture of Royal Jelly. Aynia grabbed a small ceremonial cup off of the floor. As Heather arched her back and pulled her knees up to her chest, Aynia caught the precious Royal Jelly as it flowed out of Heather's vagina.

'I've seen this somewhere,' a male voice drawled. 'Oh I know, in my fantasies. Usually I'm in the middle though.'

Aynia hopped up. 'The Mountain King!'

'You've led me on a merry chase Queen Aynia. But you should have realized that I could follow your scent through solid rock. Tell me Priestess, did you taste the Queen too? Or was this a one way party?'

The room filled with the scent of the Mountain King. Heather found herself gasping for breath again. The scent was intoxicating.

'So tell me, is her pussy like fire?' He whispered.

'Oh yes,' Heather answered. Without knowing what she was doing, she spread her legs far apart. She slid her hand between her legs, preparing herself for the Mountain King.

The Mountain King leaned over and licked Heather's lips. 'Mmm, what a lovely flavor.'

Heather reached up to bring the Mountain King's lips back to hers. Her hips worked a rhythm as her body begged to make love to him. She never saw his blade as it slipped towards the base of her skull.

'No offense, but I don't share my females, even with other females.'

Aynia gave a small scream. She lashed out with her stinger, knocking the blade away from Heather. The blow hit Heather on the side of her head. Her eyes rolled back and Heather's body slid off of the chair.

'Alone again my love.' King Liderc advanced on Aynia.

'Back away,' another male voice warned from the door.

Aynia looked over at Sarkany. Then she looked over at the Mountain King. The resemblance was uncanny.

'You!' Aynia pointed at Prince Sarkany. 'You're a goblin!' How could she not have seen the obvious before? Maybe he was able to cloud her mind.

Sarkany nodded. 'Half.'

King Liderc regarded Prince Sarkany. 'All goblins are half goblins. The only difference is where we live, and how we choose to live. Sarkany, it's been awhile.'

'And yet it's still too soon,' Sarkany replied caustically.

'You two know each other?'

'Brothers,' King Liderc confirmed.

'Half brothers,' Sarkany growled.

'How?'

'I told you that in the Romanian Hive we live in harmony with the other Sidhe, the magic folk and creatures. My mother lived in close harmony with the Mountain King.'

King Liderc laughed. 'Very close. I have eleven half brothers. And I would have had more if the Fairie Queen hadn't eventually poisoned our father.'

'She needed to breed a Princess. He wasn't allowing her to mate with her other drones,' Sarkany defended his mother.

'She didn't want the other drones! Once a Fairie female has been mastered by a goblin she never looks at a Fairie male again,' King Liderc told Aynia with a roguish leer.

'Stay away from me, both of you,' Aynia warned the two males. She slowly backed out of the room, but Sarkany and King Liderc both followed her. 'Leave me alone,' she cried out as she stumbled out of the Temple and back into the Hive Center.

Aynia fled from the two males. She was angry with herself. How could she have allowed herself to fall in love with a goblin, even if he was only half goblin? But it explained so much. This was why he knew he couldn't sire a female child. And this explained the reason why Sarkany seemed to have worked his way not only into her heart, but also into her very blood. Even with half goblin blood he was powerfully sensual and addictive. Aynia glanced down at the palm of her hand where she imagined she could still feel that first kiss from Sarkany.

'Why hasn't he killed you?' A voice asked, incredulous.

Aynia spun around. Thorn was on his knees on the ground. Carman's stinger was aimed at his neck.

'Thorn!' Aynia cried out.

'Don't bargain for me,' Thorn said before Carman yanked his head back by the hair.

'Quiet drone,' Carman snapped.

Sarkany and King Liderc ambled out of the Temple. Their strides were the same languid, fluid movement that hinted at the sexual power each of the two males possessed.

Thorn looked from the Prince to the King then met Sarkany's eyes for a second. 'Save the Queen,' he whispered.

Sarkany leaned against one of the three pillars at the entrance to the Temple. His suddenly casual air made Carman and King Liderc suspicious. 'Save her for who Thorn? For you? No. I don't think so. Save her for my half brother? He already has a female, such as she is,' Sarkany sneered at Carman.

'Don't let him talk about me that way!' Carman protested.

Sarkany ignored Carman. 'Goblin males are meant to be Kings, not consorts for females,' Sarkany said with contempt. 'That is why I raised my own army of workers to come here and take over this Hive.'

'Where is this army?' King Liderc asked warily.

'Your army killed most of them, I captured the others,' Carman informed King Liderc. 'There were only sixty Fairie in his army and they were all mere workers. Once confronted by a Queen, well, they weren't used to thinking for themselves. I ordered them to surrender and they did.'

'Stop her; she could fly away at any moment!' Carman warned King Liderc as Aynia began to back away from the front steps of the Temple.

Before King Liderc could reach Aynia Sarkany roughly grabbed her arm.

Goblins began to return to the Hive center, dragging captured Fairie with them. King Liderc turned to his goblins. 'Tie down the Queen's wings. But don't hurt her. I'll save that pleasure for myself.'

Aynia struggled but Sarkany held her fast as the goblins bound her wings closed with a leather thong. Aynia was full of fury.

'Liderc, you seem to think that this female is yours. I claim her. Besides, she is already mated.' Sarkany told his half brother.

'I can smell the truth. But we all know that there are potions she could be given to make her lose the child and go back into heat.' King Liderc stroked Aynia's cheek.

Thorn struggled against Carman. 'No! You can't do that! Leave the child alone!' He yelled.

503

'Oh? Oh,' King Liderc said with a cruel smile. 'I see, the Captain protests,' he looked over at Thorn, 'not the consort. One does not have to think hard about who sired the child. Sarkany, it would be a waste to give such a fine female over to a mere half goblin that can't even get her to spread her legs. That is why I must insist on taking her.'

'She's mine,' Sarkany said stubbornly. 'You aren't supposed to be here brother,' he growled under his breath. 'This is my Hive.'

'You're supposed to be in Ireland, aren't you? But I suppose that even you couldn't resist the lure of a virgin Queen. Scotland is mine Sarkany. And now so are this Hive, and its Queen.'

'Neither one of you get her! Kill the bitch!' Carman screamed.

King Liderc walked over to Carman and backhanded her hard across her face. 'Quiet female. I've allowed you much leeway because you carry my Prince, but don't forget your place.'

'I'm a Fairie Queen!' Carman protested.

Aynia laughed contemptuously. 'I'm the Queen. You're merely a failed Princess.'

'I'm not a failure!' Carman lunged at Aynia with her stinger.

Aynia's stinger whipped out. Despite her bound wings she still had use of her stinger and her arms. Aynia gave Sarkany a hard look and pulled her arm out of his grasp. The two Queens circled each other.

'You can't fly away this time,' Carman jeered.

'Either can you,' Aynia reminded her. With a swift jab Aynia landed a powerful shot from her stinger right on Carman's chest. But the stinger only glanced off of Carman's skin.

Carman laughed. 'Nice try bitch.' Carman lunged at Aynia.

'I don't know about you,' Sarkany turned to King Liderc, 'but I don't want my female harmed.'

'But I enjoy watching the battle,' King Liderc answered.

'She could lose your Prince.'

Liderc stopped smiling. It was difficult for a goblin to find a female who survived mating. 'Who said that they aren't both my females?'

'I did. Really, don't be tiresome. Father would have been embarrassed to see us fighting over mere females,' Sarkany reminded King Liderc.

Carman and Aynia still circled each other.

'You can't hurt me,' Carman said, 'my skin in impenetrable by your stinger.'

'So you are turning into a goblin.' Aynia's stinger lashed out through the air. The Fairies and goblins backed away to a safer distance. When two Queens dueled it was not wise to get in their way.

Aynia's stinger hit Carman with such force that it knocked her down to the ground, but Carman's skin was hard, like stone, like a goblin, and the stinger did not find its mark.

Carman scrambled to rise, but she laughed. 'Ha! You can't hurt me, but we both know that a corset can't cover everything.' She aimed her stinger for Aynia's face.

Aynia grabbed Carman's stinger with her bare hand. The sharp stinger sliced deep into Aynia's flesh as Carman tried to wrench her stinger free. Aynia hands were slick with her own blood, but she held on to Carman's stinger and twisted it with all her strength towards the ground.

Carman screamed in pain and anger. The twist of her stinger hurled her down to the ground and flipped her onto her back.

Aynia slammed Carman's stinger into stone floor. The sharp tip broke off; leaving a lethal looking jagged point that was as sharp as broken glass.

Carman pulled away from Aynia's grasp and plunged her stinger at Aynia's thigh. The stinger caught on Aynia's skirt, ripping it. Carman thought that her stinger made contact with Aynia's leg. She tried to pump poison into her sister.

Aynia yanked her clothes away from the stinger. She could see that no poison came from the damaged tip.

'You have no poison to sting with? And your skin is like stone! You are a goblin,' Aynia accused.

'So, I can't sting you and you can't sting me. We're even. How should we decide this one?' Carman asked.

'Yes, how should we decide this one?' Sarkany asked King Liderc.

King Liderc paused for a moment as if to consider. 'I have an idea. We will both release our scent. Whichever one of us Queen Aynia goes to will get to keep her.'

'The Queen is not a pet,' Thorn protested.

'Did you ask his opinion?' Sarkany asked.

'No.'

'Neither did I. Shut up Thorn,' Sarkany sneered.

'So is it agreed?' King Liderc asked.

Sarkany tried to appear unconcerned. 'If that is the only way, then I'm in.'

'It's not the only way, but it's the fun way,' King Liderc told him. 'You haven't lived until you've had a Fairie Queen crawling across the floor begging to be fucked.'

'You bastard!' Carman screamed.

King Liderc smirked. 'Come Sarkany, begin releasing your scent. I'll even give you a head start.'

The Hive center suddenly filled with the earthy musk of the goblin males. Captured Fairie females fought against their bonds, desperate to give themselves to the Mountain King.

Carman stopped where she stood, a dreamy look coming over her face.

'Bind her to a post,' the Mountain King ordered his goblins. He didn't want Carman to interfere with this contest.

It took five goblins to drag Carman to one of the pillars in front of the Temple and to tie her to it. She struggled against the bonds.

Aynia also stopped where she stood. She looked down at Thorn for a second. She shook her head as if to clear her thoughts, but suddenly her eyes became unfocused.

'No!' Thorn shouted out. 'Fight it my Queen. Try to resist!'

Goblins came over and yanked a gag into Thorn's mouth. When he could see Aynia again he saw a strange smile on her face. She turned towards Prince Sarkany and King Liderc.

With maddeningly slow movements Aynia slid off her dress. First one shoulder was lowered, then the other. She held her dress up just at her breasts for a moment, but then let it drop.

King Liderc gave a low whistle of appreciation.

Unhooking one clasp of her corset at a time, Aynia slowly walked forward.

'Come my love, come to me,' King Liderc crooned.

'Yes,' Aynia said in a whisper.

'You don't seem to be getting anywhere,' King Liderc told Sarkany with a smirk.

Sarkany closed his eyes and concentrated on the Queen. He had to win her.

Aynia pushed her corset off. As the tight undergarment passed her hips she wriggled enticingly. Thorn swallowed hard. He remembered her doing that once, just inches from his face. He'd been a fool. He should have taken her milk then. Despite the danger around him, Thorn felt himself grow hard.

'Well, at least we know she's a real redhead,' King Liderc commented.

'My King,' Aynia breathed.

'No! Aynia, no!' Sarkany and Thorn cried out at the same time.

Aynia pressed her body against the Mountain King's. His arm went around her waist and pulled her close.

'Looks like I win this time brother. Tell you what, you can have the other one,' King Liderc indicated Carman. 'I'm through with her.'

'Kiss me,' Aynia begged.

Aynia let the Mountain King roughly kiss her lips and force his tongue into her mouth. 'I love your taste,' he whispered. 'Does your pussy taste as good as your mouth?'

Aynia smiled a very cold smile as she suddenly stopped struggling against the Mountain King. 'You like that?' She purred suggestively.

'Yes I do,' he growled.

'We call that flavor Royal Jelly.'

'No!' The Mountain King dropped Aynia to the floor. She rose and backed away from his reach.

The Mountain King tried to wipe the Royal Jelly from his lips and tongue, but the damage was done. His clawed fingers tore at his skin. Every second that the Royal Jelly was on his skin it drew deeper into his cells and blood. His skin began to burn.

The Mountain King desperately pulled off his clothes to cool his skin, but in his own haste to remove the heat he flayed his own skin off. He scratched off his lips and pulled out his own tongue. Blood and bits of goblin skin flew everywhere as he insanely ripped his own flesh apart in an effort to take the Royal Jelly away.

The other goblins watched in silent horror as their King shredded his body to bone. He fell to the floor, screaming in agony. Then, as he plucked out his own heart, his screams finally fell silent.

Looking at the goblin army with frightening maliciousness, Aynia took at step in their direction. 'Which one of you goblins will challenge the Fairie Queen?' She threatened. 'Beware my kiss of death. I will take you in my embrace and you will die!'

The Goblins scrambled for the great chasm in the floor. Several collected the remnants of the body of their King, dragging it down into the darkness with them as they fled. As suddenly as they appeared the hundreds of goblins were gone.

Carman and Aynia watched the goblins go.

'Aren't you going to join your people?' Aynia asked Carman.

'They're not my people. The Fairie are my people, and I have returned to claim the Throne that is rightfully mine,' Carman addressed the remaining Hive population.

Aynia snorted with disdain. 'The Fairie will not follow you.'

'Yes they will.'

The nobles who confronted Aynia earlier in the day but ran at the sight of the goblins now slowly floated down to the Hive center. Many gaped openly at Carman. Most of them never guessed that she was still alive.

'Fellow Fairie, hear me! You have another choice. This so called Queen forgets the old ways and breaks the rules that have held our society together for a thousand years. I am a Queen who knows and cherishes the old ways. Bow to me and I can be your Queen.' Carman used the jagged edge of her broken stinger to free herself from the ties that bound her to the pillar.

'They will only follow me, not you. I am the only Fairie Queen.' Aynia said in a tone that brooked no argument.

'Come to my side,' Carman pleaded with the nobles.

'Go to her if you will,' Aynia told the undecided nobles, 'but once you choose her I will never allow you to come back to me.'

'Why would they want to go back to you?'

'Make your choice nobles,' Aynia ordered them. 'But remember, I know who sided against me this morning.'

No one, not even Thane Monarda would move.

Heather stumbled out of the Temple. She was still dazed and confused from the knock to her head. She saw that the goblins were gone, but many Fairie were still bound. Taking a knife from her corset, she first untied Thorn, and then set out to release the Hive's population from bondage.

'Come to me! Together we can destroy Aynia! Why won't the rest of you come to me?' Carman asked.

'Because you're not Fairie!'

'I am too; I'm the daughter of our mother!' Carman protested.

'You're not Fairie,' Aynia reiterated. She turned to the nobles. 'Look well on this one claiming to be Fairie Queen. Does she have the crystal wings of a Queen? No, her wings are goblin black. Is she fair? No, her skin is gray and lifeless, like a worm that crawls through the earth. And look at her eyes. Can she be in the warming rays of the sun?' Aynia looked up. Naturally so did everyone else.

Carman looked up, but the strong light cut through her brain like a knife. Putting her hands over her eyes, she gasped with pain.

'Look on her closely. She's a goblin!'

The nobles did look and they too saw the signs.

'I am not a goblin! I was held prisoner for awhile, but now I have escaped! Stay with me, stay with this Hive! I'm the strong Queen,' Carman said desperately.

'They won't stay with you,' Aynia said with contempt.

'They'll have to if I'm the only Queen!' Carman threw herself at Aynia. Aynia easily stepped out of the way.

Suddenly the Hive went dark. Everyone looked up. Everywhere Fairies screamed.

A horse came crashing down through the top of the Hive.

Fairie scattered.

Outside the Hive the English rider fell to the ground, rolled expertly into a standing position, and brought his sword up. The horse limped away from the fissure in the ground.

A Scot attacked.

All across the valley the English and the Scots fought a pitched battle.

Rain began to pour onto the battlefield. The water formed a small stream, which ran through the battlefield. Seeking a place to flow, the cold water washed into the Hive. From the rent opening in the roof of the Hive, down to the floor, a waterfall cascaded and formed a river through the Hive Center, then disappeared into the chasm created by the goblin army. It was red with blood.

On the battlefield ravens swooped down to feed on the dead and the dying.

Aynia felt a tugging sensation on her wings. Looking back over her shoulder she saw Sarkany untying the leather thong.

'Majesty, I never meant to betray you. I knew that the nobles were planning to revolt…'

Aynia placed her fingers against Sarkany's lips. 'I know. I could feel it in my blood.' She held up her hand, showing the palm he kissed the first day they met. Only now blood dripped slowly from the slice across the palm. 'We are bound together. You got very jealous when I went to the Mountain King.' She smiled at him.

'I thought that you chose him over me.'

'If I could resist your scent my love, how could I possibly fall prey to his?'

'He's so much stronger than I am.'

'Was Prince, he was. Now he's dead.' Aynia reminded Sarkany as he wiped the Royal Jelly carefully from her face.

'I didn't care to taste Lady Heather,' he explained. Then he roughly pulled her close and kissed her hungrily.

'How would you know how she tastes?' Aynia asked, but forgot her question in his embrace.

Thorn ran over. 'The workers are untying the last captives. Majesty, we must leave the Hive immediately. There is no time left. The humans have invaded Balnacra. Their blood poisons our land.'

'I know. I can smell it. We will go immediately.'

'But how will we transport the workers that don't have wings?' Thorn asked.

'You will not abandon this Hive!' Carman shouted.

Aynia stared at Carman for a moment as if considering something. 'I have an idea,' Aynia purred. 'You release your Queen's scent, and I'll release mine, and we'll see who the Hive picks to be their leader.'

Carman laughed. 'Like the boys? Sure, I'll play, only this time you won't win.'

Aynia smiled her cool smile. 'Ready?' She waited silently until Carman nodded her agreement.

'Set?'

'Get on with it,' Carman said impatiently.

'Swarm!' Aynia shouted, releasing her powerful Queen's scent into the Hive air.

Nobles and workers alike ripped their clothes off then joined hands to create a chain. Aynia leapt into the air. Those with wings followed, taking the non-flyers with them.

'No!' Carman screamed. 'No!' She could not produce a Queen's scent. There was not enough Fairie left in to her to create the intoxicating odor that would bring the Hive to her. She had become goblin.

Thorn and Sarkany reached the Queen first.

Thorn hungrily suckled from her breasts. Sarkany spread her legs and mounted her from behind.

Others rushed to join them as Aynia flew out of the Hive. Soon they were a great mass of writhing bodies.

Aynia felt no fear, only pleasure, as the orgy raged around her, through her, and in her, as she flew the Hive to safety.

Carman looked around the abandoned Hive in disbelief. Across the Hive center the façade of Parliament failed. Stones crumbled and fell, some exploding on impact with the ground. Flying chips of stone hit her face and arms and drew blood. Dust rolled over her. Once thousands of Fairie lived in this Hive, now she was the only one left. She began to laugh, at first quietly, then loudly.

Carman threw her arms wide open. 'It is all mine,' she yelled. 'At last! The Hive is mine!'

ABOUT THE AUTHOR

Raised in a family that moved constantly, the author, Ischade Bradean, studied the local lore and legends of each place she lived. She always preferred the darker, older versions of tales that were meant as much for adults as they were for children. Special favorites were the haunting tales her Romanian Grandparents told her late at night.

A social chameleon, Ischade learned how to appear to be a native as quickly as possible. Her ear for accents and ability to adapt to the people around her make her nearly invisible to the naked eye, which is what she prefers.

Ischade currently lives at 33 degrees north, her favorite latitude no matter which continent she's on.

Printed in the United States
6503